He had her in his grasp . . .

Phoebe eyed him with hostility. "So I must remain in your house, I collect, until it shall please your grace to order the carriage to come round?"

"No. If you cannot bring yourself even to speak to me, I will send for it immediately."

She now perceived that he was not only arrogant but unscrupulous. Wholly devoid of chivalry, too, or he would not have done anything so shabby as to smile at her in just that way. What was more, it was clearly unsafe to be left alone with him: his eyes might smile, but they held besides the smile a very disturbing expression . . .

*Also by Georgette Heyer
from Jove*

ARABELLA

GEORGETTE HEYER

SYLVESTER
OR
THE WICKED UNCLE

A JOVE BOOK

First Jove edition published December 1980

10 9 8 7 6 5 4 3 2 1

Printed in the United States of America

Jove books are published by Jove Publications, Inc.,
200 Madison Avenue, New York, NY 10016

SYLVESTER
OR
THE WICKED UNCLE

CHAPTER

1

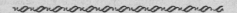

Sylvester stood in the window of his breakfast-parlour, leaning his hands on the ledge, and gazing out upon a fair prospect. No view of the ornamental water could be obtained from this, the east front of Chance, but the undulations of a lawn shaved all summer by scythemen were broken by a cedar, and beyond the lawn the stems of beech-trees, outliers of the Home Wood, shimmered in wintry sunlight. They still held their lure for Sylvester, though they beckoned him now to his coverts rather than to a land where every thicket concealed a dragon, and false knights came pricking down the rides. He and Harry, his twin, had slain the dragons, and ridden great wallops at the knights. There were none left now, and Harry had been dead for almost four years; but there were pheasants to tempt Sylvester forth, and they did tempt him, for a succession of black frosts had made the ground iron-hard, robbing him of two hunting days; and a blusterous north wind would not have invited the most ardent of sportsmen to take a gun out. It was still very cold, but the wind had dropped, and the sun shone, and what a bore it was that he should have decided that this day, out of all the inclement ones that had preceded it, should be devoted to business. He could change his mind, of course,

1

telling his butler to inform the various persons now awaiting his pleasure that he would see them on the following day. His agent-in-chief and his man of business had come all the way from London to attend upon him, but it did not occur to Sylvester that they could find any cause for complaint in being kept kicking their heels. They were in his employ, and had no other concern than to serve his interests; they would accept his change of mind as the caprice to be expected from a noble and wealthy master.

But Sylvester was not capricious, and he had no intention of succumbing to temptation. Caprice bred bad servants, and where the management of vast estates was concerned good service was essential. Sylvester had only just entered his twenty-eighth year, but he had succeeded to his huge inheritance when he was nineteen, and whatever follies and extravagances he had committed they had never led him to treat that inheritance as his plaything, or to evade the least one of its responsibilities. He had been born to a great position, reared to fill it in a manner worthy of a long line of distinguished forebears, and as little as he questioned his right to command the obedience of all the persons whose names were inscribed on his staggering payroll did he question the inescapability of the duties which had been laid on his shoulders. Had he been asked if he enjoyed his consequence he would have replied truthfully that he never thought of it; but he would certainly have disliked very much to have had it suddenly removed.

No one was in the least likely to ask him such a question, of course. He was generally considered to be a singularly fortunate young man, endowed with rank, wealth, and elegance. No bad fairy had attended his christening to leaven his luck with the gift of a hunchback or a harelip; though not above medium height he was well-proportioned, with good shoulders, a pair of shapely legs, and a countenance sufficiently pleasing to make the epithet *handsome*, frequently bestowed on it, not altogether ridiculous. In a lesser man the oddity of eyes set with the suspicion of a slant under flying black brows might have been accounted a blemish; in the Duke of Salford they were naturally held to lend distinction; and those who had admired his mother in her heyday remembered that she too had that thin, soaring line of eyebrow. It was just as though the brows had been added with a paintbrush, drawn in a sleek line upwards towards the temples. In the Duchess this peculiarity was charming; in Sylvester it was less attractive. It gave him, when he was vexed, and the upward trend was exaggerated by a frown, a slight look of a satyr.

He was about to turn away from the window when his attention was caught by a small, scampering figure. Emerging from the shelter of a yew hedge, a little boy with a cluster of golden curls set off across the lawn in the direction of the Home Wood, his nankeen-covered legs twinkling over the grass, and the freshly laundered frill of his shirt rucked up under one ear by a duffle coat, dragged over his little blue jacket by hurried and inexpert hands.

Sylvester laughed, throwing up the window. His impulse was to wish Edmund success in his adventure, but even as he leaned out he checked it. Though Edmund would not stop for his nurse or his tutor he would do so if his uncle called to him, and since he seemed to have made good his escape from these persons it would be unsportsmanlike to check him when his goal was within sight. To keep him dallying under the window would put him in grave danger of being captured, and that, reflected Sylvester, would lead to one of those scenes which bored him to death. Edmund would beg his leave to go off to the woods, and whether he gave it or withheld it he would be obliged to endure the reproaches of his widowed sister-in-law. He would be accused of treating poor little Edmund either with brutal severity, or with a heartless unconcern for his welfare; for Lady Henry Rayne could never bring herself to forgive him for having persuaded his brother (as she obstinately affirmed) to leave Edmund to his sole guardianship. It was of no use for anyone to tell Lady Henry that Harry's will had been drawn up on the occasion of his marriage, merely to ensure, in the event of accident, which no one had thought more unlikely than Harry himself, that any offspring of the match would be safe under the protection of the head of his house. However stupid Sylvester might think her she hoped she was not so green as to imagine that his attorney would have dared to insert so infamous a clause except at his express command. Sylvester, with the wound of Harry's death still raw, had allowed himself to be goaded into bitter retort: "If you imagine that I wished to have the brat thrust on to me you are even greener than I had supposed!"

He was to regret those hasty words, for although he had immediately retracted them he had never been allowed to forget

3

them; and they formed today, when the custody of Edmund had become a matter of acute importance, the foundation-stone of Lady Henry's arguments. "You never wanted him," she reminded him. "You said so yourself!"

It had been partly true, of course; except as Harry's son he had had very little interest in a two-year-old infant, and had paid no more heed to him than might have been expected of a young man. When Edmund began to grow out of babyhood, however, he saw rather more of him, for Edmund's first object, whenever his magnificent uncle was at Chance, was to attach himself as firmly as possible to him. He had qualities wholly lacking in Button, Edmund's nurse (and his father's and uncle's before him), or in Mama. He showed no disposition to fondle his nephew; he was indifferent to torn clothes; such conversation as he addressed to Edmund was brief and to the point; and while he might, in an unpropitious mood, send him somewhat peremptorily about his business, it was always possible that he would hoist him up on to his saddle before him, and canter off with him through the park. These attributes were accompanied by a less agreeable but equally godlike idiosyncrasy: he exacted instant obedience to his commands, and he had a short way of dealing with recalcitrants.

Sylvester thought that Ianthe and Button were doing their best to spoil Edmund, but while he did not hesitate to make plain to that astute young gentleman the unwisdom of employing with him the tactics that succeeded so well in the nursery it was rarely that he interfered with his upbringing. He saw no faults in Edmund that could not speedily be cured when he was rather older; and by the time he was six had grown to like him as much for his own sake as for his father's.

Edmund had disappeared from view. Sylvester pulled the window down again, thinking that he really ought to provide the brat with a livelier tutor than the Reverend Loftus Leyburn, the elderly and rather infirm cleric who was his—or, more accurately, his mother's—chaplain. He had thought it a poor arrangement when Ianthe had begged Mr. Loftus to teach Edmund his first lessons, but not a matter of sufficient moment to make it necessary for him to provoke her by refusing to agree to the scheme. Now she was complaining that Edmund haunted the stables, and learned the most vulgar language there. What the devil did she expect? wondered Sylvester.

He turned from the window as the door opened, and his

butler came in, followed by a young footman, who began to clear away the remains of a substantial breakfast.

"I'll see Mr. Ossett and Pewsey at noon, Reeth," Sylvester said. "Chale and Brough may bring their books in to me at the same time. I am going up to sit with her grace now. You might send down a message to Trent, warning him that I may want——" He paused, glancing towards the window. "No, never mind that! The light will be gone by four o'clock."

"It seems a pity your grace should be cooped up in the office on such a fine day," said Reeth suggestively.

"A great pity, but it can't be helped." He found that he had dropped his handkerchief, and that the footman had hurried to pick it up for him. He said, "Thank you", as he took it, and accompanied the words with a slight smile. He had a singularly charming smile, and it ensured for him, no matter how exacting might be his demands, the uncomplaining exertions of his servants. He was perfectly well aware of that, just as he was aware of the value of the word of praise dropped at exactly the right moment; and he would have thought himself extremely stupid to withhold what cost him so little and was productive of such desirable results.

Leaving the breakfast-parlour, he made his way to the main hall, and (it might have been thought) to another century, since this central portion of a pile that sprawled over several acres was all that remained of the original structure. Rugged beams, plastered walls, and a floor of uneven flagstones lingered on here in odd but not infelicitous contrast to the suave elegance of the more modern parts of the great house. The winged staircase of Tudor origin that led up from the hall to a surrounding gallery was guarded by two figures in full armour; the walls were embellished with clusters of antique weapons; the windows were of armorial glass; and under an enormous hood a pile of hot ashes supported several blazing logs. Before this fire a liver-and-white spaniel lay in an attitude of watchful expectancy. She raised her head when she heard Sylvester's step, and began to wag her tail; but when he came into the hall her tail sank, and although she bundled across the floor to meet him, and looked adoringly up at him when he stooped to pat, she neither frisked about him nor uttered barks of joyful anticipation. His valet was hardly more familiar with his wardrobe than she, and she knew well that pantaloons and Hessian boots

5

meant that the most she could hope for was to be permitted to lie at his feet in the library.

The Duchess's apartments comprised, besides her bedchamber, and the dressing-room occupied by her maid, an antechamber which led into a large, sunny apartment, known to the household as the Duchess's Drawing-room. She rarely went beyond it, for she had been for many years the victim of an arthritic complaint which none of the eminent physicians who had attended her, or any of the cures she had undergone, had been able to arrest. She could still manage, supported by her attendants, to drag herself from her bedchamber to her drawing-room, but once lowered into her chair she could not rise from it without assistance. What degree of pain she suffered no one knew, for she never complained, or asked for sympathy. "Very well" was her invariable reply to solicitous enquiries; and if anyone deplored the monotony of her existence she laughed, and said that pity was wasted on her, and would be better bestowed on those who danced attendance on her. As for herself, with her son to bring her all the London on-dits, her grandson to amuse her with his pranks, her daughter-in-law to discuss the latest fashions with her, her patient cousin to bear with her crotchets, her devoted maid to cosset her, and her old friend, Mr. Leyburn, to browse with her amongst her books she thought she was rather to be envied than pitied. Except to her intimates she did not mention her poems, but the fact was that the Duchess was an author. Mr. Blackwell had published two volumes of her verses, and these had enjoyed quite a vogue amongst members of the ton; for although they were, of course, published anonymously the secret of their authorship soon leaked out, and was thought to lend considerable interest to them.

She was engaged in writing when Sylvester entered the room, on the table so cleverly made by the estate carpenter to fit across the arms of her wing-chair; but as soon as she saw who had come in she laid down her pen, and welcomed Sylvester with a smile more charming than his own because so much warmer, and exclaimed: "Ah, how delightful! But so vexatious for you, love, to be obliged to stay at home on the first good shooting-day we have had in a se'enight!"

"A dead bore, isn't it?" he responded, bending over her to kiss her cheek. She put up her hand to lay it on his shoulder, and he stayed for a moment, scanning her face. Apparently he

6

was satisfied with what he saw there, for he let his eyes travel to the delicate lace confection set on her silvered black hair, and said: "A new touch, Mama? That's a very fetching cap!"

The ready laughter sprang to her eyes. "Confess that Anna warned you to take notice of my finery!"

"Certainly not! Do you think I must be told by your maid when you are looking in great beauty?"

"Sylvester, you make love so charmingly that I fear you must be the most outrageous flirt!"

"Oh, not *outrageous*, Mama! Are you busy with a new poem?"

"Merely a letter. Dearest, if you will push the table away, you may draw up that chair a little, and we can enjoy a comfortable prose."

This he was prevented from doing by the hurried entrance from the adjoining bedchamber of Miss Augusta Penistone, who begged him, somewhat incoherently, not to trouble himself, since she considered the task peculiarly her own. She then pushed the table to the side of the room, and instead of effacing herself, as he always wished she would, lingered, amiably smiling at him. She was an angular, rather awkward lady, as kind as she was plain, and she served the Duchess, whose kinswoman she was, in the capacity of a companion. Her good-nature was inexhaustible, but she was unfortunately quite unintelligent, and rarely failed to irritate Sylvester by asking questions to which the answers were patent, or commenting upon the obvious. He bore it very well, for his manners were extremely good, but when, after stating that she saw he had not gone out hunting, she recollected that one didn't hunt after severe frost and said, with a merry laugh at her mistake: "Well, that *was* a stupid thing for me to have said, wasn't it?" he was provoked into replying, though with perfect suavity: "It was, wasn't it?"

The Duchess intervened at this stage of the dialogue, urging her cousin to go out into the sunshine while it lasted; and after saying that, to be sure, she might venture to do so if dear Sylvester meant to sit with his mama, which she had no doubt of, and pointing out that Anna would come if the Duchess rang the bell, she got herself to the door, which Sylvester was holding open. She was obliged to pause there to tell him that she was now going to leave him to chat with his mama, adding: "For I am sure you wish to be private with her, don't you?"

"I do, but how you guessed it, cousin, I can't imagine!" he replied.

"Oh!" declared Miss Penistone gaily, "a pretty thing it would be if I didn't know, after all these years, just what you like! Well, I will run away, then—but you should not trouble to open the door for me! That is to treat me like a stranger! I am for ever telling you so, am I not? But you are always so obliging!"

He bowed, and shut the door behind her. The Duchess said: "An undeserved compliment, Sylvester. My dear, how came you to speak as you did? It was not kind."

"Her folly is intolerable!" he said impatiently. "Why do you keep such a hubble-bubble woman about you? She must vex you past bearing!"

"She is not very wise, certainly," admitted the Duchess. "But I couldn't send her away, you know!"

"Shall I do so for you?"

She was startled, but, supposing that he was speaking out of an unthinking exasperation, only said: "Nonsensical boy! You know you could no more do so than I could!"

He raised his brows. "Of course I could do it, Mama! What should stop me?"

"You cannot be serious!" she exclaimed, half inclined still to laugh at him.

"But I'm perfectly serious, my dear! Be frank with me! Don't you wish her at Jericho?"

She said, with a rueful twinkle: "Well, yes—sometimes I do! Don't repeat that, will you? I have at least the grace to be ashamed of myself!" She perceived that his expression was one of surprise, and said in a serious tone: "Of course it vexes you, and me too, when she says silly things, and hasn't the tact to go away when you come to visit me, but I promise you I think myself fortunate to have her. It can't be very amusing to be tied to an invalid, you know, but she is never hipped or out of temper, and whatever I ask her to do for me she does willingly, and so cheerfully that she puts me in danger of believing that she enjoys being at my beck and call."

"So I should hope!"

"Now, Sylvester——"

"My dear Mama, she has hung on your sleeve ever since I can remember, and a pretty generous sleeve it has been! You have always made her an allowance far beyond what you would have paid a stranger hired to bear you company, haven't you?"

"You speak as though you grudged it!"

"No more than I grudge the wages of my valet, if you think her worth it. I pay large wages to my servants, but I keep none in my employment who doesn't earn his wage."

There was a troubled look in the eyes that searched his face, but the Duchess only said: "The cases are not the same, but don't let us brangle about it! You may believe that it would make me very unhappy to lose Augusta. Indeed, I don't know how I should go on."

"If that's the truth, Mama, you need say no more. Do you suppose I wouldn't pay anyone you wished to keep about you double—treble—what you pay Augusta?" He saw her stretch out her hand to him, and went to her immediately. "You know I wouldn't do anything you don't like! Don't look so distressed, dearest!"

She pressed his hand. "I know you wouldn't. Don't heed me! It is only that it shocked me a little to hear you speak so hardly. But no one has less cause to complain of hardness in you than I, my darling."

"Nonsense!" he said, smiling down at her. "Keep your tedious cousin, love—but allow me to wish that you had with you someone who could entertain you better—enter into what interests you!"

"Well, I have Ianthe," she reminded him. "She doesn't precisely enter into my interests, but we go on very comfortably together."

"I am happy to hear it. But it begins to seem as if you won't have the doubtful comfort of her society for much longer."

"My dear, if you are going to suggest that I should employ a second lady to keep me company, I do beg of you to spare your breath!"

"No, that wouldn't answer." He paused, and then said quite coolly: "I am thinking of getting married, Mama."

She was taken so much by surprise that she could only stare at him. He had the reputation of being a dangerous flirt, but she had almost given up hope of his coming to the point of offering for any lady's hand in matrimony. She had reason to think that he had had more than one mistress in keeping—very expensive Cythereans some of them had been if her sister were to be believed!—and it had begun to seem as if he preferred that way of life to a more ordered existence. Recovering from her stupefaction, she said: "My dear, this is very sudden!"

"Not so sudden as you think, Mama. I have been meaning for some time to speak to you about it."

"Good gracious! And I never suspected it! Do, pray, sit down and tell me all about it!"

He looked at her keenly. "Would you be glad, Mama?"

"Of course I should!"

"Then I think that settles it."

That made her laugh. "Of all the absurd things to say! Very well! having won my approval, tell me everything!"

He said, gazing frowningly into the fire: "I don't know that there's so much to tell you. I fancy you guessed I haven't much cared for the notion of becoming riveted. I never met the female to whom I wished to be leg-shackled. Harry did, and if anything had been needed to confirm me in——"

"My dear, leave that!" she interposed. "Harry was happy in his marriage, remember! I believe, too, that although Ianthe's feelings are not profound she was most sincerely attached to him."

"So much attached to him that within a year of his death she was pining for the sight of a ballroom, and within four is planning to marry a worthless fribble! It will not do, Mama!"

"Very well, my dear, but we are talking of your marriage, not Harry's, are we not?"

"True! Well, I realized—oh, above a year ago!—that it was my duty to marry. Not so much for the sake of an heir, because I have one already, but——"

"Sylvester, don't put that thought into Edmund's head!"

He laughed. "Much he would care! His ambition is to become a mail-coachman—or it was until Keighley let him have the yard of tin for a plaything! Now he cannot decide whether to be a coachman or a guard. Pretty flat he would think it to be told that he would be obliged instead to step into my shoes!"

She smiled. "Yes, *now* he would, but later——"

"Well, that's one of my reasons, Mama. If I mean to marry I ought, I think, to do so before Edmund is old enough to think his nose has been put out of joint. So I began some months ago to look about me."

"You are the oddest creature! Next you will tell me you made out a list of the qualities your wife must possess!"

"More or less," he admitted. "You may laugh, Mama, but

10

you'll agree that certain qualities are indispensable! She must be well-born, for instance. I don't mean necessarily a great match, but a girl of my own order."

"Ah, yes, I agree with *that!* And next?"

"Well, a year ago I should have said she must be beautiful," he replied meditatively. (She is not a beauty, thought the Duchess.) "But I'm inclined to think now that it is more important that she should be intelligent. I don't think I could tolerate a hen-witted wife. Besides, I don't mean to foist another fool on to you."

"I am very much obliged to you!" she said, a good deal entertained. "Clever, but not beautiful: very well! continue!"

"No, some degree of beauty I do demand. She must have countenance, at least, and the sort of elegance which you have, Mama."

"Don't try to turn my head, you flatterer! Have you discovered amongst the débutantes one who is endowed with all these qualities?"

"At first glance, I suppose a dozen, but in the end only five."

"Five!"

"Well, only five with whom I could perhaps bear to spend a large part of my life. There is Lady Jane Saxby: she's pretty, and good-natured. Then there's Barningham's daughter: she has a great deal of vivacity. Miss Bellerby is a handsome girl, with a little reserve, which I don't dislike. Lady Mary Torrington—oh, a diamond of the first water! And lastly Miss Orton: not beautiful, but quite taking, and has agreeable manners." He paused, his gaze still fixed on the smouldering logs. The Duchess waited expectantly. He looked up presently, and smiled at her. "Well, Mama?" he said affably. "Which of them shall it be?"

CHAPTER

2

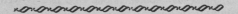

After an astonished moment the Duchess said: "Dearest, are you roasting me? You can't in all seriousness be asking me to choose for you!"

"No, not choose precisely. I wish you will advise me, though. You're not acquainted with any of them, but you know their families, and if you should have a decided preference——"

"But, Sylvester, have *you* no preference?"

"No, that's the devil of it: I haven't. Whenever I think one more eligible than any of the others as sure as check I find she has some fault or trick which I don't like. Lady Jane's laugh, for instance; or Miss Orton's infernal harp! I've no turn for music, and to be obliged to endure a harp's being eternally twanged in my own house—no, I think that's coming it a trifle too strong, don't you, Mama? Then Lady Mary——"

"Thank you, I have heard enough to be able to give you my advice!" interrupted his mother. "Don't make an offer for any one of them! You are not in love!"

"In love! No, of course I am not. Is that so necessary?"

"Most necessary, my dear! Don't, I beg of you, offer marriage where you can't offer love as well!"

He smiled at her. "You are too romantic, Mama."

"Am I? But you seem to have no romance in you at all!"

"Well, I don't look for it in marriage, at any rate."

"Only in the muslin company?"

He laughed. "You shock me, Mama! That's a different matter. I shouldn't call it romance either—or only one's first adventure, perhaps. And even when I was a greenhead, and fell in love with the most dazzling little bird of Paradise you ever saw, I don't think I really fancied myself to have formed a lasting passion! I daresay I'm too volatile, in which case——"

"No such thing! You have not yet been fortunate enough to meet the girl for whom you *will* form a lasting passion."

"Very true: I haven't! And since I've been on the town for nearly ten years, and may be said to have had my pick of all the eligible débutantes that appear yearly on the Marriage Mart, we must conclude that if I'm not too volatile I must be too nice in my requirements. To be frank with you, Mama, you are the only lady of my acquaintance with whom I don't soon become heartily bored!"

A tiny frown appeared between her winged brows as she listened to this speech. It was spoken in a bantering tone, but she found it disturbing. "Your *pick* of them, Sylvester?"

"Yes, I think so. I must have seen all the eligibles, I fancy."

"And have made quite a number of them the objects of your gallantry—if the things I hear are to be believed!"

"My aunt Louisa," said Sylvester unerringly. "What an incorrigible gossip your sister is, my dear! Well, if I have now and then shown a preference at least she can't accuse me of having been so particular in my attentions as to have raised false hopes in any maiden's bosom!"

The hint of laughter had quite vanished from her eyes. The image she cherished of this beloved son was all at once blurred; and a feeling of disquiet made it difficult for her to know what she should say to him. As she hesitated, an interruption occurred. The door was opened; a pretty, plaintive voice said: "May I come in, Mama-Duchess?" and there appeared on the threshold a vision of beauty dressed in a blue velvet pelisse, and a hat with a high poke-front which made a frame for a ravishing countenance. Ringlets of bright gold fell beside damask cheeks; large blue eyes were set beneath delicately arched

13

brows; the little nose was perfectly straight; and the red mouth deliciously curved.

"Good-morning, my love. Of course you may come in!" said the Duchess.

The vision had by this time perceived her brother-in-law, and although she did come in she said with a marked diminution of cordiality: "Oh! I didn't know you had Sylvester with you, ma'am. I beg your pardon, but I only came to discover if Edmund was here."

"I haven't seen him this morning," replied the Duchess. "Is he not with Mr. Leyburn?"

"No, and it is particularly vexatious because I wish to take him with me to visit the Arkholmes! You know I have been meaning for days to drive over to the Grange, ma'am, and now, on the first fine morning we have had for an age, no one can tell me where he is!"

"Perhaps he has slipped off to the stables, little rogue!"

"No, though, to be sure, that was what I expected too, for ever since Sylvester took to *encouraging* him to haunt the stables——"

"My dear, they all do so, and without the least encouragement!" interposed the Duchess. "Mine certainly did—they were the most deplorable urchins! Tell me, did you have that charming pelisse made from the velvets we chose from the patterns sent down last month? How well it has made-up!"

The effect of this attempt to divert the beauty's thoughts was unfortunate. "Yes, but only think, ma'am!" exclaimed Ianthe. "I had a suit made from it for Edmund to wear when he goes out with me—quite simple, but after the style of that red dress the boy has on in the picture by Reynolds. I forget where I saw it, but I thought at once how well Edmund would look in it if only it were not red but blue!"

"Wouldn't he just!" muttered Sylvester.

"What did you say?" demanded Ianthe suspiciously.

"Nothing."

"I suppose it was something ill-natured. To be sure, I never hoped that *you* would think it pretty!"

"You are mistaken. The picture you would both present would be pretty enough to take one's breath away. Assuming, of course, that Edmund could be persuaded to behave conformably. Standing within your arm, with that soulful look on his face—no, that won't do! He only wears that when he's plotting mischief. Well——"

"Sylvester, *will* you be silent?" begged the Duchess, trying not to laugh. "Don't heed him, my dear child! He's only quizzing you!"

"Oh, I know that, ma'am!" said Ianthe, her colour considerably heightened. "I know, too, who it is who teaches poor little Edmund not to mind me!"

"Oh, good God, what next?" Sylvester exclaimed.

"You do!" she insisted. "And it shows how little affection you have for him! If you cared a rap for him you wouldn't encourage him to run into heaven knows what danger!"

"*What* danger?"

"Anything might happen to him!" she declared. "At this very moment he may be at the bottom of the lake!"

"He is nowhere near the lake. If you must have it, I saw him making off to the Home Wood!"

"And you made not the smallest effort to call him back, I collect!"

"No. The last time I interfered in Edmund's illicit amusements I figured in your conversation as a monster of inhumanity for three days."

"I never said any such thing, but only that—besides, he may change his mind, and go to the lake after all!"

"Make yourself easy: he won't! Not while he knows I'm at home, at all events."

She said fretfully: "I might have known how it would be! I would as lief not to go to the Grange at all now, and I wouldn't, only that I have had the horses put to. But I shan't know a moment's peace of mind for wondering if my poor, orphaned child is safe, or at the bottom of the lake!"

"If he should fail to appear in time for his dinner, I will have the lake dragged," promised Sylvester, walking to the door, and opening it. "Meanwhile, however careless I may be of my nephew I am not careless of my horses, and I do beg of you, if you have had a pair put to, not to keep them standing in this weather!"

This request incensed Ianthe so much that she flounced out of the room in high dudgeon.

"Edifying!" remarked Sylvester. "Believing her orphaned son to be at the bottom of the lake this devoted parent departs on an expedition of pleasure!"

"My dear, she knows very well he isn't at the bottom of the lake! Can you *never* meet without rubbing against one another? You are quite as unjust to her as she is to you, I must tell you!"

He shrugged. "I daresay. If I had ever seen a trace of her vaunted devotion to Edmund I could bear with her patiently, but I never have! If he will be so obliging as to submit to her caresses she is pleased to think she dotes on him, but when he becomes noisy it is quite a comedy to see how quickly she can develop the headache, so that Button must be sent for to remove her darling! She never went near him when he had the measles, and when she made his toothache an excuse to carry him off to London, and then was ready to let the brat's tooth rot in his head rather than put herself to the trouble of compelling him to submit to its extraction——"

"I knew we should come to it!" interrupted the Duchess, throwing up her hands. "Let me tell you, my son, that it takes a great deal of resolution to drag a reluctant child to the dentist! I never had enough! It fell to Button to perform the dreadful duty—and so it would have done in Edmund's case, only that she was ill at the time!"

"I shan't let you tell me, Mama," he said, laughing. "For I *have* performed the dreaful duty, remember!"

"So you have! Poor Edmund! Swooped upon in the Park, snatched up into your curricle, and whisked off to the torture-chamber in such a ruthless style! I promise you my heart bled for him!"

"It might well have done so had you seen his face as *I* saw it! I suppose the witless abigail who had him in charge told you I *swooped* upon him? All I did was to drive him to Tilton's immediately, and what was needed was not resolution but firmness! No, Mama: don't ask me to credit Ianthe with devotion to her brat, for it sickens me! I only wish I knew who was the sapskull who told her how lovely she appeared with her child in her arms. Also that I hadn't been fool enough to allow myself to be persuaded to commission Lawrence to paint her in that affecting pose!"

"You did so to give Harry pleasure," said the Duchess gently. "I have always been glad to think it was finished in time for him to see it."

Sylvester strode over to the window, and stood looking out.

After a few minutes he said: "I'm sorry, Mama. I should not have said that."

"No, of course you should not, dearest. I wish you will try not to be so hard on Ianthe, for she is very much to be pitied, you know. You didn't like it when she began to go into society again with her mama, at the end of that first year of mourning. Well, I didn't like it either, but how could one expect such a pleasure-loving little creature to stay moping here, after all? It was not improper in her to put off her blacks." She hesitated, and then added: "It is not improper in her to be wishing to marry again now, Sylvester."

"I haven't accused her of impropriety."

"No, but you are making it dreadfully hard for her, my love! She may not be devoted to Edmund, but to take him from her entirely——"

"If that should happen, it will be her doing, not mine! She may make her home here for as long as she chooses, or she may take Edmund to live with her at the Dower House. All I have ever said is that Harry's son will be reared at Chance, and under my eye! If Ianthe marries again she is welcome to visit Edmund whenever she pleases. I have even told her she may have him to stay with her at reasonable intervals. But one thing I will never do, and that is to permit him to grow up under Nugent Fotherby's ægis! Good God, Mama, how can you think it possible I would so abuse my twin's trust?"

"Ah, no, no! But is Sir Nugent so very bad? I was a little acquainted with his father—he was so amiable that he said yes and amen to everything!—but I think I never met the son."

"You needn't repine! A wealthy fribble, three parts idiot, and the fourth—never mind! A pretty guardian I should be to abandon Edmund to his and Ianthe's upbringing! Do you know what Harry said to me, Mama? They were almost the last words he spoke to me. He said: 'You'll look after the boy, Dook.'" He stopped, his voice cracking on that last word. After a moment he said, not very easily: "You know how he used to call me that—with that twinkle in his eye. It wasn't a question, or a request. He *knew* I should, and he said it, not to remind me, but because it was a comfortable thought that came into his head, and he always told me what he was thinking." He saw that his mother had shaded her eyes with one hand, and crossed the room to her side, taking her other hand,

and holding it closely. "Forgive me! I must make you understand, Mama!"

"I do understand, Sylvester, but how can I think it right to keep the child here with no one but old Button to look after him, or some tutor for whom he's far too young? If I were not useless——' She clipped the words off short.

Knowing her as he did, he made no attempt to answer what had been left unspoken, but said calmly: "Yes, I too have considered that, and it forms a strong reason for my marriage. I fancy Ianthe would soon grow reconciled to the thought of parting with Edmund, could she but leave him in his *aunt's* charge. She wouldn't then incur the stigma of heartlessness, would she? She cares a great deal for what people may say of her—and I must own that after presenting a portrait of herself to the world in the rôle of devoted parent, I don't perceive how she *can* abandon Edmund to the mercy of his wicked uncle. My wife, you know, could very well be held to have softened my disposition!"

"Now, Sylvester——! She can never have said you were wicked!"

He smiled. "She may not have used that precise term, but she has regaled everyone with the tale of my disregard for Edmund's welfare, and frequent brutality to him. They may not believe the whole, but I've reason to suppose that even a man of such good sense as Elvaston thinks I treat the boy with unmerited severity."

"Well, if Lord Elvaston doesn't know his daughter better than to believe the farradiddles she utters I have a poor opinion of his sense!" said the Duchess, quite tartly. "Do let us stop talking about Ianthe, my love!"

"Willingly! I had rather talk of my own affairs. Mama, what sort of a female would you wish me to marry?"

"In your present state, I don't wish you to marry *any* sort of a female. When you come out of it, the sort *you* wish to marry, of course!"

"You are not being in the least helpful!" he complained. "I thought mothers always made marriage plans for their sons!"

"And consequently suffered some severe disappointments! I am afraid the only marriage I ever planned for you was with a three-day infant, when you were eight years old!"

"Come! this is better!" he said encouragingly. "Who was she? Do I know her?"

18

"You haven't mentioned her, but I should think you must at least have seen her, for she was presented this year, and had her first season. Her grandmother wrote to tell me of it, and I almost asked you——" She broke off, vexed with herself, and altered the sentence she had been about to utter. "——to give her a kind message from me, only did not, for she could hardly be expected to remember me. She's Lady Ingham's grand-daughter."

"What, my respected godmama? One of the Ingham girls? Oh, no, my dear! I regret infinitely, but—*no*!"

"No, no, Lord Marlow's daughter!" she replied, laughing. "He married Verena Ingham, who was my dearest friend, and the most captivating creature!"

"Better and better!" he approved. "Why have I never en-countered the captivating Lady Marlow?" He stopped, frown-ing. "But I have! I'm not acquainted with her—in fact, I don't remember that I've ever so much as spoken to her, but I must tell you, Mama, that whatever she may have been in her youth——"

"Good heavens, *that* odious woman is Marlow's second! Verena died when her baby was not a fortnight old."

"Very sad. Tell me about her!"

"I don't think you would be much the wiser if I did," she answered, wondering if he was trying to divert her mind from the memories he had himself evoked. "She wasn't beautiful, or accomplished, or even modish, I fear! She defeated every effort to turn her into a fashionable young lady, and never appeared elegant except in her riding-dress. She did the most outrageous things, and nobody cared a bit—not even Lady Cork! We came out in the same season, and were the greatest of friends; but while I was so fortunate as to meet Papa—and to fall in love with him at sight, let me tell you!—she refused every offer that was made her—scores of them, for she never lacked for suitors!—and declared she preferred her horses to any man she had met. Poor Lady Ingham was in despair! And in the end she married Marlow, of all people! I believe she must have liked him for his horsemanship, for I am sure there was nothing else to like in him. Not a very exciting story, I'm afraid! Why did you wish to hear it?"

"Oh, I wished to know what sort of a woman she was! Marlow I do know, and I should suppose that any daughter of his must be an intolerable bore. But your Verena's child might be the very wife for me, don't you think? *You* would be disposed to like her, which must be an object with me; and although I don't mean to burden myself with a wife who wants conduct, I should imagine that there must be enough of Marlow's blood in this girl to leaven whatever wildness she may have inherited from her mother. Eccentricity may be diverting, Mama, but it is out of place in a wife: certainly in my wife!"

"My dear, what nonsense you are talking! If I believed you meant it I should be most seriously disturbed!"

"But I do mean it! I thought you would have been pleased, too! What could be more romantic than to marry the girl who was betrothed to me in her cradle?"

She smiled, but she did not look to be much amused. His eyes searched her face; he said in the caressing tone he used only to her: "What is it, my dear? Tell me!"

She said: "Sylvester, you have talked of five girls who might perhaps *suit* you; and now you are talking of a girl of whose existence you were unaware not ten minutes ago—and as though you had only to decide between them! My dear, has it not occurred to you that you might find yourself rebuffed?"

His brow cleared. "Is *that* all? No, no, Mama, I shan't be rebuffed!"

"So sure, Sylvester?"

"Of course I'm sure, Mama! Oh, not of Miss Marlow! For anything I know, her affections may be engaged already."

"Or she might take you in dislike," suggested the Duchess.

"Take me in dislike? Why should she?" he asked, surprised.

"How can I tell? These things do happen, you know."

"If you mean she might not *fall in love* with me, I daresay she might not, though I know of no reason, if she doesn't love another man, why she shouldn't come to do so—or, at any rate, to like me very tolerably! Do you suppose me to be so lacking in address that I can't make myself agreeable when I wish to? Fie on you, Mama!"

"No," she said. "But I didn't know you had so much address that you could beguile no fewer than five girls of rank and fashion to be ready to accept an offer from you."

He could not resist. "Well, Mama, you said yourself that I make love charmingly!" he murmured.

It drew a smile from her, because she could never withstand that gleaming look, but she shook her head as well, and said: "For shame, Sylvester! Do you mean to sound like a coxcomb?"

He laughed. "Of course I don't! To be frank with you, there are not five but a dozen young women of rank and fashion who are perfectly ready to receive an offer from me. I'm not hard to swallow, you know, though I don't doubt I have as many faults as a Mr. Smith or a Mr. Jones. Mine are more palatable, however: scarcely noticeable for the rich marchpane that covers them!"

"Do you wish for a wife who marries you for the sake of your possessions?" the Duchess asked, arching her brows.

"I don't think I mind very much, provided we were mutually agreeable. Such a wife would be unlikely to enact me any tragedies, and anything of that nature, Mama, would lead to our being regularly parted within a twelvemonth. I couldn't endure it!"

"The enacting of tragedies, my son, is not an invariable concomitant of love-matches," she said dryly.

"Who should know that better than I?" he retorted, his smile embracing her. "But where am I to look for your counterpart, my dear? Show her to me, and I will engage to fall desperately in love with her, and marry her, fearing no after-ills!"

"Sylvester, you are too absurd!"

"Not as absurd as you think! Seriously, Mama, although I have seen some love-matches that have prospered, I have seen a great many that most certainly have not! Oh! no doubt some husbands and wives of my acquaintance would stare to hear me say I thought them anything but happy! Perhaps they enjoy jealousies, tantrums, quarrels, and stupid misunderstandings: I should not! The well-bred woman who marries me because she has a fancy to be a duchess will suit me very well, and will probably fill her position admirably." His eyes quizzed her. "Or would you like me to turn my coat inside out, and sally forth in humble disguise, like the prince in a fairy-tale? I never thought much of that prince, you know! A chuckle-headed fellow, for how could he hope, masquerading as a mean person, to come near any but quite ineligible females whom it would have been impossible for him to marry?"

"Very true!" she replied.

He was always watchful where she was concerned. It struck him now that she was suddenly looking tired; and he said with quick compunction: "I've fagged you to death with my non-sense! Now, why did you let me talk you into a head-ache? Shall I send Anna to you?"

"No, indeed! My head doesn't ache, I promise you," she said, smiling tenderly up at him.

"I wish I might believe you!" he said, bending over her to kiss her cheek. "I'll leave you to rest before you are assailed by Augusta again: don't let her plague you!"

He went away, and she remained lost in her reflections until roused from them by her cousin's return.

"All alone, dear Elizabeth?" Miss Penistone exclaimed. "Now, if I had but known—but in general I do believe Sylvester would stay with you for ever, if I were not obliged at last to come in! I am sure I have said a hundred times that I never knew such an attentive son. So considerate, too! There was never anything like it!"

"Ah, yes!" the Duchess said. "To me so considerate, so endlessly kind!"

She sounded a little mournful, which was unusual in her. Miss Penistone, speaking much in the heartening tone Button used to divert Edmund when he was cross, said: "He was looking particularly handsome today, wasn't he? Such an excellent figure, and his air so distinguished! What heart-burnings there will be when at last he throws the handkerchief!"

She laughed amiably at this thought, but the Duchess did not seem to be amused. She said nothing, but Miss Penistone saw her hands clasp and unclasp on the arm of her chair, and at once realized that no doubt she must be afraid that so rich a prize as Sylvester might be caught by some wretchedly designing creature quite unworthy of his attention. "And *no* fear of his marrying to disoblige you, as the saying goes," said Miss Penistone brightly, but with an anxious eye on the Duchess. "With so many girls on the catch for him I daresay you would be quite in a worry if he were not so sensible. That thought came into *my* head once—so absurd!—and I mentioned it to Louisa, when she was staying here in the summer. 'Not he!' she said—you know her abrupt way! 'He knows his worth too well!' Which set my mind quite at rest, as you may suppose."

It did not seem to have exercised the same beneficial effect on the Duchess's mind, for she put up a hand to shade her eyes. Miss Penistone knew then what was amiss: she had had one of her bad nights, poor Elizabeth!

CHAPTER

3

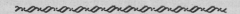

Sylvester made no further mention of his matrimonial plans; nor, since she could not fail to be cheerful whenever he came to visit her, did he suspect that his mother was troubled for him. Had he known it he would have supposed her merely to dislike the thought of his marriage, and would not have found it difficult to put any such scheme aside; if she had told him that she was more disturbed by the fear, which was taking uncomfortably strong possession of her mind, that he had become arrogant he would have been distressed to think that he could have said anything to put such a notion into her head, and would have done his best to joke her out of it. He knew it to be false: he was acquainted with several persons to whom the epithet might well apply, and he thought them intolerable. Few men were more petted and courted than he; there were not many hostesses who would not have forgiven him such slights as were not uncommonly dealt them by spoiled men of rank and fashion. But no hostess would ever be given cause to complain of Sylvester's courtesy; and no insignificant person who perhaps rendered him a trifling service, or even did no more than touch his hat to him, would have reason to think himself despised. To reserve one's civility for people of consequence was a piece of ill-breeding, dishonourable to oneself, as disgusting as to make a parade of greatness, or to curse a servant for clumsiness. Sylvester, who did not arrive at parties very late, refuse to stand up for country-dances, take his bored leave within half an hour of his arrival, leave invitations unanswered, stare unrecognizingly at one of his tenants, or fail to exchange a few words with every one of his guests on Public Days at Chance, was not very likely to believe that a charge of arrogance levelled against him was anything but a calumny, emanating probably from a tuft-hunter whom he had snubbed, or some pert mushroom of society whose pretensions he had been obliged to depress.

The Duchess knew this, and felt herself to be at a loss. She would have liked to have been able to consult with someone who had his interests as much to heart as herself, and must know better than she (since she never saw Sylvester but in her own apartments) how he conducted himself in society. There was only one such person; but although she felt both respect and affection for Lord William Rayne, Sylvester's uncle, and for two years his guardian, very little reflection was needed to convince her that any attempt to get him to enter into her rather vague apprehensions would only make him think her the victim of such crotchets as might be expected to attack an invalid. Lord William was old-fashioned, very bluff and kind, but very full of starch as well. He had some influence over Sylvester, of whom he was as fond as he was proud: a word from him would carry weight, but unfortunately one of his terse reproofs would be more easily drawn from him by what he thought a failure on his nephew's part to remember his exalted station, than by his placing himself on too high a form.

He stayed at Chance at Christmas, and so far from affording the Duchess reassurance considerably depressed her, though this was far from being his intention. He had nothing but praise to bestow on Sylvester. He told the Duchess that the boy did just as he ought, his manners being particularly correct. "Very affable and civil, you know, but knows how to keep a proper distance," said Lord William. "No need to fear he'll forget what he owes to his position, my dear sister! He tells me he's thinking of getting married. Very proper. High time he was setting up his nursery! He seems to be going about the business exactly as he should, but I dropped him a hint. Don't think it was necessary, mind, but I shouldn't like to see him make a fool of himself for want of a word of advice. But thank the lord he's got no rubbishing romantical notions in his head!"

It was the immutable custom of the House of Rayne for as many members of it as could possibly do so to gather together at Christmas under the roof of the head of the family. As the family was enormous, and most of those who congregated at Chance remained for a month, Sylvester had little leisure, and saw less of his mother than he liked. He was an excellent host, and he had an excellent supporter in his sister-in-law, who, besides having a turn for entertaining, very much enjoyed acting as deputy for the Duchess, and consequently became more cheerful as soon as the first of the visitors crossed the threshold. Her pleasure was only marred by Sylvester's refusal to invite Sir Nugent Fotherby to join the party. She argued that if he could invite her father and mother he could with equal propriety invite her affianced husband, but any intention she might have had of developing this grievance was checked by the intervention of both parents. Lord Elvaston, to whom Sir Nugent was objectionable, informed her that if he had found the fellow at Chance he would have gone home instantly, and Lady Elvaston, though willing to tolerate Sir Nugent for the sake of his vast wealth, told her that if she thought to win Sylvester round by affording him the opportunity of studying that amiable dandy at close quarters she was no better than a ninnyhammer.

Sylvester left Chance towards the end of January, a day later than his last, lingering guest. He was bound for Blandford Park, whither his hunters were sent by the direct route from Leicestershire; but he went first to London, a deviation that caused no surprise, since he told his mother he had business there. As it was hunting, not matrimony, that took him to Blandford Park she was able to see him off without any immediate apprehension of his proposing to one of the five eligible candidates for his hand. None of these ladies would be at Blandford Park; and it was in the highest degree unlikely that they were to be found in London either, at the end of January. The Duchess believed he would be granted little opportunity to commit his contemplated imprudence until the beginning of the season. But he had omitted to tell her what was his chief business in town. He went to pay a morning visit to his godmother.

The Dowager Lady Ingham lived in Green Street, in a house bursting with all the furniture and ornaments she had insisted on removing from Ingham House on the occasion of her son's marriage, and her own retirement to Green Street. Any piece for which she had a fancy she insisted was her personal property; and since neither Ingham nor his gentle bride was a match for her she bore off several heirlooms, handsomely promising, however, to bequeathe them to their rightful owner. She also removed the butler, but as he was growing old and was obstinate in his adherence to customs Lord Ingham thought obsolete, this was not felt to be a loss. He was now considerably stricken in years, went about his duties in a slow and stately manner, and discouraged the Dowager from holding any entertainments more arduous than a small soirée, or a card-party. Fortunately she had no wish to give dinner-parties, or breakfasts, excusing herself on the score of age and infirmity. She was not, in fact, much above five-and-sixty; and beyond a tendency to gout no one had any very clear idea of what her infirmities might be. She certainly walked with the aid of an ebony cane; and whenever she was confronted with any disagreeable form of exertion she was threatened with palpitations, and was obliged to send for Sir Henry Halford, who understood her constitution so well that he could always be depended on to recommend her to do precisely what she wished.

When Sylvester was ushered into her crowded drawing-room she greeted him with a snort; but she was pleased to receive a visit from him nevertheless; and after telling him acidly that she had well-nigh forgotten what he looked like she unbent sufficiently to give him her hand, and allow him to kiss it. Mollified by the grace with which he performed this courtesy she waved him to a chair on the opposite side of the fireplace and bade him tell her how his mother did.

"I left her pretty well, I think," he answered. "But tell me, ma'am, how *you* do?"

She told him. The recital lasted for twenty minutes, and might have lasted longer had she not suddenly bethought herself of something she wanted to know. She broke off her account of her aches and ails abruptly, saying: "Never mind that! What's this I'm hearing about your brother's widow? The on-dit is that she's going to marry a man-milliner. I knew his father: a namby-pamby creature *he* was, though he passed for an amiable man. They tell me the son is a Pink of the Ton. I suppose he has a genteel fortune? Old Fotherby should have cut up warm."

"Oh, as rich as Golden Ball!" Sylvester replied.

"Is he indeed? H'm!" She was evidently impressed by this, but said after a reflective moment: "In a vast hurry to be married again, ain't she? What happens to the boy?"

"He will remain at Chance, of course."

She stared at him. "What, is your poor mother to be charged with the care of him?"

"No, certainly not." He held up his quizzing-glass, twisting it between finger and thumb, and watching the flash of firelight on its magnifying lens. "I am thinking of getting married myself, ma'am."

"Well, it's high time," she responded snappishly. "The Torrington girl, I collect?"

"I suppose she might answer the purpose—if I could be sure she would not be hipped at Chance. It is an object with me, you know, ma'am, to choose a wife who will be acceptable to my mother."

If she thought this an odd reason for matrimony she did not say so. "Is your heart engaged?" she demanded.

"Not in the least," he replied. "You see what a quandary I am in! Do advise me!"

She did not speak for a minute, but he knew that she was on the alert, and was content to wait, idly swinging his quizzing-glass.

"You can pour yourself out a glass of wine!" she said suddenly. "I'll take one too—though I don't doubt I shall suffer for it."

He rose, and crossed the room to where Horwich had set a silver tray on a side-table. When he came back to the fire, and put a glass of sherry into the Dowager's hand, he said lightly: "Now, if you were only a fairy godmother, ma'am, you would wave your wand, and so conjure up exactly the bride I want!"

He returned to his chair as he spoke, and had embarked on a change of subject when she interrupted him, saying: "I may not be able to wave a wand, but I daresay I could produce an eligible bride for you." She set her glass down. "What you want, Sylvester, is a pretty-behaved girl of good birth, good upbringing, and an amiable dispositon. If your Uncle William were not a zany he would have arranged just such an alliance for you years ago, and you may depend upon it you would have been very comfortable in it. Well, I haven't meddled, though I own I've been tempted, when I've heard how you were making up to first this female and then that. However, you've now applied to me, and it's my belief that if you wish for a wife who will know what her duty is and be more acceptable than any other to your mother, you could do no better for yourself than to offer for my granddaughter. I don't mean one of Ingham's girls, but Phoebe: my Verena's child."

He was extremely annoyed. His godmother was not playing the game as he had planned it. Those carefully casual words of his should have prompted her not to hold him up at the sword's point, but to have produced her granddaughter presently (at the start of the season, perhaps) for his inspection. There was a lack of finesse about her conduct of the affair which vexed and alarmed him; for while the notion of marrying the daughter of his mother's dear friend had taken possession of his mind its hold was not so strong that it could not speedily be broken by the discovery that Miss Marlow was lacking in the qualities he considered indispensable in his wife. In Lady Ingham's bluntness he saw an attempt to force his hand, and nothing could more surely set up the back of a young man who had been, virtually, his own master from the time he was nineteen, and the master of a great many other persons as well. He said in a cool tone: "Indeed? Have I met your granddaughter, ma'am? I think I have not."

"I don't know. She was brought out last season—it should have been done before, but she contracted scarlet fever, and so it was put off for a year. She will be twenty in October: I'm not offering you a schoolroom miss. As for the rest—I imagine you must several times have been in company with her, for she was taken to all the ton parties. *I* saw to that! If I had left it to that woman Marlow married as his second the poor child would have spent her time at museums, and the Concerts of Ancient Music, for that's Constance Marlow's notion of disporting herself in town! Marlow married her before Phoebe was out of leading-strings, the more fool he! Not but what I give the woman credit for having done her duty by the child. She has been well brought-up—no question about that!" Glancing across at Sylvester she saw that he was wearing his satyr-look, and she said with the sharpness of defiance: "*I* couldn't take charge of the girl! At my age, and with my indifferent health it wasn't to be thought of!"

He said nothing, nor did the satyr-look abate. Since Lady

Ingham had made no attempt during the previous season to bring her granddaughter to his notice he concluded that Miss Marlow was probably a plain girl, unlikely to attract him. He tried to remember whether he had seen a girl with Lady Marlow on the few occasions when he had found himself in company with that forbidding lady. If he had, she held no place in his memory.

"Phoebe's not one of your beauties," said the Dowager, almost as if she had read his mind. "She don't show to advantage with her mother-in-law, but to my way of thinking she's not just in the ordinary style. If pink-and-white's your fancy, she wouldn't do for you. If you want quality, and a girl with a quick understanding, you'd like her. As for her fortune, she won't inherit much from Marlow, but her mother's dowry was tied up in her, so she'll have that, besides what I shall leave her." She was silent for a minute, but said presently: "It would please your mother, and I don't deny it would please me too. I want to see Verena's child comfortably established. She's not an heiress, but her fortune won't be contemptible; and as for her birth, Marlow's a fool, but his blood's well enough; and the Inghams may look as high as they please when it comes to matchmaking. But if an alliance with my granddaughter isn't to your taste, pray don't hesitate to tell me so!"

This set the seal on his resentment. She was apparently trying to fluster him into committing himself. A stupid move: she ought to know that hers was not the first trap set for him. He rose, smiling at her with apparently unruffled serenity, and said, as he lifted her hand to his lips: "I can't suppose, my dear ma'am, that you need my assurance that on the score of eligibility I could have no possible objection to the match. I shall only say, therefore, that I hope to have the pleasure of meeting Miss Marlow—this season, perhaps? Ah, that will be delightful!"

He left her with no clue to his sentiments, but in an angry mood that was not soothed by the reflection that he had laid himself open to her attack. She had proposed to him only what he had had in mind when he visited her, but the alacrity with which she had snapped at the chance offered her was almost as offensive as her attempt to force his hand. It was also stupid, for it inspired him with nothing more than a desire to cross Miss Marlow off the list of his eligibles, and propose without much waste of time to one of the remaining five. Unfortunately, the impropriety of such conduct made it impossible for him to administer this salutary lesson to the Dowager. She must regard it as a studied insult (which, indeed, it would be), and so wholly beneath him was it to insult her that he could only shrug, and resign himself. There was nothing to be done now until he had met Miss Marlow.

He put the matter aside, only to be confronted with it again the following week, when, upon arrival at Blandford Park, he found Lord Marlow to be one of his fellow-guests.

In itself this circumstance was not suspicous. Marlow and the Duke of Beaufort were old friends; and since Austerby, Marlow's seat, was situated in the rather indifferent country south of Calne he was a frequent visitor to Badminton during the hunting-season. The Heythrop country, which was hunted by the Duke alternately with the Badminton district, was farther from Austerby and saw his lordship less often, but he was not a stranger to the hunt. Sylvester could have believed that his presence at Blandford Park was due to the workings of chance had it not soon been borne in upon him that Marlow was there by design.

Lord Marlow was always bluff and good-natured, but he had never been on anything more than common civility terms with Sylvester, twenty-five years his junior. On this occasion, however, his object was to stand well with him, and nothing could have exceeded his affability. Sylvester saw that Lady Ingham had been busy, and had the encounter taken place anywhere but at a hunting-party he might have rebuffed his lordship's overtures with the chilling formality he was quite capable of adopting whenever it seemed expedient to him to do so. But Lord Marlow blundering jovially through the London scene and Lord Marlow bestriding one of his high-bred hunters were two very different persons. The one could be held in contempt; the other commanded the respect of every hunting-man. Whether over the black fences of Leicestershire or the stone walls of the Cotswold uplands he had few equals, and not even Lord Alvanley could match him for intrepidity. Every available penny from the yield of a fortune long since found to be inadequate was spent on his slapping hunters, of which he never had fewer than fourteen in his stables; and to be singled out by him on the field for a word of advice or approval was the ambition of every young blood seeking to emulate his prowess. Sylvester might know very well why he had suddenly become the recipient of his lordship's favours, but he could not be indifferent to the bluff word of praise, or ungrateful for the advice which taught him the trick of the stone walls. One thing leading to another, before the end of the week he was fairly caught, and had accepted an invitation to stay for a few days at Austerby when he left Blandford Park. Lord Marlow was generally thought to be a stupid man, but he was not so stupid as to let it appear that he had any other object in mind than to show Sylvester what sport was to be had in admittedly humbug country; and possibly (if it should suit him) to sell him a promising five-year-old that was not quite up to his own weight. There was to be no ceremony about this visit; they would leave Blandford Park together, and Salford would take his pot-luck at Austerby. Lord Marlow made no mention of his daughter; and in these circumstances Sylvester allowed himself to be persuaded. On the whole he was not displeased. Under his host's unexpectedly tactful handling of the affair he could make the acquaintance of Miss Marlow without in any way committing himself: a better arrangement, he was disposed to think, than a formal London party to which he would be invited for the express purpose of meeting the young lady.

CHAPTER

4

The schoolroom of Austerby was presided over by a lady of quelling aspect whose rawbone frame was invariably clad in sober-hued dresses made high to the neck and unadorned by flounces. Her sandy hair was smoothly banded under a cap; her complexion was weatherbeaten; her eyes of a pale blue; and her nose, the most salient feature of her countenance, jutted out intimidatingly. She had a gruff way of talking, and as her voice was a deep one this helped to make her seem a veritable dragon.

Appearances, however, were deceptive. Under Miss Sibylla Battery's formidable front beat a warmly affectionate heart. With the possible exception of Eliza, Lady Marlow's third and best loved daughter, her young charges all adored her; and Phoebe, Susan, Mary, and even little Kitty confided their hopes and their griefs to her, and loyally shielded her from blame in their peccadilloes.

It might have been supposed that Miss Phoebe Marlow, nineteen years of age, and a débutante of a season's standing, would have been emancipated from the schoolroom; but as she feared and disliked her stepmother, and was cordially disliked by Lady Marlow, she was glad to make Italian lessons with

Miss Battery an excuse to spend what time she could spare from the stables in the schoolroom. This arrangement suited Lady Marlow equally well, for although she had striven her utmost to rear her stepdaughter in the image of a genteel young female, none of the whippings Phoebe had received and no weight of hours spent in solitary confinement had availed to purge her of what her ladyship called her hoydenish tricks. She careered all over the country-side, mounted either on her own cover-hack, or on one of her father's big hunters; tore her clothes; hobnobbed with grooms; stitched abominably; and was (in Lady Marlow's opinion) on far too easy terms with Mr. Thomas Orde, her life-long friend and the son of the Squire. Had she had her way Lady Marlow would have very speedily put a stop to any but the mildest form of equestrian exercise; but to every representation made to him on this sore subject Lord Marlow turned a deaf ear. He was in general the most compliant of husbands, but horses were his passion, and her ladyship had learnt long ago that any attempt to interfere in what concerned the stables would fail. Like many weak men, Lord Marlow could be mulish in obstinacy. He was proud of Phoebe's horsemanship, liked to take her out with him on hunting-days, and could ill have spared her from his stables, which she managed, in theory, during his frequent absences from home, and, in practice, at all times.

Summoned peremptorily to London by Lady Ingham, Lord Marlow, an indolent man, left Austerby grumbling. He returned two days later in the best of spirits, and in unaccustomed charity with his one-time mother-in-law. Such a brilliant match as she seemed to have arranged for Phoebe he had never hoped to achieve, for Phoebe had not taken very well during her London season. Lady Marlow had drilled her into propriety; it was Lord Marlow's unexpressed opinion that she had overdone it. A little more vivacity, of which he knew Phoebe to have plenty, was needed to overcome the disadvantages of a thin, wiry figure, a brown complexion, and no more beauty than could be found in a pair of clear gray eyes, which could certainly twinkle with mischief, but which more frequently held a look of scared apprehension.

Lady Marlow was a Christian woman, and she did not grudge Phoebe her astonishing good fortune, however unworthy of it she might be. Indeed, she determined to see to it that Phoebe did nothing to alienate such an eligible suitor during his stay at Austerby. "For, you may depend upon it," she said, "that whatever whimsical notion Salford may have taken into his head of offering for the daughter of his mama's friend he will marry none but a female who conducts herself with propriety. For my part, I am persuaded this marriage has been proposed to him by Lady Ingham. Phoebe has yet to establish herself in his eyes. He met her in London in the spring—indeed, he stood up with her at Lady Sefton's ball—but if he would recognize her again it is more than I bargain for."

"You don't think, my love," his lordship ventured to suggest, "that it might be wiser not to inform her why he comes to visit us—that is, if he does come, which, you know, is not certain?"

No, her ladyship did not think so at all, unless it was my lord's wish that his daughter should instantly disgust the Duke by coming in spattered all over with mud, blurting out one of her ill-considered remarks, or giving him a very odd notion of her character by encouraging the familiarities of young Orde.

Lord Marlow wished for none of these things, and although he saw no harm in her alliance with young Orde, and knew their relationship to be that of brother and sister, he was easily brought to believe that it might be misunderstood by Salford, a pretty high stickler. He agreed that Tom's visits to Austerby, and Phoebe's to the Manor, should be discouraged, and kept to himself his earnest hope that his helpmate might not offend the Squire and his lady. Lord Marlow did not like to be on bad terms with his neighbours; besides, the Squire was the Master of the hunt, and although his lordship did most of his hunting in the shires it still would by no means suit him to fall out with the local Master. But Lady Marlow said commandingly: "Leave it to me!" and, on the whole, he was only too glad to do so.

It was agreed that nothing should be said to Phoebe until he had secured the Duke's promise to visit Austerby; but when his second groom came over from Blandford Park with a letter from him to her ladyship, warning her that when he returned at the end of the week Salford would be accompanying him, she instantly sent for Phoebe to her dressing-room.

Phoebe obeyed the summons in considerable trepidation; but when she entered the dressing-room she was greeted, if not with cordiality, at least not with the bleak look that still had the power to make her heart knock against her ribs. Lady Marlow told her to shut the door and sit down. She then noticed that one of the flounces of Phoebe's gown had come unstitched, and drew her attention to it, reading her a homily on the evils of slovenliness, and expressing the hope that she would have no occasion, in the near future, to blush for her.

"No, Mama," Phoebe said, wondering why the near future was of particular importance.

"I have sent for you," pursued her ladyship, "to inform you of a very gratifying circumstance. I do not scruple to say that the good fortune which is coming to you is a great deal more than you have done anything to deserve, and I can only trust that you may be found to be worthy of it." She paused, but Phoebe only looked rather bewildered. "I daresay," she continued, "that you may have wondered what it was that took your papa to London at this season."

Since she had not given the matter a thought Phoebe was a good deal astonished. It was not Lady Marlow's custom to encourage the girls to indulge in curiosity, and an enquiry into the nature of Papa's business in town would certainly have met with a heavy snub.

"You are surprised that I should mention the matter to you," said her ladyship, observing Phoebe's expression. "I do so because it was on your behalf that he undertook the fatigue of a journey to London. You should be very much obliged to him, which I am persuaded you must be when I tell you that he is about to arrange a very advantageous marriage for you."

Phoebe was well aware that in failing to secure at least one respectable offer during her London season she had fallen lamentably short of expectation, and this announcement made her look more astonished than ever. "Good gracious!" she exclaimed involuntarily. "But I don't think—I mean, no one made up to me, except old Mr. Hardwick, and that was only because of my mother!"

She then quailed, flushing to the roots of her hair as she came under a basilisk stare from Lady Marlow's cold eyes.

"*Made up to you——!*" repeated Lady Marlow ominously. "I need not ask from whom you learned such a vulgarism, but perhaps you will inform me how you dared permit me to hear it on your lips?"

"I beg your pardon, ma'am!" faltered Phoebe.

"Such language may do very well for young Orde," said her ladyship bitingly. "No female with the smallest claim to refinement would use it. And if you were to express yourself in such a manner to the Duke of Salford I tremble to think what the consequences might be!"

Phoebe blinked at her. "To the Duke of Salford, ma'am? But how should I? I mean, I am sure there can be no danger, for I am barely acquainted with him. I shouldn't think," she added reflectively, "that he even remembers me."

"You are mistaken," replied Lady Marlow. "He is to visit us next week, with what object I imagine you may guess."

"Well, I haven't the least notion what it may be," said Phoebe in a puzzled voice.

"He is coming with the intention of making you an offer—and you will oblige me, Phoebe, by not sitting there in a stare, and with your mouth open!"

"M-me?" stammered Phoebe. *The Duke of Salford?*

Not displeased to find her daughter incredulous, Lady Marlow bestowed than smile upon her. "I do not wonder that you should be surprised, for it is far more than *I* ever hoped for you, I can tell you. I shall expect to hear you express your gratitude to Papa for his kindness in arranging so splendid a match for you."

"I don't believe it!" Phoebe cried vehemently. "Besides, I don't want to marry the Duke of Salford!"

No sooner had the words been uttered than she trembled at her boldness, and for several moments dared not raise her eyes to the austere countenance confronting her. An awful silence greeted her rash speech, which was broken at last by Lady Marlow's demanding to know whether her ears had deceived her. Judging this question to be rhetorical Phoebe made no attempt to answer it, but only hung her head.

"A marriage of the first consequence is offered to you: a marriage that must make you the envy of a score of young females, all of them by far more handsome than you will ever be, and you have the audacity to tell me you do not want it! Upon my word, Phoebe——!"

"But, ma'am, I am persuaded it is all a mistake! Why, I only spoke to him once in my life, and that was at the Seftons' ball, when he stood up with me for one dance. He thought it a great bore, and when I saw him not three days after, at Almack's, he *cut* me!"

"Pray do not talk in that nonsensical style!" said her ladyship sharply. "Your situation in life renders you an eligible wife for a man of rank, however unsuited to a great position I may consider you to be; and I don't doubt the Duke must be aware that your upbringing has been in accordance with the highest principles."

"But there are others j-just as well brought-up, and m-much prettier!" Phoebe said, twisting her fingers together.

"You have over them what his grace apparently believes to be an advantage," responded Lady Marlow repressively. "Whether he may be right is not for me to say, though I should rather have supposed——however, on *that* subject I prefer to be silent. Your mother was a close friend of the Duke's mother, which is why you have been singled out. I tell you this so that you shall not become puffed up in your own conceit, my dear Phoebe. Nothing is more unbecoming in a young woman, I can assure you."

"Puffed up! I should rather think not!" Phoebe said hastily. "Offer for me because his mother knew mine? I—I never heard of anything so—so monstrous! When he is barely acquainted with me, and has never made the least push to engage my interest!"

"It is for that precise reason that he is coming to visit us," said Lady Marlow, with the patience of one addressing an idiot. "He desires to become better acquainted with you, and I trust you are neither so foolish nor so undutiful as to conduct yourself in a way that must make him think better of offering for your hand." She paused, scanning Phoebe's face. What she read in it caused her to change her tactics. The girl, though in general biddable enough, showed occasionally a streak of obstinacy. Lady Marlow did not doubt her ability to command her ultimate obedience, but she knew that if Phoebe were to take one of her odd notions into her head she was quite capable of repulsing the Duke before there was time to bring her back to a state of proper submission. So she began to point out the advantages of the match, even going so far as to say that Phoebe would like to be mistress of her own establishment. Winning no other response than a blank stare, she lost no time in drawing, with vigour and fluency, a grim picture of the alternative to becoming the Duchess of Salford. As this seemed to include a life of unending disgrace at Austerby (for it was not to be expected that Lord Marlow, with four more daughters to establish, would waste any more money on her ungrateful eldest-born); the reproaches of her sisters, of whose advancement she would have shown herself to be wickedly careless; and various other penalties, a number of which were not rendered less terrible for being left unnamed, it should have been enough to have brought a far more recalcitrant girl than Phoebe to her senses. She did indeed look very white and frightened, so Lady Marlow dismissed her to think it over.

Phoebe fled back to the schoolroom. Here she found not only Susan, but her two next sisters as well: thirteen-year-old Mary, and the saintly Eliza. Susan, perceiving that Phoebe was big with news, instantly banished Eliza to the nursery, and, when that affronted damsel showed signs of recalcitrance, forcibly ejected her from the room, recommending her to go and tell Mama, and to be careful how she got into bed later. This sinister warning quelled Eliza, the horrid memory of a slug found between her sheets still lively in her mind, and she prepared to join the youngest of the family in the nursery, merely apostrophizing Susan, through the keyhole, as the greatest beast in nature before taking herself off. Unfortunately, Miss Battery came along the passage at that moment and very properly consigned her to her bedroom for using language unbecoming to a young lady of quality. Eliza complained in a whining voice that Phoebe and Sukey were very unkind and would not tell her any of their secrets, but this only drew down on her a reprimand for indulging the sin of curiosity. Miss Battery led her inexorably to her bedchamber before repairing to the schoolroom.

She reached the room just as Mary, a humble-minded girl, gathered her books together, asking her sister whether she too must go away.

"Not unless Phoebe wishes it," replied Susan. *"You* don't carry tales to Mama!"

"Oh, no!" Phoebe said. "Of course I don't wish you to go, Mary! Besides, it isn't a secret. She looked round quickly as the door opened, and exclaimed: "Oh, Sibby, did *you* know? Did Mama tell you?"

"No," said Miss Battery. "I overheard something your papa said to her, though. Couldn't help but do so. I thought it not right to say anything to you, but when I heard you had been sent for to the dressing-room I guessed what it must be. Your papa has received an offer for your hand."

"No!" cried Susan. "Phoebe, has he indeed?"

"Yes—at least, I think—Oh, I don't know, but Mama seems to think he *will*, if only I will conduct myself *conformably*!"

"Oh, famous!" Susan declared, clapping her hands. "Who is he? How could you be so sly as never to breathe a word about it? Did you meet him in London? Is he passionately in love with you?"

"No," replied Phoebe baldly.

This damping monosyllable checked Susan's raptures. Miss Battery looked rather anxiously at Phoebe; and Mary said diffidently that she rather supposed that persons of quality did not fall in love.

"That's only what Mama says, and *I* know it isn't true!" said Susan scornfully. "*Is* it, ma'am?"

"Can't say," responded Miss Battery briefly. "Nor can you. Shouldn't be thinking of such things at your age."

"Pooh, I am nearly sixteen, and I can tell you I mean to get a husband as soon as I can! Phoebe, do stop being missish, and tell us who he is!"

"I'm not being missish!" said Phoebe indignantly. "I am in flat despair, and he is the Duke of Salford!"

"W-what?" gasped Susan. "Phoebe, you wretch, you're hoaxing us! Only fancy you as a duchess!"

Phoebe was not in the least offended by her burst of hearty laughter, but Mary said stoutly: "I think Phoebe would make a very *nice* duchess."

That made Phoebe laugh too, but Miss Battery nodded, and said: "So she would!"

"How can you say so?" expostulated Phoebe. "When I haven't the smallest turn for fashion, and never know what to say to strangers, or——"

"Is he fashionable?" interrupted Susan eagerly.

"Oh, excessively! That is, I don't know, but I should think he would be. He is always very well dressed, and he goes to all the ton parties, and drives a splendid pair of dapple-grays in the Park. I shouldn't wonder at it if he spent as much as a hundred pounds a year on soap in his stables."

"Well, that ought to make him acceptable to you!" observed Susan. "But what is he like? Is he young? Handsome?"

"I don't know what his age may be. He is not *old*, I suppose. As for handsome, people say he is, but *I* do not think so. In fact——" She stopped suddenly, aware of Mary's innocently enquiring gaze, and ended her description of Sylvester by saying only that she judged him to ride about twelve stone.

Mary, who had a retentive memory, said hopefully: "Papa

used to ride twelve stone when he was a young man. He said so once, and also that it is the best weight for hunting over strong country. Does the Duke hunt over strong country, Phoebe?"

Susan broke in on this with pardonable impatience. "Who cares a fig for that? I wish you won't be so provoking, Phoebe! Why don't you want him to offer for you? Is he disagreeable? For my part, if he were rich and reasonably civil I shouldn't care for anything else. Only fancy! You would have a house of your own, and as many new dresses as you wished, and very likely splendid jewels as well, besides being able to do just as you chose!"

Miss Battery eyed her with disfavour. "If you can't refrain from expressing yourself with what I can't call anything but vulgarity, Susan, I must impose silence upon you. In any event, it is past the hour, and you should be practising that sonatina."

Having in this masterly fashion disposed of Susan, Miss Battery recommended Mary to occupy herself for half an hour with the sampler she was embroidering for her Mama's birthday, and left the room, taking Phoebe with her. Firmly shutting the schoolroom door she said in a lowered voice: "Thought it best you should say no more to Susan. Good girl, but wants discretion. You're all of a twitter: why?"

"It is the most shocking thing!" Phoebe declared, looking quite distracted. "If it were anyone but Mama I should think it a take-in! But *Mama*——! Oh dear, I am utterly confounded! I feel as though my senses won't be straight again for a twelve-month!"

"Not so loud!" said Miss Battery. "Tell me in your bed-chamber! Try to recover your composure, my dear."

Thus adjured, Phoebe followed her meekly along the corridor to her bedchamber. Since one of Lady Marlow's favourite economies was to allow no fires to be kindled in any bed-chamber but her own, her lord's, and those occupied by such guests as were hardy enough to visit Austerby during the winter months, this apartment might have been considered singularly unsuitable for a *tête-à-tête*. Phoebe, however, was inured to its rigours. Miss Battery, stalking over to the wardrobe, and unearthing from it a large shawl, wrapped this round her pupil's thin shoulders, saying as she did so: "I collect you don't wish for this match. Can't deny that it's a flattering one, or that I should like to see you so well-established. Now, tell me this,

40

child: have you got some silly notion in your head about that scheme of yours to set up for yourself with me to bear you company? Because if so don't give it a thought! *I* shan't. Never supposed it would come to pass—or wished for it, if you received an agreeable offer."

"No, no, it's not that!" Phoebe said. "For if I were to be married who but you should I want to instruct my children? Sibby, do you know who Salford is?"

Miss Battery frowned at her in a puzzled way. "Who he is?" she repeated. "You said he was a duke."

Phoebe began to laugh a little hysterically. "He is Count Ugolino!" she said.

It might have been expected that this extraordinary announcement would have still further bewildered Miss Battery, but although she was certainly startled by it, she found it perfectly intelligible. Ejaculating: "Merciful heavens!" she sat down limply, and stared at Phoebe in great perturbation. She was well-acquainted with the Count: indeed, she might have been said to have been present at his birth, an event for which she was, in some measure, responsible, since she had for several years shared with Phoebe the romantic novels which were the solace of her own leisure hours. Her only extravagance was a subscription to a Bath lending library; her only conscious sin was that she encouraged Lady Marlow to suppose that the package delivered weekly by the carrier contained only works of an erudite or an elevating character. So strong was Lady Marlow's disapproval of fiction that even Miss Edgeworth's moral tales were forbidden to her daughters. Her rule was so absolute that it never occurred to her to doubt that she was obeyed to the letter; and as she was as imperceptive as she was despotic no suspicion had ever crossed her mind that Miss Battery was by no means the rigid disciplinarian she appeared.

In none of Lady Marlow's own daughters did Miss Battery discover the imaginative turn of mind so much deprecated by her ladyship; in Phoebe it was pronounced, and Miss Battery, loving her and deeply pitying her, fostered it, knowing how much her own joyless existence was lightened by excursions into a world of pure make-believe. From the little girl who scribbled fairy stories for the rapt delectation of Susan and Mary, Phoebe had developed into a real authoress, and one, moreover, who had written a stirring romance worthy of being published.

She had written it after her London season. It had come white-hot from her ready pen, and Miss Battery had been quick to see that it was far in advance of her earlier attempts at novel-writing. Its plot was as extravagant as anything that came from the Minerva Press; the behaviour of its characters was for the most part wildly improbable; the scene was laid in an unidentifiable country; and the entire story was rich in absurdity. But Phoebe's pen had always been persuasive, and so enthralling did she contrive to make the adventures of her heroine that it was not until he had reached the end of the book that even so stern a critic as young Mr. Orde bethought him of the various incidents which he saw, in retrospect, to be impossible. Miss Battery, a more discerning critic, recognized not only the popular nature of the tale, but also the flowering in it of a latent talent. Phoebe had discovered in herself a gift for humorous portraiture, and she had not wasted her time in London. Tom Orde might complain that a score of minor characters were irrelevant, but Miss Battery knew that it was these swift, unerring sketches that raised *The Lost Heir* above the commonplace. She would not allow Phoebe to expunge one of them, or a line of their wickedly diverting dialogues, but persuaded her instead to write it all out in fairest copperplate. Phoebe groaned at this tedious labour, but since neither she nor Miss Battery knew of a professional copyist, and would have been hard put to it to have paid for such a person's services, she submitted to the drudgery. After that the book was packed up, and despatched by the mail to Miss Battery's cousin, Mr. Gilbert Otley, junior partner in the small but aspiring firm of Newsham & Otley, Publishers.

Mr. Otley, receiving the manuscript and perusing the accompanying letter from Miss Battery, was unimpressed. At first glance he did not think *The Lost Heir* the sort of book he wished to handle; and the intelligence that it was the work of a Lady of Quality drew from him only a heavy sigh. However, he took *The Lost Heir* home with him, and read it at a sitting. It did not take him long to perceive that it was to some extent a *roman à clef*, for although he was unacquainted with the members of the *haut ton* he was shrewd enough to realize that the authoress in depicting many of her characters was drawing from the life. The success of *Glenarvon*, published some eighteen months previously, was still fresh in his mind; and it was this circumstance which led him, rather doubtfully, to hand *The Lost Heir* to his partner.

Mr. Harvey Newsham was unexpectedly enthusiastic; and when Mr. Otley pointed out to him that it was not such a book as they had been used to produce he replied caustically that if it enjoyed better sales than had the last three of these works he for one should not complain.

"But will it?" said Mr. Otley. "The story is no great thing, after all—in fact it's nonsensical!"

"No one will care for that."

"Well, I don't know. I should have thought it too fantastical myself. In fact, it still has me in a puzzle. How the devil did that Ugolino-fellow get hold of his nephew in the first place? And why didn't he smother him, or something, when he *had* got hold of him, instead of keeping him prisoner in that castle of his? And as for the boy's sister managing to get into the place, let alone that corkbrained hero, and then the pair of them setting sail with the boy—well, they couldn't have done it!"

Mr. Newsham dismissed such trivialities with a wave of his hand. "It doesn't signify. This female——" he jabbed a finger at Phoebe's manuscript—"knows how to do the trick! What's more, the book's stuffed with people she's met, and *that's* what will make the nobs buy it." He glanced down at the manuscript appraisingly. "In three volumes, handsomely bound," he said thoughtfully. "At the start of next season. Say April—skilfully puffed-off, of course. I think it will do, Otley!"

"It will be pretty expensive," objected Mr. Otley.

"I mean this book to be in every fashionable drawing-room, and it won't do to get it up shoddy. Colburn issued Lady Caroline Lamb's tale in tooled leather. It looked very well."

"Ay, but you may depend upon it Lady Caroline paid for it," retorted Mr. Otley.

"No reason to suppose this author won't do the same," said the optimistic Mr. Newsham. "Offer her profit-sharing terms, she to pay all losses. You know, my boy, if the book were to take, Colburn will be as surly as a butcher's dog to think it wasn't offered him!"

"So he will!" agreed Mr. Otley, cheered by this reflection. "I'll write off to my cousin next week: we don't wish to appear overanxious to come to terms. I shall tell her it ain't just in our line, besides having a good many faults."

This programme, being approved by the senior partner, was carried out; but from then on the negotiations proceeded on quite different lines from those envisaged by Mr. Otley. Miss Battery's prompt reply afforded him a new insight into that lady's character. Begging his pardon for having put him to the trouble of reading a work which she now realized to be unsuitable matter for the firm of Newsham & Otley she requested him to return it to her by the mail, care of the receiving office in Bath. Further enquiries had given her to think that the manuscript ought to be offered to Colburn, or perhaps to Egerton. She would be much obliged to him for his advice on this point, and remained his affectionate cousin, Sibylla Battery.

Recovering from this setback, Mr. Otley then entered upon some spirited bargaining, agreement being finally reached at the sum of £150, to be received by Miss Battery on behalf of the author upon receipt by the publisher of the booksellers' accounts. Left to himself Mr. Otley would have done his possible to have reduced this figure by £50, but at this stage of the negotiations Mr. Newsham intervened, giving it as his opinion that to behave scaly to a promising new author could result only in her offering her second book to a rival publisher. He would have been gratified could he but have known to what dizzy heights his generosity raised Miss Marlow's spirits. The sum seemed enormous to her; and then and there was born her determination to leave Austerby as soon as she came of age, and with Miss Battery for chaperon to set up a modest establishment of her own in which she would be able without interference to pursue her lucrative vocation.

Besides Miss Battery only Mr. Orde shared the secret of her authorship, and it was not until he had been permitted to see the proof-sheets that Mr. Orde was relieved of his suspicion that the whole affair was an attempt to hoax him. He was much more impressed by the sight of the story in actual print than he thought it proper to admit; but he very handsomely acknowledged to the proud author that he had not believed it could read half as well.

CHAPTER

5

Miss Battery, a strong-minded female, did not for many minutes allow her consternation to overpower her. Squaring her shoulders, she said: "Unfortunate! That you should have taken him in dislike, I mean. No more to be said, if that's the case. Though I don't suppose he can be as villainous as Count Ugolino. No one could be."

"Oh, no! He isn't villainous at all—at least, I shouldn't think he would be, but I'm not even acquainted with him! I only chose him for Ugolino because of the way his eyebrows slant, which makes him look just like a villain. And also, of course, because of his—his *crested* air, which made me long to give him a set-down!"

"Self-consequence?" said Miss Battery, a little at sea. "Thinks too much of his rank?"

Phoebe shook her head, frowning. "No, it isn't that. It is—yes, it is worse than that! I think it is so natural to him to have all that consequence that he doesn't give it a thought. Do you understand, Sibby?"

"No. Oughtn't to give it a thought."

"It is very difficult to explain, but I am persuaded you *will* understand, when you see him. It is as though being a duke

45

is so much a part of him that he takes it perfectly for granted, and quite unconsciously expects to be treated everywhere with distinction. I don't mean to say that his manners are not what they ought to be, for he has a great deal of well-bred ease— a sort of cool civility, you know, towards persons who don't interest him. I believe he is very amiable to those whom he likes, but the thing is—or so I fancy—that he doesn't care a button for what anyone may think of him. To be sure, *that* isn't wonderful," she added reflectively, "for the way he is courted and toad-eaten is quite repulsive! Why, when Lady Sefton brought him up to me—she is the Baroness Josceline in my story, you know: the affected, fidgety one!—she introduced him as though she were conferring the greatest favour on me!"

"That doesn't signify," interrupted Miss Battery. "Did *he* behave as though he thought it so?"

"Oh, no! He is so much accustomed to such flattery that he doesn't appear even to heed it. Being civil to poor little dabs of females who have neither beauty nor conversation is one of the tiresome duties his exalted situation obliges him to perform."

"Well, if I were you, my dear, I wouldn't fly into a pucker yet awhile," said Miss Battery with strong commonsense. "Seems to me you don't know anything about him. One thing you can depend on: if he's coming here to make you an offer he won't treat you with cool civility!"

"Even if he did not—oh, he must have changed indeed if I were to like him well enough to marry him!" declared Phoebe. "I *could* not, Sibby!"

"Then you will decline his offer," said Miss Battery, with a conviction she was far from feeling.

Phoebe looked at her rather hopelessly, but said nothing. She knew it to be unnecessary. No one understood more thoroughly the difficulties of her situation than her governess; and no one was better acquainted with the ruthlessness of Lady Marlow's imperious temper. After a few moments' reflection Miss Battery said: "Speak to your father. He wouldn't wish you to be forced into a marriage you disliked."

This advice was repeated, in substance, by young Mr. Orde, upon the following day, when Phoebe, knowing her mama to be out of the way, rode over to the Manor House to confer with him.

Thomas was the only child of the Squire of the district, a very respectable man, who contrived to maintain thirty or more couples of hounds, a score of hunters for himself, his son, and his huntsmen, several coach-horses and cover-hacks, half a dozen spaniels, and upwards of a hundred gamecocks at walk, on an income of no more than eight thousand pounds a year, and that without being obliged to stint his lady of the elegancies of life, or to allow to fall into disrepair the dwellings of his numerous tenants. His family had been established in the county for many generations, most of its members having been distinguished for their sporting proclivities, and none of them having made any particular mark in the world. The Squire was a man of excellent plain sense, much looked up to as a personage of the first consequence within his circle. While perfectly aware of his own worth, his way of life was unpretentious; although he employed, besides his huntsman, several grooms, a coachman, a gamekeeper, an experienced kennelman, and a cocker, he was content, when he travelled any distance from Somerset, to hire postilions; and his household boasted no more than three indoor menservants.

He was a fond as well as a judicious parent, and had his son shown the least leaning towards academic pursuits he would have sent him up to Oxford upon his leaving Rugby, whatever retrenchments this might have entailed. That they must have been heavy he knew, for it was impossible for such a thoroughgoing sportsman as Tom to maintain a creditable appearance at Oxford on a penny less than six hundred pounds a year, setting aside such debts as the squire thought him bound to incur. A sense of what was due to his heir enabled him to face the necessity of reducing his stable and disposing of his cocks without grumbling or trying to impress Tom with the notion that he was fortunate to possess so generous a father; but he was not at all displeased when Tom said that the thought it would be a great waste of time for him to go up to Oxford, since he was not bookish, and would very likely be ploughed there. What with cocking and coursing, fishing and flapper-shooting in the summer, hunting and pheasant-shooting through the winter, acquiring a knowledge of farming from the bailiff, and learning how to manage the estates, he thought he would be much better employed at home. He was allowed to have his way, the Squire resolving to arrange for him to be given a little town polish when he should be rather older.

Except for one or two visits to friends living in a different part of the country he had been at home for a year now, enjoying himself very much, and justifying his father's secret pride in him by taking as much interest in crops as in hounds, and rapidly becoming as popular with the villagers as he was with the neighbouring gentry.

He was a pleasant youth, sturdy rather than tall, with a fresh, open countenance, unaffected manners, and as much of the good sense which characterized his father as was to be expected of a young gentleman of nineteen summers. From the circumstances of his being an only child he had from his earliest youth looked upon Phoebe, just his own age, as a sister; and since she had been, as a child, perfectly ready to engage with him on whatever dangerous pursuit he might suggest to her, besides very rapidly becoming a first-rate horsewoman, and a devil to go, not even his first terms at Rugby had led him to despise her company.

When Phoebe divulged to him her astonishing tidings, he was as incredulous as Susan had been, for, as he pointed out with brotherly candour, she was not at all the sort of girl to achieve a brilliant marriage. She agreed to this, and he added kindly: "I don't mean to say that I wouldn't as lief be married to you as to some high flyer, for if I was obliged to marry anyone I think I'd offer for you rather than any other girl I know."

She thanked him.

"Yes, but I'm not a fashionable duke," he pointed out. "Besides, I've known you all my life. I'm dashed if I understand why this duke should have taken a fancy to you! It isn't as though you was a beauty, and whenever your mother-in-law is near you behave like a regular pea-goose, so how he could have guessed you ain't a ninnyhammer I can't make out!"

"Oh, he didn't! He wishes to marry me because his mama was a friend of mine."

"That *must* be a bag of moonshine!" said Tom scornfully. "As though anyone would offer for a girl for such a reason as that!"

"I think," said Phoebe, "it is on account of his being a person of great consequence, and wishing to make a suitable alliance, and not caring whether I am pretty, or conversible."

"He can't think you suitable!" objected Tom. "He sounds to me a regular knock-in-the-cradle! It may be a fine thing to become a duchess, but I should think you had much better not!"

"No, no, but what am I do, Tom? For heaven's sake don't tell me I have only to decline the Duke's offer, for you at least know what Mama is like! Even if I had the courage to disobey her only think what misery I should be obliged to endure! And don't tell me not to regard it, because to be in disgrace for weeks and weeks, as I would be, so sinks my spirits that I can't even *write*! I know it's idiotish of me, but I can't overcome my dread of being in her black books! I feel as if I were withering!"

He had too often seen her made ill by unkindness to think her words over-fanciful. It was strange that a girl so physically intrepid should have so much sensibility. In his own phrase, he knew her for a right one; but he knew also that in a censorious atmosphere her spirits were swiftly overpowered, none of her struggles to support them alleviating the oppression which transformed her from the neck-or-nothing girl whom no oxer could daunt to the shrinking miss whose demeanour was as meek as her conversation was insipid. He said, rather doubtfully: "You don't think, if you were to write to him, Lord Marlow would put the Duke off?"

"You know what Papa is!" she said simply. "He will always allow himself to be ruled by Mama, because he can't bear to be made uncomfortable. Besides, how could I get a letter to him without Mama's knowing of it?"

He considered for a few moments, frowning. "No. Well— You are quite *sure* you can't like the Duke? I mean, I should have supposed anything to be better than to continue living at Austerby. Besides, you said yourself you only once talked to him. You don't really know anything about him. I daresay he may be rather shy, and that, you know, might easily make him appear stiff."

"He is not shy and he is not stiff," stated Phoebe. "His manners are assured; he says everything that is civil because he places himself on so high a form that he would think it unworthy of himself to treat anyone with anything but cool courtesy; and because he knows his consequence to be so great he cares nothing for what anyone may think of him."

"You *did* take him in dislike, didn't you?" said Tom, grinning at her.

"Yes, I did! But even if I had not, how could I accept an offer from him when I made him the villain in my story?"

That made Tom laugh. "Well, you needn't tell him that, you goose!"

"Tell him! He won't need telling! I described him *exactly*!"

"But, Phoebe, you don't suppose he will *read* your book, do you?" said Tom.

Phoebe could support with equanimity disparagement of her person, but this slight cast on her first novel made her exclaim indignantly: "Pray, why should he not read it? It is going to be *published*!"

"Yes, I know, but you can't suppose that people like Salford will buy it."

"Then who will?" demanded Phoebe, rather flushed.

"Oh, I don't know! Girls, I daresay, who like that sort of thing."

"You liked it well enough!" she reminded him.

"Yes, but that was because it was so odd to think of your having written it," explained Tom. He saw that she was looking mortified, and added consolingly: "But I'm not bookish, you know, so I daresay it's very fine, and will sell a great many copies. The thing is that no one will know who wrote it, so there's no need to tease yourself over *that*. When does the Duke come to Austerby?"

"Next week. It is given out that he is coming to try the young chestnut. He is going to hunt too, and now Mama is trying to decide whether to dish up all our friends to entertain him at a dinner-party, or to leave it to Papa to invite Sir Gregory Standish and old Mr. Hayle for a game of whist."

"Lord!" said Tom, in an awed tone.

Phoebe gave a giggle. "*That* will teach him to come to Austerby in this odious, condescending way!" she observed, with satisfaction. "What is more, Mama does not approve of newfangled fashions, so his grace will find himself sitting down to dinner at six o'clock, which is not at all the style of thing he is accustomed to. And when he comes into the drawing-room after dinner he will discover that Miss Battery has brought Susan and Mary down. And then Mama will call upon me to go to the pianoforte—she has told Sibby already to be sure I know my new piece thoroughly!—and at nine o'clock Firbank will bring in the tea-tray; and at half-past nine she will tell the Duke, in that complacent voice of hers, that we keep early hours in the country; and so he will be left to Papa and piquet, or some such thing. I wish he may be heartily bored!"

"I should think he would be. Perhaps he won't offer for you after all!" said Tom.

"How can I dare to indulge that hope, when all his reason for visiting us is to do so?" demanded Phoebe, sinking back into gloom. "His mind must be perfectly made up, for he knows already that I am a dead bore! Oh, Tom, I am *trying* to take it with composure, but the more I think of it the more clearly do I see that I shall be forced into this dreadful marriage, and I feel sick with apprehension already, and there is no one to take my part, no one!"

"Stubble it!" ordered Tom, giving her a shake. "Talking such slum to me! Let me tell you, my girl, that there's not only me to take your part, but my father and mother as well!"

She squeezed his hand gratefully. "I know you would, Tom, and Mrs. Orde has always been so kind, but—it wouldn't answer! You know Mama!"

He did, but said, looking pugnacious: "If she tries to bully you into this, and your father don't prevent her, you needn't think I shall stand by like a gapeseed! If the worst comes to the worst, Phoebe, you'd best marry me. I daresay we shouldn't think it so very bad, once we had grown accustomed to it. At all events, I'd rather marry you than leave you in the suds! What the devil are you laughing at?"

"You, of course! Now, Tom, don't be gooseish! When Mama is so afraid we might fall in love that she has almost forbidden you to come within our gates! She wouldn't hear of it, or Mr. Orde either, I daresay!"

"I know that. It would have to be a Gretna Green marriage, of course."

She gave a gasp. "Gretna Green? Of all the hare-brained— No, really, Tom, how can you be so tottyheaded? I may be a hoyden, but I'm not abandoned! Why, I wouldn't do such a shocking thing even if I were in love with you!"

"Oh, very well!" he said, a trifle sulkily. "*I* don't want to do it, and if you prefer to marry Salford there's no more to be said."

She rubbed her cheek against his shoulder. "Indeed, I am very much obliged to you!" she said contritely. "Don't be vexed with me!"

He was secretly so much relieved by her refusal to accept

his offer that after telling her severely that it would be well if she learned to reject such offers with more civility he relented, owned that a runaway marriage was not quite the thing, and ended by promising to lend his aid in any scheme she might hit on for her deliverance.

None occurred to her. Lady Marlow took her to Bath to have her hair cut into a smarter crop, and to buy a new dress, in which, presumably, she was to captivate the Duke. But as Lady Marlow considered white, or the palest of blues and pinks, the only colours seemly for a débutante, and nothing showed her to worse advantage, it was hard to perceive how this staggering generosity was to achieve its end.

Two days before the arrival of Lord Marlow and the Duke it began to seem as if one at least of the schemes for his entertainment was to be frustrated. Lord Marlow's coachman, a weatherwise person, prophesied that snow was on the way; and an item in the *Morning Chronicle* carried the information that there had been heavy falls already in the north and east. A hope, never very strong, that the Duke would postpone his visit wilted when no message was brought to Austerby from its master, and was speedily followed by something very like panic. If the Duke, who was coming ostensibly to see how he liked the young chestnut's performance in the hunting-field, was undeterred by the threat of snow he must be determined indeed to prosecute his suit; and if there were no hunting to remove him during the hours of daylight from the house he would have plenty of opportunity to do it. Try as she would Phoebe could not persuade herself that the weather, which had been growing steadily colder, showed any sign of improvement; and when the Squire cancelled the first meeting of the week, and followed that up by going away to Bristol, where some business had been for some time awaiting his attention, it was easy to see that he, the best weather-prophet in the district, had no expectation of being able to take his hounds out for several days at least.

It was very cold, but no snow had fallen when Lord Marlow, pardonably pleased with himself, arrived at Austerby, bringing Sylvester with him. He whispered in his wife's ear: "You see that I have brought him!" but it would have been more accurate to have said that he had been brought by Sylvester, since he had accomplished the short journey in Sylvester's curricle, his own and Sylvester's chaise following with their valets, and all their baggage. The rear of this cavalcade was brought up, some time later, by his lordship's hunters, in charge of his head groom, and several underlings. Sylvester, it appeared, had sent his own horses back to Chance from Blandford Park. Keighley, the middle-aged groom who had taught him to ride his first pony, was perched up behind him in the curricle; but although the postilions in charge of his chaise wore his livery the younger Misses Marlow, watching the arrivals from an upper window, were sadly disappointed in the size of his entourage. It was rather less impressive than Papa's, except that Papa had not taken his curricle to Blandford Park, which, after all, he might well have done. However, his chaise was drawn by a team of splendid match-bays; the pair of beautiful gray steppers harnessed to the curricle were undoubtedly what Papa would call complete to a shade; and to judge from the way this vehicle swept into view round a bend in the avenue the Duke was no mere whipster. Mary said hopefully that perhaps this would make Phoebe like him better.

Phoebe, in fact, was not privileged to observe Sylvester's arrival, but since she had frequently seen him driving his high-perch phaeton in Hyde Park, and already knew him to be at home to a peg, her sentiments would scarcely have undergone a change if she had seen how stylishly he took the awkward turn in the avenue. She was with Lady Marlow in one of the saloons, setting reluctant stitches in a piece of embroidery stretched on a tambour-frame. She wore the white gown purchased in Bath; and as this had tiny puff sleeves, and the atmosphere in the saloon, in spite of quite a large fire, was chilly, her thin, bare arms showed an unattractive expanse of gooseflesh. To Lady Marlow's eye, however, she presented as good an appearance as could have been hoped for. Dress, occupation, and pose befitted the maiden of impeccable birth and upbringing: Lady Marlow was able to congratulate herself on her excellent management: if the projected match fell through it would not, she knew, be through any fault of hers.

The gentlemen entered the room, Lord Marlow ushering Sylvester in with a jovial word, and exclaiming: "Ah, I thought we should find you here, my love! I do not have to present the Duke, for I fancy you are already acquainted. And Phoebe, too! you know my daughter, Salford—my little Phoebe! Well, now what could be more comfortable? Just a quiet family party,

53

as I promised you: no ceremony—you take your pot-luck with us!"

Sylvester, uttering his practised civilities as he shook hands with his hostess, was out of humour. He had had time enough in which to regret having accepted Marlow's invitation, and he had been wishing himself otherwhere ever since leaving Blandford Park. His lordship's prowess in the hunting-field was forgotten, and the tedium of his conversation remembered; and long before Austerby was reached he had contrived not only to bore Sylvester, but to set up his back as well. Naturally expansive, he had not deemed it necessary, once he was sure of his noble guest, to maintain the discretion imposed on him by Lady Ingham. He had let several broad hints drop. They had fallen on infertile soil, their only effect having been to ruffle Sylvester's temper. He had told Sylvester, too, that he would find himself the only guest at Austerby, which was by no means what Sylvester had bargained for, since such an arrangement lent to his visit a particularity he had been anxious to avoid. Whatever his lordship might have said about not standing on ceremony with him he had supposed that he would find several other persons gathered at Austerby, for form's sake, if not in an endeavour to render his chief guest's stay agreeable. His lordship, concluded Sylvester, was devilish anxious to get his daughter off; but if he imagined that the head of the great house of Rayne could be jockeyed into taking one step not of his own choosing he would very soon learn his mistake. It had then occurred to Sylvester that he might be said to have taken one such step already, in coming to Austerby: a reflection which piqued him so much that he decided, a little viciously, that unless Miss Marlow proved to be something quite out of the common way he would have nothing to say to the proposed connection.

This unamiable resolve was strengthened by his first impression of Austerby. One swift glance round the entrance hall was enough to convince him that it was not at all the sort of household he liked. The furniture was arranged with rigid formality; the small fire smouldering on the hearth was inadequate to overcome the icy nature of several draughts; and although there was really no fault to be found with the butler, or with the two London-bred footmen, who relieved the gentlemen of their coats and hats, Sylvester was sure that the establishment would be found to be under-staffed. It would not surprise him to learn that a female presided over the kitchen; and he had little doubt that there was no groom of the chambers to attend to the comfort of visitors. The fact that he frequently stayed in houses by far less magnificent than his own and never gave the size and style of their domestic arrangements a thought did not, in his present mood, occur to him; and the knowledge that he was so severly critical of Lord Marlow's house would have greatly astonished a number of his less affluent friends and relations. One of his favourite cousins, a lively young woman married to an impecunious Major of Dragoon Guards, would, indeed, have been incredulous, since none of the visitors to her modest establishment was more adaptable than he, or more ready to be pleased with his entertainment. But Sylvester liked Major and Mrs. Newbury; Lord Marlow he was in a fair way to disliking cordially.

He was received by Lady Marlow in what her lord recognized as her most gracious manner. It struck Sylvester as condescending, and he was taken aback by it.

He turned from her to meet Miss Marlow, and his gloomiest forebodings were realized. She had neither beauty nor countenance, her complexion was poor and her figure worse, her dress was tasteless, and the colourless voice in which she murmured how-do-you-do confirmed him in his instant belief that she was insipid. He wondered how soon he would be able to bring his visit to an end.

"You will remember my little Phoebe, Salford," persevered Lord Marlow optimistically. "You have danced with her in London, haven't you?"

"Of course—yes!" said Sylvester. He perceived that more was required of him, and fired a shot at a fairly safe venture. "At Almack's, was it not?"

"No," said Phoebe. "At the Seftons' ball. When you saw me at Almack's I don't think you recognized me."

This girl, thought Sylvester indignantly, wants conduct as well as countenance! Is she trying to put me to the blush? Very well, Miss Marlow! Aloud, he said lightly: "How rude of me! But perhaps I *didn't* see you." Then he perceived that she had flushed up to the roots of her hair, her eyes flying to her mother-in-law's face, and he remembered that Lady Ingham had said she did not show to advantage in Lady Marlow's presence. A glance at this lady surprised a quelling stare directed at Phoebe, and he was a little sorry: enough to make

55

him add: "I have frequently been accused of cutting people at Almack's. But the Assemblies have become such shocking squeezes that it is wonderful if one can discover one's oldest friends amongst such a press of persons."

"Yes, it—it is—isn't it?" stammered Phoebe.

"Pray be seated, Duke!" commanded Lady Marlow. "You have been staying with the Beauforts. You are a hunting-man, I collect. I am not myself a friend to the sport, but Marlow is greatly addicted to it."

"Oh, you must not talk so to Salford!" said Lord Marlow. "He is a clipping rider, you know: showed us all the way!"

Beyond directing an enigmatical look at his host Sylvester made no response to this piece of flattery. Lady Marlow said that she believed the Duke of Beaufort to be a very worthy man, but as she followed up this encomium by deploring the dandyism of his heir the conversation did not prosper. Lord Marlow struck in with a sporting anecdote, and Phoebe, picking up her tambour-frame and setting another crooked stitch, sat listening for the next twenty minutes to a three-cornered dialogue that would have diverted her had it not vexed her too much to seem amusing. Lady Marlow's part in it took the form of a series of statements, which, according to her custom, she announced in a fashion that admitted of no argument; Lord Marlow, in an effort to check her, broke in whenever he could with a flow of jovial remarks and reminiscences, all of which were extremely trivial; and Sylvester, civil, and cool, and unhelpful, replied to each of his hosts in turn, and encouraged neither.

To hear her father striving with such eager anxiety to engage Sylvester's interest very soon made Phoebe angry. He was an inveterate talker, and his most fervent admirers could scarcely have called him a sensible man, but he was a much older man than Sylvester, he was doing his best to please, and she thought it detestable of Sylvester to accord him nothing but polite tolerance. Her dislike of him grew to such large proportions that when Lady Marlow announced that they dined at six o'clock she was almost disappointed to see that he bore the announcement with fortitude. Fuel for her rancour would have been supplied by the knowledge, could she but have come by it, that it was just what he had expected.

When she entered her chilly bedchamber to change her dress for dinner Phoebe found a screw of paper stuck into the frame

56

of the looking-glass, and realized, as she drew it out and unfolded it, that it must have been put there by Firbank, the butler, whose extraordinary grimaces, as she had passed him in the hall in the wake of Lady Marlow, she had been quite unable to interpret. She saw that it was from Tom, but its message was slightly disappointing. After informing her that he was on his way to dine with friends he added that he should leave betimes, and drop in at Austerby on his way home to learn how she had gone on. *"I have greased Firbank in the fist, and he will let me in the sidedoor, and says we shall be safe in the morning-room, so come there before you retire to bed. By the bye, the Mail was four hours late reaching Bath today on account of snow as far as Reading. I shouldn't wonder at it if you had this Duke of yours quartered on you for a se'enight."*

At Austerby Phoebe did not enjoy the luxury of an abigail, so there was no one to compel her to spend more time than was strictly necessary over the changing of her dress. She made haste out of her muslin frock and arrayed herself in a somewhat scrambling way in the evening-gown prescribed by Lady Marlow. It was as unbecoming to her as the muslin, but beyond combing out her ringlets and clasping a string of pearls round her throat she made no attempt to render herself more presentable. Her ears were on the prick to catch the sounds of male voices. When she heard these, and knew that her father was escorting the Duke to his bedchamber, her toilet was done. Wrapping a shawl round her shoulders she slipped out of her room, and across the hall to Lord Marlow's dressing-room.

"Papa, may I speak to you?"

His valet was with him, and he had already put off his coat, but being naturally affable he was about to welcome his daughter, when he saw that she was labouring under barely repressed agitation, and he at once felt uneasy. He said in a bluff voice: "Well, unless it is of immediate importance, my dear——"

"It is of most immediate importance, Papa!"

His uneasiness grew. "Oh, well, then——! Well, I can spare you five minutes, I daresay!"

His valet went out of the room. Hardly had he shut the door than Phoebe said breathlessly: "Papa, I wish to tell you—I cannot like the Duke of Salford!"

He stood there staring at her, at first aghast, and then, as a sense of ill-usage crept over him, with gathering choler. He

57

said explosively: "Well, upon my word, Phoebe! A fine moment you have chosen to break this news to me!"

"How could I break it to you earlier? If you had but told me before you went to Blandford Park what you intended! Papa, you know Mama would never have permitted me to send a servant there with a letter from me, begging you to go no further in the business! Oh, pray, Papa, don't be angry! Indeed, it is not my fault you were kept in ignorance of—of my sentiments upon this occasion!"

The colour in his florid cheeks darkened; he really did feel that he had been abominably used. His pride in having contrived to draw the Duke into Lady Ingham's net had been great; already he was three parts persuaded that the scheme had been all his own, and that he had been put to considerable trouble on his daughter's behalf. Now it seemed that his care was to be thrown away. That was bad; and still worse would be the awkwardness of his situation, if he were obliged to inform Sylvester that Phoebe would have none of him. In an attempt to turn aside her protests, he said: "Pooh, nonsense! The merest irritation of nerves, my dear! You are shy—yes, yes, you are shy, I say, and who should know better than your father? You have a great deal of sensibility—I always thought it had been wiser not to have told you what Salford's purpose was in visiting us, but your mama—however, that's nothing to the purpose now the mischief has been done! Your senses arc in disorder! I don't deny that your situation is embarrassing. I declare I am vexed to death that your mama should have—But you will not regard it! I assure you, I have given a great deal of thought to this matter, and am satisfied that Salford will make you an amiable husband. You will allow that I am more fitted to be the judge of a man's character than you! Well, I am satisfied with Salford: he is as sound as a roast!" He gave his hearty laugh, and added: "I am prepared to wager the day is not far distant when you will wonder how you can have been such a goose! How I shall joke you about it!"

"Papa, I cannot like him!" she repeated.

"For God's sake, girl, don't talk such fustian!" he said irascibly. "You are barely acquainted with him! A pretty pass we have come to when a chit of a girl holds up her nose at a man of Salford's estate! Let me tell you that you should rather be blessing yourself for your good fortune!"

She said imploringly: "Papa, you know I would not willingly displease you, but——"

"Very fine talking!" he interrupted. "You haven't a pennyworth's consideration for me! What a fix you would put me in! Good God, it is beyond anything! So I am to inform Salford you cannot like him! Upon my word, it puts me out of all heart, I declare to heaven it does! Here am I, putting myself to all this trouble—ay, and expense! for if Salford should take a fancy to the young chestnut I must let him have the horse at a price that will put me sadly out of pocket, of course. Not to mention the new dress that was purchased for you, and I dare not say how many bottles of the good claret! A hundred pounds I paid for one hogshead, and no more than fifty bottles left, by what Firbank tells me. Carbonnell's Best!"

"Papa——"

"Don't talk to me!" he said, lashing himself into a weak man's rage. "I have no patience left to speak to you! And what your mama will say——!"

"Oh, you won't tell her! *Surely* you won't?" she cried. "You could tell the Duke—that you find you were mistaken in my sentiments, so that he won't propose to me! Papa——!"

"If I am to be put into such a position she must know the whole!" he said, taking instant advantage of her fright. "I should be sorry indeed if I were obliged to divulge to her what has passed between us, but if you continue in this obstinacy I must do so. Now, my dear child, consider! Salford has had no opportunity to fix his interest with you: at least grant him that opportunity! If you find you are still unable to like him when he has been staying with us some few days, we will talk of this again. Meanwhile I shall say nothing of this interview to Mama, and you need not either. There, I fancy your senses are in a way to being straight again, are they not?" He gave her shoulder a pat. "Now I must send you away, or Salford will be down before me. I am not vexed with you: you have sometimes an odd kick in your gallop, but you are a good girl at heart, and you know you may trust your father!"

She went away without another word. The optimistic trend of his mind made it easy for him to believe that he had talked her into submission, but the truth was she knew him too well to persevere. His dislike of finding himself in an uncomfortable predicament was stronger than his love for his children; so far from trusting him she felt sure that before he slept that night he would have told his wife the whole. He would not bring pressure to bear upon his daughter, for that would be uncomfortable too; but he would look the other way while his wife did so.

Until the morning Phoebe thought she must be safe from attack. There was not much time left to her to think of some means of escape from a fate that had begun to seem inevitable; and she could look for no help from any inmate of Austerby. To ask it of Miss Battery would be not only to place the governess in a position of great difficulty, but to ensure her being dismissed from her post under such conditions as must make it hard indeed for her to establish herself in another household. Tom could be relied on to do whatever was required of him, but it was hard to see how his support could be of assistance. She could think of no one but her grandmother who might be able to lend her effective aid. She was not intimately acquainted with Lady Ingham, but she knew her to be well-disposed towards her, and she knew too that she held Lady Marlow in contempt and dislike. If Austerby had been within reach of London, Phoebe would have had no hesitation in claiming her protection. But Austerby was ninety miles from London. It would be useless to write a letter, for it was not to be supposed that an invalid would come posting into Somerset to rescue her in the middle of a hard winter, and although Grandmama had several times shown herself to be more than a match for Mama when they had met face to face, at a distance Mama would have everything all her own way.

Even as her spirits sank under these reflections Phoebe remembered Tom, who was coming to see her this evening. Hope began to flower; she began to weave plans; and became so absorbed in these that she forgot she had been ordered to attend Lady Marlow in her room as soon as she was dressed, and instead made her way to the gallery in which it was the bleak custom of the family to assemble before dinner.

CHAPTER

6

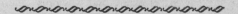

Sylvester was in the gallery, alone, and glancing through the pages of a periodical. He was standing in front of the fire, which was burning sluggishly, and every now and then gave forth a plume of smoke. He was dressed with his usual quiet elegance in a black coat and pantaloons, and a plain white waistcoat. A single fob hung at his waist, a single diamond glinted from between the folds of his neckcloth, and one ring, his heavy signet, adorned his hand. He adopted none of the extravagances of the dandy-set, but his air was one of decided fashion, and the exquisite cut of his coat made Phoebe feel more than ordinarily dowdy.

She was startled to find him in the gallery, and checked on the threshold, exclaiming involuntarily: "Oh——!"

He looked up in faint surprise. After a moment he put the periodical down, and said pleasantly: "It's a bad guest, is it not, who comes down before his host? Let me draw a chair to the fire for you! It is smoking a trifle, but not enough, I am sure, to signify."

The acid note was faint, but it did not escape her. She came reluctantly down the gallery, saying as she seated herself in the chair he had pulled forward: "All the chimneys smoke at Austerby when the wind is in the north-east."

Having received abundant evidence of the truth of this statement in the bedchamber allotted to him, he did not question it, merely replying: "Indeed? Every house has its peculiarities, I fancy."

"Do none of the chimneys smoke in your house?" she asked.

"I believe they were used to, but it was found possible to remedy the fault," he said, conveniently forgetting how often in exasperation at finding the hall at Chance dense with smoke, he had sworn to replace its medieval fireplace with a modern grate.

"How fortunate!" remarked Phoebe.

Silence fell. Miss Marlow sat gazing abstractedly at a Buhl cabinet; and his grace of Salford, unaccustomed to such treatment, eyed her in gathering resentment. He was much inclined to pick up the newspaper again, and was only deterred from doing so by the reflection that disgust at her want of conduct was no excuse for lowering his own standard of good manners. He said in the voice of one trying to set a bashful schoolgirl at her ease: "Your father tells me, Miss Marlow, that you are a notable horsewoman."

"Does he?" she responded. "Well, he told us that you showed him the way with the Heythrop."

He glanced quickly down at her, but decided, after an instant, that this remark sprang form inanity. "I imagine I need not tell you that I did no such thing!"

"Oh, no! I am very sure you did not," she said.

He almost jumped; and being now convinced that this seeming *gaucherie* was deliberate began to feel as much interested as he was ruffled. Perhaps there was rather more to this little provincial than he had supposed, though why she should utter malicious remarks he was at a loss to understand. It was coming it too strong if she was piqued by his failure to recall on what occasion he had danced with her: did she think he could remember every insignificant girl with whom he had been obliged to stand up for one country dance? And what the devil did she mean by relapsing again into indifferent silence? He tried a new tack: "It is now your turn, Miss Marlow, to start a topic for conversation!"

She withdrew her gaze from the cabinet, and directed it at

him for a dispassionate moment. "I haven't any conversation," she said.

He hardly knew whether to be diverted or vexed; he was certainly intrigued, and had just decided that although he had not the remotest intention of offering for this outrageous girl, it might not be unamusing to discover what (if anything) lay behind her odd manners when Lady Marlow came into the gallery. Finding her guest there before her she pointed out to him that he was in advance of the hour, which nettled him into replying: "You must blame the wind for being in the north-east, ma'am."

The shaft went wide. "You mistake, Duke: no blame attaches to your being so early. Indeed, I consider it a good fault! My daughter has been entertaining you, I see. What have you been talking of together, I wonder?"

"We can scarcely be said to have talked of anything," replied Sylvester. "Miss Marlow informs me that she has no conversation."

He glanced at Phoebe as he spoke, and encountered such a burning look of reproach that he repented, and tried to mend matters by adding with a laugh: "In point of fact, ma'am, Miss Marlow entered the room a bare minute before yourself, so we have had little opportunity to converse."

"My daughter-in-law is shy," said Lady Marlow, with a look at Phoebe which promised signal vengeance presently.

It occurred to Sylvester that after her first start of surprise Phoebe had not appeared to be at all shy. He remembered that Lady Ingham had said she was not just in the ordinary style, and wondered if there might be something more in her than he had as yet detected. Since she was making no effort to engage his interest he concluded that she did not know that he had come to Austerby to look her over. That made it fairly safe to try whether he could charm her out of her farouche behaviour. He smiled at her, and said: "I must hope, then, that she will not be too shy to converse with me when we are a little better acquainted."

But by the time he rose from the dinner-table all desire to become better acquainted with Phoebe had left him, and the only thing he did desire was an excuse to leave Austerby not later than the following morning. As he sat through an interminable dinner, enduring on one side a monologue delivered by his hostess, at her most consequential, on such topics of interest as the defections of the latest incumbent of the Parish, the excellence of the Bishop, the decay of modern manners, and the customs obtaining in her dear father's household; and on the other a series of sporting recollections from his host, the look of the satyr became ever more strongly marked on his countenance. Never had he been subjected to such treatment as he was meeting with at Austerby! When he accepted invitations to stay with friends he knew that he would find himself one of a party composed of agreeable persons, with whom he was well acquainted; and that every form of sport or amusement would be provided for their entertainment. One hunted, or one shot; and if the weather became inclement one played at whist, and billiards, took part in theatricals, danced at impromptu balls, and flirted desperately with the prettiest of the ladies. That was how he entertained his own guests: so much the way of his world that it never occurred to him that quite a number of the hostesses who secured him for their parties put forth their best efforts to entertain him royally. But when he found himself the sole guest at Austerby, had been promised by his host an evening's whist with two obscure country gentlemen; and, by his hostess, the felicity of meeting the Bishop of Bath and Wells, it occurred to him forcibly that in making no proper provision for his entertainment Lord Marlow had been guilty of a social solecism.

He had been received by a hostess who seemed to think she was conferring a high treat upon him. He was contemptuous of flattery, he disliked toad-eaters, he did not consciously expect to be welcomed with distinction, but to be met with condescension was a new experience which set him instantly on his high ropes.

His bedchamber was rendered untenable by the smoke which gushed from the chimney; the water in the brass ewer had been tepid, so that his valet had had to fetch a fresh supply from the kitchens; the eldest daughter of the house had uttered no more than half a dozen sentences since they had entered the dining-room; and although Lord· Marlow's wines were good, the dinner set before the company was as commonplace as it was long drawn-out.

By the time Lord Marlow, promising some rubbers of piquet later in the evening, took him to join the ladies in the drawing room, he had resigned himself to boredom; but when the first object to meet his gaze, upon entering the room, was a grim female, dressed in black bombasine and seated bolt upright in a chair slightly drawn back from the circle round the fire, he realized that he had grossly underestimated the horrors that lay before him. Besides the grim female two schoolgirls had joined the party, the elder a bouncing young woman with a high complexion, and her father's rather protuberant blue eyes; the younger a sallow girl too bashful to speak above a whisper or without blushing fierily from neck to brow. Lady Marlow made them both known to him, but ignored the claims of the grim lady to a share of his civility. He concluded that she must be the governess; and instantly determined to show his hostess what he thought of her insufferable manners. He favoured Miss Battery with a slight bow, and his most pleasant smile, and directed at Lady Marlow an enquiring look she was unable to ignore.

"Oh———! My daughters' governess," she said shortly. "Pray come to the fire, Duke!"

Sylvester, choosing instead a chair rather nearer to Miss Battery than to the fireside party, addressed a civil remark to her. She answered it with composure, but gruffly, looking at him with unnerving fixity.

Lord Marlow, always very easy and good-natured with his dependants, then added to his wife's displeasure by saying: "Ah, Miss Battery! I have not seen you since I came home! How do you go on? But I need not ask: you are always well!"

That gave Sylvester the opportunity to ask her if she were related to a family of the same name living in Norfolk. She replied: "Shouldn't think so, sir. Never heard of them until your grace mentioned them."

As the family had no existence outside his imagination this was not surprising; but his question seemed to have broken the ice: Miss Battery, appearing slightly mollified, disclosed that she came from Hertfordshire.

Lady Marlow, breaking rudely in on this, said loudly that she had no doubt the Duke would enjoy a little music, and waved Phoebe towards the pianoforte.

Phoebe was an indifferent performer, but as neither her father nor Lady Marlow was at all musical they were perfectly satisfied, as long as she did not falter, or play any unmistakably wrong notes. Sylvester was not musical either, but he had been used to listen to the first musicians of the day, and thought he had never heard anyone play with less taste or feeling. He could only be thankful that she did not play the harp; but when, in response to some affectionate urging from her father, she sang an old ballad in a small, wooden voice he was much inclined to think that even a harp might have been preferable.

At half-past eight the schoolroom party withdrew, and after half an hour's desultory conversation the tea-tray was brought in. Sylvester saw the end of his purgatory, and so it was. Punctually at half-past nine Lady Marlow informed him that they kept early hours at Austerby, bade him a formal good-night, and went away, with Phoebe following in her wake. As they mounted the stairs she said complacently that the evening had gone off very well. She added that although she feared the Duke was a man of fashion, she was on the whole pleased with him. "Your father informs me that hunting will be out of the question tomorrow," she observed. "If it should not be snowing I shall suggest to Salford that he might like to walk with you and your sisters. Miss Battery will accompany you, of course, but I shall tell her she may fall behind, with the girls, and give her a hint at the same time not to be putting herself forward, as I was excessively surprised to see her doing this evening."

This programme, which, a few hours earlier, would have appalled her, Phoebe listened to with a calm born of her fixed resolve to be gone from Austerby long before it could be put into execution. Parting from Lady Marlow at the head of the stairs she went away to her bedchamber, knowing that both Susan and Miss Battery would come to her there, and that it would consequently be dangerous to repair to the morning-room before she had received these visitors.

Susan was soon got rid of; but Miss Battery, who followed her, showed a disposition to linger. Seating herself at the foot of the bed, and tucking her heads into the sleeves of her thick woollen dressing-gown, she told Phoebe that she thought she had done Sylvester less than justice.

"Sibby! You did not *like* him?" cried Phoebe.

"Don't know him well enough to like him. I didn't *dis*like him, at all events. No reason why I should: very civil to me!"

"Yes, to vex Mama!" Phoebe said shrewdly. "He was wanting to give her a set-down all through dinner!"

"Well," said Miss Battery, "can't blame him for that! Shouldn't say so, of course, but there it is! Got a charming smile too."

"I haven't observed it."

"You wouldn't have taken him in such aversion if you had. *I* observed it. What's more," added Miss Battery candidly, "he bore your playing very well, you know. Most truly the gentleman! He must be bent on making you an offer to have solicited you for another song."

She remained for several more minutes, but finding Phoebe deaf to whatever she chose to advance in Sylvester's favour she presently went away; and Phoebe, after a discreet interval, slipped out of her room, and along the corridor to the west wing of the house. Here, besides the schoolroom, the nurseries, and various bedchambers, the morning-room was situated, a shabby apartment which, while still dignified by its original title, had dwindled into a mere sewing-room. It was lit by an oil lamp set in the middle of a bare table; and by this indifferent light young Mr. Orde, his overcoat buttoned up to his throat, sat reading a book of Household Hints, which was all the literature the room afforded. He seemed to have found it rewarding, for upon Phoebe's entrance he looked up, and said with a grin: "I say, Phoebe, this is a famous good book! It tells you how to preserve tripe to go to the East Indies—which is just the sort of thing one might want to know any day of the week. All you need do is to *Get a fine Belly of Tripe, quite fresh——*"

"Ugh!" shuddered Phoebe, carefully shutting the door. "How horrid! Do put the book away!"

"All in good time! If you don't want to know how to preserve tripe, what about an *Excellent Dish for six or seven Persons for the Expense of Sixpence*? Just the thing for the ducal kitchens, *I* think! It's made with calf's lights, and bread, and fat, and some sheeps' guts, and——"

"How can you be so absurd? Stop reading that nonsense!" scolded Phoebe.

"Nicely cleaned," pursued Tom. "And if you don't fancy sheeps' guts you may take hogs', or——"

But at this point Phoebe seized the book, and after a slight struggle for possession he let her have it.

"For heaven's sake don't laugh so loud!" she begged him. "The children's bedchamber is almost opposite this room! Oh, Tom, you can't conceive what a shocking evening I've spent! I begged Papa to send the Duke away, but he wouldn't, so I have made up my mind to go away myself."

He was conscious of a sinking feeling at the pit of his

stomach, but replied staunchly: "Well, I told you I was game. I only hope we don't find the roads snow-bound in the north. Gretna Green it shall be!"

"Not so loud! Of course I'm not going to Gretna Green!" she said in an indignant under-voice. "Keep your voice low, Tom! If Eliza were to wake and hear us talking she would tell Mama, as sure as check! Now listen! I thought it all out at dinner! I must go to London, to my grandmother. She told me once that I might depend on her to do all she could for me, and I think—oh, I am sure she would support me in this, if only she knew what was happening! The only thing is—Tom, you know Mama buys all my dresses, and lets me have very little pin-money! Could you—would you lend me the money for the coach-fare? I think it costs about five-and-thirty shillings for the ticket. And then there is the tip to the guard, and——"

"Yes, of course I'll lend you as much rhino as you want!" Tom interrupted. "But you can't mean to travel to London on the stage!"

"Yes, I do. How could I go post, even if I could afford to do so? There would be the hiring of the chaise, and then all the business of the changes—oh, no, it would be impossible! I haven't an abigail to go with me, remember! I shall be much safer in the common stage. And if I could contrive to get a seat in one of the fast day coaches——"

"Well, you couldn't. They are always booked up as full as they can hold in Bath, and if you aren't on the way-bill—— Besides, if the snow is as deep beyond Reading as they say it is those coaches won't run."

"Well, never mind! Any coach will serve, and I don't doubt I shall be able to get a place, because people won't care to travel in this weather, unless they are obliged. I have made up my mind to it that I must be gone from here before anyone can prevent me, very early in the morning. If I could reach Devizes—it is nearer than Calne, and I know some of the London coaches do take that road—only I shall have a portmanteau to carry, and perhaps a bandbox as well, so—— Oh, Tom, could you, could you, do you think, take me to Devizes in your gig?"

"Will you *stop* fretting and fuming?" he said severely. "I'll take you anywhere you wish, but this scheme of yours—— You know, I don't wish to throw a rub in the way, but I'm afraid it may not hold. This curst weather! A pretty piece of business it would be if you were to get no farther than Reading! It might well turn out so, and then it would be all holiday with you."

"No, no, I have thought of that already! If the coach goes on, I shall stay with it, but if the snow is very bad I know just what I must do. Do you remember Jane, that used to be the maid who waited on the nursery? Well, she married a corn-chandler, in a very good way of business, I believe, and lives at Reading. So, you see, if I can't travel beyond Reading I may go to her, and stay with her until the snow has melted!"

"Stay in a corn-chandler's house?" he repeated, in accents of incredulity.

"Good God, why should I not? He is a very respectable man, and as for Jane, she will take excellent care of me, I can assure you! I suppose you had rather I stayed in a public inn?"

"No, that I wouldn't! But——" He paused, not liking the scheme, yet unable to think of a better.

She began to coax him, representing to him the advantages of her plan, and all the hopelessness of her situation if she were forced to remain at Austerby. He was easily convinced of this, for it did indeed seem to him that without her father's support her case was desperate. Nor could he deny that her grandmother was the very person to shield her; but it took a little time to persuade him that neither danger nor impropriety would attend her journey to London in a stage-coach. It was not until she told him that if he would not lend her his aid she meant to trudge to Devizes alone that he at last capitulated. Nothing remained, after that, but to arrange the details of her escape, and this was soon accomplished. Tom promised to have his gig waiting in the lane outside one of the farm gates of Austerby at seven o'clock on the following morning; Phoebe pledged herself not to keep him waiting there; and they parted, one of them full of confidence, the other trying to smother his uneasiness.

She was punctual at the rendezvous; he was not; and for twenty nerve-racking minutes she paced up and down the lane, in the lee of the hedge, her imagination running riot amongst the various disasters which might have overtaken him. The most likely of these was that he had overslept, a probability which added rage to her anxiety. It had been dark when she herself had dressed, and packed her night gear into the already bulging portmanteau, but by seven o'clock it was daylight, and at any moment, she felt, she might be discovered by some villager or farm-hand to whom she must be well known. The day was cheerless, the wind blowing from the north, and the clouds ominously thick. Anger and apprehension steadily mounted, but both were forgotten in surprise when Tom arrived on the scene, driving, instead of his gig, his father's curricle, with those two tidy brown steppers, Trusty and True, harnessed to it.

He pulled up beside her and commanded her, without preamble, to go to the horses' heads. She obeyed, but said, as he cast off the rug wrapped about his legs and jumped down into the road: "But, Tom, how is this? Why have you brought the curricle? I am persuaded you ought not!"

He had picked up her portmanteau, and was lashing it quickly in place. "Yes, I ought. Did you think I was never coming? I'm sorry to be so late, but, you see, I had to go back. We must put this bandbox under the seat." He stowed it away as he spoke, and came striding up to her. "I'll take 'em. Do you jump up, and take the ribbons! Take care! they haven't been out since my father went away, and they're as lively as be-damned! You will find my father's old driving-coat: put it on, and wrap that fur rug well round you! And don't waste time disputing!" he added.

She did as he bade her, but she was considerably astonished, and demanded, as soon as he had climbed up beside her, and taken the reins from her competent hands: "Have you run mad, Tom? What in the world——"

"No, of course I haven't. The thing is I was the most complete gudgeon last night, not to have seen what I ought to do. Plain as a pikestaff, but it never occurred to me till I had actually set out to come to you. Mind you, I wasn't easy in my mind! Kept on waking up all night, wondering what I should do. It only came to me when I was on my way here, driving the gig. So I turned sharp about, scribbled a note for my mother, got Jem to fig out Trusty and True——"

"But why?" she interrupted.

"Going to take you to London myself," he replied briefly.

Her first feeling was one of gratitude, but she was instantly assailed by qualms, and said: "No, no, you can't do so, Tom!"

"Nonsense, what could be easier? Trusty and True are good for two full stages, and very likely more, if I don't press them. After that, of course, I must hire job-horses, but unless we

70

learn at Reading that the road from there is too deep to make the attempt we shall be in London by tonight. I shan't try it, mind, if we get bad news at Reading! If that should be the case, I'll take you to this corn-chandler of yours, and put up myself at the Crown. The only thing is that you may find it pretty cold."

"Oh, *that* doesn't signify! But indeed, Tom, I think you ought not! Perhaps——"

"Well, it makes no odds what you think," he returned. "I'm going to do it."

"But Mrs. Orde—your father——"

"I *know* my father would say I shouldn't let you go alone; and as for Mama, she won't be thrown into a pucker, because I dashed off a note to her, telling her she need not be. And don't you fly into one of your fusses either! I didn't say where I was taking you, but only that I was obliged to rescue you from that Duke, and very likely should be away from home for a little while. So that's all right and tight."

She could not be perfectly satisfied, but since there was plainly no hope of turning Tom from his purpose, and she was besides thankful not to be obliged to journey alone to London, she said no more to dissuade him.

"That's a good girl!" he said, correctly interpreting her silence. "Lord, I call it a famous lark, don't you? If only we don't run into snow, and I must own I don't like the look of the sky above half."

"No, nor I, but if we can but reach Reading I shan't care for anything else, for even if it was discovered which way we were gone I don't think I should be looked for there."

"Oh, we shall reach Reading!" Tom said cheerfully.

She drew a long breath, and said in a thankful tone: "Tom, I can't *tell* you how much I'm obliged to you! To own the truth, I didn't at all want to go all by myself, but now—oh, now I can be easy!"

7

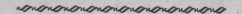

Breakfast was served at Austerby, on all but hunting-days, at ten o'clock, which, in Sylvester's opinion, was at least an hour too early. In general, the custom obtaining at country house-parties was for guests to breakfast at eleven, or even twelve o'clock. Lady Marlow knew it, but she told Sylvester that she disapproved of such hours. Sylvester, to whom the imperative summons of the bell had been an offence, received this information with a slight smile, and a polite inclination of the head, but offered no comment.

It was not long before Lord Marlow, noticing the absence of his daughter, wondered aloud where she could be. Her ladyship, speaking with careful restraint, replied that she fancied she must have gone out for a walk.

"Gone out for a walk!" repeated Lord Marlow, chuckling. "Not she! Gone down to the stables, more like. You must know, Salford, that there is no keeping that girl of mine away from the horses. I wish you might have seen her in the field. A capital seat, good, even hands, and the most bruising little rider you ever saw! Never any need to tell her to throw *her* heart over! Anything her horse can take she will too: stake-and-bound, a double, an in-and-out, a ridge and furrow—all one to Phoebe! I've seen her laid on her back in a ditch, but much she cared!"

Oblivious to his wife's attempts to catch his eye, he would have continued talking in this strain had Firbank not come into the parlour just then, with the intelligence that Mrs. Orde wished to speak to him.

He was surprised, and Lady Marlow still more so. She thought it an extraordinary circumstance, and said: "Depend upon it, she wishes to see *me*, Marlow. I do not know why she should disturb us at such an hour. It is not at all the thing. Inform Mrs. Orde, Firbank, that I am at breakfast, but will come to her presently."

He withdrew, but came back again almost immediately, looking harassed, and with a plump, bright-eyed lady hard on his heels.

"I regret, ma'am, to be obliged to break in on you with so little ceremony," announced Mrs. Orde, who appeared to be labouring under strong emotion, "but my business will not await your pleasure!"

"Not at all! Delighted to welcome you, ma'am!" said Lord Marlow hastily. "Always happy to be of service! You wish to see me—precisely, yes!"

"On a matter of the utmost urgency!" she said. "Your daughter, sir, has run away with my son!"

The company was not unnaturally startled into silence by this announcement. Without giving her hosts time to recover from the shock Mrs. Orde loosed the vials of her pent-up wrath upon them. "I don't know why you should look amazed!" she declared, her eyes snapping at Lady Marlow. "You have left no stone unturned to achieve this result! *I* guessed how it would be from the instant my son told me what his reception has been in this house for the past ten days! I pass over the insulting nature of your conduct, ma'am, but I shall take leave to inform you that nothing is farther from the wishes of his parents than an alliance between Tom and your family! I am excessively attached to Phoebe, poor child, but his father and I have other plans for Tom, and they don't, let me assure you, include his marriage at the age of nineteen!"

"Nonsense! Such a thought was never in either of their heads!" exclaimed Lord Marlow, in an attempt to stem this blistering eloquence.

He was promptly demolished. "No! Never until her ladyship

planted it there!" Mrs. Orde said fiercely. "If *I* had viewed their friendship with apprehension I should have thought myself a ninny-hammer to have acted as she has! And what has been the result? Exactly what might have been foreseen!"

"Upon my word!" broke in Lady Marlow. "I could almost believe you to have taken leave of your senses, ma'am! A very odd rage you have flown into, and all because my daughter-in-law (as I do not doubt!) has gone out riding with Mr. Thomas Orde!"

"Gone out riding!" Mrs. Orde exclaimed contemptuously. "She has run away from this house, and for that, Lady Marlow, *you* are to blame, with your Turkish treatment of her, poor little soul! Oh, I have no patience to talk to you! My errand is not to you, but to Phoebe's father! Read *that*, my lord!"

With these peremptory words she thrust a single sheet of paper into Lord Marlow's hand. While he perused the few lines Tom had scrawled to allay any anxiety his mother might feel, Lady Marlow commanded him to show her the note, and Sylvester retired discreetly into the window embrasure. A man of delicacy, he knew, would seize this opportunity to withdraw from the parlour. He accepted with fortitude the realization that he was lacking in delicacy, and wondered whether there was any chance of his being allowed a glimpse of a missive which was exercising so powerful an effect upon his host.

"My dear Mama," Tom had scribbled, *"I am obliged to go away without taking leave of you, but do not be in a worry. I have taken my father's curricle, and may be absent for some few days, I cannot say precisely how many. Things have come to such a pass at Austerby that there is no bearing it. I must rescue Phoebe, and am persuaded you and my father will understand how it is when you know the whole, and think I did right, for you have always held her in affection."*

As he read these lines Lord Marlow's cheeks lost some of their ruddy colour. He allowed his wife to twitch the paper out of his hand, stammering: "Impossible! I do not credit it! P-pray, where could they have gone?"

"Exactly! *Where?*" demanded Mrs. Orde. "That question is what brings me here! If my husband were not in Bristol at this moment—but so it is always! Whenever a man is most needed he is never to be found!"

"I do not know what this message means," announced Lady Marlow. "I do not pretend to understand it. For my part I

74

strongly suspect Mr. Thomas Orde to have been inebriated when he wrote it."

"How dare you?" flashed Mrs. Orde, her eyes sparkling dangerously.

"No, no, of course he was not!" interposed Lord Marlow hurriedly. "My love, let me beg of you—Not but what it is so extraordinary that—Though far be it from me to suggest——"

"Oh!" cried Mrs. Orde, stamping her foot, "don't stand there in that addle-brained fashion, saying nothing to the purpose, my lord! Is it *nothing* to you that your daughter is at this very moment *eloping*? You must go after her! Discover where she meant to go! Surely Susan might know! Or Miss Battery! She may have let fall a hint—or one of them, better acquainted with her than you, might guess!"

Lady Marlow was inclined to brush this suggestion aside, but her lord, the memory of his overnight interview with Phoebe lively in his mind, was by this time seriously alarmed. He said at once that Susan and Miss Battery should be sent for, and hastened to the door, shouting to Firbank. While a message was carried up to the schoolroom, Mrs. Orde at once relieved her overcharged nerves and paid off every arrear of a debt of rancour that had been mounting in her bosom for years by telling Lady Marlow exactly what she thought of her manners, conduct, insensibility, and gross stupidity. Lord Marlow was inevitably drawn into the altercation; and in the heat of battle Sylvester's presence was forgotten. He did nothing to attract attention to himself. The moment for that had not yet come, though he had every hope that it was not far distant. Meanwhile he listened to Mrs. Orde's masterly indictment of his hostess, gratefully storing up in his memory the several anecdotes illustrative of Lady Marlow's depravity, every detail of which Mrs. Orde had faithfully carried in her mind for years past.

She was silenced at last by the entrance into the room of Miss Battery, accompanied not only by Susan but by Eliza as well. To this circumstance Lady Marlow took instant and pardonable exception; but when she would have dismissed her Miss Battery said grimly: "I thought it my duty to bring her to your ladyship. She says she knows where her sister has gone. Don't think it, myself."

"Phoebe would never tell *Eliza*," asserted Susan. "And particularly when she never breathed a word to *me*!"

"I *do* know where she has gone!" said Eliza. "And I was going to tell Mama, because it is my duty to do so."

"Yes, well, never mind that!" said Lord Marlow testily. "If you know, tell me at once!"

"She has gone to Gretna Green with Tom Orde, Papa," said Eliza.

The tone in which she uttered this staggering information was so smug that it goaded Susan into exclaiming impetuously: "*I* know that's a rapper, you odious little mischief-maker, you!"

"Susan, you will go to my dressing-room and remain there until I come to you!" said Lady Marlow.

But greatly to her surprise Lord Marlow came to Susan's rescue. "No, no, this matter must be sifted! It's my belief Sukey is in the right of it."

"Mine too," interpolated Miss Battery.

"Eliza is a very truthful child," stated Lady Marlow.

"How do you know she is gone to Gretna Green?" demanded Mrs. Orde. "Did she tell you so?"

"Oh, no, ma'am!" said Eliza, looking so innocent that Susan's hand itched to slap her. "I think it was a secret between her and Tom, and it has made me very unhappy, because it is wrong to have secrets from Mama and Papa, isn't it, Mama?"

"Very wrong indeed, my dear," corroborated Lady Marlow graciously. "I am glad to know that *one* at least of my daughters feels as she ought."

"Yes, very likely," said Lord Marlow without any marked display of enthusiasm, "but how do you come to know this, girl?"

"Well, Papa, I don't like to tell tales of my sister, but Tom came to see her last night."

"Came to see her last night? When?"

"I don't know, Papa. It was very late, I think, because I was fast asleep."

"Then you couldn't have known anything about it!" interrupted Susan.

"Be silent, Susan!" commanded Lady Marlow.

"I woke up," explained Eliza. "I heard people talking in the morning-room, and I thought it was robbers, so I got up, because it was my duty to tell Papa, so that he could——"

"Oh, you wicked, untruthful brat!" gasped Susan. "If you

had thought that you would have put your head under the blankets in a quake of fright!"

"Am I to speak to you again, Susan?" demanded Lady Marlow.

"Perfectly true," said Miss Battery. "Never had such an idea in her head. Not at all courageous. Got up out of curiosity."

"Oh, what does it signify?" cried Mrs. Orde. "Tom must have come to see Phoebe on his way home last night, that much is certain! You heard them talking in the morning-room, did you, Lizzy? What did they say?"

"I don't know, ma'am. Only that just as I was about to run to find Papa I heard Tom speak, quite loud, so I knew it wasn't house-breakers. He said he hoped there wouldn't be snow in the north, because it must be Gretna Green."

"Good God!" ejaculated Lord Marlow. "The young—— And what had Phoebe to say to that, pray?"

"She told him not to speak so loud, Papa, and then I heard no more, for I went back to bed."

"Yes, because try as you might you *couldn't* hear any more!" said Susan.

"You behaved very properly," said Lady Marlow. "If your sister is saved from the dreadful consequences of her conduct she will owe it to your sense of duty. I am excessively pleased with you, Eliza."

"Begging your pardon, ma'am," said Miss Battery, "*I* should like to know why Eliza's sense of duty didn't prompt her to come immediately to my bedchamber to inform me of what was going forward! Don't scruple to tell you, ma'am, that I don't think there's a word of truth in the story."

"Yes, by God!" said Lord Marlow, kindling. "So should I like to know that! *Why* didn't you rouse Miss Battery immediately, Eliza? Susan's right! You made up the whole story, didn't you? Eh? Answer me!"

"I didn't! Oh, Mama, I didn't!" declared Eliza, beginning to cry.

"Good gracious, my lord!" cried Mrs. Orde. "I should hope that it would be beyond the power of a child of her age to *imagine* such a tale! Pray, what should she know of Gretna Green? I do not doubt her: indeed, the terrible suspicion had already crossed my mind! What else can we think, in face of what my son wrote? If he felt himself obliged to *rescue her*, how could he do so except by marrying her? And where could he do *that*, being under age, except across the Border? I beg of you—I *implore* you, sir!—to go after them!"

"Go after them!" ejaculated his lordship, his face alarmingly suffused with colour. "I should rather think so, ma'am! Implore me, indeed! Let me tell you you have no need to do *that*! My daughter to be running off to Gretna Green like an——Oh, let the pair of them but wait until I catch up with them!"

"Well, they won't do that!" said Mrs. Orde, with some asperity. "And if you *do* catch them (which I don't consider certain, for you may depend upon it they have several hours' start of you, and will stay away from the post roads for as far as they may) you will be so good as to remember, sir, that my son is little more than a schoolboy, and has acted, I don't question, from motives of the purest chivalry!"

At this point, perceiving that his host, having forgotten all about him, was preparing to storm out of the room, Sylvester judged it to be time to make his presence felt. Coming back into the centre of the room, he said soothingly: "Oh, I should think he would catch them quite easily, ma'am! The strongest probability is that they will run into a snow-drift. I believe it has been snowing for several days in the north. My dear Lord Marlow, before you set out in pursuit of the runaways you must allow me to take my leave of you. In such circumstances I daresay you and her ladyship must be wishing me at Jericho. Accept my thanks for your agreeable hospitality, my regret for its unavoidable curtailment, and my assurance—I trust unnecessary!—that you may rely upon my discretion. It remains only for me to wish you speedy success in your mission, and to beg that you will not delay your departure on my account."

With these words, delivered very much in the grand manner, he shook hands with Lady Marlow, executed two slight bows to Mrs. Orde and Miss Battery, and was gone from the room before his host had collected his wits enough to do more than utter a half-hearted protest.

His valet, a very correct gentleman's gentleman, received the news of his immediate departure from Austerby with a deferential bow and an impassive countenance; John Keighley, suffering all the discomfort of a severe cold in his head, bluntly protested. "We'll never reach London, your grace, not with the roads in the state they're in, by all accounts."

"I daresay we shan't," replied Sylvester. "But do you think I can't reach Speenhamland? I'll prove you wrong!"

Swale, already folding one of Sylvester's coats, heard this magical word with relief. Speenhamland meant the Pelican, a hostelry as famous for the excellence of its accommodation as for the extortionate nature of its charges. Far better entertainment would be found there than at Austerby, as well for his grace's servants as for his grace himself.

Unmoved by this reflection, Keighley objected: "It's more than thirty miles from here, your grace! You'll have to change horses, and postilions too, because the boys couldn't do it, not if we run into snow."

"Oh, I'm not travelling in the chaise!" said Sylvester. "I'll take the curricle, of course, and drive myself. You will come with me, and Swale can follow in the chaise. Tell the boys they must go as far as they can without a change. They are to bring my own team on by easy stages to the Pelican, and if I'm not there, to town. Swale, put up all I might need for several days in one of my portmanteaux!"

"If your grace should wish me to travel in the curricle I shall be happy to do so," said Swale, with less truth than heroism.

"No, Keighley will be of far more use to me," replied Sylvester.

His devoted retainer grunted, and went off to the stables. Within half an hour, resigned to his fate, he was seated beside his master in the curricle, gloomily surveying the prospect, which had by this time become extremely threatening. He had added a large muffler to his attire, and from time to time blew his nose on a handkerchief drenched with camphor. Upon Sylvester's addressing a chatty remark to him, he said primly: "Yes, your grace." To a second effort to engage him in conversation he replied: "I couldn't say, your grace."

"Oh, couldn't you?" Sylvester retorted. "Very well! Say what you wish to: that it's devilish cold, and I'm mad to make the attempt to get to the Pelican! It's all one to me, and will very likely make you feel more amiable."

"I wouldn't so demean myself, your grace," replied Keighley, with dignity.

"Well, that's a new come-out," commented Sylvester. "I thought I was in for one of your scolds." Receiving no response to this, he said cajolingly: "Come out of the sullens, John, for God's sake!"

Never, from the day when a very small Sylvester had first

coaxed him to do his imperious will, had Keighley been able to resist that note. He said severely: "Well, if ever there was a crack-brained start, your grace! Driving right into a snow-storm, like you are! All I say is, don't you go blaming me if we end up in a drift!"

"No, I won't," Sylvester promised. "The thing was, you see, it was now or never—or at least for a week. You may have been enjoying yourself: I wasn't! In fact, I'd sooner put up at a hedge tavern."

Keighley chuckled. "I suspicioned that was the way of it. I didn't think we should be there long: not when I heard about the smoke in your grace's bedchamber. Nor Swale didn't like it, being very niffy-naffy in his ways."

"Like me," remarked Sylvester. "In any event, I could hardly have remained, when his lordship was suddenly called away, could I?"

"No, your grace. Particularly seeing as how you wasn't wishful to."

Sylvester laughed; and good relations being restored between them they proceeded on their way in perfect amity. It was snowing in Devizes, but they reached Marlborough in good time, and at the Castle Inn stopped to rest the horses, and to partake of a second breakfast. Roaring fires and excellent food strongly tempted Sylvester to remain there, and he might have done so had it not occurred to him that it was situated rather too near to Austerby for safety. The arrival of the Bath Mail clinched the matter. It was several hours late, but Sylvester learned from the coachman that although the road was bad in parts, it was nowhere impassable. He decided to push on. Keighley, fortified by a potation of gin, beer, nutmeg, and sugar, which he referred to as hot flannel, raised no objection; so the horses were put to again.

It was heavier going over the next ten miles, and once beyond the Forest of Savernake Sylvester was obliged, once or twice, to pull up, while Keighley got down from the curricle to discover the line of the road. Hungerford was reached, however, without mishap. Sylvester's famous dapple-grays, with a light vehicle behind them, were tired, but not distressed. If rested for a space, he judged them to be perfectly capable of accomplishing the next stage, which would bring him to Speen-hamland, and the Pelican.

By the time they set forward again on their journey it was

past four o'clock, and to the hazards of the weather were added those of failing daylight. With the sky so uniformly overcast Keighley was of the opinion that it would be dark before they reached Newbury, but he knew his master too well to waste his breath in remonstrance. Sylvester, who could have numbered on one hand the occasions when he had been ill enough to coddle himself, was neither disconcerted by the blinding snow, nor troubled by its discomforts. Keighley, his cold at its zenith, wondered whether he could be persuaded to draw rein at the Halfway House, and would not have been altogether sorry had they foundered within reach of this or any other hostelry. Neither he nor Sylvester was familiar with the road, but fortune favoured them, just when it became most difficult. They met a stage-coach making its slow and perilous progress towards Bath, and were able to follow its deep tracks for several miles, before these became obliterated by the falling snowflakes. They were still discernible when Keighley's sharp eyes saw the wreck of a curricle lying in the ditch, and remarked that someone had had a nasty spill. The curricle was covered with snow, but it was plainly a sporting vehicle, and had just as plainly been travelling eastward. Sylvester was assailed suddenly by a suspicion. He pulled up, the better to scrutinize the derelict. "It's a curricle, John."

"Yes, your grace," agreed Keighley. "Broken shaft, let alone the near-side wheels, which I dare say are smashed. Now, for goodness' sake, do you take care how you go! Nice bobbery if we was to end up the same way!"

"I wonder?" said Sylvester, unholy amusement in his voice. "I shouldn't suppose there could be many desperate enough to take a curricle out in this weather. I *wonder?*"

"But they was making for the Border, your grace!" said Keighley, betraying a knowledge he had hitherto discreetly concealed.

"That was only what Miss Eliza said. I thought young Orde must be a regular greenhead to have supposed there was the least chance of his getting within two hundred miles of the Border. Perhaps he isn't a greenhead, John! I think we are going to make his acquaintance. I *am* glad we decided to push on to the Pelican!"

"Begging your grace's pardon," said Keighley grimly, "*we* didn't decide no such thing! What's more, if I may make so bold as to say so, you don't want to make his acquaintance.

Nor you don't want to meet Miss again—not if *I* know anything about it!"

"I daresay you know all about it," retorted Sylvester, setting his horses in motion again. "You usually do. What happened when they ran into the ditch?"

"I don't know, your grace," replied Keighley irascibly. "Maybe there was a coach passed, and they got into it."

"Don't be a clunch! What became of the horses? They don't belong to Master Tom, but to his father. He'd take precious good care of 'em, wouldn't he?"

"He would, if his father's the cut of your grace's honoured father," acknowledged Keighley, with mordant humour. "Lord what a set-out we did have, that time your grace took the young bay out, and——"

"Thank you, I haven't forgotten it! Master Tom, John, got his horses disentangled from that wreck, and led them to the nearest shelter. There can't have been any broken legs, but I fancy they didn't come off entirely scatheless. Keep your eyes open for a likely farm, or inn!"

Keighley sighed, but refrained from comment. In the event no great strain was imposed upon his visionary powers, for within half a mile, hard by a narrow lane which crossed the post road, a small wayside inn stood, set back a few yards from the road, with its yard and several outbuildings in its rear.

"Aha!" said Sylvester. "Now we shall see, shan't we, John? Hold 'em for me!"

Keighley, receiving the reins, was so much incensed by this wayward conduct that he said with awful sarcasm: "Yes, your grace. And if you was to be above an hour, should I walk them, just in case they *might* happen to take cold?"

But Sylvester, springing down from the curricle, was already entering the Blue Boar, and paid no heed to this sally.

The door opened on to a passage, on one side of which lay the tap, and on the other a small coffee-room. Opposite, a narrow staircase led to the upper floor, and at the head of it, looking anxiously down, stood Miss Phoebe Marlow.

CHAPTER

8

The startled exclamation which broke from her, and the look of dismay which came into her face, afforded Sylvester malicious satisfaction. "Ah, how do you do?" he said affably.

One hand gripping the banister-rail, a painful question in her eyes, she uttered: "Mama——?"

"But of course! Outside, in my curricle." Then he saw that she had turned perfectly white, and said: "Don't be such a goose-cap! You can't suppose I would drive your mother-in-law thirty yards, let alone thirty miles!"

Her colour came rushing back; she said: "No—or she consent to drive in a curricle! What—what brings you here, sir?"

"Curiosity, ma'am. I saw the wreck on the road, and guessed it to be Mr. Orde's curricle."

"Oh! You didn't—you were not——" She stopped in some confusion; and then, as he looked up at her in bland enquiry, blurted out: "You didn't come to find me?"

"Well, no!" he answered apologetically. "I am merely on my way to London. I am afraid, Miss Marlow, that you have been labouring under a misapprehension."

"Do you mean you were not going to make me an offer?" she demanded.

"You *do* favour the blunt style, don't you? Bluntly, then, ma'am, I was not."

She was not at all offended, but said, with a sigh of relief: "Thank goodness! Not but what it is still excessively awkward. However, you are better than *nobody*, I suppose!"

"Thank you!"

"Well, when I heard you come in I hoped you had been that odious ostler."

"What odious ostler?"

"The one who is employed here. Mrs. Scaling—she's the landlady—sent him off to Newbury to purchase provisions when she feared they might be snowed up here for weeks, perhaps, and he has not come back. His home is there, and Mrs. Scaling thinks he will make the snow an excuse for remaining there until it stops. And the thing is that he has taken the only horse she keeps! Tom—Mr. Orde—won't hear of my trying if I can ride Trusty—and I own it *would* be a little difficult, when there's no saddle, and I am not wearing my riding-dress. And no one ever *has* ridden Trusty. True would carry me, but that's impossible: his left hock is badly strained. But that leg is certainly broken, and it *must* be set!"

"Whose leg?" interrupted Sylvester. "Not the horse's?"

"Oh, no! It's not as bad as *that*!" she assured him. "Mr. Orde's leg."

"Are you sure it's broken?" he asked incredulously. "How the deuce did he get here, if that's the case? Who got the horses out of their traces?"

"There was a farm-hand, leading a donkey and cart. It was that which caused the accident: Trusty holds donkeys in the greatest aversion, and the wretched creature brayed at him, just as Tom had him in hand, as I thought. Tom caught his heel in the rug, I think, and that's how it happened. The farm-hand helped me to free Trusty and True; and then he lifted Tom into his cart, and brought him here, while I led the horses. Mrs. Scaling and I contrived to cut off Tom's boot, but I am afraid we hurt him a good deal, because he fainted away in the middle of it. And here we have been ever since, with poor Tom's leg not set, and no means of fetching a surgeon, all because of that abominable ostler!"

"Good God!" said Sylvester, struggling with a strong desire to laugh. "Wait a minute!"

With these words, he went out into the road again, to where

Keighley awaited him. "Stable 'em, John!" he ordered. "We are putting up here for the night. There is only one ostler, and he has gone off to Newbury, so if you see no one in the yard, do as seems best to you!"

"Putting up *here*, your grace?" demanded Keighley, thunderstruck.

"I should think so: it will be too dark to go farther in another couple of hours," replied Sylvester, vanishing into the house again.

He found that Phoebe had been joined by a stout woman with iron-gray curls falling from under a mob cap, and a comely countenance just now wearing a harassed expression. She dropped a curtsey to him; and Phoebe said, with careful emphasis: "This is Mrs. Scaling, sir, who has been so very helpful to *my brother* and to me!"

"How kind of her!" said Sylvester, bestowing upon the landlady the smile which won for him so much willing service. "Their parents would be glad to know that my imprudent young friends fell into such good hands. I have told my groom to stable the horses, but I daresay you will tell him just where he may do so. Can you accommodate the pair of us?"

"Well, I'm sure, sir, I should be very happy—only this is quite a simple house, such as your honour—— And I've took and put the poor young gentleman in my best room!" said Mrs. Scaling, considerably flustered.

"Oh, that makes no odds!" said Sylvester, stripping off his gloves. "I think, ma'am, it would be as well if you took me up to see your brother."

Phoebe hesitated, and when Mrs. Scaling bustled off to the back premises, said suspiciously: "Why do you wish to see Tom? Why do you wish to remain here?"

"Oh, it's not a question of wishing!" he returned, a laugh in his eyes. "Pure fellow-feeling, ma'am! What a dog I should be to leave the poor devil in the hands of two females! Take me up! I promise you, he will be very glad to see me!"

"Well, I don't think he will," said Phoebe, regarding him in a darkling way. "And *I* should like to know why you talked of us to Mrs. Scaling as though you had been our grandfather!"

"I feel like your grandfather," he replied. "Take me up to the sufferer, and let us see what can be done for him!"

She still seemed to be doubtful, but after a moment's indecision she said ungraciously: "Oh, very well! But I won't have him ranted at, or reproached, mind!"

"Good God, who am I to give him a trimming?" Sylvester said, following her up the narrow stair.

Mrs. Scaling's best bedchamber was a low-pitched room in the front of the house. A fire had been lit in the grate, and the blinds drawn across the dormer window to shut out the bleak dusk. An oil lamp had been set on the dressing-table, and a couple of candles on the mantelshelf, and as the window-blinds and the curtains round the bed were of crimson the room presented a pleasantly cosy appearance. Tom, fully dressed except for his boots and stockings, was lying on the bed, with a patchwork quilt spread lightly over his legs, and his shoulders propped up by several bulky pillows. There was a haggard look on his face, and the eyes which he turned towards the door were heavy with strain.

"Tom, this—this is the Duke of Salford!" said Phoebe. "He *would* have me bring him up, so—so here he is!"

This startling intelligence made Tom wrench himself up on to his elbow, wincing, but full of determination to protect Phoebe from any attempt to drag her back to Austerby. *"Salford?"* he ejaculated. "You mean to tell me—— Come over here, Phoebe, and don't you be afraid! He has no authority over you, and so he knows!"

"Now, don't you enact me a high tragedy!" said Sylvester, walking up to the bed. "I haven't any authority over either of you, and I'm not the villain of this or any other piece. How do you do?"

Finding that a hand was being held out to him Tom, much disconcerted, took it, and stammered: "Oh, how—how do you do, sir? I mean——"

"Better than you, I fear," said Sylvester. "In the devil of a hobble, aren't you? May I look?" Without waiting for an answer he twitched the quilt back. As Tom instinctively braced himself, he glanced up with a smile, and said: "I won't touch it. Have you been much mauled?"

Tom grinned back at him rather wanly. "Oh, by Jove, haven't I just?"

"Well, I am very sorry, but we had to get your boot off, and we did *try* not to hurt you," said Phoebe.

"Yes, I know. It wasn't so much that as that booberkin

thinking he knew how to set a bone, and Mrs. Scaling believing him!"

"It sounds appalling," remarked Sylvester, his eyes on the injured leg, which was considerably inflamed, and bore the marks of inexpert handling.

"It was," asseverated Tom. "He is Mrs. Scaling's son, touched in his upper works, I think!"

"Well, he is a natural," amended Phoebe. "Indeed, I wish I hadn't allowed him to try what he could do, but he was not at all unhandy with poor True, which made me think he would very likely know how to set your leg, for such persons, you know, frequently have that kind of knowledge." She saw that Sylvester was regarding her with mockery, and added defensively: "It *is* so! There is a natural in our village who is better than any horse-doctor!"

"You should have been a horse, Orde," said Sylvester. "How many hours is it since this happened?"

"I don't know, sir. A great many, I daresay: it seems like an age," replied poor Tom.

"I am not a doctor—even a horse-doctor—but I fancy the bone should be set as soon as possible. We shall have to see what we can do. Oh, don't look so aghast! *I'm* not going to make the attempt! We need Keighley—my groom. I shouldn't be at all surprised if he knows how to do the trick."

"Your groom?" said Phoebe sceptically. "How should we know anything of the sort, pray?"

"Perhaps he doesn't, in which case he will tell us so. He put my shoulder back once, when I was a boy and dislocated it, and I recall that when the surgeon came he said he could not have done it better himself. I'll call him," said Sylvester, walking to the door.

He went out, and Tom turned wondering eyes towards Phoebe. "What the deuce brought him here?" he asked. "I thought he had been chasing us, but if that was the way of it what makes him care a button for my leg?"

"I can't think!" said Phoebe. "But he didn't come in search of me, that I *do* know! In fact, he says he didn't come to Austerby to offer for me at all. I was never more relieved in my life!"

Tom looked at her in a puzzled way, but since he was a good deal exhausted by all he had undergone, and his leg was paining him very much, he felt unequal to further discussion, and relapsed into silence.

In a short space of time Sylvester came back, bringing Keighley with him, and carrying a glass half full of a rich brown liquid, which he set down on a small table beside the bed. "Well, Keighley says that if it is a simple fracture he can set it for you," he remarked cheerfully. "Let us hope it is, therefore! But I can't help feeling that the first thing to do is to get you out of your clothes, and into your night-shirt. You must be excessively uncomfortable!"

"Oh, I do *wish* you will persuade him to be undressed!" exclaimed Phoebe, regarding Sylvester for the first time with approval. "It is precisely what Mrs. Scaling and I wanted to do for him at the outset, but nothing would prevail upon him to agree to it!"

"You amaze me!" said Sylvester. "If I find him similarly obstinate Keighley and I will strip him forcibly. Meanwhile, Miss Marlow, *you* may go downstairs—if you will be so obliging!—and assist Mrs. Scaling to tear up a sheet for bandages. No, I know you don't wish to leave him to our mercy, but, believe me, you are shockingly in the way here! Go and brew him a posset, or some broth, or whatever you think suitable to this occasion!"

She looked a trifle mulish, but a chuckle from Tom clinched the matter. "Oh, do go away, Phoebe!" he begged.

She went, but the incident did nothing to put her in charity with Sylvester, politely holding the door for her, and saying with odious kindness, as she passed him: "You shall come back presently!"

Tom, however, was so grateful that he began to think Sylvester a very tolerable sort of a man; and when Sylvester, turning away from the door, winked at him, he grinned, and said shyly: "I'm much obliged to you, sir! She's a good girl— as good as ever twanged, in fact—but—but——"

"I know," said Sylvester sympathetically. "They *will* be ministering angels!"

"Yes," agreed Tom, somewhat uneasily eyeing Keighley, who, having shed his coat, was now rolling up his shirtsleeves in an ominous manner.

"You want to bite on the bullet, sir," recommended Keighley. "Because I'll have to find out just what you have broke in your leg, if you've broke anything, which I've only got your word for, when all's said."

Tom assented to this, clenched his teeth and his fists, and endured in sweating silence while Keighley discovered the exact nature of his injury. The rough cart-journey, and the inexpert attempts of Will Scaling to set the broken bone, had caused considerable inflammation. Keighley said, as he straightened himself: "Properly mauled you they did, sir! True enough, you've broke your fibula—which is what you might call Dutch comfort, because it might have been worse. Now, if that jobbernoll below stairs has sawn me off a nice splint, like I told him to do, we'll have you going along like winking in a pig's whisper, sir!"

"Are you sure of that, John?" Sylvester asked. "It won't do to be making a mull of it!"

"I shan't do that, your grace. But I'm thinking it would be as well if the young gentleman was put to bed. I'll have to slit his breeches up the left side, but I can get 'em off easier without his leg being splinted."

Sylvester nodded; Tom said faintly: "My razor is on the dressing-table. You may as well use it. It's ruined already, cutting my boot."

"Don't let that vex you!" said Sylvester. "You can borrow one of mine."

Tom thanked him. He submitted to being stripped, and put into his nightshirt, and owned, upon being lowered again on to the pillows, that he felt a degree more comfortable. Keighley then went away to collect splints and bandages; and Tom, a little white about the gills, said with what jauntiness he could muster that he would be devilish glad when it was over.

"I should think you would be," agreed Sylvester. He picked up the glass he had brought into the room, and held it out. "Meanwhile, here's a drink to fortify you. No daylights, mind!"

Tom looked rather dubiously at the dark potion, but took the glass, and raised it to his lips. Then he lowered it again. "Yes, but it's rum, isn't it, sir?"

"Yes. Don't you like it?"

"Well, not above half. But the thing is I should be as drunk as a wheelbarrow if I drank all this!"

"That isn't of the slightest consequence. Oh, are you thinking of what Miss Marlow might say? You need not: I shan't let her come back until you've slept it off. Don't argue with me! Just drink it, and be thankful."

Keighley, returning to find his patient happily, if somewhat muzzily, smiling, said with approval: "That's the dandy! Properly shot in the neck, ain't you, sir? It won't make any odds to you *what's* done to you. Now, if your grace will lend a hand——?"

If Tom was not quite as insensible as Keighley optimistically prophesied, the rum undoubtedly made it much easier for him to bear the exquisite anguish of the next minute or two. He behaved with great fortitude, encouraged by Keighley, who told him he was pluck to the backbone. The ordeal was soon at an end. It left him feeling limp and rather sick. His leg ached; and he found that everything he tried to look at swam so giddily before him that he was obliged to close his eyes, yielding to the powerful effect of rum. Keighley, observing with satisfaction that he was sinking into stertorous sleep, nodded at Sylvester, and said briefly: "He'll do now, your grace."

"I hope he may, but it will be as well if we get a surgeon to him," replied Sylvester, frowning down at Tom. "If anything were to go amiss, I've no mind to be responsible. He's under age, you know. I wonder why the devil I embroiled myself in this affair?"

"Ah!" said Keighley, snuffing the candles. "Just what I've been asking myself, your grace!"

They left the room together, and descended the stairs to the coffee-room. Here they found Phoebe, sitting before a brisk fire, and looking anxious. Sylvester said: "Well, Keighley has set the bone, and Orde is now asleep. For anything I know, there's nothing more to be done, but at the same time—What's the weather like?" He stepped up to the window, and drew the blind aside. "Still snowing, but not dark yet. What do you wish, Miss Marlow?"

She had smiled at Keighley, and thanked him; but at these words she cast him an apologetic glance, and said: "I should *wish* to bring a doctor to see him, because if it hadn't been for me it would never have happened, and I know Mrs. Orde would do so. It is the most vexatious thing! Mrs. Scaling only spoke to me of a doctor at Newbury, and now I've discovered that there is a Dr. Upsall, living at Hungerford! If I had known of him earlier I might have walked there, for I don't think it's much above four miles. Mrs. Scaling didn't think to tell me

90

of him, because from what she says I collect he is above her touch."

"Let us hope he doesn't consider himself above mine. Do you suppose the half-wit capable of guiding one to his house?"

"I should think he would be. He says so, at all events. But it is growing dark, and perhaps the doctor might not choose to venture out, for a stranger?"

"Nonsense!" Sylvester said. "It is his business to venture out. He will be well paid for his trouble. You had better put the horses to immediately, John—and tell young Scaling he is to go with you! You may present my card to this Dr. Upsall, and say that I shall be obliged to him if he will come here at once."

"Very good, your grace," Keighley said.

Phoebe, who had listened to Sylvester's orders in gathering indignation, waited only until Keighley had left the room before exclaiming in accents of strong censure: "You cannot mean to send that unfortunate man out in this weather!"

He looked surprised. "You said you wished a doctor to see Orde, didn't you? I own, I wish it too, and though he might take no particular harm through waiting until the morning it is quite possible, you know, that the road may be impassable by then."

"Indeed, I wish him to see a doctor!" she said. "And if you will trust your horses to me I'll fetch him myself—since *you* do not care to go!"

"I?" he demanded. "Why should I do any such thing?"

"Can't you see that your groom has the most shocking cold?" she said fiercely. "He is looking worn to a bone already, and here you are, sending him out again without a thought to what may come of it! I suppose it is of no consequence if he contracts an inflammation of the lungs, or falls into a confirmed consumption!"

He flushed angrily. "On the contrary! I should find it excessively inconvenient!"

"Oh, surely you have other grooms? I am persuaded there could never be a want of servants to spare you the least exertion!"

"Many other grooms! But only one Keighley! It may interest you to know, Miss Marlow, that I have a considerable regard for him!"

"Well, it doesn't interest me, because I don't believe it!"

she said warmly. "You couldn't have brought him thirty miles in an open carriage on such a day if you had a *regard* for him! Would *you* have set out from Austerby if you had had a bad cold? No such thing!"

"You are mistaken! I should! I never pay the least heed to such trifling ailments!"

"*You* are not fifty years old, or more!"

"Nor is Keighley! Fifty years old indeed! He is not much above forty!" said Sylvester furiously. "What's more, if he had thought himself too unwell to travel he would have told me so!"

Her lips curled derisively. "Would he?"

"Yes, he——" Sylvester stopped suddenly, staring at her with very hard, frowning eyes. A dull colour crept into his cheeks; he said stiffly: "He should have done so, at all events. He knows very well I wouldn't—Good God, you seem to think me an inhuman taskmaster!"

"No, only *selfish*!" she said. "I daresay you never so much as noticed that the poor man had caught cold."

A retort sprang to his lips, but he checked it, his colour deepening as he recollected feeling vexed with Keighley for contacting an epidemic cold, and hoping that he would not take it from him.

But no sooner had Phoebe uttered her last stricture than she too suffered an uncomfortable recollection. Flushing far more vividly than Sylvester, she said on a conscience-stricken voice: "I beg your pardon! It was very bad of me to have said that, when—when I am so much obliged to you! Pray forgive me, sir!"

"It is of no consequence at all, Miss Marlow," he replied coldly. "I should be grateful to you for calling my attention to Keighley's state. Let me assure you that you need feel no further anxiety! I am far too selfish to wish to have him laid up, and shall certainly not send him to Hungerford."

Before she could reply to this Keighley came back into the room, muffled in his heavy driving-coat. "Beg pardon, your grace, but I went off without the card."

"I've changed my mind, John," Sylvester said. "I'll go myself."

"*Go yourself*, your grace?" repeated Keighley. "And may I make so bold as to ask why? If your grace don't care to have me driving the grays, I hope your grace will pardon me if I was to say that it won't be *quite* the first time I've done so! P'raps your grace would as lief drive them without me in the curricle at all?"

This withering sarcasm had the effect of clearing the frown from Sylvester's brow. "Exactly so!" he said, his eyes quizzing his offended henchman. "I am going alone! Oh, no I'm not! I shall have the half-wit with me, shall I not? I hope he may not murder me, or anything of that nature! No, don't argue with me! Miss Marlow believes you to be sinking into a confirmed consumption, and I will *not* have your death upon my conscience! Besides, what *should* I do without you? Where is my greatcoat?"

Keighley turned an amazed and slightly reproachful gaze upon Phoebe. "*Me*? Lor', ma'am, there's nothing amiss with me barring a bit of a cold in my head! Now, if your grace will give me your card, I'll be off! And no more funning, *if* you please, because if I don't get started quick there's no saying but what *I'll* end in the ditch, and a nice set-out that would be!"

"No, I am quite determined you shan't go," Sylvester said. "Did you put my coat in my bedchamber? Where *is* my bedchamber? Direct me to it instantly, and be off to put the horses to! Good God! Ought I, perhaps, to do that too? Miss Marlow, do you think——?"

Keighley intervened before Phoebe was obliged to answer a question she suspected to be deliberately provocative. Reiterating his request to Sylvester to stop funning, he added a strongly worded protest against the impropriety of his chasing all over the country after a mere sawbones. Such unbecoming conduct, he said severely, would not do.

"I'm the best judge of that," returned Sylvester. "Put the horses to, at once, if you please!"

He strode to the door, but was arrested by Phoebe, who said suddenly: "Oh, pray——! I don't wish to charge you with an office you might think troublesome, but—but if you *are* going to Hungerford, would you be so very obliging as to try if you can procure for me a few ounces of muriate of ammonia, a pint of spirit of wine, and some spermacctti ointment?"

Sylvester's lip twitched, and he burst out laughing. "Oh, certainly, Miss Marlow! Are you sure there is nothing else you would wish me to purchase for you?"

"No," she replied seriously. "Mrs. Scaling has plenty of

vinegar. And if you can't come by the ointment, she will let me have some lard instead—only I can't be sure it is perfectly free from salt. It is to put on Trusty's foreleg," she explained, seeing that he was still much inclined to laugh. "It is badly grazed: I fancy poor True may have kicked him, when he was struggling to get out of the ditch."

"I'll come and take a look at that, miss," said Keighley, his professional interest aroused. "Showing red, is it? It'll have to be fomented before the ointment's put on it."

"Oh, yes, I have been doing so, every hour, and True's hock as well! I should be very much obliged to you, if you will look at it, Keighley, and tell me if you think I should apply a bran poultice tonight."

"Render Miss Marlow all the assistance you can, John, but first put the grays to!" interrupted Sylvester. "See to it that fires are lit in our rooms, bespeak dinner, and a private parlour—no, I expect there isn't one in so small a house: you had better tell the landlady I'll hire this room—don't disturb Mr. Orde, and have everything ready for a bowl of punch as soon as I return. And don't let Miss Marlow keep you out in the draughty stable too long!"

On this Parthian shot he departed, closely followed by Keighley, who did not cease to expostulate with him until he was actually preparing to mount into the curricle.

"Be damned to you, John, *no!*" he said. "You will stay here, and nurse your cold. Why didn't you tell me you were out of sorts, you stupid fellow? I could have taken Swale with me, and left you to follow in the chaise."

He sounded a little contrite, which would have surprised Keighley had he not been so much revolted by the thought of relinquishing his post to Swale that he never noticed Sylvester's unusual solicitude. By the time he could trust himself to repudiate the disgraceful suggestion in anything but terms quite unsuited to his position, Sylvester had swung himself up into the curricle, and set his pair in motion. Beside him, Will Scaling, a shambling and overgrown youth of somewhat vacuous amiability, grinned hugely, and sat back with all the air of one prepared to enjoy a high treat.

CHAPTER

9

It was nearly eight o'clock before Sylvester returned to the
Blue Boar, and for a full hour Phoebe had been picturing just
such an accident as had befallen Tom, and wishing that she
had not sent him forth on his errand. When he did at last arrive
he took her by surprise, for the snow muffled the sound of the
horses' hooves, and he drove his curricle straight into the yard,
and came into the house through the back-door. She heard a
quick stride in the passage, and looked up to see him standing
in the doorway of the coffee-room. He had not stayed to put
off his long driving-coat, which was very wet, and had snow
still clinging to its many shoulder-capes. She started up, exclaiming: "Oh, you are safely back! I have been in such a
fidget, fearing you had met with an accident! Have you brought
the doctor, sir?"

"Oh, yes, he is here—or he will be, in a few minutes. I
came ahead. Is there a fire in your bedchamber, Miss Marlow?"

"Yes, but——"

"Then may I suggest that you retire there until the surgeon
has departed? I haven't mentioned your presence here to him,
for although your brother and sister story may do well enough
for the landlady, it is quite possible, you know, that a doctor

living at Hungerford might recognize one or other of you. You will agree that the fewer people to get wind of this escapade of yours the better."

"I shouldn't think he would know either of us," she replied, with what he considered to be quite unbecoming *sangfroid*. "However, I daresay you are right, sir. Only, if I am not to see the doctor, will you take him up to Tom, if you please, and hear what he thinks we should do for him?"

"I've told Keighley to do so. He knows much more about such matters than I do. Moreover, I want to put off these wet clothes. Have you dined?"

"Well, no," she owned. "Though I ate a slice of bread-and-butter just after you went away."

"Good God! Why didn't you order dinner when you wished for it?" he said, rather impatiently.

"Because *you* bespoke it for when you should return. Mrs. Scaling has only one daughter to help her, you know, and she couldn't dress *two* dinners. In fact, she has been in a grand fuss ever since she discovered who you are, because, of course, she is not at all in the habit of entertaining dukes."

"I hope that doesn't mean that we shall get a bad dinner."

"Oh, no, on the contrary! She means to feed you in the most *lavish* way!" Phoebe assured him.

He smiled. "I'm happy to know it: I could eat an ox whole! Stay in this room until you hear Keighley take the surgeon upstairs, and then slip away to your own. I suppose I must, in common charity, give the man a glass of punch before he sets out for Hungerford again, but I'll get rid of him as soon as I can." He nodded to her, and went away, leaving her with her mind divided between resentment at his cool assumption of authority and relief that some at least of her burden of responsibility had been lifted from her shoulders.

When the surgeon presently left Tom, she ventured to go and tap on the door of the best bedroom. Tom bade her come in, and she entered to find him sitting up in bed, much restored by his long sleep, but fretting a good deal over her predicament, his own helplessness, and the condition of his father's horses. She was able to give him a comfortable account of the horses; as for herself, she said that since they could scarcely have hoped to reach Reading she was quite as well off at the Blue Boar as she would have been at an inn in Newbury.

"Yes, but the Duke!" Tom objected. "I must say, there was

never anything more awkward! Not but what I'm devilish obliged to him. Still——!"

"Oh, well!" said Phoebe. "We must just make the best of him! And his groom, you know, is a most excellent person. He put the poultice on Trusty's fore, and he says if we keep the wound pliant with spermacetti ointment until it is perfectly healed, and then dress it with James's blister, he thinks there will be no blemish at all."

"Lord, I hope he may be right!" Tom said devoutly.

"Oh, yes, I am persuaded he is!" She then bethought her that the horses had not been the only sufferers in the spill, and conscientiously enquired after Tom's broken fibula.

He grinned his appreciation of this palpable afterthought, but replied that the surgeon had not meddled with Keighley's handiwork, beyond applying a lotion to the inflamed surface, and bandaging the leg to a fresh and less makeshift splint. "But the devil of it is that he says I must lie abed for at least a week. And even then I shall be in no case to drive you to London. Lord, I hadn't thought I was such a clunch as to overturn like that! I am as sorry as could be, but that's no use! What are we to do?"

"Well, we can't do anything at present," she answered. "It is still snowing, you know, and I shouldn't wonder at it if we were to find ourselves beleaguered by the morning."

"But what about the Duke?"

She considered the Duke. "Oh, well, at least I'm not afraid of him! And I must own that although I cannot approve of his conduct—he seems to think he can have anything he wants, you know!—he *has* made us excessively comfortable. Only fancy, Tom! I have a fire in my bedchamber! A thing Mama never allowed at home, except when I have been ill! Then he said he must have a private parlour, and would hire the coffee-room, I daresay not so much as considering whether it might not be inconvenient for Mrs. Scaling to give it to him—and of course she didn't dare say a word, because she is so much dazzled by his being a duke that she would give up the whole house to him if he should take it into his head to wish for it."

"I expect he will pay her handsomely—and who would be coming here on such a night?" said Tom. "Are you going to sit down to dinner with him? Shall you find it awkward?"

"Well, I daresay it may be a trifle awkward," she acknowledged. "Particularly if he should ask me why I am on my way

97

to London. However, he may not do so, because he will very likely still be in a miff with me."

"In a miff with you? Why?" demanded Tom. "He didn't seem to me as though he cared a groat for your having run away!"

"Oh, no! Only we quarrelled, you see. Would you believe it? He had the intention of sending poor Keighley to fetch the surgeon! It put me in such a passion that there was no bearing it, and—well, we came to cuffs! But he *did* go himself, in the end, so I don't regret it. In fact," she added reflectively, "I am glad of it, because I was feeling miserably shy before I quarrelled with him, and there is *nothing* like quarrelling with a person to set one at one's ease!"

Unable to take this philosophic view of the matter, Tom said, in a shocked voice: "Do you mean to tell me you sent him out just to fetch the surgeon for me?"

"Yes, why not?" said Phoebe.

"Well, my God, if that's not the outside of enough! as though he had been *anybody*! You are the most outrageous girl, Phoebe! I shouldn't think he would ever wish to offer for you after such treatment as that!"

"Well, what a good thing that would be! Not that I think he ever did wish to offer for me. It is the strangest business! I wonder why he came to Austerby?"

Speculation on this point was interrupted by the entrance of Keighley, bearing a heavily laden tray. Neither his injury nor his subsequent potations having impaired Tom's appetite, he temporarily lost interest in any other problem than what might be concealed beneath the several covers on the tray. Keighley, setting the whole down on the table by the bed, asked him in a fatherly way if he was feeling peckish; and upon being assured by Tom that he was, smiled benevolently at him, and said: "That's the barber! Now, you keep still, sir, and leave me to fix you up so as you can manage! As for you, miss, the covers are set downstairs, and his grace is waiting for you."

Dismissed in this kind but firm manner Phoebe withdrew, promising in response to a somewhat peremptory command from Tom to return to him as soon as she should have dined. Tom had suddenly been attacked by qualms. Phoebe was at once too innocent and too intimate with him to see anything equivocal in her position; he was fully alive to its impropriety, and he felt that he ought to keep her under his eye. Sylvester had certainly seemed to him to be a very good sort of a man, but he did not know him, after all: he might be a hardened rake, and if that were so a very uncomfortable time Phoebe would have of it, alone with him in the coffee-room, while her supposed protector lay tied by the leg in the best bedroom.

Had he but known it, Sylvester was not feeling at all amorous. He was tired, hungry, and in a fair way to regretting the impulse which had made him stop at the Blue Boar. To assist in an elopement was conduct quite unbecoming his position; moreover, it would lay him open to censure, which would not be easier to bear because it was justified. He was frowning down into the fire when Phoebe came into the room, and although he looked up at her entrance the frown did not immediately leave his brow.

She read in it condemnation of her attire, for she was still wearing her stuff travelling dress. He, on the other hand, had changed his buckskins and frockcoat for pantaloons and a long-tailed coat of fine blue cloth, and had arranged a fresh necktie in intricate folds about his throat. It was morning dress, but it made her feel dowdy. To her vexation she found herself explaining that she had not changed her own dress because she would be obliged to go out again to the stable.

He had not noticed what she was wearing, and he replied in the light, indifferent tone which always set up her back: "My dear Miss Marlow, there is no occasion to change your dress that I know of—and none for you to visit the stable again tonight, let me add!"

"I must be satisfied that Trusty has not contrived to rid himself of his poultice," she said firmly. "I have very little faith in Will Scaling."

"You may have complete faith in Keighley."

She made no reply to this, for while she felt that Keighley, who was developing a cough, ought not to leave the house, she was reluctant to reopen a quarrel just as she was about to sit down to dinner with Sylvester. She glanced uncertainly at him, and saw that the frown had yielded to a look of slight amusement. Having no idea that her countenance was a tolerably exact mirror for her thoughts, or that he had correctly interpreted the changes of expression that flitted across it, she was surprised, and looked enquiringly at him, her head a little tilted to one side.

She put him in mind of some small, brown bird. He laughed, and said: "You look like—a sparrow! Yes, I know just what you are wondering whether or not to say. As you wish, Miss Marlow: I will cast an eye over the horses before I go to bed, and if I find that that singularly inappropriately named horse has eaten his poultice I will engage to supply him with a fresh one!"

"Do you know how to mix a bran poultice?" she asked sceptically.

"Better than you, I daresay. No, I don't, in general, apply them myself, but I hold it to be an excellent maxim that every man should know more than his grooms, and be as well able to deal with whatever need may arise in his stables. When I was a boy the farrier was one of my closest friends!"

"Do you have your own farrier?" she asked, diverted. "My father does not, and it is something I have always wished for! But you will not mix a poultice in those clothes!"

"Rather than incur your displeasure I will even do that!" he assured her. "It will expose me to Keighley's displeasure, of course, but I shan't regard that. Which puts me in mind of something I have to tell you. I find that the grooms' quarters here are not at all what Keighley is accustomed to: there is, in fact, only the room in which the ostler sleeps and that, being above that very ill-built stable, is extremely cold. I know you will agree that that will not do, and I hope you won't dislike the arrangement I have made, which is that the daughter of the house is to give up her chamber to Keighley, and herself sleep on a trestle-bed in your room."

"Why shouldn't she sleep in her mother's room?" objected Phoebe, by no means pleased with this further example of Sylvester's high-handed ways.

"There is not space enough," said Sylvester.

"Or Keighley might share Will Scaling's room?"

"He would be afraid to."

"Nonsense! the poor boy is perfectly harmless!"

"Keighley has the greatest dislike of half-wits."

"Then why don't you let him set up a trestle-bed in *your* room?" she demanded.

"Because I should be very likely to catch his cold," explained Sylvester.

She sniffed, but appeared to find this answer reasonable, for she said no more. A welcome interruption was provided by the arrival upon the scene of Miss Alice Scaling, panting under the load of a tray piled high with covered dishes. She was a strapping girl, with apple-red cheeks, and a wide grin, and when she had dumped the tray down on the sideboard she paused a moment to fetch her breath before bobbing a curtsey to Sylvester, and reciting: "Mother's compliments, and there's chickens, and rabbit-stew, and a casserole of rice with the giblets, and curd pudding, and apple fritters, and please to say if your honour would fancy the end of the mutton-pie Mother and me and Will had to our dinner." A hissing admonition from the passage caused her to amend this speech. "Please to say if *your grace* would fancy it! There's a tidy bit of it left, and it's good," she added confidentially.

"Thank you, I am sure it is," he replied. "I hardly think we shall need it, however."

"You're welcome if you do," said Miss Scaling, setting out the dishes on the table with hearty good-will. "And no need to fear going short tomorrow, because you're going to have a boiled turkey. I shall wring his neck first thing in the morning, and into the pot he'll go the instant he's plucked and drawed. That way he won't eat tough," she explained. "We hadn't meant to have killed him, but Mother says dukes is more important than a gobble-cock, even if he *is* a prime young 'un. And after that we'll have Mr. Shap's pig off of him, and there'll be the legs and the cheeks, and the loin, and the chitterlings and all, your honour! No, your *grace*! I do be forgetting!" she said, beaming apologetically.

"It makes no matter what you call me, but pray don't wring your turkey's neck on my account!" he said, with a quelling glance at Phoebe, who showed every sign of succumbing to an unseemly fit of giggling.

"What's a turkey?" said Miss Scaling, in a large-minded spirit. "Happen we can come by another of *them*, but dukes ain't found under every bush, that's what Mother says."

On this piece of worldly wisdom she withdrew, pulling the door shut behind her with enough vigour to drown Phoebe's sudden peal of laughter.

"What an atrocious girl you are!" remarked Sylvester. "Don't you know better than to laugh at yokels?"

"It was your face, when she said you were more important than a gobble-cock!" explained Phoebe, wiping her eyes. "Has anyone ever told you that before?"

"No, never. I take it to be a handsome compliment. But she mustn't slay that turkey."

"Oh, you have only to give her the price of another bird and she will be perfectly satisfied!"

"But nothing would prevail upon me to eat a bird that had been thrust warm into the pot!" he objected. "And what are chitterlings?"

"Well, they are the *inside* parts of the pig," said Phoebe, bubbling over again.

"Good God! Heaven send it may stop snowing before we come to *that*! In the meantime, shall I carve these chickens, or will you?"

"Oh, no! You do it, if you please!" she replied, seating herself at the table. "You cannot imagine how hungry I am!"

"I can, for I am very hungry myself. I wonder why quite half this bird has been removed? Oh, I suppose it was for Orde! How is he, by the bye?"

"Well, he seems to be going on quite prosperously, but the doctor said he must not get up for a week. I don't know how I shall contrive to keep him in bed, for he will find it a dead bore, you know."

He agreed to this, reflecting, however, that Tom would not be the only one to find a prolonged sojourn at the inn a dead bore.

Conversation during the meal was desultory, Sylvester being tired and Phoebe careful to inaugurate no topic for discussion that might lead him to ask embarrassing questions. He asked her none, but his mind was not so much divorced from interest in her adventure as she supposed. Between the snow and Tom's broken leg it seemed probable that they would all of them be chained to the Blue Boar for some appreciable time. Sylvester had taken his own measures to invest Phoebe's situation with a certain measure of propriety, but very little doubt existed in his brain that it was the part of a man of the world at least to do what lay within his power to frustrate an elopement. The evils of so clandestine an adventure might not be apparent to a country-bred boy of nineteen, but Sylvester, older than Tom by far more than the eight years that lay between them, was fully alive to them. He supposed he could do no less than bring them to Tom's notice. He had not the smallest intention of discussing the affair with Phoebe: an awkward task in any circumstances, and in her case likely to prove fruitless, since her entire freedom from the confusion natural to a girl discovered in an escapade she must know to be grossly improper argued a singularly brazen disposition.

As soon as dinner was over she withdrew to Tom's room, to find that he had been devoting considerable thought to her predicament. One aspect of it had struck him forcibly, and he lost no time in presenting it to her.

"You know what we were saying, when Keighley brought in my dinner? About the Duke's not wishing to offer for you? Well, if that's the case, Phoebe, you need not go to London after all! What a pair of gudgeons we were not to have thought of that before! I have been racking my brains to hit upon a way of getting you there, too!"

"I did think of it," replied Phoebe. "But even though the Duke won't be a danger I am quite determined to go to my grandmother. It isn't only being afraid of Mama, Tom—though when I consider how angry she will be with me for running away, I own I feel *sick* with terror!—it is—oh, having once escaped I cannot—*will* not—go back! You see, even Papa doesn't love me very much. Not enough to support me, when I implored him to do so. When he held it over my head that if I wouldn't accept an offer from Salford he would tell Mama I felt myself freed from *every* bond."

"But you aren't, Phoebe," Tom pointed out. "You are under age, and he is your father, you know. Your grandmother has no power to keep you against his will."

"Oh, no! And perhaps, if he truly wished for my return, I should go back willingly. But he won't. If I can prevail upon Grandmama to keep me with her I think Papa will be as glad as Mama to be rid of me. At any rate, he won't care whether I am at Austerby or not, except that he will miss me a little when he discovers how unreliable Sawley is when there is no one to watch over the stables."

Tom did not know what to say to this. He had thought it reasonable enough that she should have fled from her home when faced (as she had believed) with a distasteful marriage; but that she should do so for no other reason than that she was not happy there shocked him a little. He could not approve; on the other hand he was well aware of the misery she would be made to suffer if she were forced to return to Austerby after such an exploit, and he was much too fond of her to withhold whatever help he could render. So he said presently: "What can I do, Phoebe? I've made a mull of it, but if there *is* anything I can do I promise you I will."

She smiled warmly at him. "You didn't make a mull of it: it was all that wretched donkey! Perhaps, if we are not discovered before you are able to help yourself, I might still go to London on the stage-coach, and you will buy my ticket for me. But there is no question of that yet."

"No, not while the snow lasts. And in any event——"

"In any event I hope you don't think I would leave you in this case! I'm not so shabby! No, don't tease yourself, Tom! I shall come about, see if I don't! Perhaps, when the Duke goes away—I should think he would do so as soon as it may be possible, wouldn't you?—he will carry a letter to Grandmama for me."

"Phoebe, has he said anything? About your having run away, I mean?" Tom asked abruptly.

"No, not a word! Isn't it fortunate?" she replied.

"I don't know that. Seems to me—Well, he must think it excessively odd! What happened at Austerby, when it was discovered that you had gone away? Hasn't he even told you that?"

"No, but I didn't ask him."

"Good God! I hope he does not think—Phoebe, did he say if he meant to come up to visit me presently?"

"No, do you wish him to?" she asked. "Shall I send him to you? That is, if he has not already gone to look at Trusty for me. He promised he would do so, and put on a fresh poultice if it should be needed."

"Phoebe!" uttered Tom explosively. "If you made him do so it was perfectly outrageous! You are treating him as though he were a lackey!"

She gave an involuntary chuckle. "No, am I? I daresay it would do him a great deal of good, but I didn't make him go out to attend to the horses. He offered to do so, and I own I was surprised. Why do you wish him to visit you?"

"That's my concern. Keighley will be coming in before he goes to bed, and I'll ask him to convey a civil message to the Duke. You are not to go downstairs again, Phoebe. Understand?"

"No, I am going to bed," she replied. "I am so sleepy I can hardly keep my eyes open. But what do you think? That odious man has had Alice Scaling give up her bedchamber to Keighley and set up a trestle for herself in mine! Without so much as asking my leave, and all because he is too proud to let Keighley have a trestle-bed in *his* room! He said it was because he feared to catch his cold, but I know better!"

"So do I—much better!" said Tom. "Lord, what a goose you are! You go to bed! And mind, Phoebe! be civil to the Duke when you meet him again!"

She was granted the opportunity to obey this order sooner than he had expected, for at that moment Sylvester walked in, saying: "May I come in? How do you go on, Orde? You look a degree better, I think."

"Yes, pray do come in!" said Phoebe, before Tom could speak. "He was wishing you would come to visit him. Have you been out to the stable yet?"

"I have, ma'am, and you may go to bed with a quiet mind. Trusty shows no disposition to rid himself of his poultice. There is some heat still in his companion's hock, but nothing to cause uneasiness."

"Thank you! I am truly obliged to you!" she said.

"So am I, sir—*most* truly obliged to you!" said Tom. "It is devilish kind of you to put yourself to all this trouble! I don't know how to thank you."

"Well, I *have* thanked him," said Phoebe, apparently feeling that any further display of gratitude would be excessive.

"Yes, well, it's time you went to bed!" said Tom, directing a speaking look at her. "His grace will excuse you, so you may say good-night, and be off!"

"Yes, Grandpapa!" said Phoebe incorrigibly. "Good-night, my lord Duke!"

"Sleep well, Sparrow!" retorted Sylvester, holding the door for her.

To Tom's relief she went away without committing any more solecisms. He drew a long breath, as Sylvester shut the door, and said: "I am very conscious, my lord Duke, that an explanation——"

"Call me Salford," interrupted Sylvester. "Did the sawbones subject you to further tortures? I trust not: he told me that Keighley had done all he should."

"No, no, he only bound it up again when he had put some lotion on it!" Tom assured him. "And that puts me in mind of something else! I wish you had not gone out in such weather to fetch him, sir! I was excessively shocked when I heard of it! Oh, and you must have paid him his fee, for I did not! If you will tell me what it was——"

"I will render a strict account to you," promised Sylvester, pulling up a chair to the bedside, and sitting down. "That hock, by the bye, will have to be fomented for a day or two, but there should be no lasting injury. A tidy pair, so far as I could judge by lantern-light."

"My father bought them last year—proper high-bred 'uns!" Tom said. "I wouldn't have had this happen to them for a thousand pounds!"

"I'll go bail you wouldn't! A harsh parent?"

"No, no, he's a prime gun, but——!"

"I know," said Sylvester sympathetically. "So was mine, *but*——!"

Tom grinned at him. "You must think me a cowhanded whipster! But if only that curst donkey hadn't brayed—However, it's no use saying that: my father will say I made wretched work of it, and the worst of it is I think I did! And what sort of a case I should have been in if you hadn't come to the rescue, sir, I don't know!"

"If you must thank anybody, thank Kieghley!" recommended Sylvester. "I couldn't have set the broken bone, you know."

"No, but it was you who fetched Upsall, which was a great deal too kind of you. There's another thing, too." He hesitated, looking rather shyly at Sylvester, and colouring a little. "Phoebe didn't understand—she isn't by any means fly to the time of day, you know!—but I did, and—and I'm very much obliged to you for what you've done for her. Sending that girl to sleep with her, I mean. I don't know if it will answer, or if—Well, the thing is, sir—now that we are in such a rare mess do you think I ought to marry her?"

Sylvester had been regarding him with friendly amusement, but this naïve question brought a startled frown to his face. "But isn't that your intention?" he asked.

"No—oh, lord, no! I mean, it *wasn't* my intention (though I did offer to!) until we were grassed by that overturn. But now that we're cooped up here perhaps I ought, as a man of honour—Only ten to one she'll refuse to marry me, and then where shall we be?"

"If you are not eloping, what *are* you doing?" demanded Sylvester.

106

"I guessed that was what you must be thinking, sir," said Tom.

"I imagine you might. Nor am I the only one who thinks it!" said Sylvester. "When I left Austerby I did so because Marlow had already set out for the Border in pursuit of you!"

"No!" exclaimed Tom. "Well, what a gudgeon! If he thought Phoebe had run off with me why the deuce hadn't he the wit to enquire for me at the Manor? My mother could have told him all was well!"

"I can only say that she did not appear to me to have perfectly understood that," responded Sylvester dryly. "As it chanced it was she who came to Austerby, bringing with her the letter you had written to her. You young idiot, I don't know precisely what you told her, but it certainly didn't persuade her that all was well! It threw her into a state of great affliction—and what she said to Lady Marlow I shall always be happy to think I was priviliged to hear!"

"Did she give her snuff?" asked Tom appreciatively. "But she *can't* have thought I had eloped with Phoebe! Why, I particularly told her there was no need for her to be in a fidget! Lord Marlow might, I daresay, but not Mama!"

"On the contrary! Lord Marlow pooh-poohed the suggestion. He was only brought to believe it on the testimony of one of his younger daughters. I forget what her name is: a sanctimonious schoolgirl whose piety I found nauseating."

"Eliza," said Tom instantly. "But she knew nothing about it! Unless she was listening at the keyhole, and if that was the case she must have known we hadn't gone to the Border."

"She was, but she insisted that she had heard you say you were going to Gretna Green."

Tom frowned in an effort of memory. "I suppose I might have said so: I know I couldn't see any other way out of the fix. But Phoebe had a much better scheme, as it happened, which I own I was devilish glad to hear! I'm as fond of her as I could be—well, I've run tame at Austerby ever since I was breeched, you know, and she's like my sister!—but I'm damned if I want to marry her! The thing was I promised I'd help her, and the only way I could think of to do it was by doing so."

"Help her to do what?" interrupted Sylvester, considerably mystified.

"To escape from Austerby. So——"

"Well, I blame no one for wishing to do that, but what the devil made you choose such a moment? Didn't you know there was snow in the air?"

"Yes, of course I did, sir, but I *had* no choice! The need was urgent—or, at least, Phoebe thought it was. If I hadn't taken her she meant to go to London by herself, on the common stage!"

"Why?"

Tom hesitated, glancing speculatively at Sylvester. Sylvester said encouragingly: "I won't cry rope on you!"

The smile won Tom; he said in a burst of confidence: "Well, the truth is the whole thing was a fudge, but Lady Marlow told Phoebe you were going to Austerby to make her an offer! I must say it sounded like a hum to me, but it seems Lord Marlow thought so too, so one can't blame Phoebe for being taken in, and cast into flat despair because of it."

"In fact," said Sylvester, "an offer from me would not have been welcome to her?" _

"Oh, lord, no!" said Tom. "She said nothing would induce her to marry you! But I daresay you may have seen how it is in that house: if you had meant to offer for her Lady Marlow would have bullied her into submitting. The only thing was for her to run away." He stopped, uneasily aware of having said more than was discreet. There was an odd expression in Sylvester's eyes, hard to interpret but rather disquieting. "You know what females are, sir!" he added, trying to mend matters. "It was all nonsense, of course, for she scarcely knew you. I hope—I mean—perhaps I shouldn't have told you!"

"Oh, why not?" Sylvester said lightly, smiling again.

CHAPTER

10

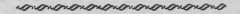

Tom was relieved to see the smile, but he was not wholly reassured. "I beg pardon!" he said. "I thought it wouldn't signify, telling you how it was, if you *didn't* wish to offer for her—and you don't, do you?"

"No, certainly not! What did I do to inspire Miss Marlow with this violent dislike of me?"

"Oh, I don't know! Nothing, I daresay," said Tom uncomfortably. "I expect you are not just her style, that's all."

"Not timbered up to her weight, in fact. Where, by the way, are you meaning to take her?"

"To her grandmother. She lives in London, and Phoebe is persuaded she will take her part—or that she *would* have done so, if it had been necessary."

Sylvester's eyes lifted suddenly to Tom's. "Do you mean Lady Ingham?" he asked.

"Yes," Tom nodded. "The other one died years ago. Are you acquainted with Lady Ingham, sir?"

"Oh, yes!" replied Sylvester, a laugh in his voice. "She is my godmother."

"Is she, though? Then you must know her pretty well. Do you think she will let Phoebe stay with her? Phoebe seems to

109

think there can be no doubt, but *I* can't help wondering whether she won't think it pretty shocking of her to have run off from home, and perhaps send her back again. What do *you* think, sir?"

"How can I say?" countered Sylvester. "Miss Marlow, I collect, still holds by her scheme, even though the menace of an offer from me doesn't exist?"

"Oh, yes! I did suggest to her that she need not go to London after all, but she says she will do so, and I must say I think she should—if only the old lady will receive her kindly! You know, sir, Lady Marlow is a regular brute, and it's not a particle of use thinking Marlow will protect Phoebe, because he won't! Phoebe knows there's no help to be got from him— well, he told her so, when she begged him to stand by her!— and now she says she shan't go back on any account. Only what's to be done? Even if the snow melted tomorrow I can't escort her, and I *know* I ought not to let her go alone. But if that detestable woman catches her here the trap will be down!"

"Not so much fretting and fussing, Galahad!" said Sylvester. "There's no immediate danger, and before it becomes imminent I don't doubt you will have hit upon an answer to the problem. Or I might do so for you."

"How?" asked Tom quickly.

"Well," replied Sylvester, getting up, "somewhere between this place and Austerby I have a chaise. I have left orders at the Bear, in Hungerford, that when it arrives there my servants are to be directed to this inn. In the circumstances, I shall be delighted to convey Miss Marlow to her grandmother!"

Tom's face lightened; he exclaimed: "Oh, by Jove, would you do that, sir? It would be the very thing—if she will go with you!"

"Let me beg you not to fidget yourself into a fever on the chance that she won't! You had much better try if you can go to sleep. I only hope you may not be too uncomfortable to do so."

"Oh, no! That is, Dr. Upsall left some stuff he said I should drink: syrup of poppies, or some such thing. I daresay I shall sleep like a log."

"Well, if you should wake, and wish for anything, knock on the wall behind you," said Sylvester. "I shall hear you: I am a tolerably light sleeper. I'll send Keighley to you now. Goodnight!"

He went away with a nod and a smile, leaving Tom to his various reflections. Prominent amongst these was a determination to endure hours of wakefulness rather than to drag his noble acquaintance from his bed. Thanks, however, to Keighley, interpreting the surgeon's instructions liberally, he very soon succumbed to a large dose of the narcotic prescribed for him, and slept the night through. His dreams were untroubled, for although, when Sylvester left him, he thought over all that he had disclosed, and wished the greater part of it unsaid, he was soon able to persuade himself that he had been grossly indulging his imagination when he had read danger in that queer look of Sylvester's. When he came to consider the matter he could not remember that he had said anything to arouse anger in Sylvester. It was not given to Tom, rating himself modestly, to understand the emotions of one who had been encouraged all the years of his adult life to set his value high.

But the discovery that Phoebe had decided he was not at all the sort of man she wished to marry had made Sylvester furious. While he believed her to be eloping with her true love he bore her no ill-will; but the case was now altered, and the more he thought of it the more did the wound to his self-esteem smart. He had chosen to single out from amongst the débutantes a little dab of a country girl, without style or countenance, and she had had the impertinence to snub him. She had done it in such a way, too, as to make a fool of him, and that was not an injury he could easily forgive. It was possible to forgive it when he supposed her to be in love with another man; but when he learned that her flight from her home—an outrageous action which only a passionate attachment to Tom could in some measure excuse—was due to a dread of being compelled to receive his addresses he was not only unable to forgive it, but became possessed of a strong desire to teach Miss Marlow a lesson. To be sure, her crest would very soon be lowered if she thought any match half as brilliant would be offered her, but that was not quite what Sylvester wanted. Something of greater importance than his consequence had been hurt. That he could shrug away; he could not shrug off the knowledge that she apparently found him repulsive. She had had the insolence to criticize him, too; and she did not scruple to show him that she held him cheap. What was it Tom had said? *Nothing would induce her to marry you!* A little too cock-sure,

Miss Marlow! The opportunity will not be granted you—but let us see if you can be made to feel sorry!

Sylvester dropped asleep on this vengeful thought; and since no summons was rapped on the wall dividing his room from Tom's, he did not wake until Keighley brought his breakfast to him at ten o'clock next morning. He then discovered that his faithful henchman was not only looking heavy-eyed, but had lost his voice as well. He said: "Go back to bed at once, John! Good God, I *have* knocked you up! You ought to have a mustard-plaster on your chest. Tell Mrs. Scaling to fetch one up to you—and go away!"

Keighley started to whisper reassurance, but was stopped by a paroxysm of coughing.

"John, don't be a nodcock! Do you think I want your death at my door? Go to bed! And tell them to kindle a fire in your room—*my* orders!"

"How *can* I lay up, your grace?" whispered Keighley. "Who's to look after Mr. Orde if I do?"

"To hell with Mr. Orde! Can't the half-wit attend to him? Well, if he can't, I must. What has to be done for him?"

"I've done all that's needful for the moment, your grace, and seen to the grays, but——"

"Then you have nothing further to worry about, and may go to bed without more ado. Now, don't be a gudgeon, John! You will only give him your cold if you hang about him!"

"He's got it," croaked Keighley.

"No, has he? Well, *I* have no wish to catch it, so don't let me see you again until you're rid of it!" He saw that Keighley was torn by a longing for his bed and a determination not to leave his post, and said threateningly: "If I have to get up to you, John, you'll be sorry!"

That made Keighley laugh, which brought on another paroxysm. This left him feeling so exhausted that he was very glad to obey his master.

An hour later, Sylvester, beautiful to behold in a frogged dressing-gown of crimson and gold brocade, strolled into Tom's room, saying cheerfully: "Good-morning, Galahad! So you've taken Keighley's cold, have you? What a mutton-headed thing to do! Did you sleep well?"

"Oh, like a top, thank you, sir! As for the cold, if I *must* stay in bed I might as well have a cold as not. But I'm devilish sorry for Keighley: he's as sick as a horse!"

"You will soon be devilish sorry for yourself, for I've sent him to bed, and you will be obliged to endure my ministrations in place of his. What, as a start, can I do for you?"

"Good God, nothing!" replied Tom, looking horrified. "As though I would let you wait on me!"

"You won't have any choice in the matter."

"Yes, yes, I will! The boy can do all I want, sir!"

"What, the half-wit? If you think that a choice I'll thank you not to be so insulting, Thomas!"

Tom laughed at that, but insisted that for the moment at least he needed nothing, except (with a sigh) something to do.

"That's what we shall all of us be pining for, if the snow lasts," said Sylvester. "If Mrs. Scaling cannot supply us with a pack of cards we shall be obliged to make up charades, or something of that nature. Do you care to read *The Knight of St. John*? It came out last year, and is by the author of *The Hungarian Brothers*. I'll fetch it for you."

Tom was no great reader, but when Sylvester, handing him the first volume of Miss Porter's latest romance, said: "I don't like it as well as *The Hungarian Brothers*, but it's quite a lively tale," he realized that the work was not, as he had feared, a history, but a novel, and was much relieved. He accepted it with thanks, and then, after a thoughtful moment, asked Sylvester if he read many novels.

"Any that come in my way. Why?"

"Oh, I don't know!" Tom said. "I thought perhaps you might not."

Sylvester looked a little surprised, but said after a moment: "Oh, did you think that because my mother is a poetess I might have a turn for verse? No: nothing of the sort!"

"*Is* she?" said Tom, awed.

"Yes, indeed she is. And I assure you she does not despise novels! I fancy she buys almost all that are published. She is an invalid, you see, and reading is her greatest solace."

"Oh!" said Tom.

"I must go and look to my horses," said Sylvester. "I collect that Miss Marlow is in the stables already, probably fomenting that hock. I only hope I may not fall under her displeasure for making so belated an appearance!"

He went away to finish dressing; and then, after consigning Keighley to Mrs. Scaling's care, went out to join Phoebe. It was still snowing hard, but a brazier was burning in the stable.

Phoebe, having turned True in his stall, and removed his quarterpiece, was vigorously brushing him.

"Good-morning!" said Sylvester, removing his coat, and rolling up his sleeves. "I'll do that for you, Miss Marlow. How is the hock?"

"Better, I think. I have just been fomenting it again. I don't think Tom would like it if I let you dress the horses, Duke."

"Then don't tell him," said Sylvester, taking the brush away from her. "Doesn't he think me capable of the task?"

"Oh, it isn't that! He has a great respect for your consequence, you see, and perhaps wouldn't think it proper for you to do it! But in general he is not at all stupid, I assure you!"

The smile that went with this remark was so ingenous that Sylvester was obliged to laugh. Phoebe would have set to work on Trusty with the currycomb, but was deterred by Sylvester's pointing out to her that her skirt was already covered with True's hairs. He recommended her to change her dress, giving the one she had on to Alice to brush, but she replied that as the only other dress she had with her was of muslin, she rather thought she might freeze to death in it. "Besides, Alice has gone to tell old Mr. Shap that we must have his pig. It isn't full-grown, so perhaps he won't sell it."

"Why not?"

"Because he would get more of it later, of course. And also he may be in a bad skin."

"In a *what*?"

She looked up, twinkling, from the task of picking the short hairs out of her skirt. "I think it means that he has a sullen disposition! But I expect Alice will get the pig: she is a most redoubtable girl!"

"You and she should deal extremely," he commented, turning True about, and stripping off the rest of his clothing.

At that she raised her head again, tilting it enquiringly. "Do you mean that I am redoubtable? Oh, you are quite mistaken!"

"Am I? Then let us say intrepid!"

She sighed. "I wish I were! The case is that I am a wretched coward."

"Your father gives you quite another character."

"I don't fear fences."

"What, then?"

"People—some people! To—to be slain by unkindness."

He looked at her with a slight frown; but before he could

114

ask her to explain what she meant they were interrupted by Alice, who came in, stamping her feet to rid her pattens of the clogged snow, and followed by an ancient with very few teeth but a crafty eye. This individual she introduced as a nasty, twitty old maw-worm, disclosing that he wouldn't sell his pig until convinced that it would be eaten by a duke, and not by a Captain Sharp, masquerading as such.

Considerably taken aback, for he had never before had his credentials doubted, much less been taken for a Captain Sharp, Sylvester said: "Well, I don't know how I should be able to convince him! Unless he'd like one of my visiting-cards?"

But this Mr. Shap rejected, informing the company that he wasn't a lettered man. He apparently felt this to be a triumph, for he then fell into a fit of cackling mirth. Assured by Phoebe that Sylvester was a duke, he told her, but kindly, that she had been took in by a lot of slum. "You don't want to listen to this great fussock here, missie!" he said, jerking his thumb at Alice. "She's got a brother what's dicked in the nob, and a proper jobbernoll *she* is! Ah!"

He then nodded his head cunningly several times, and demanded to be told who had ever heard of a duke dressing his horses. But by this time Sylvester had taken the purse from his coat-pocket, and said briefly: "What's the figure?"

Mr. Shap, with great promptness, named a price which drew a shriek of scandalized wrath from Alice. She begged Sylvester not to be choused out of his money by a wicked old lick-penny; but Sylvester, who was tired of Mr. Shap, dropped three sovereigns into his gnarled hand, and told him to be off. Such openhanded conduct caused Mr. Shap to dang himself if it weren't a duke after all; and after giving Sylvester a fatherly admonition not to allow himself to be clerked by Widow Scaling, he hobbled off, calling, in a cracked, senile voice, to Will to come and fetch away the pig.

"Well," said Alice, preparing to follow him, "I'm proper set about he should have behaved like a smidge, but one thing's sure, your honour! with you paying him so handsome he knows you are a duke, and so he'll tell everyone." She nodded, her eyes sparkling with joyful anticipation. "Happen we'll have 'em all up to the tap today, wishful for to see you with their own eyes!" she told Sylvester. "Why, there's been nothing like it, not since we had the girl with two heads putting up here! Her dad was taking of her to London, being wishful to put her into a big fair they do be having there. We had half Hungerford here, as well as Kintbury, and not a drop of liquor left in the house by ten o'clock."

The fascinated horror with which Sylvester listened to these artless confidences had long since proved to be too much for Phoebe's gravity. Alice, grinning sympathetically upon her mirth, went off to supervise the transport of Mr. Shap's pig; and Sylvester demanded, with some asperity, whether his attractions were rated above or below those of a freak.

"Oh, below!" Phoebe answered, wiping her streaming eyes. "For you are not in yourself remarkable, you know! Your oddity is in being out of place. I daresay, had you been putting up at the Pelican, your presence in the district wouldn't have aroused the least interest."

"How much I wish we were all of us at the Pelican!" he exclaimed. "Only think how different our lot would be! No, *don't* let us think of it!"

"I don't mean to," responded Phoebe cheerfully. "The Pelican would not do for me at all, in such a situation. But if Keighley is better tomorrow, I shouldn't wonder at it if you were able to reach Speenhamland. It can't be many miles ahead, after all!"

"And abandon you and Thomas to your fates? If that's the opinion you hold of me I am able to understand your reluctance to receive my addresses, Miss Marlow!"

She blushed fierily, for although Tom had warned her of his indiscretion she had been encouraged by Sylvester's previous manner to believe that he would not refer to it. "I beg pardon! Of course I did not—it wasn't—I mean, it was all a stupid mistake, wasn't it?" she stammered.

Venturing to look up into his face she saw that his eyes were gleaming with mockery; and she could not doubt that he was enjoying her discomfiture. But as resentment rose in her breast the malice vanished from his expression; and she perceived that he really had got an enchanting smile. This was surprising. She had not before encountered that engaging look; and a moment earlier there had been no trace of it. She was suspicious of it, and yet could not help responding to it.

"Yes, just a stupid mistake!" he said reassuringly. "Shall I promise not to pay my addresses to you? I am perfectly ready to do so, if it will make you more comfortable."

But she only laughed at this, and got up, saying that she

116

had no longer any fears on that head. She went away then, and when he saw her next it was an hour later, in Tom's room, polishing with a scrap of sandpaper the spillikins Tom was cleverly whittling from some wood begged from Mrs. Scaling. Tom looked up, smiling, and said: "Can you play spillikins, sir? I was used to be a dab at the game, and am issuing a challenge to all comers!"

"I don't fear you," responded Sylvester, handing him a large pewter tankard. "Home-brewed, Thomas—the best thing we've yet had here!—Your skill may be superior, but I'll swear I'm the more in practice! Unless you have young brothers and sisters, in which case I may hedge off a trifle."

"No, I haven't," grinned Tom. "Have you?"

"No, but I have frequently played with my nephew," Sylvester replied.

His attention was just then diverted by a kick on the door, followed by a demand from Will Scaling to be admitted. He turned to open the door, and so did not see the looks of consternation which his words brought to his young friends' faces. By the time he had foiled an attempt by Will to dump a heavy nuncheon-tray down on Tom's legs they had revived sufficiently from the shock of discovering that he had a nephew to be able to meet his casual glance with the appearance at least of composure. They were granted no opportunity for an exchange of more than looks until later in the day, for Sylvester returned with Phoebe to Tom's room after their nuncheon, and only left it when it became time to attend again to the horses. Mrs. Scaling having unearthed from the recesses of a cupboard a pack of somewhat greasy playing-cards the beleaguered travellers were not restricted to spillikins or paper games, but embarked on several desperate gambling ventures, using dried peas for counters, and managing the cards and the bets of all the imaginary persons created by them to make up the correct number of gamesters. This was the sort of fooling that might have amused them for a few minutes, but Phoebe's talent for endowing her creations with names and characteristics invested the nonsense with wit; and when Sylvester, not slow to follow her lead, invented two eccentrics on his own account the game rapidly became a sort of charade, exercising the histrionic ability of the two players, and keeping Tom, who did not aspire to such heights, in a continuous chuckle. But although Tom laughed he thought it a dangerous diversion, for every now and then Phoebe could not resist indulging her genius for mimicry. Tom recognized several characters from *The Lost Heir;* he was unacquainted with the originals, but to judge by Sylvester's swift response Phoebe hit them off very recognizably.

"For the lord's sake take care what you're about!" Tom warned her, as soon as Sylvester had left the room. "If he *should* read your book I wouldn't wager a groat against the chance of his recalling all this mummery of yours, and then putting two and two together, for he's no fool! You know, Phoebe, I do think you should make a push to alter that book! I mean, after the way he has behaved to us it seems the shabbiest thing to make him out a villain! I can't think why you should have done so, either, or have supposed him to be insufferably proud. Why, he hasn't the least height in his manner!"

"I must own I never expected him to be so amiable," she acknowledged. "Not but what to be assuming the airs of a great man in such a place as this would be quite absurd, and I give him credit for knowing it."

"Phoebe, you must change the book!" he urged. "First, we know that he reads novels, and now he says he has a nephew! Lord, I didn't know where to look!"

"No, I was ready to sink myself," she agreed. "However, I don't think it signifies so very much. Everyone has nephews, after all! I daresay he may have several of them, but the thing is, remember, that Maximilian was wholly in Count Ugolino's power, being an orphan. There can be no resemblance!"

"What *is* Salford's family?" Tom asked.

"Well, I don't know precisely. There are quite a number of Raynes, but how nearly they may be related to him I haven't a notion."

"I must say, Phoebe, I think you should have discovered just how it was before you put him into your book!" said Tom, in accents of strong censure. "Surely your father must have a *Peerage?*"

"I don't know if he has," she said guiltily. "I never thought—I mean, when I wrote the book I didn't imagine it would be published! I own, I wish now that I hadn't made Salford the villain, but, after all, Tom, if I can but change his *appearance* no one will ever guess who Ugolino is! It is all the fault of his wretched eyebrows: if Salford had not had that *tigerish* look I should never have thought of making him a villain!"

"What a bag of moonshine!" Tom exclaimed. "Tigerish look, indeed! He has a most agreeable countenance!"

"Now that is coming it *too* strong!" interrupted Phoebe, roused to indination. "His *smile* is agreeable, but in general his expression is one of haughty indifference! I had nearly said *disdain*, but he is not disdainful of his fellows because he scarcely notices them."

"I suppose you think he has scarcely noticed me?" said Tom, with heavy sarcasm.

"No, because he took a fancy to you, and so it pleases him to treat you with flattering distinction. And also," Phoebe pursued, her eyes narrowing as though to bring Sylvester's image into perspective, "I believe it piqued him to be told that I disliked him."

"I wish I had not said anything about that!"

"Oh, don't tease yourself over it! I am persuaded it has done him a great deal of good!" she said blithely. "I assure you, Tom, when I met him previously, in London, his manners were very different. *Then* he had no thought of engaging the good opinion of such a poor little dab as I am; *now* he bestows every degree of attention on me, until I daresay I shall soon find myself obliged to be in raptures about him."

"You may well!" returned Tom. "Let me tell you, Phoebe, that if you do contrive to reach London it will be thanks to his good offices, not to mine! He says he will escort you there in his chaise, so for the lord's sake be civil to him!"

"No!" she exclaimed. "Did he say so indeed? Well, I must own that that's excessively handsome of him, but it won't answer, of course: I can't leave you here alone, and in such a case! Why, what a monster I should be to think of doing anything so inhuman!" She added naughtily: "So I need not be civil after all, need I?"

11

Sylvester, when presently applied to, gave his support to both contestants. He said that Tom must certainly not be abandoned to his fate; but he also said that Phoebe had no need to delay her journey on that account, since he himself would remain at the Blue Boar, delegating to Keighley the task of conveying her to her grandmother. She could not but be grateful to him for so practical a solution to her difficulty, her only remaining anxiety being the fear that she would be overtaken by her father before the arrival of Sylvester's chaise at the Blue Boar.

"I can only say, Miss Marlow," responded Sylvester to this confidence, "that if the first vehicle to reach us from the west is not my chaise two Houndslow-bred postilions will shortly be seeking situations in some other household than mine!"

In fact, his chaise arrived two days later, within a very short time of the snow's ceasing to fall. Since it had taken the postilions more than two hours to accomplish the stage between Marlborough and Hungerford, Swale's graphic description of the perils overcome in the cause of duty were not needed to convince Phoebe that the condition of the roads was still too bad to make her father's appearance on the scene anything but a remote contingency.

Sylvester sent his chaise on to the Halfway House, a couple of miles up the road, but kept Swale at the Blue Boar. Swale, discovering that he must share a bedchamber with Keighley, and eat all his meals in the kitchen, was so much affronted that he hovered for as much as thirty seconds on the brink of tendering his resignation to his noble employer. He bowed stiffly when commanded to wait upon Mr. Orde, and sought solace for his lacerated sensibilities in treating that hapless young gentleman with such meticulous politeness that Tom was very soon begging Sylvester to leave him to the less expert but less intimidating ministrations of Will Scaling. Tom's shyness of Sylvester had not survived forty-eight hours of depending upon him for his every need; and within an hour of having lodged this laughing complaint with him he was taking him roundly to task for having acted upon it in an ill-judged manner. "The lord knows what you said to the poor fellow, but if I'd guessed you would say anything at all I never would have told you about it!" he said. "It was worse than anything! He has been in here, begging my pardon, and telling me a bamboozling tale of having been feeling out of sorts, and hoping I shan't have cause to complain to you *again*! Lord! I promise you I was never more mortified in my life! A pretty sneaksby you made me, Salford! Did you threaten to turn him off, just because he don't care to wait on me?"

"I'm not so high-handed, Thomas. I only asked him to tell me if he was quite happy in my service."

"Oh, was *that* all?" exclaimed Tom. "No wonder he was looking so tyburn-faced! And you say you're not high-handed! Well, *I* think you're *mediaeval*!"

That made Sylvester laugh. "But in what way am I mediaeval? I pay him a handsome wage, you know."

"But you didn't hire him to take care of me!"

"My dear Thomas, what in the world has he to do besides?" Sylvester interrupted, a little impatiently. "All the work he has to do for *me* in this hedge-tavern could not occupy him for as much as a couple of hours out of the twenty-four!"

"No, but he is *your* valet, not mine! You might as well have ordered him to groom your horses, or sweep the floor. And beyond all else you told him he must share Keighley's room! Now, Salford, you *must* know that your valet is much above your groom's touch!"

"Not in my esteem."

"Very likely not, but——"

"But nothing, Thomas! In my own household my esteem is all that signifies. Does that seem mediaeval to you? If it seems so to Swale he may leave me: he's not my slave!" He smiled suddenly. "Keighley is more my slave, I assure you—and I never engaged him, and could never dismiss him. Now, what is there in that to make you frown at me?"

"I wasn't—I mean, I can't explain it, only my father always says one should take care not to offend the sensibilities of inferior persons, and though I daresay you didn't intend to do so, it does seem to me as if—— But I should not say so!" Tom ended, rather hurriedly.

"Well, you have said so, haven't you?" said Sylvester, quite gently, but with the smile hardening on his lips.

"I beg your pardon, sir!"

Sylvester made no reply to this, but remarked in a thoughtful tone: "To have become acquainted with you and with Miss Marlow ought to do me a great deal of good, I hope. What a number of faults I have of which I was never previously made aware!"

"I don't know what more I can do than beg your pardon," Tom said stiffly.

"Why, nothing! Unless you like to instruct me how I should treat my servants?" He paused, as Tom looked at him with belligerence in his eyes, and his lips very resolutely closed, and said quickly: "Oh, no! What an unhandsome thing to say to you! Forgive me: I didn't mean it!"

There could be no resisting that coaxing note, or the softened expression, half contrite, half quizzical, that put to rout the satyrlook. Tom had been conscious of a thin film of ice behind which Sylvester had seemed to withdraw; he had resented it; but it had melted, and he found himself no longer angry, but stammering: "Oh, stuff! Besides, I had no business to be criticizing you! Particularly," he added rather naïvely, "when you have been so devilish kind to me!"

"Humdudgeon!"

"No, it ain't. What's more——"

"If you mean to be a dead bore, Thomas, I'm off!" Sylvester interrupted. "And let me tell you that if you are trying to turn me up sweet you will be speedily bowled out! *Kind* was not the epithet you chose to describe my charitable attempt to make your bed more comfortable this morning!"

"Oh, well, I see I can't please you!" Tom said, grinning. "First, I'm ungrateful, and now I'm a dead bore! But I'm not ungrateful, you know. I thought the trap was down when you arrived here, and so it was, for I'm in no case to help Phoebe. But you mean to do so, don't you?"

"Do I? Oh, convey her to London! Yes, I'll do that," Sylvester replied. "If she still wishes it—though what she now hopes to achieve by it I don't immediately perceive."

Tom was unable to enlighten him, but Phoebe told him frankly that she hoped never to return to Austerby. This was sufficiently startling to make him put up his brows. She said, her eyes searching his face: "My grandmother told me once that she wished she might have me to live with her—had always wished it! Only when my mother died it was not possible, from some cause or another, for her to make that offer to Papa. And then, you know, he married Mama, which made it, she thought, unnecessary, as well as grossly uncivil, to remove me from Austerby."

A slightly sardonic gleam of amusement flickered in his eyes. "But she did not, last year, invite you to remain with her?" he suggested.

A look of anxiety came into her face; her eyes, still fixed on his, seemed to question him. She said: "No. But she thought—Sir Henry Halford warning her against any unusual exertion—well, she thought it not right to ask Papa to leave me in her charge, since she is unequal to the task of taking me to balls, and—— But I think—I am sure—she didn't perfectly enter into my sentiments upon that head! I don't care for balls, or fashionable life. At least, it was very agreeable when I went out with my aunt Ingham, for she is excessively good-natured, and doesn't scold, or watch one all the time, or—— But indeed I don't hanker after gaiety, and although, at that time, it didn't occur to me to ask her if I might live with her, when——" She paused, feeling the ice thin under her feet, and coloured.

"When you feared to be forced into a distasteful marriage?" he supplied helpfully.

Her colour deepened, but his words brought her engaging twinkle into her eyes. "Well, yes!" she acknowledged. "When *that* happened, I thought suddenly that if Grandmama would let me reside with her I need not be a trouble, but, on the contrary, *useful*, perhaps. And, in any event, it won't be so very long now before I come of age, and then I hope—I believe—the case will be quite altered, and I need be a charge on no one."

He instantly suspected her of having formed an attachment for some hopeless ineligible, and asked her bluntly if she had matrimony in view.

"Matrimony! Oh, no!" she responded. "I daresay I shall never be married. I have another scheme—quite different!" She added, in some confusion: "Excuse me on that head, if you please! I had not meant to speak of it, and must not! Pray do not regard it! Only tell me if you think—for perhaps you are better acquainted with her than I—that my grandmother will like to have me to live with her?"

He believed that there was nothing Lady Ingham would like less; but he believed also, and maliciously, that she would find it impossible to repulse her granddaughter; and he replied, smiling: "Why not?"

She looked relieved, but said very earnestly: "Every day I spend away from Austerby strengthens my resolve never to go back there! I was never so happy in my life before! You can't understand how that should be so, I daresay, but I have felt, these last few days, as though I had escaped from a cage!" Her solemnity vanished. "Oh! what a trite simile! Never mind!"

"Very well," he said. "Keighley shall escort you to London as soon as the roads are passable."

She thanked him, but said doubtfully: "And Tom?"

"I shall send a message to his parents, when you are gone. Don't you trust me? I shan't leave him until I have handed him over to his father."

"Yes, indeed I trust you. I was wondering only whether I ought to accept so much help from you—using your chaise—depriving you of your groom!" She added naïvely: "When I was not, at first, very civil to you!"

"But you are never civil to me!" he complained. "You began by giving me a heavy set-down, and you followed that with a handsome trimming! And now you threaten to deny me a chance to retrieve my character!" He laughed, seeing her at a loss for words, and took her hand, and lightly kissed it. "Cry friends, Sparrow! Am I so *very* bad?"

"No! I never said that, or thought it!" she stammered. "How could I, when I scarcely knew you?"

"Oh, this is worse than anything!" he declared. "No sooner seen than disliked! I understand you perfectly: I have frequently

124

met such persons—only I had not thought myself to have been one of them!"

Goaded, she retorted: "One does not, I believe!" Then she immediately looked stricken, and faltered: "Oh, dear, my *wretched* tongue! I beg your pardon!"

The retort had made his eyes flash, but the look of dismay which so swiftly succeeded it disarmed him. "If ever I met such a chastening pair as you and Orde! What next will you find to say to me, I wonder? Unnecessary, I'm persuaded, to tell you not to spare me!"

"Now *that* is the most shocking injustice!" she exclaimed. "When Tom positively toad-eats you!"

"*Toad-eats* me? You can know nothing of toad-eaters if that is what you think!" He directed a suddenly penetrating look at her, and asked abruptly: "Do you suppose that that is what I like? to be toad-eaten?"

She thought for a moment, and then said: "No, not precisely. It is, rather, what you *expect*, perhaps, without liking or disliking."

"You are mistaken! I neither expect it nor like it!"

She bowed her head, it might have been in acquiescence, but the ghost of a smile on her lips nettled him.

"Upon my word, ma'am——!" he said angrily, and there stopped, as she looked an enquiry. A reluctant laugh was dragged out of him. "I recall now that I was told that you were not just in the common way, Miss Marlow!"

"Oh, no! Did someone *indeed* say that of me?" she demanded, turning quite pink with pleasure. "Who was it? Oh, do pray, tell me!"

He shook his head, amused by her eagerness. It was such a mild compliment, yet here she was, all agog to learn its source, looking like a child tantalized by a toy held out of her reach. "Not I!"

She sighed. "How infamous of you! Were you hoaxing me?"

"Not at all! Why should I?"

"I don't know, but it seems as though you might do so. People don't say pretty things of me—or, if they do, I never heard of it." She pondered it. "Of course, it might mean that I was merely *odd*—in a gothic way," she said doubtfully.

"Yes—or outrageous!"

"No," she decided. "It couldn't have meant that, because

I wasn't outrageous when I went to London. I behaved with perfect propriety—and insipidity."

"You may have behaved with propriety, but insipidity I cannot allow!"

"Well, you thought so at the time!" she said tartly. "And, to own the truth, I *was* insipid. Mama was watching me, you see."

He remembered how silent and stupid she had appeared at Austerby, and said: "Yes, you must certainly escape from her. But not on the common stage, and not unescorted! Is that agreed?"

"Thank you," she replied meekly. "I own it will be more comfortable to travel post. When shall I be able to set forward, do you think?"

"I can't tell that. No London vehicles have gone by yet, which leads me to suppose that the drifts must be lying pretty thick beyond Speenhamland. Wait until we have seen the Bristol Mail go past!"

"I have a lowering presentiment that we shall see Mama's travelling-carriage instead—and it will *not* go past," stated Phoebe, in a hollow tone.

"I pledge you my word you shan't be dragged back to Austerby—and *that* you may depend on!"

"What a very rash promise to make!" she observed.

"Yes, isn't it? I am fully conscious of it, I assure you, but having given my word I am now hopelessly committed, and can only pray to heaven I may not find myself involved in any *serious* crime. You think I'm funning, don't you? I'm not, and will immediately prove my good faith by engaging Alice's services."

"Why, what can she do?" demanded Phoebe.

"Go with you as your maid, of course. Come, come, ma'am! After such a strict upbringing as you have endured is it for me to tell you that a young female of your quality may not travel without her abigail?"

"Oh, what fustian!" she exclaimed. "As though I cared for that!"

"Very likely you do not, but Lady Ingham will, I promise you. Moreover, if the road should be worse than we expect you might be obliged to spend a night at some posting-house, you know."

This was unanswerable, but she said mutinously: "Well, if

126

Alice doesn't choose to go I shan't regard such nonsensical stuff!"

"Oh, now you are glaringly abroad! Alice will do precisely what I tell her to do," he replied, smiling.

The easy confidence with which he uttered these words made her hope very much that he would meet with a rebuff from Alice, but nothing so salutary happened. Learning that she was to accompany Miss to the Metropolis, Alice fell into blissful ecstasy, gazing upon Sylvester with incredulous wonder, and breathing reverently: *"Lunnon!"* When it was disclosed to her that she should be given five pounds to spend, and her ticket on the stage for her return-journey, she became incapable of speech for several minutes, being afeared, as she presently informed her awed parent, to bust her stay-laces.

The thaw set in, and with it arrived the errant ostler, full of hair-raising accounts of the state of the road. Mrs. Scaling told him darkly that he would be sorry presently that he had not made a push to return immediately to the Blue Boar; and when he learned what noble guests she was entertaining he was indeed sorry. But when he discovered that the stables had fallen under the governance of an autocrat who showed no disposition to abdicate in his favour, but, on the contrary, every disposition to set him to work harder than he had ever done, he was not so sorry. He might have missed handsome largesse, but he had also missed several days of being addressed as "my lad", and having his failings crisply pointed out to him, and being commanded to perform all over again such tasks as Keighley considered him to have scamped. Nor were his affronted sensibilities soothed by the treatment he received at Swale's hands. Swale was forced to eat his dinner in the kitchen amongst the vulgar, but no power known to man could force him to notice the existence of a common ostler. So aloof was his demeanour, so disdainful his glance, that the ostler at first mistook him for his master. He discovered later that the Duke was more approachable.

The first vehicles to pass the inn came from the west, a circumstance which made Phoebe very uneasy; but a day later the Bristol Mail went by, at so unusual an hour that Mrs. Scaling said they might depend upon it the road was still mortal bad to the eastward. "Likely as not they've been two days or more getting here," she said. "They do be saying in the tap that there's been nothing like it since four years ago, when the

127

river froze over in London-town, and they had bonfires on it, and a great fair, and I don't know what-all. I shouldn't wonder at it, miss, if you was to be here for another se'enight," she added hopefully.

"Nonsense!" said Sylvester, when this was reported to him. "What they say in the tap need not cast you into despair. Tomorrow I'll drive to Speenhamland, and discover what the mail-coachmen are saying."

"If it doesn't freeze again tonight," amended Phoebe, a worried frown between her brows. "It was shockingly slippery this morning, and you will have enough to do in holding those grays of yours without having that added to it! I *could* not reconcile it with my conscience to let you set forth in such circumstances!"

"Never," declared Sylvester, much moved, "did I think to hear you express so much solicitude on my behalf, ma'am!"

"Well, I can't but see what a fix we should be in if anything should happen to you," she replied candidly.

The appreciative gleam in his eyes acknowledged a hit, but he said gravely: "The charm of your society, my Sparrow, lies in not knowing what you will say next—though one rapidly learns to expect the worst!"

It did not freeze again that night; and the first news that greeted Phoebe, when she peeped into Tom's room on her way downstairs to breakfast, was that he had heard a number of vehicles pass the inn, several of which he was sure came from the east. This was presently confirmed by Mrs. Scaling, who said, however, that there was no telling whether they had come from London, or from no farther afield than Newbury. She was of the opinion that it would be unwise to venture on such a hazardous journey until the snow had entirely gone from the road; and was regaling Phoebe with a horrid story of three outside passengers on the stagecoach who had died of the cold in just such weather, when Sylvester arrived on the scene, and put an end to this daunting history by observing that since Miss Phoebe was not proposing to travel to London on the roof of a stage-coach there was no need for anyone to feel apprehensive on her account. Mrs. Scaling reluctantly conceded this point, but warned his grace that there was a dangerous gravel-pit between Newbury and Reading, very hard to see when there had been heavy falls of snow.

"Like the coffee-pot," said Sylvester acidly. "I don't see

that at all—and I should wish to do so immediately, if you please!"

This had the effect of sending Mrs. Scaling scuttling off to the kitchen. "Do you suppose there really is any danger of driving into a gravel-pit, sir?" asked Phoebe.

"No."

"I must say, it sounds very unlikely to me. But Mrs. Scaling seems to think——"

"Mrs. Scaling merely thinks that the longer she can keep us here the better it will be for her," he interrupted.

"Well, you need not snap *my* nose off!" countered Phoebe. "Merely because you have come down hours before you are used to do!"

"I beg your pardon, ma'am!" he said frigidly.

"It's of no consequence at all," she assured him, smiling kindly at him. "I daresay you are always disagreeable before breakfast. Many people are, I believe, and cannot help themselves, try as they will. I don't mean to say that you do try, of course: why should you, when you are not obliged to be conciliating?"

It was perhaps fortunate that the entrance of Alice at this moment obliged Sylvester to swallow the retort that sprang to his lips. By the time she had withdrawn again he had realized (with far less incredulity than he would have felt a week earlier) that Miss Marlow was being deliberately provoking; and he merely said: "Though *I* may not be obliged to conciliate, you should reflect, ma'am, that it is otherwise with *you*! I rose at this unseasonable hour wholly on your behalf, but I might yet decide not to go to Newbury after all."

"Oh, are you capricious as well?" asked Phoebe, raising eyes of innocent enquiry to his face.

"As well as what?" demanded Sylvester. He saw her lips part, and added hastily: "No, don't tell me! I can hazard a tolerably accurate conjecture, I imagine!"

She laughed, and began to pour out the coffee. "I won't say another word till you've come out of the sullens," she promised.

Though strongly tempted to reply in kind, Sylvester decided, upon reflection, to hold his peace. Silence prevailed until, looking up from his plate a few minutes later, he found that she was watching him, with so much the air of a bird

129

hopeful of crumbs that he burst out laughing, and exclaimed: "Oh, you—*Sparrow*! What an abominable girl you are!"

"Yes, I am afraid I am," she said, quite seriously. "And nothing seems to cure me of saying things I ought not!"

"Perhaps you don't *try* to overcome the fault?" he suggested, quizzing her.

"But, in general, I *do* try!" she assured him. "It is only when I am with persons such as you and Tom—I mean——"

"Ah, just so!" he interrupted. "When you are with persons whose opinions are of no particular consequence to you, you allow rein to your tongue?"

"Yes," she agreed, pleased to find him of so ready an understanding. "That is the matter in a nutshell! Will you have some more bread-and-butter, sir?"

"No, thank you," he responded. "I find I have quite lost my appetite."

"It would be wonderful if you had not," she said cheerfully. "Cooped up in the house as you have been all this while! Will you set out for Newbury *soon*? I daresay it is foolish of me, but I can't be easy! Whatever should I do if Mama were to arrive while you are gone?"

"Hide in the hay-loft!" he recommended. "But if she has a particle of commonsense she won't make the smallest push to recover you!"

CHAPTER

12

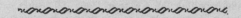

Having watched Sylvester depart, Phoebe sat down to play piquet with Tom. The sound of wheels outside made her once or twice look up apprehensively, but the approach of a ridden horse along the road caused her no alarm. She heard, but paid no heed; and so it was that Mr. Orde, walking into the room without ceremony, took her entirely by surprise. She gave a gasp, and dropped the cards she was holding. Tom turned his head, and exclaimed in dismay: *"Father!"*

The Squire, having surveyed the truants with the air of one who had known all along how it would be, shut the door, and said: "Ay! Now, what the devil do you mean by this, either of you?"

"It was my fault! Oh, pray don't be vexed with Tom!" begged Phoebe.

"No, it was not!" asserted Tom. "It was mine, and I made a mull of it, and broke my leg!"

"Ay, so I know!" said his fond parent. "I may think myself fortunate you didn't break your neck, I suppose. Young cawker! And what did my horses break?"

"No, no, only a strained hock!" Phoebe assured him. "And

I have taken the greatest care—Oh, pray let me help you out of your coat, dear sir!"

"It's no use trying to flummery me, girl!" said the Squire severely, but accepting her aid. "A pretty riot and rumpus you've caused, the pair of you! Let alone being the death of your father!"

"Oh, *no*!" cried Phoebe, blenching.

He relented, seeing that he had really frightened her, and patted her whitened cheek. "No, it ain't as bad as that, but you know what he is when anything ails him!"

"Father, we were *not* eloping!" Tom interrupted.

The Squire threw him a glance of affectionate scorn. "A tinker's budget, Tom: I never supposed you was. Perhaps you'll tell me what the devil you *were* doing—besides driving my new curricle into the ditch, and smashing two of its wheels?"

"I was taking Phoebe to London, to her grandmother. She would have gone on the common stage if I had not, sir!"

"And indeed it wasn't Tom's fault that we ended in a ditch, sir!" interpolated Phoebe. "He was driving to an inch until we met that evil donkey!"

"Met a donkey, did you? Oh!" said the Squire. "Well, there was *some* excuse for you, if that was the case."

"No, there wasn't," said Tom frankly. "I ought to have managed better, and I had rather I had broke both my legs than have let True strain his hock!"

"Well, well!" said his father, visibly mollified. "Thank the lord you didn't! I'll take a look at that hock presently. I was afraid I should find it to be a case of broken knees."

"Mr. Orde," Phoebe said anxiously, "pray tell me!—Does Papa know where I am?"

"Well, of course he does!" replied the Squire. "You couldn't expect I wouldn't tell him, now, could you?"

"Who told you, Father?" Tom demanded. "I collect it must have been Upsall, but I never saw him before in my life, and none of us disclosed my name to him! And Phoebe he didn't set eyes on!"

But the news had come from the doctor, of course. He had not discovered the identity of his patient, but he knew who was the elegant young man who had commanded his attendance at the Blue Boar; and it was rather too much to expect of a humble country practitioner that he would refrain from letting it be known as widely as possible that he had lately been called by

132

His Grace of Salford. The news had spread, in the mysterious country-fashion; and if, by the time it reached the Squire's ears, it had become garbled almost out of recognition it still retained enough of the truth to convince that shrewd gentleman that the supposed scion of the house of Rayne, who had overturned some vehicle on the Bath Road, was none other than his own son.

No, he had not been much surprised. Reaching the Manor not many hours after Tom had left it, he had been met by a distracted helpmate, who poured horrifying tidings into his incredulous ears. But he hoped he knew Tom well enough to be sure he had not eloped. A pretty gudgeon he had thought Marlow, to be hoaxed by such a tale! He had assumed his heir to be well able to take care of himself, as the lord knew (with an ironical eyebrow cocked at Tom) he ought to have been! He had awaited events. The first of these had been the return of Marlow to Austerby with a bad chill, and no news of the fugitives. If her ladyship were to be believed, the chill had developed into a congestion of the lung: at all events, his lordship was feeling devilish sorry for himself, and no wonder, lying in a room so hot as to make him sweat like a gamecock. So far as the Squire had been able to discover, Phoebe had run away to escape a proposal from the Duke of Salford. Well, he had thought that an unlikely tale at the outset; and since he had ascertained that he had been right in thinking that it was on Tom's behalf Salford had called in the sawbones he knew it for a Banbury story. And now he would be obliged to them if they would explain to him what the devil *had* made them go off in such a crackbrained style.

It was really very difficult to explain it to him; and not surprising that he should presently declare himself unable to make head or tail of the story. First, this Duke of Phoebe's was a monster from whose advances she had been obliged to fly; next, he was transformed without cause into a charming fellow with whom she had been consorting on terms of amity for the best part of a se'enight.

"*I* never said he was charming," objected Phoebe. "That was Tom. He toad-eats him!"

"No such thing!" said Tom indignantly. "*You* don't treat him with common civility!"

"Now, that's enough!" interposed the Squire, inured to sudden squabbles between his heir and his heir's lifelong friend.

"All I know is that I'm very much obliged to the Duke for taking care of as silly a pair of children as ever I knew! Well, I told her ladyship we should find it to be much ado about nothing, and so it is! It's not my business to be giving you a scold, my dear, but there's no denying you deserve one! However, I shall say no more to either of you. A broken leg is punishment enough for Tom; and as for you—well, there's no sense in saying her ladyship ain't vexed with you, because she is—very!"

"I'm not going back to Austerby, sir," said Phoebe, with the calm of desperation.

The Squire was very fond of her, but he was a parent himself, and he knew what he would think of any man who aided a child of his to flout his authority. He said kindly, but with a firm note in his voice which Tom at least knew well, that she was certainly going back to Austerby, and under his escort. He had promised Marlow that he would bring his daughter safely back to him, and that was all there was to be said about it.

In this he erred: both Phoebe and Tom found much more to say; but nothing they could say availed to turn the Squire from what he conceived to be his duty. He listened with great patience to every argument advanced, but at the end of an impassioned hour he patted Phoebe's shoulder, and said: "Yes, yes, my dear, but you must be reasonable! If you wish to reside with your grandmother you should write to her, and ask her if she will take you, which I'm sure I hope she may. But it won't do to go careering over the country in this way, and so she would tell you. As for expecting me to abet you—now, you don't want for sense, and you know I can't do it!"

She said despairingly: "You don't understand!"

"*Won't* understand!" muttered Tom savagely.

"Don't, Tom! Perhaps, if I write to her, Grandmama might—Only they will be so dreadfully angry with me!" A tear trickled down her cheek; she wiped it away, saying as valiantly as she could: "Well, at least I have had one very happy week. When must I go, sir?"

The Squire said gruffly: "Best to do so as soon as possible, my dear. I shall hire a chaise to convey you, but Tom's situation makes it a trifle awkward. Seems to me I ought first to consult with this doctor of his."

She agreed to this; and then, as another tear spilled over,

ran out of the room. The Squire cleared his throat, and said: "She will feel better when she's had her cry out, you know."

It was Phoebe's intention to do just this, in the privacy of her bedchamber; but she found Alice there, sweeping the floor, and retreated to the stairs, just as the door leading to the back of the inn opened, and Sylvester came into the narrow passage. She stopped, halfway down the stairs, and he looked up. He saw the tear-stains on her cheeks, and said: "What's the matter?"

"Tom's papa," she managed to reply. "Mr. Orde . . ."

He was frowning now, the slant of his brows accentuated. "Here?"

"In Tom's room. He—he says——"

"Come down to the coffee-room!" he commanded.

She obeyed, blowing her nose, and saying in a muffled voice: "I beg your pardon: I am *trying* to compose myself!"

He shut the door. "Yes, don't cry! What is it that Orde says?"

"That I must go home. He promised Papa, you see, and although he is very kind he doesn't understand. He is going to take me home as soon as he can."

"Then you haven't much time to waste," he said coolly. "How long will it take you to make ready?"

"It doesn't signify. He has to go to Hungerford first to see Dr. Upsall, as well as to hire a chaise."

"I am not talking of a journey to Austerby, but of one to London. Isn't that what you want?"

"Oh, yes, yes, indeed it is! Do you mean—But he won't permit me!"

"Must you ask his leave? If you choose to go, my chaise is at the Halfway House, and I will drive you there immediately. Well?"

A faint smile touched his lips, for these words had acted on her magically. She was suddenly a creature transformed. "*Thank you!* Oh, how good you are!"

"I'll tell Keighley not to stable the grays. Where's Alice?"

"In my bedchamber. But will she——"

"Tell her she may have precisely fifteen minutes in which to pack up what she may need, and warn her that we shan't stay for her," he said, striding to the door.

"Mrs. Scaling——?"

135

"I'll make all right with her," he said, over his shoulder, and was gone.

Alice, at first bemused, no sooner learned that she would not be waited for than she cast her duster from her with the air of one who had burnt her boats, and said tersely: "I'll go if I bust!" and rushed from the room.

Fearing that at any moment the Squire might come to find her, Phoebe dragged her portmanteau from under the bed and began feverishly to cram her clothes into it. Rather less than fifteen minutes later both damsels crept down the stairs, one clutching a portmanteau and a bandbox from under whose lid a scrap of muslin flounce protruded, the other clasping in both arms a bulky receptacle made of plaited straw.

The curricle was waiting in the yard, with Keighley at the grays' heads and Sylvester standing beside him. Sylvester laughed when he saw the two dishevelled travellers, and came to relieve Phoebe of her burdens, saying: "My compliments! I never thought you would contrive to be ready under half an hour!"

"Well, I'm not," she confessed. "I was obliged to leave several things behind, and—oh, dear! part of my other dress is sticking out of the bandbox!"

"You may pack it again at the Halfway House," he said. "But straighten your hat! I will not be seen driving a lady who looks perfectly demented!"

By the time she had achieved a more respectable appearance the luggage had been stowed under the seat, and Sylvester was ready to hand her up. Alice followed her, and in another minute they were away, Keighley swinging himself up behind as the curricle moved forward.

"Shall I reach London tonight, do you think, sir?" Phoebe asked, as soon as Sylvester had negotiated the narrow entrance to the yard.

"I hope you may, but it's more likely you will be obliged to rack up for the night somewhere. There's no danger of running into drifts now, but it will be heavy going, with the snow turning everywhere into slush. You must leave it to Keighley to decide what is best to do."

"The thing is, you see, that I haven't a great deal of money with me," she confided shyly. "In fact, very little! So if we *could* reach London——"

"No need to tease yourself over money. Keighley will attend

136

to all such matters as inn charges, tolls, and changes. You will take my own team over the first few stages, but after that it must be hired cattle, I'm afraid."

"Thank you! you are very good," she said, rather overwhelmed. "Pray desire him to keep account of the money he may have to lay out!"

"He will naturally do so, Miss Marlow."

"Yes, but I mean——"

"Oh, I know what you mean!" he interrupted. "You would like me to present you with a bill, and no doubt I should do so—if I were a job-master."

"I may be very much beholden to you, Duke," said Phoebe coldly, "but if you speak to me in that odiously snubbing way I shall—I shall——"

He laughed. "You will what?"

"Well, I don't yet know, but I shall think of something, I promise you! Because you are quite at fault! I fancy it may be proper for you to pay the post charges, but it would be most improper for you to pay my bill at an inn!"

"Very well. If there should be such a bill I will hand it to you when next we meet."

She inclined her head graciously. "I am obliged to you, sir."

"Is that the way I speak when I am being odiously snubbing?" enquired Sylvester.

She gave a tiny chuckle, and said handsomely: "I must own that you are not at all stupid!"

"Oh, no, I'm not stupid! I have a good memory, too. I haven't forgotten how well you contrived to hit off a number of our acquaintances, and I make no secret of my uneasiness. You have an uncomfortable knack of hitting off just what is most ridiculous in your victims!"

She did not reply. Glancing down at her he saw a very grave look in her face. He wondered what she had found to disturb her in his bantering speech, but he did not ask, because they had by this time reached the Halfway House, and he was obliged to give his attention to the ostler, who came running to hold the grays.

It was not long before the chaise stood waiting to convey the travellers to London. Alice, who had sat lost in a beatific dream in the curricle, was quite overcome by the sight of the elegant equipage in which she was now to travel, with the crest

137

upon its panel, its four magnificent horses stamping and fretting and tossing up their heads, its smart postilions, the deep squabs of the seats, and the sheepskin that covered the floor. To Phoebe's dismay she burst into tears. However, when anxiously begged to say what was distressing her she replied, between snorting sobs, that she was thinking of the neighbours, denied the privilege of watching her drive off like a queen.

Relieved, Phoebe said: "Well, never mind! you will be able to tell them all about it when you go home again! Jump up, and don't cry any more!"

"Oh, no, miss! But I do be so happy!" said Alice, preparing to clamber into the chaise.

Phoebe turned, and looked at Sylvester, waiting to hand her up the steps. Her colour rose; she put out her hand, and as he took it in his, said haltingly: "I have been trying to think how to tell you how—how *very* grateful I am, but I can't find the words. But, oh, I *thank* you!"

"Believe me, Sparrow, you make too much of a very trifling service. Convey my compliments to Lady Ingham, and tell her that I shall do myself the honour of calling on her when I come to town. In my turn, I will convey yours to Thomas and his father!"

"Yes, pray do! I mean, you will tell Tom how it was, won't you? And perhaps you could convey my *apologies* to the Squire, rather than my compliments?"

"Certainly, if that is your wish."

"Well, I think it would be more civil. I only hope he won't be out of reason vexed!"

"Don't tease yourself on that head!"

"Yes, but if he should be I know you will give him one of your freezing set-downs, and *that* I couldn't bear!" she said.

"I thought it would not be long before you came to the end of your unnatural civility," he observed. "Let me assure you that I have no intention of conducting myself with anything less than propriety!"

"That's *exactly* what I dread!" she said.

"Good God, what an abominable girl you are! Get into the chaise before I catch the infection!" he exclaimed, between amusement and annoyance.

She laughed, but said, apologetically, as he handed her up: "I wasn't thinking! *Truly* I meant not to say one uncivil thing to you!"

138

"You are certainly incorrigible. *I*, on the other hand, am so magnanimous as to wish you a safe and speedy journey!"

"Magnanimous indeed! Thank you!"

The steps were let up; Alice's voice was the last to be heard before the door was shut. "Hot bricks, and a fur rug, miss!" disclosed Alice. "*Spanking*, I call it!"

Phoebe leaned forward to wave farewell, the ostlers let go the wheelers' heads, and the chaise started to move, swaying on its excellent springs. Sylvester stood watching it until it disappeared round a bend in the road, and then turned to Keighley, waiting beside him, the bridle of a hired riding-hack in his hand. "Get them to London tonight if you can, John, but run no risks," he said. "Money, pistols—I think you have everything."

"Yes, your grace, but I wish you'd let me come back!"

"No, wait for me at Salford House. I can't take both you and Swale. Or, at any rate, I won't! Curricles were never meant to carry three persons."

Keighley smiled grimly, as he hoisted himself into the saddle. "I thought your grace was being a trifle crowded," he remarked, with a certain amount of satisfaction.

"And hope it may be a lesson to me! Be damned to you!" retorted Sylvester.

He accomplished the short journey back to the Blue Boar at a leisurely trot, his mind occupied, not altogether pleasurably, with the events of the past week. He ought never to have stopped at the Blue Boar. He wondered what could have possessed him, and was much inclined to think it had been perversity: John had tried to dissuade him—*damn* John for being in the right of it, as usual!—and he had done it as much to tease him as for any other reason. Well, he had been well served for that piece of mischief! Once he had found young Orde in such a fix he had been fairly caught: only a monster could have abandoned the boy to his fate. Besides, he liked Thomas, and had not foreseen that his act of charity would precipitate him into the sort of imbroglio he particularly disliked. He could only be thankful that he was not a frequent traveller on the Bath Road: he had given them plenty to talk about at the Halfway House, and to afford the vulgar food for gossip was no part of his ambition. That hurly-burly girl! She wanted both manners and conduct; she was disagreeably pert, and had no beauty: he cordially disliked her. What the devil had made him come to her rescue, when all his saner self desired was to see her thoroughly set-down? There had not been the least necessity—except that he had pledged his word. But when he had seen her on the stairs, so absurdly woebegone but trying rather pathetically to smile, he hadn't recollected that foolish promise: he had acted on impulse, and had only himself to thank for the outcome. Here he was, tied still to a primitive inn, and a young man whose welfare was no concern of his; deprived of his groom; open to the justifiable censure of some unknown country squire—the sort of worthy person, in all probability, whom he entertained at Chance on Public Days; and the subject (if he knew his world) of scandalous conjecture. In some form or another the story would be bound to leak out. The best he could hope for was to be thought to have taken leave of his senses; the worst, that for all his famed fastidiousness he had fallen laughably in love with a dab of a female without style or countenance, who scorned his supposed advances.

No, decided Sylvester, turning neatly into the yard of the Blue Boar: that was rather too much to expect him to bear! Miss Marlow should *not* exhibit her poor opinion of him to the interested ton. Miss Marlow, in fact, should exhibit something very different from contempt: he was damned if he was going to be the only one to learn a salutary lesson!

His expression, when he alighted from the curricle, and stood watching, with a merciless eye, the exact carrying out of his curt orders, was unamiable enough to make the ostler break into a sweat of anxiety; but when he presently strolled into Tom's room all traces of ill-humour had vanished from his countenance.

He entered upon a scene of constraint. The Squire, peckish after his ride, had just disposed of a substantial nuncheon, and Tom, having talked himself out of arguments, had been preserving for the past ten minutes a silence pregnant with resentment. He looked round at the opening of the door, his eyes still smouldering, and as soon as he saw that it was Sylvester who had come in, burst out: "Salford! The—the most *damnable* thing! Perhaps you can prevail upon my father to listen to reason! I never would have believed it possible he could—oh, this *is* my father!"

"I don't know what you would never have believed possible," said the Squire, getting up from his chair, and bowing to Sylvester, "but let me tell you, my boy, *I* wouldn't have believed you had only to be away from home for a week to lose your manners! I should think your grace must be wondering if he was reared in a cow-byre, and I'm sure I don't blame you. He wasn't, however—and a thundering scold he'd get from his mother if *she* were here!" He saw that Sylvester, advancing into the room, was holding out his hand, and shook it warmly. "I'm honoured to make your grace's acquaintance— and feel myself to be devilish obliged to you, as you may guess! You've been a great deal too kind to Tom, and how to thank you I don't know!"

"But there's no need to thank me at all, I assure you, sir," Sylvester said, at his most charming. "I've spent a most entertaining week—and made a new friend, whom I can't allow you to scold! It would be most unjust, you know, for he abandoned his really oppressive civility only at my request. Besides, he has endured six days of boredom without a murmur of complaint!"

"Ay, and serve him right!" said the Squire. "A bad business this, my lord Duke! I left Marlow in a rare taking, I can tell you. Well, well! he's the best man to hounds I ever saw, but I never thought his understanding more than moderate. Gretna Green, indeed! Of all the hare-brained notions to have taken into his head!"

"I wish to God I *had* taken her to Gretna Green!" said Tom savagely. "Salford, my father is determined to carry her back to Austerby! I can't make him understand that only a regular brute would do so, after such an escapade as this!"

"Now, now!" said the Squire. "There's been no harm done, and no one but ourselves any the wiser—thanks to his grace!— and so I shall tell her ladyship."

"As though she would pay the least heed! And what a figure *I* must cut! I wouldn't let her go on the stage, and if I had she would have been with Lady Ingham days ago! I promised to take her there myself, and all I've done is to land her in a worse case than ever! *Father*——"

"Calm yourself, Galahad!" interposed Sylvester. "There is really no occasion to be cast into despair. Miss Marlow left for London an hour ago."

An astonished silence succeeded these words. Tom broke it with a shout of triumph. "Oh, you *Trojan*, Salford!"

This made Sylvester laugh; but an instant later he was putting up his brows, for the Squire, after staring at him fixedly, said bluntly: "If that was your grace's doing, as I collect it must have been, I shall take leave to tell you it was wrong of you, my lord Duke—very wrong!"

Tom, recognizing that look of withdrawal, intervened quickly. "You mustn't say that, Father—indeed you must not! Pray——"

"I shall say just what I think, Tom," said the Squire, still looking at Sylvester from under his brows. "If his grace don't like it, why, I'm sorry for it, but I've said it, and I stand by it!"

Tom glanced apprehensively at Sylvester, but his intervention had been more successful than he knew. Meeting his eyes Sylvester realized, with a slight shock, that he was trying to prevent the Squire's being wounded by a snub. He had been unaware of his own stiffening; for an instant he remembered Phoebe's words. He had dismissed them as an impertinent attempt to vex him; he wondered now if it could be true that he, who prided himself on his good manners, appeared to others to be insufferably high in the instep. He said, smiling: "Well, I *don't* like it, for you are doing me an injustice, sir! *You* may have pledged your word to Marlow, but *I* pledged mine to his daughter!"

"Ay, that's very pretty talking!" retorted the Squire. "But what the devil am I to tell him, Duke?"

"If I were you," replied Sylvester, "I rather think I should merely tell him that I had been unable to bring Miss Marlow back with me because she had already left for town—on a visit to her grandmother."

The Squire, having thought this over, said slowly: "I could say that, of course. To be sure, they don't know Phoebe has been here all along—and it would be as well, I daresay, if they never did get to know of it. At the same time, I don't like hoaxing Marlow, for that's what I should be doing, no question about it!"

"But, Father, what good would it do to tell them you found Phoebe here?" asked Tom. "Now that she's gone, it could only do harm!"

"Well, that's true enough," admitted the Squire. "What *am* I going to tell them?"

"That Miss Marlow travelled to town in my chaise, escorted by my head groom, and attended by a respectable abigail,"

142

replied Sylvester fluently. "Not even Lady Marlow could demand a greater degree of propriety, surely?"

"Not if she don't set eyes on the respectable abigail!" murmured Tom.

"Don't put mistaken notions into your father's head, Thomas! Let me reassure you, sir! The landlady's daughter has gone with Miss Marlow. She is unquestionably respectable!"

"Yes, but such a toad-eater!" said Tom wickedly. "Saying you were more important than a gobble-cock——!"

CHAPTER

13

Contrary to Sylvester's expectation Phoebe reached her grandmother's house at half past ten that evening. She had been travelling for nearly eight hours, for the state of the roads had compelled the postilions to proceed at a very sober pace, and she was as weary as she was anxious. Her initial reception in Green Street was not encouraging. While she waited in the chaise, with the window let down, watching him, Keighley trod up the steps to the front door and plied the heavy knocker resoundingly. A long, long pause followed, and a nerve-racking fear that Lady Ingham was out of town assailed Phoebe. But just as Keighley raised his hand to repeat his summons she saw him check, and lower his arm again. The quelling noise of bolts being drawn back was next heard, and Phoebe, craning eagerly forward, saw her grandmother's butler standing on the threshold, with a lamp in his hand, and heaved a sigh of relief.

But if she expected to receive a welcome from Horwich she was the more deceived. Persons who demanded admittance at unseasonable hours were never welcome to him, even when they arrived in a chaise-and-four and escorted by a liveried servant. A street lamp illumined the chaise, and he perceived that for all the dirt that clung to the wheels and panels it was

144

an extremely elegant vehicle: none of your job-chaises, but a carriage built for a gentleman of means and taste. A glimpse of a crest, half concealed by mud, caused him to unbend a trifle, but he replied coldly to Keighley's enquiry that her ladyship was not at home to visitors.

He was obliged to admit Phoebe, of course. He did it with obvious reluctance, and stood, rigid with disapproval, while she thanked Keighley for his services, and bade him good-bye with what he considered most unbecoming friendliness.

"I will ascertain whether her ladyship will receive you, miss," he said, shutting the door at last upon Keighley. "I should inform you, however, that her ladyship retired to rest above an hour ago."

She tried not to feel daunted, and said as confidently as she could that she was sure her grandmother would receive her. "And will you, if you please, look after my maid, Horwich?" she said. "We have been travelling for a great many hours, and I expect she will be glad of some supper."

"I will that, and no mistake!" corroborated Alice, grinning cordially at Horwich. "Don't you go putting yourself out, though! A bit of cold meat and a mug of porter will do me fine."

Phoebe could not feel, observing the expression on Horwich's face, that Sylvester had acted wisely in sending Alice to town with her. Horwich said in arctic accents that he would desire the housekeeper—if she had not gone to bed—to attend to the Young Person presently. He added that if Miss would be pleased to step into the morning-room he would send her ladyship's maid up to apprise my lady of Miss's unexpected arrival.

But by this time Phoebe's temper had begun to mount, and she surprised the venerable tyrant by saying tartly that she would do no such thing. "You need not put yourself to the trouble of escorting me, for I know my way very well! If her ladyship is asleep I shall not wake her, and if she is not I don't need Muker to announce me!" she declared.

Her ladyship was not asleep. Phoebe's soft knock on her door was answered by a command to come in; and she entered to find her grandmother sitting up in her curtained bed, with a number of pillows to support her, and an open book in her hands. Two branches of candles and the flames of a large fire lit the scene, and cast into strong relief her ladyship's aquiline profile. "Well, what is it?" she said testily, and looked round. "*Phoebe*! Good God, what in the world——? My dear, dear child, come in!"

A weight slid from Phoebe's shoulders; her face puckered, and with a thankful cry of: "Oh, *Grandmama*!" she ran forward.

The Dowager embraced her warmly, but she was not unnaturally alarmed by so sudden an arrival. "Yes, yes, of course I am glad to see you, my love! But tell me at once what has happened! Don't try to break it to me gently! Not, I do trust, a fatal accident to your papa?"

"No—oh, no! nothing of *that* nature, ma'am!" Phoebe assured her. "Grandmama, you told me once that I might depend on you if—if ever I needed help!"

"That Woman!" uttered the Dowager, sitting bolt upright.

"Yes, and—and Papa too," said Phoebe sadly. "That was what made it so desperate! Something happened—at least, I believed it was going to happen—and I couldn't *bear* it, and so—and so I ran away!"

"Merciful heavens!" exclaimed Lady Ingham. "My poor child, what have they been doing to you? Tell me the whole!"

"Mama told me that Papa had arranged a—a very advantageous marriage for me with the Duke of Salford," began Phoebe haltingly. She was conscious that her grandmother had stiffened, and paused nervously. But the Dowager merely adjured her to continue, so she drew a breath, and said earnestly: "I *couldn't* marry him, ma'am! You see, I had only met him once in my life, and I disliked him excessively. Besides, I knew very well that he didn't so much as remember me! Even if I had liked him I couldn't have borne to marry a man who only offered for me because his mother wished him to!"

The Dowager, controlling herself with a strong effort, said: "Is that what That Woman told you?"

"Yes, and also that it was because I had been brought up as I should be, which made him think I should be *suitable*!"

"Good God!" said the Dowager bitterly.

"You—you do understand, don't you, ma'am?"

"Oh, yes! I understand only too well!" was the somewhat grim response.

"I was persuaded you would! And the dreadful thing was that Papa was bringing him to Austerby to propose to me. At least, so Mama said, for Papa had told her so."

"When I see Marlow—*Did* he bring Salford to Austerby?"

"Yes, he did, but how he came to make such a mistake—unless, of course, Salford did mean to offer for me, but changed his mind as soon as he saw me again, which, I must say, no one could wonder at. I don't know precisely how it may have been, but Papa was sure he meant to make me an offer, and when I told him what my sentiments were, and begged him to tell the Duke—he would not," said Phoebe, her voice petering out unhappily. "So I knew then that there wasn't anybody, except you, Grandmama, who could help me. And I ran away."

"*Alone?*" demanded the Dowager, horrified. "Never tell me you've come all that distance on the common stage and by yourself!"

"No, indeed I haven't!" Phoebe hastened to reassure her. "I came in Salford's chaise, and he made me bring a—a maid with me, besides sending his groom to look after *everything* for me!"

"*What?*" said the Dowager incredulously. "Came in *Salford's* chaise?"

"I—I must explain it to you, ma'am," said Phoebe, looking guilty.

"You must indeed!" said the Dowager, staring at her in the liveliest astonishment.

"Yes. Only, it—it is rather a long story!"

"In that case, my love, be good enough to pull the bell!" said the Dowager. "You will like a glass of hot milk after your journey. And I think," she added, in fainter accents, "that I will take some myself, to sustain me."

She then (to Phoebe's alarm) sank back against her disordered pillows, and closed her eyes. However, upon the entrance of Miss Muker presently, she opened them again, and said with surprising vigour: "You may take that sour look off your face, Muker, and fetch up two glasses of hot milk directly! My granddaughter, who has come to pay me a visit, has endured a most fatiguing journey. And when you have done that, you will see that a warming-pan is slipped between the sheets of her bed, and a fire lit, and everything made ready for her. In the best spare bedchamber!"

When my lady spoke in that voice it was unwise to argue with her. Muker, who had responded to Phoebe's greeting in a repressive voice, and with the slightest of curtsies, received her orders without comment, but said with horrid restraint:

147

"And would Miss wish to have the Female which I understand to be her maid attend her here, my lady?"

"No, pray send her to bed!" said Phoebe quickly. "She—she is not precisely my maid!"

"So, if I may say so, miss, I apprehend!" said Muker glacially.

"Disagreeable creature!" said the Dowager, as the door closed behind her devoted abigail. "Who is this Female, if she is not your maid?"

"Well, she's the landlady's daughter," Phoebe answered. "Salford *would* have me bring her!"

"Landlady's daughter? No, don't explain it to me yet, child! Muker will come back with the hot milk directly, and something seems to tell me that if we suffer an interruption I shall become perfectly bewildered. Take that ugly pelisse off, my love—good gracious, where did you have that dreaful gown made? Has That Woman *no* taste? Well, never mind! Whatever happens I'll set *that* to rights! Draw that chair to the fire, and then we can be comfortable. And perhaps if you were to give me my smelling-salts—yes, on that table, child!—it would be a good thing!"

But although the story presently unfolded to her might have been thought by some to have been expressly designed to cast into palpitations any elderly lady in failing health, the Dowager had no recourse to her vinaigrette. The tale was so ravelled as to make it necessary for her to interpolate a number of questions, and there was nothing in her incisive delivery of these to suggest frailty either of body or intellect.

The most searching of her enquiries were drawn from her by the intrusion into the recital of Mr. Thomas Orde. She appeared to be much interested in him; and while Phoebe readily told her all about her oldest friend she kept her eyes fixed piercingly upon her face. But when she learned of Tom's nobility in offering a clandestine marriage to her granddaughter ("which threw me into whoops, because he isn't *nearly* old enough to be married, besides being just like my brother!") she lost interest in him, merely requesting Phoebe, in a much milder tone, to continue her story. There was nothing to be feared, decided her ladyship, from young Mr. Orde.

The last of her questions was posed almost casually. "And did Salford chance to mention me?" she asked.

"Oh, yes!" replied Phoebe blithely. "He told me that he

was particularly acquainted with you, because you were his godmother. So I ventured to ask him if he thought you might— might *like* to let me reside with you, and he seemed to think you *would*, Grandmama!"

"Did he indeed?" said the Dowager, her countenance inscrutable. "Well, my love——" with sudden energy—"he was perfectly right! I shall like it excessively!"

It was long before her ladyship fell asleep that night. She had been provided by her innocent granddaughter with food for much thought, and still more conjecture. Lord and Lady Marlow were soon dismissed from her mind (but a large part of the following morning was going to be pleasurably spent in the composition of a letter calculated to bring about a dangerous relapse in his lordship's state of health); and so too was young Mr. Orde. What intrigued Lady Ingham was the position occupied by Sylvester in the stirring drama disclosed to her. The rôle of *deus ex machina*, which he appeared to have undertaken, sounded most unlike him; nor could she picture him living in what she judged to be the depths of squalor, and spending his time between the stables and a sickroom. In fact, the only recognizable thing he seemed to have done was to encourage Phoebe to seek refuge in Green Street. That, thought the Dowager indignantly, rang very true! She had no doubt, either, that he had done it out of pure malice. Well! he would shortly discover that he had shot wide of the mark. She was delighted to welcome Phoebe. She wondered that it should not have occurred to her that the very thing needed to relieve the intolerable boredom she had been suffering during the past few months, when the better part of her acquaintance had retired into the country, was the presence in her house of a lively granddaughter. She now perceived that to keep Phoebe with her would be in every way preferable to the fatigue of a journey to Paris, a project which she had had in doubtful contemplation ever since one of her chief cronies had written thence to urge her to join the throng of well-born English who were disporting themselves so agreeably in that most delightful of capitals. She had been tempted, but there were grave drawbacks to the scheme. It would mean putting oneself beyond the reach of dear Sir Henry; Muker would be certain to dislike it; and whatever poor Mary Berry might allege to the contrary it was the Dowager's unalterable conviction that the escort of a gentleman was indispensable to any lady bent on foreign travel. One could admittedly engage a courier, but to do so merely added to one's expenditure, since the gentleman was still necessary, to keep a watchful eye on the activities of this hireling. No: on every count it would be better to adopt Phoebe, and try what *she* could achieve for the child. Once she had rigged her out becomingly she would positively enjoy taking her, whenever her health permitted, into society.

Here her ladyship's thoughts suffered a check. She had no intention of allowing Phoebe to abjure the world (as Phoebe had suggested), but although her health might benefit by chaperoning the child to one or two private balls, nothing could be more prejudicial to it than interminable evenings spent at Almack's Assembly Rooms, or at parties given by hostesses with whom she was barely acquainted. But the check was only momentary: the Dowager remembered the existence of her meek daughter-in-law. Rosina, with two girls of her own to chaperon, could very well take her niece under her wing: such an arrangement could make no possible difference to her.

This was a small matter, and soon disposed of; far more important, and far more difficult to solve, was the riddle of Sylvester's behaviour.

He was coming to visit her. She had received this message with every appearance of indifference, but she had pricked up her ears at it. He was, was he? Well, it would go against the grain to do it, but if he did come she would receive him affably. Perhaps, if she saw him, she might be able to discover just what game he was playing. His actions invited her to suppose that he had fallen in love with Phoebe, and was bent on displaying himself to her in his most pleasing colours. But if Phoebe's account of what had passed during his stay at Austerby were to be believed it was hard to detect what he had seen in her to captivate him. The Dowager did not think he had gone to Austerby with the intention of liking what he found there, for she was well aware that she had erred a trifle in her handling of him, and set up his back. It had been quite a question, when she had seen that sparkle of anger in his eyes, whether she should push the matter farther, or let it rest.

CHAPTER

14

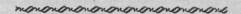

On the following morning Phoebe found her grandmother in brisk spirits, and very full of plans for the day. Foremost amongst these was a visit to a silk-warehouse and another to her ladyship's own modiste. "To dress you becomingly is the first necessity, child," said the Dowager. "The sight of you in that shabby gown makes me nervous!"

The prospect of choosing fashionable raiment was enticing, but Phoebe was obliged to beg her grandmother to postpone this programme. She had promised to show Alice all the most notable sights of London, and, in particular, to take her to the Pantheon Bazaar.

She had a little difficulty in persuading the Dowager to consent to any part of this scheme, for it did not at all suit that lady's sense of propriety to permit her granddaughter to wander about, seeing the lions, with no other escort than a raw country-girl. She told Phoebe that Alice would enjoy herself more in the company of one of the maidservants, but was persuaded finally to sanction an expedition to the Pantheon Bazaar, having recollected that before she herself could prosecute her various designs she must write a letter to Lord Marlow, and another to her daughter-in-law. Phoebe's own letter to her papa was already written; and she was able to frustrate the Dowager's intention to send her forth in her town carriage by reminding her how much her coachman was likely to object to having his horses kept standing in inclement weather. Phoebe had a piece of very secret business to transact, and she by no means wished Lady Ingham's coachman to report to his mistress that her first port of call had been the offices of Messrs. Newsham & Otley, Publishers.

She entered those premises with high hopes, and left them in a mood of such black foreboding as made it hard for her to enter into Alice's raptures at all that met her eyes. It had not occurred to Phoebe that it might be too late for her to delete from her forthcoming romance every mention of Count Ugolino's distinctive eyebrows.

But so it was. Mr. Otley, confronted by a nameless lady in an ugly stuff gown who announced herself to be the authoress of *The Lost Heir,* almost burst with curiosity. He and his senior partner had often speculated on the identity of that daring authoress, but neither of them had supposed that she would prove to be nothing more than a dowdy schoolgirl. His manner underwent a change, and a note of patronage crept into his voice. Phoebe's disposition was friendly to a fault, but she was quite unused to being addressed in just such a way by persons of Mr. Otley's order. Mr. Otley, encountering an amazed stare, hastily revised his first impression, and decided that it might be wise to call in the senior partner.

Mr. Newsham's manner was perfect: a nice blend of the respectful and the fatherly. Had it been possible he would have delayed publication gladly, and as gladly have incurred the expense of having the book entirely reset. But, alas! The date of issue was fixed, a bare month ahead, the edition fully prepared. Nothing could have been more unfortunate, but he ventured to think that she must still be pleased by the result of his labours.

Well, she was pleased. So handsome were they, those three slim volumes, elegantly attired in blue leather, the fore-edges of the pages gilded, and the title enclosed in a scroll! It didn't seem possible that between those opulent covers reposed a story of her weaving. When the volumes were put into her hands she gave an involuntary gasp of delight; but when she opened the first volume at random her eyes fell upon a fatal paragraph.

Count Ugolino's appearance was extraordinary. His figure was elegant, his bearing graceful, his air that of a well-bred man, and his lineaments very handsome; but the classical regularity of his countenance was marred by a pair of feline orbs, which were set beneath black brows rising steeply towards his temples, and which were sinister in expression. Matilda could not repress a shudder of revulsion.

Nor could Matilda's creator, hurriedly shutting the volume, and looking imploringly up at Mr. Newsham. "I *cannot* allow it to be published!"

It took patience and time to convince Phoebe that it was not in her power to arrest publication, but Mr. Newsham grudged neither. His tongue was persuasive, and since he was astute enough to perceive that an optimistic forecast of the book's chances of success would only dismay her he explained to her how rarely it was that a first novel enjoyed more than a modest sale, and how improbable it was that it would come under the notice of persons of ton.

She was a little reassured, but when she parted from him it was with the resolve to write immediately to Miss Battery, imploring her to use her influence with her cousin to arrest publication. For his part, having bowed her off the premises, Mr. Newsham instantly sought out the junior partner, demanding: "Didn't you tell me that that cousin of yours is governess in a nobleman's household? Who is he? Mark my words, that chit's his daughter, and we've got a hit!"

"Who is the fellow—I mean the real fellow—she wants to alter?" asked Mr. Otley uneasily.

"I don't know. Only one of the nobs," replied his partner cheerfully. "*They* don't bring actions for libel!"

It was nearly a week later when Miss Battery's letter reached her one-time pupil, and by then Phoebe, caught up in what seemed to her a whirl of fashionable activity, had little time to spare for her literary troubles. It was impossible to be apprehensive for very long at a time when her life had been miraculously transformed. Lady Marlow's unsatisfactory daughter-in-law had become her grandmother's pet, and it was wonderful what a change it wrought in her. Lady Ingham was well-satisfied. Phoebe would never be a beauty, but when she was prettily dressed, and not afraid of incurring censure every time she unclosed her lips, she was quite a taking little thing.

A touch of town-bronze was needed, but she would soon acquire that.

Miss Battery wrote affectionately but not helpfully. More conversant than Phoebe with the difficulties of publishing, she could only recommend her not to tease herself too much over the remote possibility of the Duke's reading her book. Very likely he would not; and if he did Phoebe must remember that no one need know she was the authoress.

That was consoling, but Phoebe knew she would feel guilty every time she met Sylvester, and almost wished the book unwritten. After his kindness to have portrayed him as a villain was an act of treachery; and it was no use, she told herself sternly, to say that she had done this before she became indebted to him, for that was mere quibbling.

The season had not begun, but the unusually hard weather was driving a number of people back to town. Several small parties were being given; Grandmama prophesied that long before Almack's opening night the season would be in full swing, and she wish to lose no time in making it known that she now had her granddaughter living with her. In vain did Phoebe assure her that she did not care for balls. "Nonsense!" said her ladyship.

"But it's true, ma'am! I am always so stupid at big parties!"

"Not when you know yourself to be as elegantly dressed as any girl in the room—and very much more elegantly than most of 'em!" retorted the Dowager.

"But, Grandmama!" said Phoebe reproachfully. "I meant to be a comfort to you: not to go out raking every night!"

The Dowager glanced sharply at her, saw that the saintly tone was belied by eyes brimming with mischief, and thought: If Sylvester has seen *that* look——! But why the deuce hasn't he paid us a visit yet?

Phoebe wondered why he had not, too. She knew of no reason why he should wish to see her again, but he had asked her to tell Grandmama that he would call on her when he came to town, and surely he must have reached town days ago? Tom, she knew, was at home; so the Duke could not still be at the Blue Boar. She was not in the least affronted, but she found herself wishing several times that he would call in Green Street. She had such a lot to tell him! Nothing of importance, of course: just funny things, such as Alice's various remarks, which Grandmama had not thought very funny (Grandmama had not taken kindly to Alice), and how Papa had written her a thundering scold, not for having run away from Austerby, but for having done so without first telling him where she kept the key to the chest containing the horse-medicines. Grandmama had not thought that funny either; and a joke lost some of its savour when there was no one with whom one could share it. It was a pity the Duke had not come to London after all.

In point of fact he had come, but he had left again almost immediately for Chance, one of the first scraps of news that had greeted him on arrival at Salford House being that Lady Henry was also in town, with her child, staying with Lord and Lady Elvaston. Since she had not mentioned to him that she had formed any such intention this made him very angry. Her comings and goings were no concern of his (though she had no right to remove Edmund without his permission), but he thought it unpardonable that she should have left the Duchess during his absence, and without a word of warning to him. He posted back to Leicestershire; but as he found his mother not only in good spirits but looking forward to a visit from her sister he did not remain for more than a few days at Chance. During his stay he made no mention of his visit to Austerby. The Duchess was left with the impression that he had been all the time at Blandford Park; and since he had straitly charged Swale and Keighley to preserve discreet silence he was reasonably sure that no account of his adventures would filter through the household channels to her ears.

Just why he was reluctant to divulge to her an episode which would certainly amuse her was a question he found difficult to answer; and since a fleeting apprehension of this occurred to him he did not tax his brain with it. After all, it could afford her no pleasure to know that he had passed the daughter of her dearest friend under review and found her to be unworthy to become his wife.

In London he found quite a pile of invitations awaiting him, including a graceful note from Lady Barningham, bidding him (if he did not disdain a small, informal party) to a little dance at her house that very evening. Now, Lady Barningham's daughter was the vivacious girl who came second on the list of the five candidates for his hand. Having formed no other plan than to look in at one or other of his clubs, he decided to present himself at the Barninghams' house, where he could be sure of meeting several friends, and sure also that his hostess would accept his excuses for having left her invitation unanswered.

He was right on both counts. His arrival coincided with that of Lord Yarrow, who hailed him on the doorstep, and demanded where the devil he had been hiding himself; he found two more of his intimates in the drawing-room; and was received by a hostess who told him that his apologies were unnecessary—indeed, absurd, for he must know that this dance was the merest impromptu. What *was* one to do, Duke, in March, of all impossible months, and with London still so thin of company?

"You have hit on the very thing, of course," he replied. "I have nothing to do but be glad I reached London in time to present myself, and was so fortunate as to escape a deserved scold!"

"As though we were not well enough acquainted to dispense with ceremony! I warn you, you will find none here tonight! I perform no introductions, but leave you to choose whom you will for your partner, since I fancy all are known to you."

In high good-humour was her ladyship, but careful not to betray her triumph to jealous eyes. With Salford one never knew, and a hint of complacence now would be remembered by the dear friends who were present, if he let another season go without making Caroline an offer, or offered instead for Sophia Bellerby, or the lovely Lady Mary Torrington. It would not do to indulge optimism too far. She had done that last year, and his grace had not come up to the scratch; and however pleased he seemed to be in Caroline's company no one could accuse him of making her his sole object. Not one of the twelve young ladies present would go home feeling that he had slighted her; three of them at least had enjoyed charming flirtations with him.

She would have been dismayed had she known that Sylvester had discovered a sad fault in Miss Barningham. She was too compliant. He had only to lift his brows, to say: "You cannot be serious!" and she was ready in an instant to allow herself to be converted. She was not going to argue with him, she knew his intellect to be superior. Well! if people (unspecified) supposed him to like that sort of flattery they were mistaken: it was a dead bore. Not that he had not enjoyed the party: he had spent an agreeable evening amongst friends; and it had been pleasant, after his experience in Somerset, to be welcomed with such cordiality. He wondered how he would be received in Green Street, and smiled wryly as he recollected what cause he had given his godmother to regard him with a hostile eye.

But there was no trace of hostility in Lady Ingham's face or manner when he was ushered into her drawing-room; indeed, she greeted him with more enthusiasm than her granddaughter. He found both ladies at home, but Phoebe was engaged in writing a note for the Dowager, and although she rose to shake hands, and smiled at Sylvester in a friendly way, she asked him to excuse her while she finished her task.

"Come and sit down, Sylvester!" commanded Lady Ingham. "I have been wishing to thank you for taking care of Phoebe. You may guess how very much obliged to you I am. According to what she tells me she wouldn't be with me today if it hadn't been for your kind offices."

"Now, how, without disrespect, does one tell one's godmother that she is talking nonsense?" countered Sylvester, kissing her fingers. "Does Miss Marlow make a long stay, ma'am?"

"She is going to make her home with me," replied the Dowager, smiling blandly at him.

"But how delightful!" he said.

"What a hoaxing thing to say!" remarked Phoebe, hunting in the writing-table for a wafer. "You can't pretend *you* thought it delightful to endure my company!"

"I have no need to pretend. Do you think we didn't miss you abominably? I promise you we did!"

"To make a fourth at whist?" she said, pushing back her chair.

He rose as she came to the fire, retorting: "No such thing! Whist was never in question. Mr. Orde remained with us only one night."

"What, did he take Tom home immediately?"

"No, he left him with me while he himself went home to allay the anxieties of Mrs. Orde and your father. He came back three days later, and bore Thomas off most regally, in an enormous carriage, furnished by Mrs. Orde with every imaginable comfort, from pillows to smelling-salts."

"Smelling-salts! Oh, no!"

"I assure you. Ask Thomas if he didn't try to throw them out of the window! Tell me how you fared! I know from

Keighley that you did reach town that night: were you very tired?"

"Yes, but I didn't care for that. And as for Alice, I think she would have driven on for hours, and still enjoyed it! Oh, I must tell you that you have been eclipsed in her eyes, Duke!"

"Ah, have I?" he said, eyeing her suspiciously. "By a freak?"

She laughed. "No, no, by *Horwich*!"

"Come, that's most encouraging! What did he do to earn her admiration?"

"He behaved to her in the most odious way imaginable! As though she had been a cockroach, she told me! I was afraid she must be wretchedly unhappy, but I don't think anything she saw in London impressed her half as much! She confided to me that he was much more her notion of a duke than you are!"

He burst out laughing, and demanded further news of Alice. But the Dowager said that rustics didn't amuse her, so, instead, Phoebe told him about her father's letter, and he incensed the Dowager by enjoying that hugely. Even less than by rustics was she amused by Lord Marlow's fatuity.

Sylvester did not remain for long, nor was he offered the chance of a *tête-à-tête* with Phoebe. The only *tête-à-tête* granted him was a brief one with the Dowager, who found an excuse to send Phoebe out of the room for a few minutes, so that she could say to him: "I'm glad you didn't tell the child she had me to thank for your visit to Austerby. I'm sorry for that, Sylvester, and think the better of you for having sent her to me, when I don't doubt you were feeling vexed with me. Mind, if I'd known she'd met you already, and not fancied you, I would never have done it! However, there's no harm done, and no need to think of it again. *She* won't, and you may depend on it I shan't either. Now that I know her better I see you wouldn't suit at all. I shouldn't wonder at it if she's going to prove as hard to please as her mother was."

He was spared having to answer this speech by Phoebe's coming back into the room. He rose to take his leave, and, as he shook hands with Phoebe, said: "I hope we may meet again soon. You will be attending all the balls, I expect. I hardly dare ask you—if I really did cut you at Almack's!—if you will stand up with me?"

"Yes, of course," she responded. "It wouldn't be very civil in me to refuse, would it?"

"I might have known it!" he exclaimed. "How *could* I be such a flat as to offer you the chance to give me one of your set-downs?"

"I didn't!" she protested.

"Then heaven help me when you do!" he said. "Goodbye! Don't grow *too* civil, will you? But I need not ask that: you won't!"

15

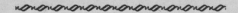

Before Phoebe saw Sylvester again she had encountered another member of his family: accompanying her grandmother on a morning visit she met Lady Henry Rayne.

Several ladies had elected to call on old Mrs. Stour that day, but the younger generation was represented only by Lady Henry and Miss Marlow. Lady Henry, brought by her mama, was so heartily bored that even the entrance of an unknown girl came to her as an alleviation. She seiz~d the first opportunity that offered of changing her seat for one beside Phoebe's, saying, with her pretty smile: "I think we have met before, haven't we? Only I am so stupid at remembering names!"

"Well, not precisely," replied Phoebe, with her usual candour. "I never saw you but twice in my life, and I wasn't introduced to you. Once was at the Opera House, but the first occasion was at Lady Jersey's ball last year. I am afraid it was the circumstance of my staring at you so rudely which makes you think we have met! But you looked so beautiful I couldn't drag my eyes away! I beg your pardon! you must think me very impertinent!"

Not unnaturally Ianthe found nothing impertinent in this speech. Her own words had been a mere conversational gambit;

she had no recollection of having seen Phoebe before, but she said: "Indeed I didn't! I am sorry we were never introduced until today. I am not often in London." She added, with a wistful smile: "I am a widow, you know."

"Oh——!" Phoebe was genuinely shocked. It seemed incredible, for she had supposed Ianthe to be little older than herself.

"I was hardly more than a child when I was married," explained Ianthe. "I am not so very old now, though I have been a widow for several years!"

"I thought you were my own age!" said Phoebe frankly.

No more was needed to seal the friendship. Ianthe, laughing at this misapprehension, disclosed that her only child was six years of age; Phoebe exclaimed: "Oh, no! impossible!" and stepped, all unknown to herself, into the rôle of Chief Confidante. She learned within the space of twenty minutes that the life of a recluse had been imposed on Ianthe by her husband's family, who expected her to wear out the rest of her widowhood in bucolic seclusion.

"I wonder you should yield to such barbarous notions!" said Phoebe, quite appalled.

"Alas, there is *one* person who holds a weapon I am powerless to withstand!" said Ianthe in a melancholy tone. "He is the sole arbiter of my poor child's destiny. Things were so left that I found myself bereft at one stroke of both husband and son!" She perceived a startled look on Phoebe's face, and added: "Edmund was not left to my guardianship. I must not say more, and should not have said as much, only that I knew, as soon as we met, that you would understand! I am persuaded I can trust you! You cannot conceive the relief of being able to speak openly: in general I am obliged to be reserved. But I mustn't talk any more about my troubles!"

She was certainly unable to do so, for at that moment her attention was drawn to Lady Elvaston, who had risen to take leave of her hostess. She too got up, and put out her hand to Phoebe, saying in her soft voice: "I see Mama is ready to go, and so I must say goodbye. Do you make a long stay in town? It would be so agreeable to meet again! Perhaps you would give me the pleasure of coming to see me one day? I should like you to see my little boy."

"Oh, is he with you?" exclaimed Phoebe, a good deal surprised. "I had collected—I mean, I should like very much to visit you, ma'am!"

"My bringing him to town was not at all approved of, I can assure you," responded Ianthe plaintively. "But even his guardian can scarcely forbid me to take him to stay with my parents! Mama quite dotes on him, and would have been so grieved if I hadn't brought him with me!"

She pressed Phoebe's hand, and floated away, leaving Phoebe a prey to doubt and curiosity.

From the outset Phoebe had been fascinated by her beauty; within a minute of making her acquaintance she had been captivated by her appealing manners, and the charm of a smile that hinted at troubles bravely borne. But Phoebe was a shrewd observer; she was also possessed of strong commonsense; and while the romantic side of her nature responded to the air of tragic mystery which clung about Ianthe the matter-of-fact streak which ran through it relentlessly pointed out to her certain anomalies in what had been disclosed, and compelled her to acknowledge that confidences uttered upon so short an acquaintance were not, perhaps, to be wholly credited.

She was anxious to discover Ianthe's identity. She now knew her to be a member of the Rayne family, but the family was a large one, and in what degree of relationship to Sylvester Ianthe stood she had no idea. Her grandmother would no doubt be able to enlighten her.

Lady Ingham was well able to enlighten her. "Ianthe Rayne?" she said, as they drove away from Mrs. Stour's house. "A pretty creature, isn't she? Gooseish, of course, but one can't but pity her. She's Elvaston's daughter, and married poor Harry Rayne the year she was brought out. He died before their son was out of short coats. A dreadful business! I fancy they never discovered what ailed him: you would have said there was not a healthier young man alive! Something internal: that's all I ever heard. Ah, if they had but called in dear Sir Henry Halford!"

"I knew she had been married to a member of that family, ma'am, but—who *was* her husband?"

"Who was he?" repeated the Dowager. "Why, Sylvester's younger brother, to be sure! His twin-brother, too, which made it worse."

"Then the child—Lady Henry's little boy——?" Phoebe faltered.

"Oh, there's nothing amiss with him that ever I heard!" replied the Dowager, leaning forward to obtain a clearer view of a milliner's shop-window as she spoke. "My love, I wonder if that chip-straw—no, those pink flowers wouldn't become you! What were you saying? Oh, Harry's son! A splendid little fellow, I'm told. I've never seen him myself: he lives at Chance."

"And he is—I understood Lady Henry to say—the Duke's ward?"

"Yes, and his heir as well—not that that is likely to signify! Was Ianthe complaining to you about that business?" She glanced at Phoebe, and said bluntly: "You would be ill-advised to refine too much on what she may have said to you, my love. The truth is that she and Sylvester can never deal together. *She* fell into a pelter as soon as she found how things were left— well, I must own I think she should have been joined with Sylvester in the guardianship!—and *he* don't take the trouble to handle her tactfully."

"I can readily believe that!" Phoebe interjected. "Is he fond of the little boy, ma'am?"

"I daresay he may be, for Harry's sake—though they say the boy is the image of his mother—but the fact is, my dear, young men don't commonly dote on nursery brats! He will certainly do his duty by the boy."

"Mama did her duty by me," said Phoebe. "I think I understand what Lady Henry's feelings must be."

"Fiddle!" said the Dowager. "I don't scruple to tell you, my love—for you are bound to hear it—that they are at odds *now* because the little ninny has got a second marriage in her eye, and knows Sylvester won't let her take the boy away from Chance."

"Oh!" Phoebe exclaimed, her eyes flashing. "How could he be so inhuman? Does he expect her to remain a widow all her life? Ah, I suppose it should be enough for her to have been married to a Rayne! I don't believe there was ever anyone more arrogant!"

"Before you put yourself in a taking," said the Dowager dryly, "let me tell you that if it is arrogance which prompts Sylvester to say he won't have his heir brought up by Nugent Fotherby it is a fortunate circumstance for the boy that he *is* arrogant!"

"Nugent Fotherby?" gasped Phoebe, her righteous wrath

suddenly and ludicrously arrested. "Grandmama, you can't mean it? That absurd creature who can't turn his head because his shirt points are too high, and who let Papa chouse him out of three hundred guineas for a showy chestnut anyone but a flat must have seen was short of bone?"

Somewhat taken aback, the Dowager said: "I don't know anything about horses. And as for your father, if he persuaded Fotherby to buy one that was unsound I call it very shabby dealing!"

"Oh, *no*, ma'am!" Phoebe said earnestly. "I assure you there is nothing wrong in *that!* If a man who can't tell when a horse isn't fit to go chooses to set up as a knowing one he must expect to be burnt!"

"Indeed!" said the Dowager.

Phoebe was silent for a minute or two; but presently she said thoughtfully: "Well, ma'am, I don't think one can precisely blame Salford for not wishing to let his nephew grow up under such a man!"

"I should think not indeed! What's more, I fancy that on that head Sylvester and Elvaston are at one. Of course Elvaston don't like the match, but I daresay he'll swallow it."

"Well, Papa wouldn't't!" said Phoebe frankly. "In fact, he told me once that if ever I took it into my head to marry a bleater who, besides being a man-milliner and a cawker who don't know a blood-horse from a commoner, encourages every barnacle on the town to hang on him, he would wash his hands of me!"

"And if that is the language he sees fit to teach you, the sooner he does so the better!" said her ladyship tartly.

Much abashed, Phoebe begged her pardon; and continued to meditate in silence for the rest of the drive.

Her thoughts were not happy, but it was not Lady Henry's lapse of taste which cast a damper over her spirits. It was the existence of Lady Henry's fatherless child.

Dismay had been her first reaction to the evil tidings; it was succeeded by a strong conviction that Fate and Sylvester between them had contrived the whole miserable business for no other purpose than to undo her. She had long known Fate for her enemy, and Fate was clearly responsible for Coincidence. As for Sylvester, however much it might seem to the casual observer that he was hardly to be blamed for possessing a nephew who was also his ward, anyone with the smallest knowledge of his character must recognize at a glance that it was conduct entirely typical of him. And if he had not wished to figure as the villain in a romance he should not have had satanic eyebrows—or, at any rate, amended the ill-used authoress, he should have exerted himself to be more agreeable to her at Lady Sefton's ball, instead of uttering formal civilities, and looking at her with eyes so coldly indifferent that they seemed scarcely to see her. It would never then have occurred to her to think him satanic, for when he smiled he did not look in the least satanic. Far otherwise, in fact, she decided, realizing with faint surprise that although he had frequently enraged her during their sojourn at the Blue Boar she had never, from his first entering that hostelry, perceived anything villainous in his aspect.

This reflection led her to recall how much she stood in his debt, which resulted in a fit of dejection hard to shake off. Only one alleviating circumstance presented itself to her: he need never know who had written *The Lost Heir*. But that was a very small grain of comfort, since his ignorance would not make her feel less treacherous.

It was probable that if they had not chanced to meet again only two days later nothing further would have come of Ianthe's desire to know Phoebe better; but Fate once more took a hand in Phoebe's affairs. Sent out under the escort of Muker to execute some commissions for her grandmother in Bond Street, she came abreast of a barouche, drawn up beside the flagway, just as Ianthe, a picture of lovely maternity, was helping her child to climb into it. When she saw Phoebe she exclaimed, and at once shook hands. "How charming this is! Are you bent on any very important errand? Do come home with me! Mama has driven out to Wimbledon to visit one of my sisters, so we shall be quite alone, and can enjoy such a comfortable chat!" She hardly waited for Phoebe to accept the invitation, but nodded to Muker, saying that Miss Marlow should be sent home in the carriage later in the day, and made Phoebe get into the carriage, calling on Master Rayne to say how do you do politely.

Master Rayne pulled off his tasselled cap, exposing his sunny curls to the breeze. His resemblance to his mother was pronounced. His complexion was as delicately fair, his eyes as large and as deeply blue, and his locks as silken as hers; but a sturdy frame and a look of determination about his mouth and chin saved him from appearing girlish. Having subjected Phoebe to a dispassionate scrutiny he decided to make her the recipient of an interesting confidence. "I am wearing gloves," he said.

"So you are! Very smart ones too!" she replied admiringly.

"If I was at home," said Master Rayne, with a darkling glance at his parent, "I wouldn't have to wear them."

"Now, Edmund——!"

"But I expect you are enjoying your visit to London, are you not?" asked Phoebe, diplomatically changing the subject.

"Indeed he is!" said Ianthe. "Only fancy! his grandpapa promises to take him riding in the Park one morning, doesn't he, my love?"

"If I'm good," said Edmund, with unmistakable pessimism. "But I won't have my tooth pulled out again!"

Ianthe sighed. "Edmund, you know Mama said you should not go to Mr. Tilton this time!"

"You said I shouldn't go when we came to London afore," he reminded her inexorably. "But Uncle Vester said I should. And I did. I do not like to have my tooth pulled out, *even* if I am let keep it in a little box, and people do *not* throw it away," said Edmund bitterly.

"No one does," intervened Phoebe. "I expect, however, that you were very brave."

"Yes," acknowledged Edmund. "Acos Uncle Vester said he would make me sorry if I wasn't, and I don't like Uncle Vester's way of making people sorry. It hurts!"

"You see!" said Ianthe in a low voice, and with a speaking look at Phoebe.

"Keighley said I was brave when I fell off my pony," disclosed Edmund. "Not one squeak out o' me! Full o' proper spunk I was!"

"*Edmund*!" exclaimed Ianthe agrily. "If I have told you once I won't have you repeating the vulgar things Keighley says to you I have told you a hundred times! Beg Miss Marlow's pardon this instant! I don't know what she must think of you!"

"Oh, no, pray do not bid him do so!" begged Phoebe, perceiving the mulish set to Master Rayne's jaw.

"Keighley," stated Edmund, the light of battle in his eye, "is a prime gun! He is my *partickler* friend."

"I don't wonder at it," returned Phoebe, before Ianthe could pick up this gage. "I am a little acquainted with him myself, you know, and I am sure he is a splendid person. Did he teach you to ride your pony? I wish you will tell me about your pony!"

Nothing loth, Edmund embarked on a catalogue of this animal's points. By the time Lord Elvaston's house in Albemarle Street was reached an excellent understanding flourished between him and Miss Marlow, and it was with considerable reluctance that he parted from her. But his mother had had enough of his company, and she sent him away to the nursery, explaining to Phoebe that if she allowed him to remain with her once he would expect to do so always, which would vex Lady Elvaston. "Mama doesn't like him to play in the drawing-room, except for half an hour before he is put to bed."

"I thought you said that she doted on him!" said Phoebe, forgetting to check her unruly tongue.

"Oh, yes! Only she thinks that it isn't good for him to be put forward too much!" said Ianthe, with commendable aplomb. "Now I am going to take you upstairs to my bed-chamber, so that you may put off your hat and pelisse, for I don't mean to let you run away in a hurry, I can tell you!"

It was indeed several hours later when the carriage was sent for to convey Phoebe to Green Street; and she was by that time pretty fully informed of all the circumstances of Ianthe's marriage, widowhood, and proposed remarriage. Before they had risen from the table upon which a light nuncheon had been spread she knew that Sylvester had never wanted to be saddled with his brother's child; and she had been regaled with a number of stories illustrative of his harsh treatment of Edmund, and the malice which prompted him to encourage Edmund to defy his mother's authority. Count Ugolino was scarcely more repulsive than the callous individual depicted by Ianthe. Had he not been attached to his twin-brother? Oh, well, yes, in his cold way, perhaps! But never would dearest Harry's widow forget his unfeeling conduct when Harry, after days of dreadful suffering, had breathed his last. "Held up in his arms, too! You would have supposed him to be made of marble, my dear Miss Marlow! Not a tear, not a word to *me!* You may imagine how wholly I was overset, too—almost out of my senses! Indeed, when I saw Sylvester lay my beloved husband down, and heard his voice saying that he was dead—in the most *brutal* way!—I was cast into such an agony of grief that the doctors were alarmed for my reason. I was in hysterics for three days, but he cared nothing for that, of course. I daresay he never even knew it, for he walked straight out of the room without one look towards me, and I didn't set eyes on him again for weeks!"

"Some people, I believe," Phoebe said, rendered acutely uncomfortable by these reminiscences, "cannot bring themselves to permit others to enter into their deepest feelings. It would not be right—excuse me!—to suppose that they have none."

"Oh, no! But reserve is repugnant to me!" said Ianthe, rather unnecessarily. "Not that I believe Sylvester to have feelings of that nature, for I am sure I never knew anyone with less sensibility. The only person he holds in affection is his mama. I own him to be quite devoted to *her—absurdly* so, in my opinion!"

"But you are fond of the Dutchess, I collect?" Phoebe asked, in the hope of giving Ianthe's thoughts a happier direction. "She is kind to you?"

"Oh, yes, but even she does not perfectly understand the misery of my situation! And I dare not hope that she will even try to prevail upon Sylvester not to tear my child from my arms, because she quite idolizes him. I pity his wife! She will find herself expected to defer in everything to Mama-Duchess!"

"Well, perhaps he won't have a wife," suggested Phoebe soothingly.

"You may depend upon it he will, just to keep poor little Edmund out of the succession. Mama is persuaded that he is hanging out for one, and may throw the handkerchief at any moment."

"I daresay! It takes two to make a marriage, however!"

"Do you mean he might meet with a *refusal*?"

"Why not?" said Phoebe.

"*Sylvester?* With all that he has to offer? Of course he won't! I wish he might, for it would do him good to be rebuffed. Only ten to one if it did happen he would set to work to make the girl fall in love with him, and then offer for another!"

"I see no reason for anyone to fall in love with him," declared Phoebe, a spark in her eye.

"No, nor do I, but you would be astonished if you knew how many girls have positively *languished* over him!"

"I should!" said Phoebe fervently. "For my part I should suppose them rather to have fallen in love with his rank!"

"Yes, but it isn't so. He can make girls form a tendre for him even when they have started by not liking him in the least. He knows it, too. He bet Harry once that he would succeed in attaching Miss Wharfe, and he *did*!"

"*Bet*——?" gasped Phoebe. "How—how infamous! How could any gentleman do such a thing?"

"Oh, well, you know what they are!" said Ianthe erroneously. "I must own, too, that Miss Wharfe's coldness was one of the ondits that year: she was a very handsome girl, and a great heiress as well, so of course she had *dozens* of suitors. She snubbed them all, so that it got to be a famous jest. They used to call her the Impregnable Citadel. Harry told Sylvester—funning, you know: they were always funning!—that even he would not be able to make a breach in the walls, and Sylvester instantly asked him what odds he was offering against it. I believe they were betting heavily on it in the clubs, as soon as it was seen that Sylvester was *laying siege* to the Citadel. Men are so odious!"

With this pronouncement Phoebe was in full agreement. She left Albemarle Street, amply provided with food for thought. She was shrewd enough to discount much that had been told her of Sylvester's treatment of his nephew: Master Rayne did not present to the world the portrait of an ill-used child. On the other hand, his mama had unconsciously painted herself in unflattering colours, and emerged from her various stories as a singularly foolish parent. Probably, Phoebe decided, Sylvester was indifferent to Edmund, but determined, in his proud way, to do his duty by the boy. That word had no very pleasant connotation to one who had had it ceaselessly dinned in her ears by an unloving stepmother, but it did not include injustice. Lady Marlow had always been rigidly just.

It was Ianthe's last disclosure that gave Phoebe so furiously to think. She found nothing in it to discount, for the suspicion had already crossed her mind that Sylvester's kindness had been part of a deliberate attempt to make her sorry she had so rudely repulsed him. His manners, too, when he had called in Green Street, even the lurking smile in his eyes when he had looked at her, were calculated to please. Yes, Phoebe admitted, he *did* know how to fix his interest with unwary females. The question was whether to repulse him, or whether, safe in the knowledge that he was laying a trap for her, to encourage his attentions.

169

The question remained unanswered until the following day, when she met him again. She was riding with her Ingham cousins in the Park in a sedate party composed of herself, Miss Mary and Miss Amabel, young Mr. Dudley Ingham, and two grooms following at a discreet distance; and she was heartily bored. The Misses Ingham were very plain, and very good, and very dull; and their brother, Lord Ingham's promising second son, was already bidding fair to become a solid member of some future government; and the hack provided for her use was an animal with no paces and a placid disposition.

Sylvester, himself mounted on a neatish bay, and accompanied by two of his friends, took in the situation in one amused glance, and dealt with it in a way that showed considerable dexterity and an utter want of consideration for Lord Yarrow and Mr. Ashford. Without anyone's knowing (except himself) how it had come about, the two parties had become one; and while his hapless friends found themselves making polite conversation to the Misses Ingham, Sylvester was riding with Phoebe, a little way behind.

"Oh, my poor Sparrow!" he said, mocking her. "Never have I encountered so heartrending a sight! A job-horse?"

"No," replied Phoebe. "My cousin Anne's *favourite* mount. A very safe, comfortable ride for a lady, Duke."

"I *beg* your pardon! I have not seen him show his paces, of course."

She cast him a glance of lofty scorn. "He has none. He has a very elegant shuffle, being just a trifle tied in below the knee."

"But such shoulders!"

Gravity deserted her; she burst into laughter, which made Miss Mary Ingham turn her head to look at her in wondering reproof, and said: "Oh, dear, did you ever set eyes on such a flat-sided screw?"

"No—or on a lady with a better seat. The combination is quite shocking! Will you let me mount you while you are in town?"

She was so much astonished she could only stare at him. He smiled, and said: "I keep several horses at Chance for my sister-in-law's convenience. She was used to ride a great deal. There would be nothing easier than for me to send for a couple to be brought up to London."

"Ride Lady Henry's horses?" she exclaimed. "You must be mad! I shouldn't dream of doing such a thing!"

"They are not her horses. They are mine."

"You said yourself you kept them for her use: she must consider them as good as her own! Besides, you must know I couldn't permit you to mount me!"

"I suppose you couldn't," he admitted. "I hate to see you so unworthily mounted, though."

"Thank you—you are very good!" she stammered.

"I am *what?* Sparrow, I do implore you not to let Lady Ingham teach you to utter civil whiskers! You know I am no such thing, but, on the contrary, the villain whose evil designs drove you from home!" He stopped, as her eyes flew involuntarily to meet his. The look held for no more than an instant, but the expression in her eyes drove the laughter from his own. He waited for a moment, and then asked quietly: "What is it? What did I say to make you look at me like that?"

Scarlet-cheeked, she said: "Nothing! I don't know how I looked."

"Very much as I saw you look once at your mother-in-law: stricken!"

She managed to laugh. "How absurd! I am afraid you have too lively an imagination, Duke!"

"Well, I *hope* I may have," he returned.

"There can be no doubt. I was—oh, shocked to think that after all that has passed you could suppose me to regard you in the light—in the light of a villain. But you were only funning, of course."

"I was, but I'm not funning when I tell you that I was not *maliciously* funning—to distress you."

She turned her head to look at him again, this time in candid appraisal. "No. Although it is a thing you *could* do, I fancy."

"You may believe that I did not."

"And *you* may believe I don't think you villainous!"

"Oh, that is a much harder task!" he protested, rallying her. "When I think of the reception I was accorded at that appalling inn I have the gravest misgivings!"

She laughed, but tacitly refused the challenge. He did not pursue the subject; and after riding beside him in silence for a few minutes she introduced another, saying: "I had almost forgotten to tell you that I had the pleasure of meeting your nephew yesterday, Duke! You must be very proud of him: he is a most beautiful child!"

"He is a very spoilt one. Are you acquainted with my sister-in-law?"

"I made her acquaintance a few days ago, and she was so kind as to invite me to spend the afternoon with her yesterday."

"Ah, *now* I understand the meaning of that stricken look!" he remarked. "Did I figure as the Unfeeling Brother-in-law, or as the Wicked Uncle?"

She was not obliged to answer him, for as the words left his tongue his attention was diverted. A lady who was walking beside the carriage-way just then waved to him. He recognized his cousin, Mrs. Newbury, and at once desired Phoebe to rein in. "If you are not already known to one another I should like to introduce you to Mrs. Newbury, Miss Marlow. She is quite the most entertaining of my cousins: I am persuaded you would deal extremely!—Georgie, what a stunning sight! How comes it about that you are walking in this demure style? No faithful husband to ride with you? Not *one* cicisbeo left to you?"

She laughed, stretching up her hand to clasp his. "No, isn't it infamous? Lion has a spell of duty, and *all* my cicisbeos have failed me! Those who are not still buried in the country have their feet in mustard-baths, so that I've sunk to walking with a mere female. No, you can't see her, because we have parted company."

He had leaned down to take her hand, and now, just before he released it, he pressed it meaningly, saying: "Sunk indeed! Are you acquainted with Miss Marlow, or may I introduce her to you?"

"So that is who you are!" she said, smiling up at Phoebe. "To be sure, I should have guessed it, for I have just been exchanging bows with your cousins. You are Lady Ingham's granddaughter, and—you are riding Anne Ingham's deplorable slug! But you should not be: it is quite shocking! Even under that handicap you take the shine out of us all."

"I have been trying to persuade her to let me have the privilege of mounting her, but she insists it will not do," Sylvester said. "I have now a better notion, however. I fancy your *second* hack would be just the thing for her."

Mrs. Newbury owned only one hack, but she had been on the alert from the moment of having her hand significantly squeezed, and she took this without a blink, interrupting

Phoebe's embarrassed protests to say warmly: "Oh, don't say you won't, Miss Marlow! You can't think how much obliged to you I shall be if you will but ride with me sometimes! I detest walking, but to ride alone, with only one's groom following primly behind, is intolerable! I am pining for a good gallop, too, and that can't be had in Hyde Park. Sylvester, if I can prevail upon Miss Marlow to go, will you escort the pair of us to Richmond Park upon the first real spring day?"

"But with the greatest pleasure, my dear cousin!" he responded.

"Do say you would like it!" Mrs. Newbury begged Phoebe.

"I should like it of all things, ma'am, but it is quite dreadful that you should be obliged to invite me!"

"But I promise you I'm not! Sylvester knew I should be charmed to have a companion—and, you know, I could have said my other horse was lame, or sold, if I had wished to! I shall come to pay Lady Ingham a morning-visit, and coax her into giving her consent."

She stepped back then, and as they parted from her cast a quizzing look up at Sylvester. He met it with a smile, so she concluded that he was pleased, and went on her way, wondering whether he was indulging a fit of gallantry, or if it was possible that he was really trying to fix his interest with Miss Marlow. It seemed unlikely, but no more unlikely than his having singled her out for his latest flirt. Or was he merely being kind to Lady Ingham's countrified little granddaughter? Oh, no! not Sylvester! decided Mrs. Newbury. He could be kind, but only where he liked. Well, it was all very intriguing, and for her part she was perfectly ready to lend him whatever aid he wanted. One did not look gifthorses in the mouth, certainly not a gift-horse of Sylvester's providing.

CHAPTER

16

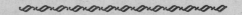

The encounter in the Park decided the matter: Sylvester was not to be immediately rebuffed. He had certainly made it almost impossible for Phoebe to do so, but this was a consideration that only occurred to her after she had made her decision. Without standing the smallest danger of losing her heart to him, she found his company agreeable, and would be sorry to lose it. If he was trying to serve her as he had served the unknown Miss Wharfe there could be no better way of discomfiting him than by receiving his advances in a spirit of cool friendliness. This was an excellent reason for tolerating Sylvester; within a very short time Phoebe had found another. With the return to London of so many members of the ton quite a number of invitations arrived in Green Street; and Phoebe, attending parties in some trepidation, rapidly discovered the advantages attached to her friendship with him. Very different was her second season from the first! Then she had possessed no acquaintance in town; she had endured agonies of shyness; and she had attracted no attention. Now, though the list of her acquaintances was not large, she attracted a great deal of attention, for she was Salford's latest flirt. People who had previously condemned Phoebe as a dowd with neither beauty nor style to recommend her now discovered that her countenance was expressive, her blunt utterances diverting, and her simplicity refreshing. Unusual: that was the epithet affixed to Miss Marlow. It emanated from Lady Ingham, but no one remembered that: a quiet girl with no pretension to beauty must be unusual to have captured Sylvester's fancy. There were many, of course, who could not imagine what he saw in her; she would never rival the accredited Toasts, or enjoy more than a moderate success. Happily she was satisfied merely to feel at home in society, to have made a few agreeable friends, and never to lack a partner at a ball. No lady whose hand was claimed twice in one evening by Sylvester need fear that fate. Nor did Sylvester stand in danger of being rebuffed while he continued to treat her with just the right degree of flattering attention. His motive might be perfidious, but it could not be denied that he was a delightful companion; and one, moreover, with whom it was not necessary to mind one's tongue. His sense of humour, too, was lively: often, if a fatuous remark were uttered, or someone behaved in a fashion so typical as to be ludicrous, Phoebe would look instinctively towards him, knowing that he must be sharing her amusement. It was strange how the dullest party could be enjoyed because there was one person present whose eyes could be met for the fraction of a second, in wordless appreciation of a joke unshared by others: almost as strange as the insipidity of parties at which that person was not present. Oh, no! Miss Marlow, though fully alive to his arrogance, his selfishness, and his detestable vanity had no intention—no *immediate* intention—of repulsing Sylvester.

Besides, he had provided for her use a little spiriting mare with a silken mouth, perfect in all her paces, and as full of playfulness as she could hold. Phoebe had cried out involuntarily when first she had seen the Firefly: how could Mrs. Newbury bear to let another ride her beautiful mare? Mrs. Newbury did not know how it was, but she preferred her dear old Jupiter. Phoebe understood at once: she herself owned a cover-hack long past his prime but still, and always, her favourite hack.

It was not long before she had discovered the truth about

the Firefly. Major Newbury, very smart in his scarlet regimentals, had seen his wife and her new friend off on their almost daily ride one day. He had come out on to the step leading up to the door of his narrow little house, and no sooner had he set eyes on the Firefly than he had exclaimed: "Is that the mare Sylvester gave you, Georgie? Well, by Jove——!"

Phoebe had been standing just far enough away to make it possible that she had not heard either this remark or the Major's subsequent, and conscience-stricken: "Eh? Oh——! Just so, my love! Forgot!" For a rather dreadful moment she had wondered what she ought to do; then she had made up her mind to pretend she had not heard, prompted as much by consideration for Georgiana as by reluctance to forgo her rides.

Sylvester had been right when he had prophesied that she and Georgiana would deal extremely: each took an instant liking to the other; and since the Dowager raised no objection Phoebe became a frequent guest in the Newburys' haphazard house. Lady Ingham said they were a ramshackle pair; Phoebe, who had hitherto attended only large, formal parties in London, thought them delightful, and enjoyed nothing so much as the evenings she spent in their very ill-run house. One never knew what might happen at one of Georgie's parties, said Lord Yarrow, declaring that he had once arrived five minutes after the crystal chandelier in the drawing-room had crashed to the floor, and had found Georgie standing like Dido amongst the ruins of Carthage, only rather more composed. Sylvester agreed that this had been a remarkably good party, but contended that by far the best evening he had yet spent in the establishment was that on which the new butler, having admitted him into the hall, had fallen flat on his face in a drunken stupor. Phoebe had never dreamed that people could be as gay and as unceremonious as they were in Georgie's house. Nor had she ever liked Sylvester as well as when she saw him there, amongst his intimates. It might be another instance of his pride that he should show his most agreeable side only to his relations and his closest friends, but it was impossible to deny that that side was endearing.

He was just as charming when the projected expedition to Richmond Park took place, and even more surprisingly, since the original party was augmented by three persons, one of whom was not very acceptable to him. He welcomed the news that Major Newbury was to join it; when his sister-in-law, hearing of the scheme, announced that she would come too, with her brother Charles, he bore it with equanimity; but when the day dawned, and it was discovered that Ianthe, instead of by her brother, was escorted by Sir Nugent Fotherby, even the Major, not famed for perspicacity, informed his wife, in a penetrating whisper, that he had a very good mind to tip the double, since he clearly saw that this expedition of pleasure was bitched at the outset.

For an anxious minute it did indeed seem that it was doomed to failure. It had been arranged that Ianthe and her brother would meet the rest of the party at the Roehampton Gate, having sent their horses on in charge of a groom: a last-minute alteration in plan which was only made known to Sylvester when he arrived at the Newburys' house to escort the party. He looked vexed when the message was repeated to him, and exclaimed: "Good God, Georgie, why didn't you tell Ianthe that if she didn't choose to go with us she might remain at home? She'll keep us waiting an hour, and very likely more!"

"I daresay she will, but it's of no use to fly into a pet with me," responded Georgiana calmly. "I received her note not twenty minutes ago, and all I could do was to send the footman back to her with a reminder that since you held the tickets of admission she must take care not to be late."

"Much good that will do!" he observed.

But when they reached the Roehampton Gate he was agreeably surprised to find his sister-in-law already there, and was beginning to feel quite in charity with her when he suddenly perceived that the sprig of fashion with her was not her brother but Sir Nugent Fotherby. He stiffened, the expression of easy good-humour on his face changing in a flash to one of haughty astonishment. Phoebe, obliged to repress a strong desire to tell him precisely what she thought of such odious self-consequence, could only be sorry for Sir Nugent.

Her pity was wasted. Sir Nugent knew that Sylvester did not like him, but it never crossed his mind that Sylvester, or anyone else, held him in contempt. If he could have been brought to believe it, he would have known that Sylvester was queer in his attic, and he would have been very much shocked. When Sylvester raised his quizzing-glass he was not at all unnerved, because it was plain that Sylvester was studying the exquisite folds of his neck-cloth. He was not surprised; he would have been disappointed if what had cost him so much time and skill to arrange had attracted no attention. It was not everyone who could tie an Oriental: he was pretty sure Sylvester couldn't; and if Sylvester were to ask him how it was done he would be obliged to tell him that it took years to learn the art, and often several hours of concentrated effort to achieve a respectable result when one had learnt it. Other men might envy Sir Nugent; they could not despise him, for his pedigree was impeccable, his fortune exceeded sixty thousand pounds a year, and he had it on the authority of those boon-companions whom Lord Marlow rudely stigmatized as barnacles that, just as in all matters of fashion he was the finest Pink of the Ton, in the world of sport he figured as a Nonpareil, a regular Top-of-the-Trees, a Sure Card, up to all kinds of slums, never to be beaten on any suit.

His imperviousness to insult saved the day's pleasure from wreck. He seized the earliest opportunity that offered of edging his showy chestnut alongside Sylvester's hack for the purpose of drawing his attention to the circumstance of his having, as he phrased it, brought Lady Henry bang up to the mark on time.

"You are to be congratulated," said Sylvester, in a discouraging tone.

"Devilish good of you to say so, Duke!" responded Sir Nugent, acknowledging the tribute with a slight bow. "Don't mind owning it wasn't easy. Took a devilish deal of address. If there *is* a thing I pride myself on it's that. 'Lady Henry,' I said—well, not to cut a wheedle with you, Duke, I put it a devilish sight stronger than that! 'My love,' I said, 'we shan't turn his grace up sweet if we keep him kicking his heels at the rendezvous. Take my word for it!' She did."

In spite of himself Sylvester's face relaxed. "She did?"

"She did," asseverated Sir Nugent gravely. "'My sweet life,' I said—you've no objection to that, Duke?"

"Not the least in the world."

"You haven't?" exclaimed Sir Nugent, slewing his body round to stare at Sylvester, an exertion which the stiff points of his collar and the height of that Oriental Tie made necessary.

"Why should I?"

"You've put your finger on the nub, Duke!" said Sir Nugent. "Why should you? *I* can't tell, and I believe I've cut my wisdoms. 'My love,' I said (if you've no objection) 'you've got a maggot in your Idea-pot.'"

"And what had she to say to that?" enquired Sylvester, conscious of a wish that Phoebe had not cantered ahead.

"She denied it," said Sir Nugent. "Said you were bent on throwing a rub in our way."

"Oh?"

"Just what I said myself! 'Oh!' I said."

"Not 'my love'?"

"Not then. Because I was surprised. You might say I was betwattled."

"Like a duck in a thunderstorm."

"No," said Sir Nugent, giving this his consideration. "I fancy, Duke, that if you were to ask all round the ton if Nugent Fotherby had ever looked like any species of fowl in such a situation the answer would be, in a word, No!"

"Well, I haven't the least desire to throw a rub in the way of your marriage to my sister-in-law. You may marry her with my good-will, but you will not prevail upon me to relinquish my nephew into your care."

"But that's another nub!" objected Sir Nugent. "You may say it's the primest nub of all! Her la'ship won't give him up!"

"A man of your address must surely be able to persuade her to do so."

"Well, that's what I thought myself," said Sir Nugent. "Queer creatures, females! Devilish attached to the infantry. Let us discuss the matter!"

"No. Let us do no such thing!" interrupted Sylvester. "Talking to me will pay no toll. I have only this to say: I have neither the power nor the desire to scotch your marriage to Ianthe, but there is no argument you can advance that will induce me to delegate the least part of my authority over Edmund to you or to anyone! Try if you can twist Ianthe round your thumb: don't waste your time on me!"

He spurred his horse forward as he spoke, and cantered on to overtake the rest of the party.

Phoebe, meanwhile, after enjoying an all too brief gallop, had been forced to pull up, and to continue at a walking-pace beside Ianthe, who wanted to talk about herself, and had found Georgiana an unresponsive audience. She disclosed that she had brought Sir Nugent in place of her brother because she was convinced that Sylvester's dislike of him arose from mere prejudice. He was barely acquainted with Sir Nugent: did not Phoebe think that if he were given this opportunity of getting to know him better he might well reconsider his cruel decision to part a mother from her child?

Phoebe found it impossible to answer this question, since a flat negative was clearly ineligible. Fortunately Ianthe was more interested in her own opinion than in Phoebe's, and had posed the question in a rhetorical spirit. Without waiting for an answer, she continued: "For my part, I am persuaded that Sylvester must be agreeably surprised in him. I don't mean to say that his understanding is superior, for it is not—in fact, he has a great deal less than commonsense, and is sometimes quite addle-brained—but if I don't care for that I'm sure I don't know why Sylvester should! His disposition is amiable, and his manners excessively polished and civil. He is a man of rank, and of the first stare of fashion; and if he does associate with inferior persons, and fritter a fortune away in gaming-hells, *that* will cease when he is married. And as for his race-horses, he is so wealthy that losses on the Turf can't signify. In any event, it is nonsensical to suppose that it would do Edmund the least harm. Besides, even Sylvester must own that there can be no one better able to teach Edmund just how he should go on in all matters of taste and ton! He is always in the high kick of fashion, and makes the other men appear positively *shabby*! You have only to look at him!"

Phoebe looked instead at her, and in wonder. Beside Sylvester's quiet elegance and Major Newbury's military cut she had been thinking that Sir Nugent presented all the appearance of a coxcomb. He was a tall man, rather willowy in build, by no means unhandsome, but so tightly laced-in at the waist, so exaggeratedly padded at the shoulders, that he looked a little ridiculous. From the striking hat set rakishly on his Corinthian crop (he had already divulged that it was the New Dash, and the latest hit of fashion) to his gleaming boots, everything he wore seemed to have been chosen for the purpose of making him conspicuous. His extravagantly cut coat was embellished with very large and bright buttons; a glimpse of exotic colour hinted at a splendid waistcoat beneath it; his breeches were of white corduroy; a diamond pin was stuck in the folds of his preposterous neckcloth; and he wore so many rings on his fingers, and so many fobs and seals dangling at his waist, that he might have been taken for a jeweller advertizing his wares.

Phoebe was not obliged to make any comment on Ianthe's last observation, for Sylvester overtook them just then, and a minute later Sir Nugent ranged alongside, trying to convey to Ianthe by a series of shrugs and grimaces, which nearly overset Phoebe's gravity, that his mission had not prospered. She stole an apprehensive glance at Sylvester, fearing that Sir Nugent had put him out of temper, and was relieved to see no trace of the cold look of indifference she so much disliked. He looked rather amused, and when he addressed Sir Nugent it was in a light, good-humoured tone. Encouraged by this, Sir Nugent, who had been looking dejected, brightened, and asked him for his opinion of the horse he was riding. He won so courteous a reply that Phoebe took her underlip firmly between her teeth, and stared resolutely ahead. Sir Nugent, gratified by Sylvester's praise, drew his attention to the chestnut's manifold excellences, and confided that he had bought the animal at a devilish long price. A stifled sound from Phoebe, who knew just how long a price he had paid, made Sylvester's lips quiver, but he said, without a tremor: "Did you indeed?"

It might have been thought odd conduct in a sporting man to use his hunters for hacking at the end of the hunting season, but this idiosyncrasy was not as inhumane as it seemed to the uninitiated. Sir Nugent was a member of several hunts, and he owned an astonishing number of horses, which he stabled all over the country, and seldom rode. When he did turn out it was rarely that he went beyond the first few fields, for, like Mr. Brummell when he had led the ton, he wore white tops to his boots, and feared to get them splashed. Lord Marlow's showy chestnut certainly looked to be more in need of exercise than of rest, and succeeded, by sidlings, plungings, and head-tossing, in giving Sir Nugent an uncomfortable ride.

As soon as he could contrive to do it without the appearance of incivility, Sylvester suggested to Phoebe that they should shake the fidgets out of the horses. She agreed to it in a strangled voice; the Firefly broke into a canter, lengthened her stride to a gallop; and in a few moments carried Phoebe far beyond earshot of Ianthe and Sir Nugent. Beside her thundered Sylvester's black, but neither she nor Sylvester spoke until they presently reined in at the end of the stretch of greensward. Then, as Phoebe bent forward to pat the Firefly's neck, Sylvester said in a voice of mock censure: "Miss Marlow, I had occasion once to reprove you for laughing at rustics! *Now* I find you laughing at the very finest Pink that blooms in the Ton! You are incorrigible!"

"Oh, I didn't!" she protested, gurgling irrepressibly. "You know I didn't!"

"Do I, indeed? I promise you I was in the liveliest dread that you would start at any moment to giggle. If you had seen your own face——!"

"Well, I own it was a very close-run thing with me," she admitted. "How you were able to answer him so gravely I can't imagine!"

"Oh, he has been on the town for as long as I have, so that I have grown inured to him! I can understand, of course, that the first sight of his magnificence must come as a severe shock."

She laughed. "Yes, but I can't plead that excuse. I was for ever seeing him last year. In fact, I——"

"In fact you——?" he prompted, after waiting for a moment for her to finish the sentence.

She had broken off in confusion, the words: *I put him into my book* only just bitten back in time. She said now, with a tiny gasp: "Grew so accustomed to him that I began not to notice him! Except when he came to a ball in a green velvet coat, and a waistcoat embroidered all over with pink roses!"

He did not immediately reply, and glancing a little nervously at him she saw that the flying line of his brows was accentuated by a slight frown which drew down their inner corners. He looked steadily at her, and said: "Yes? But that isn't what you were going to say, is it?"

She hoped her countenance did not betray her, and said, with a fair assumption of ease: "No, but I daresay I ought not to tell you what *that* was. You won't repeat it? It was not his appearance which nearly had me in whoops, but that peacocky chestnut of his, and the things he said of him! He bought him from Papa, and paid three hundred guineas for him! And thinks himself a *downy one*!

He burst out laughing, and she hoped the dangerous moment had passed. But although he laughed at Marlow's successful essay in flat-catching, he said: "I am still wondering what it was that you really meant to say, Sparrow."

She was thankful to see Major and Mrs. Newbury cantering

towards them. There was time only to return a light rejoinder before Georgie called out to them, with news of a charming glade to be visited. They waited for Ianthe and Sir Nugent to come up with them, and there was no further opportunity for private talk.

The incident cast a cloud over Phoebe's pleasure. She could not be comfortable. To uneasiness was added a strong sense of guilt, which was not rendered less by the flattering distinction with which Sylvester was treating her. It was scarcely to be called gallantry, though he showed her wishes to be his first object; he quizzed rather than flirted; but there was a smiling look in his eyes when they met hers, and an informality in his manners that made her feel as if she had known him for a very long time. There had been a moment, before the Newburys had joined them, when she had hovered on the brink of telling him just what she had done. She had been strongly tempted, and the temptation recurred several times, only to be driven back by fear of what the consequences might be. When Sylvester looked at her with warmth in his eyes she felt that she could tell him anything, but she had seen him wear quite another expression; and she knew just how swiftly and with what perfect civility he could retire behind a film of ice.

She was still in a state of wretched indecision when she parted from him at the end of the day; but as she trod up the steps of Lady Ingham's house she thought suddenly that if anyone could advise her it must be her grandmother; and she determined, if her mood was propitious, to tell her the whole.

She found the Dowager in perfect good-humour, but a trifle preoccupied. She had received a visit from an old friend, just returned from a protracted sojourn in Paris, and Mrs. Irthing's account of the delightful time she had spent there, the charming nature of the parties given by dear Sir Charles Stuart and Lady Elizabeth at the Embassy—just as it was used to be before that horrid Bonaparte spoilt everything with his vulgar ways!—the exclusiveness of society—so different from London, where one was increasingly at the mercy of mushrooms and tuft-hunters!—the comfort of the hôtels, and the amazing quality and style of the goods in all the shops had reawakened her desire to remove to Paris for a few months herself. It was just the right time of year for such a visit; the Ambassador and his wife were old friends of hers; and Mrs. Irthing had been charged with messages for her from quite a number of French acquaintances whom she had not met for years but who all remembered her and wished that they might have the felicity of seeing her again. Well, she wished it too, and was much inclined to think it would do her a great deal of good to go abroad for a spell. She did not regret having assumed the charge of her granddaughter, of course, but it did just cross her mind that Phoebe might very well reside with Ingham and Rosina while she was away. A moment's reflection, however, caused her to abandon this scheme: Rosina was a fool, in no way to be trusted with the delicate task of promoting a marriage between Phoebe and Sylvester. The Dowager was feeling very hopeful about this affair, but there was no doubt that it needed skilful handling. Rosina would be bound to blunder; moreover, nothing was more likely to cause Sylvester to shy off than to find Phoebe always in company with her good, dull cousins. No, it would not do, the Dowager decided. It would not do to take Phoebe to Paris either: the Dowager was no believer in the power of absence over the heart, particularly when the heart in question belonged to Sylvester, who had so many girls on the catch for him.

The project had to be abandoned, but Mrs. Irthing's visit had roused many memories. The Dowager fell into a reminiscent vein, and it was not until she and Phoebe removed to the drawing-room after dinner that she emerged from it, and bade Phoebe tell her about her own day. Phoebe said that she had enjoyed herself very much, and then, drawing a resolute breath, took the plunge. "Grandmama, there is something I must tell you!"

She would not have been surprised if her confession of having commenced author had met with censure; but the Dowager, once assured that a strict anonymity had been preserved, was rather amused. She even said that she had always known Phoebe to be a clever little puss.

Possibly she considered it unlikely that her granddaughter's book would be read by any member of the ton; possibly she thought it even more unlikely that a portrait drawn by so inexperienced a hand would be recognizable. She only laughed when Phoebe told her the dreadful truth. But when Phoebe asked her if she thought Sylvester ought to be warned of what was hanging over his head she said quickly: "On no account in the world! Good God, you must be mad to think of such a thing!"

"Yes, ma'am. Only—I can't be comfortable!" Phoebe said.

"Nonsense! He will know nothing about it!" replied the Dowager.

CHAPTER

17

Unlike Lord Byron, Phoebe could not say that she awoke one morning to find herself famous, for clever Mr. Newsham had allowed no clue to her identity to escape him. He saw no profit in allowing it to be known that a schoolroom chit had written *The Lost Heir*: far better, he told his partner, to set the ton wondering. Poor Mr. Otley, protesting in vain that none but sapskulls would sport the blunt to the tune of eighteen shillings for a romance by an unknown author, resigned himself to ruin, and watched with a jaundiced eye the efforts of the senior partner to puff off the book to the ton.

But Mr. Newsham had been right all along. The skilful letters he had written to influential persons, the flattery he had expended, the mysterious hints he had dropped, bore abundant fruit. The list of private subscribers presently caused Mr. Otley's eyes to start in his head. "Ay! and that's only the beginning!" said Mr. Newsham. "These are the nobs who would melt a fortune not to be behindhand in the mode. All females, of course: *I* knew they wouldn't risk the chance that a *roman à clef* might not take! By the bye, I've discovered who that fellow with the eyebrows is: none other than his grace of Salford, my boy! If that ain't enough to make the nobs mad after the book, tell me what is!"

Since Mr. Newsham continued to correspond only with Miss Battery, Phoebe never knew that her book had been launched until she saw the three handsome volumes in Lady Sefton's drawingroom. "Dear Lady Ingham, has this audacious book come in your way? But I need not ask! Is it not the wickedest thing imaginable?" cried her ladyship, with much fluttering of her fan and her eyelids. "Odious creature, whoever she is!— and it is *not* Caro Lamb, or that Irish woman: that I know for a fact! Setting us all in the pillory! I forgive her only for her sketch of poor dear Emily Cowper! I own I laughed myself into stitches! She has not the least notion of it, of course— thinks it meant for the likeness of Mrs. Burrell! But Ugolino— oh, dear, dear, *what* must be his feelings if ever the book should come in his way? And that it must, you know, because everyone is talking about it!"

Too soon for her peace of mind did Phoebe prove the truth of this statement. Some, like the haughty Countess Lieven, shrugged it off, calling it an almond for a parrot; some delighted in it; some were shocked by it; but all were eager to discover its authorship. Never, thought Phoebe, could an author have watched the success of her first venture with more consternation! All her pride and pleasure in it were destroyed, and by one tiny thing that might so easily have been changed! Could she but have removed from the book every mention of a pair of eyebrows the rest would have been forgiven her, for only in that one portrait had she been blind to the virtues of her victims.

Lady Ingham, startled to find that the whole town (or as much of it as signified) was discussing her granddaughter's novel, demanded a copy of it from the reluctant author. Phoebe, who had received a set, forwarded to her by Miss Battery, shrinkingly presented her ladyship with the three elegant volumes.

The Dowager read it through, for some time anxiously watched by her trembling granddaughter, whose nerves suffered severely from the rapid transitions from hope to despair engendered by the Dowager's frequent utterances. A chuckle sent her spirits up; an ejaculated "Good God!" brought them down with a rush; and she was obliged many times to slip out of the room, unable to bear the suspense.

"Recognize himself?" said the Dowager, when she had come to the end. "Of course he will! Lord, child, how came you to commit such an imprudence? What a mercy that the whole thing is such a farrago of nonsense! I shouldn't wonder at it if Sylvester treats it as beneath his notice. We must hope he will, and at all events it need never be known that you wrote it. Who knows the truth besides your governess?—I collect she is to be trusted?"

"Indeed, she is, ma'am! The only other is Tom Orde."

The Dowager clicked her tongue. "I don't like that! Who's to say that a young rattle won't boast of being acquainted with the author when he finds you've become famous? You must write to him instantly, Phoebe, and warn him!"

Phoebe was hot in defence of her old playfellow, but it was not her championship that allayed the Dowager's alarm: it was the appearance on the scene of Tom himself, accompanied by his father, and managing to walk very creditably with the aid of a stick.

No sooner were the guests announced than Phoebe flew across the room to hug first one and then the other. The Squire, kissing her in a fatherly way, said: "Well, puss, and what have you to say for yourself, eh?" and nothing could have been more brotherly than Tom's greeting. "Hallo, Phoebe!" said Tom. "Take care what you're about, now! Don't you go rumpling my neckcloth, for the lord's sake! Well, by Jove!" (surveying her) "I'm dashed if you don't look quite modish! Won't Susan stare when I tell her!"

Nothing lover-like about Tom, decided the Dowager, turning her attention to the Squire.

It could not have been said that Lady Ingham and Mr. Orde had much in common, but her ladyship, welcoming the Squire kindly for Phoebe's sake, soon found him to be a blunt, sensible man, who seemed to feel just as he ought on a number of important subjects, notably the folly of Lord Marlow, and the pretentiousness, sanctimonious hypocrisy, and cruelty of his spouse. They soon had their heads together, leaving Tom and Phoebe to talk undisturbed in the window-bay.

Knowing his Phoebe, Tom had come in the expectation of being pelted with questions about everyone at Austerby and at the Manor, but except for a polite enquiry after Mrs. Orde's health, and an anxious one about Trusty and True, Phoebe asked him none. She was in regular communication with Miss

Battery, an excellent correspondent, had received several letters from Susan, and even one or two scribbled notes from Lord Marlow, his lordship's happy disposition having led him to believe, within a very short time, that if he had not actually connived at his daughter's flight to her grandmother, at least this adventure had had his approval. Phoebe was more interested to learn what had brought Tom to town, and for how long he meant to remain.

Well, the Squire had had business to transact, and it was so abominably slow at home, when one couldn't yet ride, or fish, or even walk very far, that there was no bearing it, so Tom had come to London with his father. They were putting up at Reddish's Hotel, and meant to stay for at least a se'ennight. The Squire had promised to take his son to visit one or two places he had long wanted to see. No, no, not *edifices!* He had seen them years ago! *Interesting* places, such as the Fives Court, and Jackson's Saloon, and Cribb's Parlour, and the Castle Tavern. Not in Phoebe's line, of course. And he was going to call on Salford.

"He told me to be sure and do so if ever I was in town, so I shall. He wouldn't have said it if he hadn't meant it, do you think?"

"Oh, no, but he has gone out of town," Phoebe replied. "I am not perfectly sure when he means to return, but I daresay it will be before you go away: he spoke of it as if he meant only to be gone a short while. He is at Chance, visiting his mother."

"Do you see him, then?" Tom asked, surprised.

"Yes, frequently," Phoebe answered, blushing faintly. "I have come to know one of his cousins, you see, and—and so we often meet. But, oh, Tom, the most terrible thing has happened, and if you do see Salford you must take the greatest care not to betray me! I *dread* his return, for how to look him in the face I don't know!"

"Betray you?" demanded Tom, astonished. "What the deuce are you talking about?"

"My wretched, wretched book!"

"Your—Oh, that! Well, what of it?"

"It is a success!" said Phoebe, in a voice of tragedy.

"Good God, you don't mean it? I wouldn't have believed it!" exclaimed Tom, adding still more infelicitously: "Though

189

I must say it has a devilish handsome binding: Sibby showed it to me, you know."

"It isn't the binding people are talking about!" said Phoebe, with asperity. "They are talking about the characters in it, and the author! Everyone wants to know who wrote it! *Now* do you understand?"

Tom did understand. He pursed his lips in a silent whistle, and after a minute said: "Has Salford read it?"

"No—at least—no, he can't have done so yet, surely! He went away almost immediately after it was published."

"I wonder if he'll guess?" said Tom slowly. "You needn't be afraid I shall let it out, but it wouldn't surprise me if—— You know what I should do if I were you?" She shook her head, her eyes fixed on his face. "I'd make a clean breast of it," said Tom.

"I did think of doing so, but when I remember what I wrote——" She broke off with a shudder.

"Devilish difficult thing to do," he agreed. "All the same——"

"I don't think I could," she confessed. "If he were to be angry——! It makes me sick only to imagine it! And my grandmother says on no account must I tell him."

"Well, I daresay she knows best," responded Tom somewhat dubiously. "What will you do if he charges you with it? Deny it?"

"Oh, don't, Tom!" begged Phoebe.

"Yes, but you'd best make up your mind," he insisted. "I shouldn't think, myself, that he'll believe you: you never could tell a bouncer without looking guilty!"

"If he asks me," said Phoebe despairingly, "I must tell the truth."

"Well, perhaps he won't ask you," said Tom, perceiving that she was looking rather sickly already. "But take care you don't mention it to anyone else, that's all! Ten to one you'll blurt it out to somebody! *I* know you!"

"Blurt it out! No, indeed!" she assured him.

She thought there could be little fear of it, but some severe trials had to be undergone, when she found herself obliged to endure in silence such discussions about her book as made her long to cry out: *No! I never meant it so!* For the one feature of *The Lost Heir* which aroused the curiosity of society was the character of Count Ugolino. The levelheaded might dismiss it as a piece of impertinence; Sylvester's friends might be up in arms; but it seemed to Phoebe that the idiots who asserted there was never smoke without a fire were legion. She was speedily made to realize that she had not been Ianthe's only confidante. Before ever *The Lost Heir* was written Ianthe had apparently blackened Sylvester's character to as many persons as would listen to her grievances. "Oh, the *circumstances* have been changed, of course!" some avid-eyed female would say. "I don't mean to say that Salford has done the same as Ugolino—well, he *couldn't*, nowadays! But as soon as I read the book I remembered how poor Lady Henry told me once..."

"*Could* it be true that Lady Henry's son is the real Duke of Salford?" breathed the credulous. "They were twins, were they not, Salford and Lord Henry?"

That lurid fancy had almost proved to be Phoebe's breaking-point. But for her grandmother's quelling eye she believed she must have spoken. It caught hers in the very nick of time, and she remained silent. That eye was absent when she heard the same lurid fancy on Ianthe's lips.

"Whoever it was who wrote the book," said Ianthe impressively, "knows a great deal about the Raynes! That much is certain! Everyone says it is a female: do *you* think so, Miss Marlow?"

"Yes—and a shockingly silly female!" said Phoebe. "It is the most absurd thing I ever read!"

"But it isn't!" insisted Ianthe. "Chance is not a castle, of course, and Sylvester couldn't possibly keep poor little Edmund *hidden*, and Edmund hasn't got a sister, but that's nothing! I have read the book twice now, and I believe there is a warning in it!"

"A warning?" echoed Phoebe blankly.

"To me," nodded Ianthe. "A warning that danger threatens my child. There can be no doubt that Matilda is meant to be me, after all."

These naïve words struck Phoebe dumb for several moments. It had not previously occurred to her that Ianthe might identify herself with *The Lost Heir*'s golden-haired sister. Having very little interest in mere heroes and heroines she had done no more than depict two staggeringly beautiful puppets, endow them with every known virtue, and cast them into a series of hair-raising adventures from which, she privately considered, it was extremely improbable they would ever have extricated themselves.

"Though Florian is not Fotherby, of course," added Ianthe, unconsciously answering the startled queston in Phoebe's mind. "I think he is just a made-up character. Poor Nugent wouldn't *do* for a hero. Besides, he is Baron Macaronio: everyone knows *that!*"

The unruffled complaisance in her face and voice provided Phoebe with the second shock of the day. This one was not of long duration, however, a bare minute's reflection sufficing to inform her that the grossest of libels could be pardoned in an author who painted Lady Henry herself in roseate hues.

"And Harry was Sylvester's twin-brother," pursued Ianthe.

"Count Ugolino's brother was not his twin!" Phoebe managed to say.

"No, but I daresay the author was afraid to make it all precisely the same. The thing is, Ugolino was a usurper."

"Lady Henry!" said Phoebe, speaking in a voice of careful control. "You cannot seriously suppose that Salford is a usurper!"

"No, except that there *have* been such things, and he was a twin, and I have often thought, when he has encouraged Edmund to do dangerous things, like riding his pony all over the park, all by himself, and climbing trees, that he would be positively glad if the poor little fellow were to fall and break his neck!"

"Oh, hush!" Phoebe exclaimed. "Pray, pray do not say so, Lady Henry! You are funning, I know, but indeed you should not!"

An obstinate look came into Ianthe's lovely face. "No, I am not. I don't say it *is* so, for I can't think Mama-Duchess would have changed the twins—for why should she? But Sylvester has never liked Edmund! He said himself he didn't want him, and although he pretended afterwards that he hadn't meant it I have always known it was the truth! Well, *why* does he hate Edmund?"

"Lady Henry, you must not indulge your fancy in this way!" Phoebe cried, quite appalled. "How can you suppose that a foolish romance bears the least relation to real life?"

"*The Lost Heir* is no more foolish than *Glenarvon,* and you can't say that bore no relation to real life!" countered Ianthe instantly.

Phoebe said: "I know—I have reason to know—that the author of the book was wholly ignorant of any of the circumstances attaching to Salford, or to any member of his family!"

"Nonsense! How can you know anything of the sort?"

Phoebe moistened her lips, and said in a shaking voice: "It so happens that I am acquainted with the author. I mustn't tell you, and you won't ask me, I am persuaded, or—or mention it!"

"Acquainted with the author?" Ianthe gasped. "Oh, *who* is she? You can't be so cruel as not to tell me! I won't breathe a *word*, dear Miss Marlow!"

"No, I must not. I should not have spoken at all, only that I felt myself obliged, when I found you had taken such a fantastic notion into your head! Lady Henry, my friend had never seen Salford but once in her life: knew nothing more of him than his name! She was struck by his strange eyebrows, and when she came to write that tale she remembered them, and thought she would give Ugolino brows like that, never dreaming that anyone would think——"

"But she must have known more!" objected Ianthe, staring rather hard at Phoebe. "She knew he was Edmund's guardian!"

"She did not. It was—she told me—nothing but the unhappiest of coincidences!"

"I don't believe it! It could not have been so!"

"But it was, it *was*!" Phoebe said vehemently. "I know it for a fact!"

There was a momentary silence. As she stared, a look of comprehension stole into Ianthe's eyes. "Miss Marlow! *You* are the author!"

"No!"

"You are! I know you are! Oh, you sly thing!" cried Ianthe.

"I tell you, *no*!"

"Oh, you won't take me in, I promise you! I see it all now! What a rage Sylvester would be in if he knew—when he has been so condescending as to make you the latest object of his gallantry, too! I only wish he may discover it." She saw the widening look of horror in Phoebe's eyes, and said: "*I* shan't tell him, of course: you may be easy on that head!"

"Indeed, I hope you won't tell anyone, for it is untrue, and absurd as well!" replied Phoebe, trying to speak as though she were amused. "And pray don't mention either that I am acquainted with the real author! I need not ask you: you must perceive how very disagreeable it would be for me—bound not to divulge the secret, and—besieged with questions, as I should be!"

"Oh, no, of course I shall not! Only fancy being able to write books! I am sure I could never do so. How clever you must be! But were you really ignorant of the circumstances? It is the oddest thing! How in the world do you contrive to think of such exciting adventures? I hadn't the least guess how Matilda and Florian would contrive to rescue poor Maximilian, you know. I could not put the last volume down until they ran the boat ashore, and Florian cried: *'Safe! Safe, Matilda! At last we stand where Ugolino holds no sway!'* I almost shed tears, it was so affecting!"

She rattled on in this way for some minutes. Phoebe was powerless to stop her. She could only repeat that she was not the book's author, which made Ianthe laugh; and derive a little doubtful comfort from Ianthe's assurance that she would not breathe a syllable to a soul.

18

The first repercussions of this interlude began to be felt by
Phoebe almost at once. She saw one or two covert glances
directed at her, and guessed several times that she was the
subject of a whispered confidence. She was rendered acutely
uncomfortable; and when, in a few days, she received the
coldest and most infinitesimal of bows from two of the Patron-
esses of Almack's, and the cut direct from Lady Ribbleton,
only and formidable sister of the Duchess of Salford, she could
no longer attempt to persuade herself that she was imagining
the whole. She did her best to maintain an air of cheerful
unconcern, but she quaked inwardly. Only one person ventured
to ask her if it were true that she had written *The Lost Heir*,
and that an ingenuous young lady embarking on her first season, who was at once frowned down by her mama. Phoebe
exclaimed with a tolerable assumption of amazement: *"I?"* and
at least had the satisfaction of knowing that she had lulled one
person's suspicions. Mrs. Newbury, the only other who might,
perhaps, have openly taxed her with what she was fast coming
to consider her crime, had been confined to the house by some
indisposition, and might be presumed to know nothing about
the gathering rumours.

The Dowager learned of the turn affairs had taken from her daughter-in-law, to whom had been entrusted the task of chaperoning Phoebe. It was with great diffidence that Rosina approached her, for it seemed very shocking to her that such a suspicion should attach to Phoebe, and she sometimes wondered if she had misunderstood certain remarks that had been made to her. No one had asked her any questions, or said anything to which exception could have been taken. Only there had been hints.

The Dowager, demanding the truth from Phoebe, heard what had passed between her and Ianthe, and was pardonably angry. If she understood the feelings which had compelled Phoebe to come so close to disclosing her secret she did not betray this, saying impatiently that no one whose opinion was worth a groat would be likely to set any store by the silly things Ianthe said of Sylvester. As for placing the smallest reliance on Ianthe's ability to keep such a tit-bit of news to herself, she wondered that Phoebe could be such a greenhead. She forgave her only because she had had at least enough sense to remain constant in denial.

"She cannot say that you told her you were the author, and as for the rest, the only thing to be done is to say that you *think* you know who the author is. That may readily be believed! I am sure there must be a score of persons who are saying the same. If people can be made to believe that Ianthe, after her usual fashion, added straws of her own providing to a single one dropped by you, until she had furnished herself with a nest, so much the better! If they don't think that, they may well think that it was you who exaggerated, pretending to know more than others, to be interesting. Yes, my love, I've no doubt you had rather not appear in such a light, but that you should have thought of before. Don't fall into flat despair! The case is not desperate, if only you will do as I bid you." She tapped her fan on her knee with a gesture of exasperation. "I might have known what would come of it if I let Rosina take care of you! Idiotish woman! *I* could have scotched the business days ago! Well, never mind that now! When is the Castlereaghs' ball? Tomorrow? Good! It will be the first crush of the season, and nothing could be better! I shall take you to it myself, child, and see what I can achieve!"

"Grandmama—must I go to it?" Phoebe faltered. "I had so much rather not!"

"Not go to it? Good God, do you want to *confirm* suspicion? You will wear your new dress—the pretty green one, with the pearl embroidery!—and you will—you *must!*—appear perfectly unconscious. I, on the other hand, am going to be very conscious—and never so much diverted in my life! That ought to take the trick! And it will be well if it does," she added, a trifle grimly. "I don't scruple to tell you, my love, that if this scandal is not put an end to I have grave fears that even my influence may not avail to procure you vouchers for Almack's. I imagine you must know what *that* would mean!" She saw that Phoebe was looking crushed, and relented, leaning forward to pat her hand, and saying: "There! No more scolding! Dear me, what a pity Tom cannot dance, with that leg of his! I declare, I would invite him to go with us to the Castlereaghs', just to put some heart into you, silly child!"

The Dowager had taken a great fancy to young Mr. Orde, but she would have found it difficult under any circumstances to have persuaded him to attend a dress-party at which he would have been obliged, as he phrased it, to do the pretty to a lot of fashionable strangers. Such affairs, he told Phoebe firmly, were not in his line: he was never more glad of a lame leg.

So Tom went off on the fateful night to be choked by the new gas-lighting at Drury Lane; and Phoebe was escorted by the Dowager, shortly after ten o'clock, to the Castlereagh mansion.

The Dowager saw immediately how close to the brink of social disaster Phoebe had approached, and her keen eyes snapped dangerously as they marked the various dames who dared to look coldly at her granddaughter. These ladies should shortly be made to regret their insolence: one might have chosen to retire a little from the world of fashion, but one was not yet quite without power in that world! She saw, with satisfaction, that Phoebe's chin was up; and, with relief, that her hand was soon solicited for the country-dance that was then forming.

Phoebe's partner, a young gentleman very conscious of his first longtailed coat and satin knee-breeches, was shy, and in striving to set him at his ease Phoebe forgot her own nervousness, and smiled, and chatted with all the unconcern that her grandmother could have wished her to show. It was when she was halfway down the second set that she saw Sylvester, and felt her heart bump against her ribs.

He was talking to his hostess, in a knot of persons by the door. He was laughing, tossing a retort over his shoulder to some friend, shaking hands with another: in spirits, she thought hopefully. He glanced round the ballroom, but cursorily; their eyes did not meet. She wondered if he would presently look for her, and hardly knew which would be the sterner trial: to be ignored by him, or to be obliged to face him.

The next dance was a waltz. She did not think that Sylvester had yet seen her, but as the fiddlers struck up he came across the floor to where she sat beside the Dowager, and said: "How do you do, ma'am? I am charged with all kinds of messages for you from my mother. You will like to know that I left her well—wonderfully well! Miss Marlow, may I have the honour?"

As she rose to her feet she looked fleetingly up at him, and again felt that sickening thud of the heart. His lips smiled, but there was a glitter in his eyes that was strange to her, and frightening, and the suggestion of a quiver about his up-cut nostrils.

He led her on to the floor, and into the dance. She hoped he could not feel the flurry of her pulses, and forced herself to speak. "I did not know you had returned to town, Duke."

"Didn't you? I came back from Chance yesterday, on purpose to attend this party. I am glad you are here—and admire your courage."

She knew that her hand was trembling in his light clasp, but she tried to rally herself. "Oh, I am not now so shy as I was used to be!"

"Obviously you are not. You must allow me to offer you my compliments, and to felicitate you on having made so notable a hit."

"I cannot imagine what you mean!"

"Oh, I think you can! You have written a romance that has set the ton by the ears: a feat indeed! Very clever, Miss Marlow, but could you find no better name for me than Ugolino?"

"You are mistaken—quite mistaken!" she stammered.

"Don't lie to me! Believe me, your face betrays you! Did you suppose I should not guess the truth? I am not a fool, and I have a tolerably good memory. Or did you think I should not read your book? If that was so you have been unfortunate. I might not have read it had my mother not desired me to do so. She wished—not unnaturally—to know what I had done to arouse such enmity, whom it was I had so bitterly offended. I was quite unable to answer the first of her questions. The second, I must confess, found me equally at a loss until I had read your book. I could have answered it then, of course, had I chosen to do so."

"Oh, I am sorry, I am sorry!" she whispered, in an anguished tone.

"Don't hang your head! Do you wish the whole room to know what I am saying to you?"

She raised it. "I tried to alter it. It was too late. I ought never to have done it. I didn't know—never dreamed——Oh, how can I explain to you? What can I say?"

"Oh, there is a great deal you might say, but it is quite unnecessary to do so! There is only one thing I am curious to know, for tax my memory as I may I cannot find the answer. What *did* I do, Miss Marlow, to deserve to be set in the pillory?"

"Nothing, nothing!"

"*Nothing?* I am aware that you took me in dislike at our first meeting; you have told me that I did not recognize you when we met for the second time. Was that all your reason for making me the model for your villain? Did you, for such small cause, put yourself to the labour of discovering the affairs of my family so that you might publish a spiteful travesty of them to the world?"

"No! Had I known—oh, how can you think I would have written it if I had known you had a nephew—were his guardian? I had not the least suspicion of it! It was coincidence: I chose you for Ugolino because—because of the way your eyebrows slant, and because I thought you arrogant! I never dreamed then the book would be published!"

"Doing it rather too brown, are you not? You can't really suppose I shall swallow *quite* so unlikely a story!"

She looked up, and saw that while he talked to her, between his teeth, he was smiling still. The sensation of moving through a nightmare threatened to overpower her. She said faintly: "It's true, whatever you believe. When I found out—about Edmund—I was ready to sink!"

"But not ready to stop the publication of this sad coincidence."

"I couldn't do so! They would not even let me alter it! the book was already bound, Duke! When I reached London it was

199

the first thing I did. I went immediately to the publishers—indeed, indeed, I did!"

"And, of course, it never occurred to you that if I were warned I might prove more successful than you in arresting publication," he said affably.

"No. *Could* you have done so?" she asked wonderingly.

"Oh, that is much better!" he approved, his eyes glinting down at her. "That innocent stare is excellent: you should cultivate it!"

She flushed vividly. "Please say no more! Not here—not now! I can't answer you. It was wrong of me—inexcusable! I—I *bitterly* regret it!"

"Why, yes, I imagine you might well! How many people have cut you tonight?"

"Not for that reason!" she answered hotly. "You know I didn't mean that! Do you think I am not fully sensible of your kindness, when you found us—Tom and me—and did so much for us?"

"Oh, don't give that a thought!" he replied. "What a stupid thing to say!—you didn't, of course."

She winced. "Oh, stop, stop! I never meant to do you an injury! I might as easily have made you the model for my hero!"

"Ought I to be grateful? Is it beyond your comprehension that to discover myself figuring in a novel—and, if you will forgive me, *such* a novel!—in *any* guise is an experience I find nauseating? You might have endowed me with every virtue imaginable, but I should still have considered it a piece of intolerable impertinence!"

She was beginning to feel as physically sick as she had so often felt when rated by her stepmother. "Take me back to my grandmother!" she begged. "I don't know why you asked me to dance with you! Could you not have chosen another occasion to say what you wished to me?"

"Easily, but why should I? I shall restore you to Lady Ingham when the music ceases: not before! You are ungrateful, Sparrow: you shouldn't be, you know!"

"Don't call me that!" she said sharply, stung by his tone.

"No, it doesn't suit you," he agreed. "What will you have me call you? Jay?"

"Let me go! You may ignore me—you need not insult me!"

His clasp on her hand tightened unkindly. "You may be

thankful I haven't ignored you. Do you know what would have happened had I done so? Do you know how many pairs of eyes were watching to see just what I should do? I asked you to dance because if I had not, every suspicion that you are indeed the author of that book would have been confirmed, and you would have found yourself, by tomorrow, a social outcast. You would have been well-served, and I own I was strongly tempted. But I should think myself as contemptible as your villainous Count if I stooped to such a paltry revenge! You may be sure of my support, Miss Marlow. What I may choose to say to you you will have to learn to accept with a good grace. I'll call in Green Street tomorrow to take you driving in the Park: that ought to convince the doubters!"

It was too much. She wrenched herself out of his hold, heedless alike of her surroundings and the consequences, and hurried off the floor to her grandmother's side, so blinded by the tears she was unable to keep back that she blundered into several couples, and did not see how everyone was staring, first at her, and then at Sylvester, left ridiculously alone in the middle of the ballroom floor, his face white with fury.

CHAPTER

19

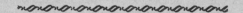

Lady Ingham was indisposed; Sir Henry Halford had said that on no account must her ladyship be agitated; her ladyship was not receiving visitors today. Miss Marlow was indisposed too and was laid down on the sofa in the Small Parlour; Miss Marlow was not receiving visitors today.

These melancholy tidings, delivered by Horwich in a voice of sepulchral gloom, daunted one of the two callers standing on the steps of the house in Green Street, but left the other unmoved. "Her ladyship will receive me," said Mrs. Newbury briskly. "Very proper of you to warn me, however, Horwich! I shall take care not to agitate her."

"I could not take it on myself to answer for her ladyship, madam. I will enquire."

"Quite unnecessary! Is her ladyship in her dressing-room? I will go up, then."

Emboldened by the success achieved by this bright-eyed lady the second caller said firmly: "Miss Marlow will receive me! Be so good as to take my card up to her!"

Mrs. Newbury ran up the stairs, and having tapped on the dressing-room door peeped in, saying softly: "Dear Lady Ingham, may I come in? I am persuaded you won't be vexed with me—say you are not!"

The blinds had been drawn halfway across the two windows; a strong aroma of aromatic vinegar pervaded the air; and a gaunt figure advanced, hissing that her ladyship must not be disturbed.

"Is that you, Georgiana?" faintly demanded the Dowager from the sofa. "I am too unwell to see anyone, but I suppose you mean to come in whatever I say. No one cares how soon I am driven into my grave! Set a chair for Mrs. Newbury, Muker, and go away!"

The grim handmaid disapprovingly obeyed this order; and Georgiana, her eyes becoming accustomed to the gloom, trod over to the sofa, and sat down by it, saying coaxingly: "I have not come to tease you, ma'am—only to help you, if I can!"

"No one can help me," said the sufferer, with awful resignation. "I need not ask if it is all over town!"

"Well, I should think it would be," said Georgiana candidly. "Charlotte Retford came to see me this morning, and I must own she said that people *are* talking. She described to me what happened last night, and—oh, I thought I must come to see you, because even if Phoebe did write that book I can't but like her still, and, whatever Lion may say about not meddling, if I can help her I will!"

"I imagine no one can now doubt that she wrote it," said the Dowager. "When I think of all I did for her last night, even convincing Sally Jersey that the whole thing was a hum, set about by that pea-goose, Ianthe Rayne—Where are my salts?"

"Why did she write it, ma'am?" asked Georgiana. "One would say she must detest Sylvester, but *that* she doesn't!"

The Dowager, between sniffs at her vinaigrette, enlightened her. After that she took a sip of hartshorn and water, and lay back with closed eyes. Mrs. Newbury sat wrapped in meditation for a few minutes, but presently said: "I shouldn't think that Sylvester will betray her, whatever she may have said to him."

"She betrayed herself! Leaving him in the middle of the floor as she did! I did my best, Georgiana, but what was the use of saying she was faint when there was Sylvester, looking like a devil? I will never forgive him, never! To overset her *there*! Heaven knows I don't excuse the child, but what *he* did was wicked! And I can't even take comfort from the reflection that she made a laughing-stock of him, because she ruined herself in doing it!" said the Dowager.

"He must have been very angry," said Georgiana, frowning. "Too angry to consider what might be the consequence of dashing her down in public. For it was not at all like him, you know, ma'am. Nothing disgusts him more than a want of conduct! I wonder if Lion was right after all?"

"Very unlikely!" snapped the Dowager.

"Well, that's what I thought," agreed the Major's fond spouse. "He said it was a case between them. In fact, he laid me a bet, because I wouldn't allow it to be so. I know just how Sylvester behaves when he starts one of his *à suivie* flirtations, and it was not at all like that. Can it be that he had formed a serious attachment?"

The Dowager blew her nose. "I thought it as good as settled!" she disclosed. "The wish of my heart, Georgie! Everything in such excellent train, and all shattered at a blow! Dare I suppose that his affections will reanimate towards her? No! They will not!"

Georgiana, with the sapient Lion's comments in mind, was glad that Lady Ingham had supplied the answer to her own question. "Dished!" had said the Major. "Pity! Nice little gal, I thought. Won't pop the question to her now, of course. Couldn't have found a surer way to drive him off than by making him ridiculous."

"What to do I don't know!" said the Dowager. "It is of no use to tell me she should brave it out: she ain't the sort of girl who could carry it off. Besides, she'll be refused vouchers for Almack's. I shan't even try for them: nothing would delight that odious Burrell creature more than to be able to give me a setdown!"

"No, that won't do," said Georgiana. "I have a better scheme, ma'am: that's why I came! Take her to Paris!"

"Take her to Paris?" repeated the Dowager.

"Yes, ma'am, to Paris!" said Georgiana. "Do but consider! Phoebe can't remain mewed up within doors, and to send her home would be worse than anything, because it would be to abandon every hope of re-establishing her presently. Paris would be the very thing! Everyone knows that you have had some thought of removing there. Why, I heard you talking of it myself, to Lady Sefton!"

"Everyone may know it, but everyone would also know why I had gone there."

"That can't be helped, dear ma'am. At least they will know that *you* have not cast Phoebe off. And you know how quickly the most shocking scandals are forgotten!"

"This one won't be."

"Yes, it will. I promise you I shall be busy while you are away, and you know that no one can be more valuable than I in this affair, because I am Sylvester's cousin, and what I say of him will be believed rather than what Ianthe says. I shall set it about that that scene last night was the outcome of a quarrel which began before Sylvester went away to Chance, and had nothing to do with *The Lost Heir*. I shall say that that was why he went to Chance: what could be more likely? *And,*" said Georgiana, in a voice of profound wisdom, "I shall tell it all in the *strictest* confidence! To one person, or perhaps two, just to make sure of the story's spreading."

There was a short silence. The Dowager broke it. "Pull the blinds back!" she commanded. "What does Muker mean by leaving us to sit in the dark, stupid woman? You're a flighty, ramshackle creature, Georgie, but one thing I'll allow! You have a good heart! But will anyone believe Phoebe didn't write that book?"

"They must be *made* to, even if I have to say I too know who is the real author! If Sylvester had taken it in good part—made a joke of it, as though he didn't care a button, and had been in the secret the whole time—it wouldn't have signified a scrap, because he was the only person unkindly used in the book, and if he hadn't taken it in snuff all the others whom Phoebe dug her quill into must have followed his example."

"Don't talk to me of Sylvester!" said the Dowager, with loathing. "If I hadn't set my heart on his marrying Phoebe I should be in transports over her book! For she hit him off to the life, Georgie! If he ain't smarting still I don't know him! Oh, drat the boy! He might have spared a thought for me before he provoked my granddaughter to enact a Cheltenham tragedy in the middle of a ballroom!"

Perceiving that slow, unaccustomed tears were trickling down her ladyship's cheeks, Georgiana overcame a desire to retort in defence of Sylvester, and made haste to soothe her, and to turn her thoughts towards Paris.

"Yes, but it's useless to think of it," said the Dowager,

dabbing at her eyes. "I cannot go without some gentleman to escort me! Poor Ingham would turn in his grave! Don't talk to me of couriers! I won't have strangers about me. And I am a wretched traveller, always seasick, and as for depending on Muker, she, you may lay your life, will be in the sullens, because she don't want to go to France!"

Georgiana was rather daunted by this. After having her suggestion that the present Lord Ingham might escort his parent spurned she was at a loss, and could only say that it seemed a pity if the scheme must fail after all.

"Of course it is a pity!" said the Dowager irascibly. "But with my constitution it would be madness for me to attempt the journey without support! Sir Henry wouldn't hear of it! If Phoebe had a brother——" She broke off, and startled Georgiana by exclaiming: "Young Orde!"

"I beg your pardon, ma'am?"

The Dowager sat up with surprising energy. "The very person! I will write at once to Mr. Orde! Where are they putting up? Reddish's! Georgie, my love, the ink, my pen, paper, wafers! In that desk! No! I will get up! Here, take all this away, child!"

"But who *is* he?" asked Georgiana, receiving from the Dowager a fan, a vinaigrette, a bottle of eau-de-Cologne, another of sal volatile, and three clean handkerchiefs.

"He's as good as a brother. Phoebe's known him all her life!" replied the Dowager, beginning to divest herself of various scarves, shawls, and rugs. "A very pretty-behaved boy! Wants town-polish, but most gentlemanly!"

Georgiana put up her brows. "A fresh-faced young man, with a shy smile? Does he walk with a limp?"

"Yes, that's he. Just give me your hand—or no! Where has Muker put my slippers?"

"Then I fancy he is with Phoebe at this very moment," said Georgiana. "We met on the doorstep: I wondered who it could be!"

The Dowager sank back again. "Why didn't you tell me so before?" she demanded. "Ring the bell, Georgie! I'll have him up here at once!"

Georgiana obeyed, but said, as she did so: "To be sure, ma'am—if you think it right to take him?"

"Right? Why shouldn't it be? It will do him good to see something of the world! Oh, are you thinking they might fall in love? No fear of that, I assure you—though why I should say *fear* I don't know," added her ladyship bitterly. "After last night I should be thankful to see her married to anyone!"

Tom, entering the dressing-room a few minutes later, was looking grave. He cast an awed glance at the battery of medicines and restoratives set out on the table beside the Dowager's sofa, but was relieved to hear himself hailed in robust accents. When asked abruptly, however, if he would escort her ladyship and Miss Marlow to Paris he looked to be more appalled than pleased; and although, when the inducement of a week in Paris as her ladyship's guest was held out to him, he stammered that he was much obliged, it was plain that this was a mere expression of civility.

"Let me tell you, Tom, that foreign travel is a necessary part of every young man's education!" said the Dowager severely.

"Yes, ma'am," said Tom. He added more hopefully: "Only I daresay my father would not wish me to go!"

"Nonsense! Your father is a sensible man, and he told me he thought it time you got a little town bronze. Depend upon it, he can very well spare you for a week or two. I shall write him a letter, and you may take it to him. Now, boy, don't be tiresome! If you don't care to go on your own account you may do so on Phoebe's."

The matter being put thus to him Tom said that of course he was ready to do anything for Phoebe. Then he thought that this was not quite polite, so he added, blushing to the roots of his hair, that it was excessively kind of her la'ship, he was persuaded he would enjoy himself excessively, and his father would be excessively obliged to her. Only perhaps he ought to mention that he knew very little French, and had not before been out of England.

These triflings objections waved aside, the Dowager explained why she was so suddenly leaving London. She asked him if Phoebe had told him of the previous night's happenings. That brought the grave look back into his face. He said: "Yes, she has, ma'am. It's the very deuce of a business, I know, and I don't mean to say that it wasn't wrong of her to have written all that stuff about Salford, but it was just as wrong of him to have given her a trimming in public! I—I call it a dashed ungentlemanly thing to have done, because he must have *meant* to sink her to the ground! What's more, I wouldn't have thought

207

it of him! I thought he was a first-rate sort of a man—a regular Trojan! Oh lord, if only she had told him! I had meant to have visited him, too! I shan't now, of course, for whatever she did I'm on Phoebe's side, and so I should tell him!"

"No, I shouldn't visit him just yet," said Georgiana, regarding him with warm approval. "He *is* a Trojan, but I am afraid he may be in a black rage. He wouldn't otherwise have behaved so improperly last night, you know. Poor Phoebe! Is she very much afflicted?"

"Well, she was in the deuce of a way when I came," replied Tom. "Shaking like a blacmanger! She does, you see, when she's been overset, but she's better now, though pretty worn down. The thing is, Lady Ingham, she wants me to take her home!"

"Wants you to take her *home*?" exclaimed the Dowager. "Impossible! She cannot want that!"

"Yes, but she does," Tom insisted. "She will have it she has disgraced you as well as herself. And she says she had rather face Lady Marlow than anyone in London, and at all events she won't have to endure Austerby for long, because as soon as they pay her!—she and Sibby will live together in a cottage somewhere. She means to write another novel immediately, because she has been offered a great deal of money for it already!"

The disclosure of this fell project acted alarmingly on the Dowager. To Tom's dismay she uttered a moan, and fell back against her cushions with her eyes shut. Resuscitated by smelling-salts waved under her nose, and eau-de-Cologne dabbed on her brow, she regained enough strength to tell Tom to fetch Phoebe to her instantly. Georgiana, catching the doubtful glance he cast at her, picked up her gloves and her reticule, and announced that she would take her leave. "I expect she feels she had rather not meet me, doesn't she? I perfectly understand, but pray give her my love, Mr. Orde, and assure her that I am still her friend!"

The task of persuading Phoebe to view with anything less than revulsion the prospect of being transported from the fashionable world of London to that of Paris was no easy one. In vain did the Dowager assure her that if some ill-natured gossip should have written the story of her downfall to a friend in Paris it could be denied; in vain did she promise to present her to King Louis; in vain did she describe in the most glowing terms the charm and gaiety of French society: Phoebe shuddered at every treat held out to her. Tom, besought by the Dowager to try what he could achieve, was even less successful. Adopting a bracing note, he told Phoebe that she must shake off her blue devils, and try to come about again.

"If only I might go home!" she said wretchedly.

That, said Tom, was addle-brained, for she would only mope herself to death at Austerby. What she must do was to put the affair out of her head—though he thought she should perhaps write a civil letter of apology to Salford from Paris. After that she could be comfortable, for she would not be obliged to meet him again for months, if Lady Ingham hired a house in Paris, as she had some notion of doing.

But the only effect of this heartening speech was to send Phoebe out of the room in floods of tears.

It was left to the Squire to bring her to a more submissive frame of mind, which he did very simply, by telling her that she owed it to her grandmother, after causing her so much trouble, to cheer up and do as she wished. "For it's my belief," said the Squire shrewdly, "that she wants to go as much for her own sake as yours. I must say I should like Tom to get a glimpse of foreign parts, too."

That settled it: Phoebe would go to Paris for Grandmama's sake, and try very hard to enjoy it. Her subsequent efforts to appear cheerful were heroic, and quite enough (said Tom) to throw the whole party into the dismals.

Between Phoebe's brave front and Muker's undisguised gloom the Dowager might well have abandoned the scheme had it not been for the support afforded her by young Mr. Orde. Having consented to go with her, Tom resigned himself with a good grace, and threw himself into all the business of departure with so much energy and good-humour that he soon began to rival Phoebe in the Dowager's esteem. With a little assistance from the Squire, before that excellent man returned to Somerset, he grappled with passports, customs, and itineraries; ascertained on which days the mails were made up for France, and on which days the packets sailed; calculated how much money would be needed for the journey; and got by heart such French phrases as he thought would be most useful. A Road Book was his constant companion; and whenever he had occasion to pull out his pocket-book a shower of leaflets accompanied it.

It did not take him long to discover that the task of conveying Lady Ingham on a journey was no sinecure. She was exacting, and she changed her mind almost hourly. No sooner had he gone off with her old coachman to inspect her traveling-carriage (kept by her longsuffering son in his coach-house and occupying a great deal of space which he could ill-spare) than she decided that it would be better to travel post. Off went Tom in a hack to arrange for the hire of a chaise, only to find on his return to Green Street that she had remembered that since Muker would occupy the foreward seat they would be obliged to sit three behind her, which would be intolerable.

"I am afraid," said Lord Ingham apologetically, "that you have taken a troublesome office upon yourself, my boy. My mother is rather capricious. You mustn't allow her to wear you to death. I see you are lame, too."

"Oh, that's nothing, sir!" said Tom cheerfully. "I just take a hack, you know, and rub on very well!"

"If I can be of assistance," said Lord Ingham, in a dubious tone, "you—er—you must not hesitate to apply to me."

Tom thanked him, but assured him that all was in a way to be done. He could not feel that Lord Ingham's assistance would expedite matters, since he knew by now that the Dowager invariably ran counter to his advice, and was exasperated by his rather hesitant manners. Lord Ingham looked relieved, but thought it only fair to warn Tom that there was a strong probability that the start would be delayed for several days, owing to the Dowager's having decided at the last minute that she could not leave town without a gown that had not yet been sent home by her dressmaker, or some article that had been put away years before and could not now be found.

"Well, sir," said Tom, grinning, "she had the whole set of 'em turning the house out of the windows to find some cloak or other when I left, but I'll bring her up to scratch: see if I don't!"

Lord Ingham shook his head, and when he repaired to Green Street on the appointed day to bid his parent a dutiful farewell it was in the expectation of finding the plans changed again, and everything at odds. But Tom had made his word good. The old-fashioned coach stood waiting, piled high with baggage; and Lord Ingham entered the house to find the travellers fully equipped for the adventure, and delayed only by the Dowager's sudden conviction that her curling-tongs had been forgotton, which entailed the removal of everything from her dressing-case, Muker having packed them at the bottom of it.

Lord Ingham, eyeing young Mr. Orde with respect, was moved to congratulate him. Young Mr. Orde then confided to him that it had been a near-run thing, her la'ship having been within amesace of crying off as late as yesterday, when the weather took a turn for the worse. "But I managed to persuade her, sir, and I think I shall be able to get her aboard Thursday's packet all right and tight," said optimistic Tom.

Lord Ingham, casting an apprehensive glance at the hurrying clouds, thought otherwise, but refrained from saying so.

CHAPTER

20

Lord Ingham was right. The first glimpse caught of the sea afforded the Dowager a view of tossing gray waters, flecked with foam; and long before she was handed down from the coach at the Ship Inn she had informed Tom that a regiment of Guards would not suffice to drag her on board the packet until the wind had abated. Two days of road travel (for to avoid fatigue she had elected to spend one night at Canterbury) had given her the headache; and during the rest of the journey she became steadily more snappish. Her temper was not improved, on alighting at Dover, by having the hat nearly snatched from her head by a gust of wind; and it seemed for several minutes as though she might reenter the coach then and there, and return to London. Fortunately Tom had written to bespeak accommodation for the party; and the discovery that the best bedchamber had been reserved for her, and the best parlour, with fires kindled in both, mollified her. A dose of the paregoric prescribed by Sir Henry Halford, followed by an hour's rest, and an excellent dinner did much to restore her, but when Tom told her that the packet had sailed for Calais that day as usual, from which circumstance it might be inferred that no danger of shipwreck attended the passage, she replied discouragingly: "Exactly what I am afraid of!"

On the following morning, in conditions described by knowledgeable persons as fair sailing weather, Tom made the discovery that fair sailing weather, in Lady Ingham's opinion, was flat calm. April sunshine lit the scene, but Lady Ingham could see white crests on the sea, and that was enough for her, she thanked Tom. An attempt to convince her that a passage of perhaps only four hours with a little pitching would be preferable to being cooped up in a stuffy packet for twice as long succeeded only in making her pick up her vinaigrette. She begged Tom not to mention that horrid word *pitching* again. If he and Phoebe had set their hearts on the Paris scheme she would not deny them the treat, but they must wait for calm weather.

They waited for five days. Other travellers came and went; Lady Ingham and Party remained at the Ship; and Tom, forewarned that the length of the bills presented at this busy hostelry was proverbial, began to entertain visions of finding himself without a feather to fly with before he had got his ladies to Amiens.

Squally weather continued; the Dowager's temper worsened; Muker triumphed; and Tom, making the best of it, sought diversion on the waterfront. Being a youth of an enquiring turn of mind and a friendly disposition he found much to interest him, and was soon able to point out to Phoebe the various craft lying in the basins, correctly identifying brigantines, hoys, sloops, and Revenue cutters for her edification.

The Dowager, convinced that every haunt of seafaring persons teemed with desperate characters lying in wait to rob the unwary, was strongly opposed to Tom's prowling about the yard and basins, but was appeased by his depositing in her care the packet of bills she had entrusted to him. It would have been better, in her opinion, had he and Phoebe climbed the Western Heights (for that might have blown Phoebe's crotchets away), but she was forced to admit that for a man with a lame leg this form of exercise was ineligible.

It seemed a little hard to Phoebe that she should be accused of having crotchets when she was taking such pains to appear cheerful. She only once begged to be allowed to go back to Austerby; and since this lapse was the outcome of her grandmother's complaining that she had allowed Mrs. Newbury to over-persuade her, it was surely pardonable. "Pray, pray, ma'am don't let us go to Paris on my account!" she had said imploringly. "I only said I would go because I thought you wished it! And I don't think Tom cares for it either, in his heart. Let him take me home instead!"

But the Dowager had been pulled up short by this speech. She was not much given to considering anyone but herself, but she was fond of Phoebe. Her conscience gave her a twinge, and she said briskly: "Fiddle-de-dee, my love! Of course I wish to go, and so I shall as soon as the weather improves!"

It began to seem, on the fifth day, that they were doomed to remain indefinitely at Dover, for the wind, instead of abating, had stiffened, and was blowing strongly off-shore. Tom's waterfront acquaintances assured him that he couldn't hope for a better to carry him swiftly across the Channel, but Tom knew that it would be useless to repeat this to the Dowager, even if she had not been keeping her bed that day. She was bilious. Sea-air, said Muker, always made my lady bilious, as those who had waited on her for years could have told others, had they seen fit to ask.

So Phoebe, having the parlour to herself, tried for the fourth time to compose a letter to Sylvester that should combine contrition with dignity, and convey her gratitude for past kindness without giving the least hint that she wished ever to see him again. This fourth effort went the way of its predecessors, and as she watched the spoiled sheets of paper blacken and burst into flame she sank into very low spirits. It was foolish to fall into a reminiscent mood when every memory that obtruded itself (and most of all the happy ones) was painful, but try as she would to look forward no sooner was she idle than back went her thoughts, and the most cheerful view of the future which presented itself to her was a rapid decline into the grave. And the author of all her misfortunes, whose marble heart and evil disposition she had detected at the outset, would do no more than raise his fatal eyebrows, and give his shoulders the slight, characteristic shrug she knew so well, neither glad nor sorry, but merely indifferent.

She was roused from the contemplation of this dismal picture by Tom's voice, hailing her from the street. She hastily blew her nose, and went to the window, thrusting it open, and looking down at Tom, who was standing beneath it, most improperly hallooing to her.

"Oh, there you are!" he observed. "Be quick, and come out, Phoebe! Such doings in the harbour! I wouldn't have you miss it for a hundred pounds!"

"Why, what?"

"Never mind what! Do make haste, and come down! I promise you it's as funny as any farce *I* ever saw!"

"Well, I must put on my hat and pelisse," she said, not wanting very much to go.

"Lord, you'd never keep a hat on in this wind! Tie a shawl over your head!" he said. "And don't dawdle, or it will all be over before we get there!"

Reflecting that even being buffeted by a cold wind would be preferable to further reverie, she said that she would be down in a trice, shut the window again, and ran away to her bedchamber. The idea of tieing a shawl round her head did not commend itself to her, but the Dowager had bought a thick travelling cloak with a hood attached for her to wear on board the packet, so she fastened that round her throat instead, and was hastily turning over the contents of a drawer in search of gloves when she was made to jump almost out of her skin by hearing herself unexpectedly addressed.

"May I make so bold as to enquire, miss, if you was meaning to go out?"

Phoebe looked quickly round, exclaiming: "Good gracious, what a start you gave me, Muker! I never heard you come in!"

"No, miss?" said Muker, standing with primly folded arms on the threshold. "And was you meaning to go out, miss?"

Her tone was very much that of a gaoler. It nettled Phoebe, but although she flushed a little she said only: "Yes, I am going for a walk," because she knew that Muker's dislike of her arose from jealousy, for which she was more to be pitied than blamed.

"May I ask, miss, if her ladyship is aware of your intention?"

"You may ask, but I don't know why you should, or why I should answer you," replied Phoebe, her temper rising.

"I shouldn't consider it consistent with my duty, miss, to permit you to go out without her ladyship was aware of it."

"Oh, *wouldn't* you?" retorted Phoebe, by this time roused to real wrath. "Try if you can stop me!"

Muker, thrust with some violence out of the way, followed her from the room, two spots of colour flaming on her cheekbones. "Very well, miss! Very well! Her ladyship shall hear of this! I should have thought she had had enough to worrit her, poor dear, without——"

"How dare you speak to me in that insolent way?" Phoebe interrupted, pausing at the head of the stairs to look back. "If my grandmother should wish to know where I am gone, you will please tell her that she need have no anxiety, since I am with Mr. Orde!"

"Hurry, Phoebe!" said Tom, from the hall below. "It will be too late soon!"

"I'm coming!" she answered, running down to join him.

"What an age you've been!" he said, pushing her through the doorway into the street. "You had better hold that cloak tightly round you, or you'll be blown away. What's the matter?"

"That odious Muker!" she fumed. "Daring to tell me *she* would not permit me to go out!"

"Oh, never mind her!" said Tom, limping along as fast as he could. "Sour old squeeze-crab! You wait till you see the pantomime in the harbour! I shouldn't wonder at it if we find the whole town's turned out to watch it by the time we get there. Lord, I hope they haven't got the thing aboard yet!"

"*What* thing?" demanded Phoebe.

"Some sort of a travelling carriage," replied Tom, with a chuckle.

"Oh, Tom, you wretch, is *that* all?"

"All! It's no ordinary carriage, I can tell you. It belongs to some fellow who has chartered a schooner to take his coach and his family to Calais, and there's him, and a little chitty-faced fellow that looks like a valet, and——but you'll see! When I left they were all arguing whether it oughtn't to be got aboard in slings, and there was a string of porters carrying enough champagne and hampers of food for a voyage to India! There! what did I tell you? Half the town at least!"

If this was an exaggeration there was certainly a crowd of people watching with deep interest the activities of those preparing to get a large travelling carriage aboard the *Betsy Anne*. The little man described by Tom as a valet was keeping a vigilant eye on this astonishing vehicle, every now and then darting forward to ward off the urchins who wanted to look inside it, and saying in a tearful falsetto: "I forbid you to lay your greasy hands on it! Go away! Go away, I say!"

His agitation was pardonable, for never was there so glossy

216

and so exquisite a chariot, double-perched, slung high between high wheels, fitted with patent axles, and embellished with a gilded iron scroll-work all round the roof. The body was painted a bright tan, with the wheels and the panels of sky-blue; and the interior, which, besides a deeply cushioned seat, included a letdown table, appeared to be entirely lined with pale blue velvet.

"Cinderella's coach!" said Phoebe promptly. "Who in the world can have ordered such a ridiculous thing?"

On board the schooner all was bustle and noise, the crew being much impeded in their tasks by the number of porters who got in their way, and voicing their disapproval in loud and frank terms.

"Getting ready to set sail," said Tom. "I should laugh if they were to miss the tide!"

As Phoebe's amused eyes ran over the crowded deck they alighted on the figure of a small boy, who was critically observing the various activities in progress. For one instant she stared unbelievingly, and then she clutched Tom's arm, exclaiming: *"Edmund!"*

"Eh?" said Tom. He saw that she was looking at the small boy as though she saw a ghost. *"Now* what's the matter?" he demanded.

"Edmund Rayne! Salford's nephew!" she stammered. "There—on the boat!"

"Is it?" said Tom, glancing at the child. "Are you poz?"

"Yes, yes, how could I mistake? Oh, Tom, I have the most dreadful fear—What was he like, the man who owns that coach?"

"Like a counter-coxcomb!" replied Tom. "I never saw such a quiz!"

She turned pale. "Fotherby! Then Lady Henry must be aboard. Did you see her? Very fair—very beautiful?"

"No, I only saw the dandy, and the valet, and that fellow over there, whom I take to be the courier. Why, you don't mean to say you think they're eloping?"

"I don't know that, and I don't care! They are kidnapping Edmund, and—oh, Tom, it is *my* fault! I am going aboard!"

He detained her. "No, you don't! How could it be your fault, pray? I wish you won't fall into such distempered freaks, Phoebe!"

"Don't you *see,* Tom? I told you what it was that made my book so particularly abominable!"

"I haven't forgotten. But your book ain't to be blamed for Lady Henry's running off with that Jack-a-dandy. If you've got some notion of trying to interfere, let me tell you, I shan't let you make such a cake of yourself! It's none of your business."

She said with determined calm: "Tom, if it is as I believe, and Lady Henry is taking that child out of England, I am so much to blame that I think I shall never hold up my head again. *I* put the scheme into her head! It was never there before she read my book. Oh, she told me herself how much struck she was by the end of it, and I never guessed, never suspected——!"

"Took the scheme out of a trumpery novel? She couldn't be such a greenhead!"

"She is just such a greenhead! I don't know how it will be, if they get Edmund to France, whether it will be possible for Salford to recover him, or even to find him, but only think what it must mean! More trouble, more scandal, and all to be laid at my door! I can't bear it, Tom! You must let me go aboard that boat! Perhaps, if I could prevent this, he—people— might not think so badly of me. Tom, I've wished the book had never been written over and over again, but I can't unwrite it, and don't you think that this—if I could stop it—would be a sort of—of atonement?"

He was struck by her earnest manner, and even more by the expression in her eyes, which was almost tragic. After a moment he said: "Well—if you think you should, I suppose— Come to think of it, if the boy is being taken out of the country without his guardian's leave it's against the law! So we have got *some* right to meddle. I only hope we don't catch cold at it, that's all!"

But Phoebe had already stepped on to the gangway. As she reached the deck Sir Nugent Fotherby emerged from a doorway behind the ladder leading to the quarterdeck, and at once perceived her.

After looking at her through his quizzing-glass for a minute he came forward, bowing, and saying in a pleased voice: "Miss Marlow! How-de-do? 'Pon my soul, I take it very kind in you to have called, and so, I venture to say, will her la'ship! Happy to welcome you aboard! Tidy little craft, ain't she? Chartered her, you know: couldn't take her la'ship on the common packet!"

"Sir Nugent, will you have the goodness to lead me to Lady Henry?" said Phoebe, ignoring these civilities.

"Greatest pleasure on earth, ma'am! But—you won't take it amiss if I give you a hint?—*not* Lady Henry!"

"I see. I should have said Lady Fotherby, perhaps?"

"No," replied Sir Nugent regretfully. "*Not* Lady Fotherby. Lady Ianthe Fotherby. *I* don't like it as well, but her la'ship informs me that to be called Lady Ianthe again makes her feel ten years younger, which is a gratifying circumstance, don't you think?"

At this point they were interrupted. Master Rayne had approached, and he planted himself squarely before Sir Nugent, demanding: "When are we going to see the circus?"

Master Rayne had to look a long way up to Sir Nugent's face, but his gaze was stern and unwavering, and under it Sir Nugent was visibly embarrassed. "Oh—ah—the circus!" he said. "Precisely so! The circus!"

"You said we were going to the circus," said Edmund accusingly. "You said if I didn't kick up riot and rumpus I should go to the circus."

"Did I?" said Sir Nugent, eyeing him uneasily. "Said that, did I?"

"Yes, you did," asserted Edmund. "Turnin' me up sweet!" he added bitterly.

"Well, there you have the matter in a nutshell," responded Sir Nugent confidentially. "Must realize it was a devilish awkward situation, my dear boy!"

"You told me a whisker," stated Edmund. "You are a Bad Man, and I won't have you for a new papa. *My* papa didn't tell whiskers."

"Be reasonable!" begged Sir Nugent. "You must own it was the only thing to be done, with you saying you didn't wish to go driving with us, and threatening to raise a dust! Why, you'd have had the whole houschold out on us!"

"I want to go home," said Edmund.

"Do you, my dear?" interpolated Phoebe. "Then I will ask you mama to let me take you home! Do you remember me? You told me all about your pony!"

Edmund considered her. Apparently he remembered her with kindness, for his severity relaxed, and he politely held out his hand. "You are the lady which knows Keighley. I will let you take me home. An' p'raps if you tell me some more about *your* pony I won't feel sick," he added.

"Very bad traveller," said Sir Nugent in an audible aside. "Seems to turn queasy every time he goes in a chaise. Dashed unfortunate, because it fidgets her la'ship. Pity we couldn't have brought his nurse, but her la'ship said no. No use trying to bribe her: had to bamboozle her instead. Meant he should travel with her la'ship's maid, but at the last moment we were queered upon that suit too. Maggoty female couldn't be brought up to the scratch! Said she was scared to go on a ship. 'What would have happened if Nelson had been scared to go on a ship?' I said. She said she didn't know. 'The Frogs would have landed,' I said. 'No one to stop 'em,' I said. No use. Said she couldn't stop 'em even if she did go to sea. Bit of a doubler, that, because I don't suppose she could. So there we were, floored at all points."

"Who is this gentleman?" suddenly demanded Edmund.

"That is Mr. Orde, Edmund. Sir Nugent, will you——"

"I'm glad he asked that," said Sir Nugent. "Didn't quite like to do it myself. Happy to make your acquaintance, sir! Daresay her la'ship would say the same, but she's rather fagged. Gone to lie down in her cabin. Allow me to escort you, ma'am!"

"I'll wait for you here, Phoebe," Tom said. "Come on, Master Poll Parrot, you may bear me company!"

Sir Nugent, handing Phoebe down the short companion-way, told her that Ianthe found her quarters rather constricted but was bearing every inconvenience with the fortitude of an angel. He then opened one of the two doors at the bottom of the companionway and announced: "A visitor, my love!"

Ianthe had been lying on one of the two berths in what seemed to Phoebe quite a spacious cabin, but upon hearing these words she uttered a shriek, and sat up, her hands clasped at her bosom. But as soon as she saw who it was who had entered, her fright vanished, and she exclaimed: "Miss Marlow! Good God, how comes this about? Oh, my dear Miss Marlow, how glad I am to see you! To think that you should be the first to felicitate me! For you must know that Nugent and I were married by special licence yesterday! We fled immediately from the church door, in the travelling chariot Nugent has had built for me. Was it not particularly touching of him? It is lined with blue, to match my eyes! Nugent, do go and tell them to make less noise! I shall be driven distracted by it! Shouting, and tramping, and clanking, and creaking till I could scream! You must tell the sailors that I have the head-ache, and cannot endure such a racket. Dear Miss Marlow, I thought you had gone to Paris a week ago!"

"We have been delayed. Lady Ianthe, I wish you very happy, but—excuse me—!—that was not my purpose in coming aboard. I saw Edmund, and realized what must be the reason for his being here. You will think me impertinent, but you must not steal him out of England! Indeed, indeed you must not!"

"Not steal him out of England? Why, how *can* you say so when it was you who showed me what I must do?"

"Oh, don't say so!" Phoebe cried sharply.

Ianthe laughed. "But of course it was you! As soon as I read how Florian and Matilda smuggled Maximilian on to that boat——"

"I implore you, stop!" begged Phoebe. "You cannot think that I meant that nonsense to be taken seriously! Lady Henry, you must let me take Edmund back to London! When I wrote that Ugolino couldn't pursue Maximilian out of his own country it was make-believe! But this is real life, and I assure you Salford can pursue you—perhaps even have you punished by the law!"

"He won't know where we are," replied Ianthe confidently. "Besides, Sylvester hates scandal. I am persuaded he would endure anything rather than let the world know the least one of the family secrets!"

"Then how could you serve him such a trick?" demanded Phoebe hotly. "The Duchess too! You cannot have considered what distress you will cause her if you hold by this scheme!"

Ianthe began to pout. "She is not Edmund's mama! I think you are being very unjust! You don't care for my distress! You cannot enter into the feelings of a mother, I daresay, but I should have thought you must have known I could never abandon my child to Sylvester. And don't tell me you didn't mean Maximilian for Edmund, because everyone knows you did!"

"Yes!" flashed Phoebe. "Because you told everyone so! Oh, haven't you harmed me enough? You promised me you wouldn't repeat what passed between us——"

"I didn't repeat it! The only person I told was Sally Derwent, and I particularly warned her not to mention it to a soul!" interrupted Ianthe, much aggrieved. "How can you be so unkind to me? As though my nerves were not worn down enough! I have had to bring Edmund without Button, and I am obliged to do everything for him, because he is so cross and naughty with poor Nugent, and I scarcely closed my eyes all night, because we were travelling, and I had to hold Edmund in my lap, and he kept waking up and crying, and saying he wanted to be sick, till I was fagged to death! If I told him one fairytale I told him fifty, but he would do nothing but say he wished to go home, till I could have slapped him! And that odious abigail refusing at the last minute to go with me, and now you reproaching me—oh, it is too bad! I don't know how I shall manage, for I am feeling very unwell already! Why can't those horrid sailors keep the boat *still*? Why does it rock up and down when it isn't even moving yet? I know I shall be prostrate the instant we set sail, and then who is to take care of Edmund?"

This impassioned speech ended in a burst of tears, but when Phoebe, seizing on the final woe, represented to the injured beauty how imprudent it would be to embark with Edmund upon a rough sea passage without providing him with an attendant, Ianthe declared herself ready to sacrifice her health, comfort, and even her sanity rather than give up her child; adding, however, with a slight lapse from nobility: "People would say I cared more for riches than Edmund!"

Since this seemed more than likely Phoebe found it difficult to reassure her; but before she had uttered more than a dozen words Ianthe was struck by a brilliant notion, and started up from her berth, her face transfigured. "Oh, Miss Marlow, I have hit on the very thing! We will take you with us! Just as far as to Paris, I mean. There can be no objection: you mean to go there, and I am sure there is no occasion for you to travel with Lady Ingham if you don't choose to do so! She may join you in Paris—you can stay at the Embassy until she comes: that may easily be arranged!—and she must surely be able to undertake the journey without you. She has her abigail to go with her, remember! I am persuaded she would be the first to say I ought not to be obliged to travel without a female to support me. Oh, Miss Marlow, do, pray, say you will stay with me!"

Miss Marlow was still saying that she would do no such

thing when Sir Nugent once more begged his bride's permission to come in.

He was followed by Tom, whom he at once presented, with great punctilio. Tom said that he begged her ladyship's pardon for intruding upon her, but had come to tell Phoebe it was time to be going ashore again. A speaking look directed at his childhood's friend conveyed to her the information that his attempts to bring Sir Nugent to a sense of his wrongdoing had met with failure.

Beyond bestowing a mechanical smile upon him, Ianthe paid him little heed, addressing herself instead to Sir Nugent, and eagerly explaining to him her brilliant notion. In him she found her only supporter: not only did he think it a stroke of genius, but he called upon Phoebe and Tom to applaud it. He won no response. Politely at first, and later with distressing frankness, Tom explained to him why he thought it rather the hall-mark of folly. He said that he would neither accompany the party to France nor remain behind to tell Lady Ingham why her granddaughter had abandoned her, and from this standpoint nothing would move him.

He had entered the cabin with the intention only of taking Phoebe ashore. In his view, there was nothing more to be done, and she might wash her hands of the affair with a clear conscience. But as Ianthe reiterated her former arguments, several times asserting that it was absurd of Phoebe to have scruples now, when everyone knew she had instigated the plot, his sentiments soon underwent a change. He saw all the force of what Phoebe had previously urged, and ranged himself on her side, even going so far as to talk of laying information with the nearest magistrate.

"Very ungentlemanly thing to do," said Sir Nugent, shaking his head. "Don't think you should. Besides, there's no sense in it: *you* go to the magistrate, *we* set sail, and then where are you?"

Tom, who was becoming heated, retorted: "Not if I don't go ashore till you've lost the tide! What's more I'll take the boy with me, because I've a strong notion it would be perfectly lawful to do so, and if you try to stop me it will very likely be a felony!"

"You rude, odious——Nugent! Where *is* Edmund?" cried Ianthe. "How could you leave him alone? Good God, he may have fallen overboard! Bring him to me this instant, unless you want me to run mad with anxiety!"

"No, no, don't do that, my love! Plenty of sailors to fish him out again, you know," Sir Nugent assured her. "Not but what I'll fetch him to you, if you *want* him!"

"*He* won't fall overboard," said Tom, as Sir Nugent departed on his errand.

"You know nothing about it!" snapped Ianthe. "*I* am his mother, and I shan't know one moment's peace until he is safe in my arms."

She repeated this statement with even more emphasis when Sir Nugent presently reappeared with the comforting intelligence that Edmund, safe in the valet's charge, was watching the men bring the carriage aboard; but when she learned that an attempt to pick him up had led him to kick his new papa severely before assuming an alarming rigidity, she seemed to feel that his presence in the cabin would not be conducive to peace, for she said only that if he began to scream it would be more than her nerves could endure without breaking under the strain.

Harping on this string, Phoebe then did her best to convince her that this sad accident would inevitably befall her if she were obliged to look after Edmund during the passage. She received unexpected support from Sir Nugent, who said that the more he considered the matter the more he thought it would be a devilish good notion to let Miss Marlow take Edmund home. "What I mean is," he explained, "it's a notion that took very well with him. He seems set against going to France. I daresay he don't like foreigners. Very understandable: I don't know that I like 'em myself."

This treachery naturally incensed Ianthe beyond measure. Having poured forth the vials of her wrath upon him, she said tragically that everyone was against her, and burst into a fit of hysterical tears. Feeling the battle to be almost won, Phoebe redoubled her efforts to persuade her, while Tom applied himself to the task of bringing over the waverer. With four people engaged in hot argument the sounds of increased activity on deck passed unheeded. The swell that had all the time been gently rocking the schooner had for several minutes been growing heavier, but it was not until the *Betsy Anne* took a plunge which made him stagger that Tom realized what must be happening.

"My God!" he gasped. "We're *moving*!"

21

Sir Nugent gave a chuckle. "Told 'em to cast off when I went up to fetch Edmund," he explained. "Told *you* he was watching the carriage go aboard! Diddled the dupes, my lady! Ah, I fancy Nugent Fotherby has rather more of quickness than most, eh?"

"Then you *didn't* mean to let Miss Marlow take Edmund away? Oh, Nugent!" said Ianthe admiringly.

"Did it pretty neatly, didn't I? Wouldn't you say I did it neatly, Orde?"

Tom, who had managed to reach the porthole without losing his balance, saw gray seas tumbling past, and turned a face pale with anger towards Sir Nugent. "I'd say you're a damned nail!" he replied fiercely.

"Not in front of ladies!" protested Sir Nugent.

"You must be mad!" Phoebe cried. "Turn back! Good God, you can't carry us off like this! Grandmama—all our baggage——! Do you realize that my grandmother has no notion where I am, and neither Tom nor I has a stitch to wear but what we have on our backs? Tell the captain he must turn about!"

"He won't do it," said Sir Nugent.

"Oh, won't he?" said Tom, making his precarious way to the door. "We'll see to that!"

Sir Nugent obligingly opened the door for him, saying amiably: "No sense in stopping him. Let us discuss the matter while he's gone!"

Tom, reaching the deck, found that the *Betsy Anne* was clear of the mouth of the Tidal Harbour, with the wind filling her sails. He had negotiated the companion-way, but the ladder leading to the quarterdeck presented a worse problem to a man with a stiff leg. He was obliged to shout at the stalwart individual above him, which set him, he felt, at a disadvantage. Certainly the ensuing dialogue was not a success. Admitting that he was the skipper, the stalwart individual seemed to be amused by Tom's demand to be set ashore. He asked if Tom had chartered the *Betsy Anne*, and upon being reassured said that that had removed a weight from his mind.

"Now, listen!" said Tom, keeping his temper. "You'll find yourself in trouble if you don't put back!"

"I'll find myself in trouble if I do!" responded the skipper.

"No, you won't. If you take me, and the lady who is with me, to France against our will, it's kidnapping!"

"Is it, now?" said the skipper, impressed. "That's bad, that is."

"As bad as it could be!"

The skipper shook his head. "It don't bear thinking on. And yet I don't seem to recall as you was forced to come aboard. Nor yet I never see anyone a-luring of you. Dang me if I see anyone *arsting* you! All I see was you and the young lady coming aboard without so much as a by-your-leave! Maybe I'm mistook, though."

"No, damn you, you aren't!" said Tom, incurably honest. "Now, be a good fellow, and put back! You wouldn't wish to upset the lady, and if she's taken off to France she'll be in the devil of a fix!"

"I'll tell you what!" offered the skipper handsomely. "You come up here, sir, and I'll hand the ship over to you! I ain't seaman enough to put into Dover with the wind in this quarter, but then I've only *been* at sea a matter of forty years."

Aware of several grinning faces turned his way Tom flushed. "Do you mean you can't put back?"

"*I* can't!" said the skipper.

"Hell and the devil!" ejaculated Tom. "Now we are in the

suds!" He burst out laughing. "Lord, what a mess! Hi, skipper! I'd like to come up there presently to watch how you do the trick!"

"You're welcome," responded the skipper.

Returning to the cabin, Tom found Ianthe reclining once more on her berth, a bottle of smelling-salts clutched in her hand. This had apparently been abstracted from a large dressing-case, which was standing open on the deck with a number of its expensive contents spilled round it. A dazzling array of gold-topped bottles, initialled with sapphires, met Tom's awed gaze, and he blinked. Sir Nugent, observing this, said with simple pride: "Something like, eh? My own design. I daresay they showed me fifty cases, but 'No,' I said. 'Not up to the rig! Trumpery,' I said. 'Nothing for it but to design a case myself,' I said. *This* is the result. Same thing happened when I wanted a carriage for her la'ship. 'Windus,' I said, 'it must be of the first stare. None of these will do,' I said. 'Build me one to my design!' Which he did. I am very fond of designing things."

"Well, I wish you will design us out of this rare mess you've pitched us into!" said Tom. "It's no go, Phoebe: the skipper says he can't put back: wind's in the wrong quarter."

"Then what in heaven's name are we to do?" she cried.

"Make the best of it. Nothing else we can do," he answered ruefully.

He was mistaken. The door was just then rudely thrust open, and the valet appeared on the threshold, his aspect alarming, his eyes glazed. He clung with one hand to the door, and over his shoulder drooped a small, wilted figure. "Sir—my lady— the young gentleman!" he said, in a strange voice. "Must request you——*take him quick!*"

"My child!" shrieked Ianthe, struggling up. "Is he *dead*?"

"No, of course he is not!" said Phoebe hurriedly relieving the valet of his burden.

"I regret, sir—shall not be available—rest of the passage!" gasped the valet, clinging now with both hands to the door.

"Well, of all things!" exclaimed Sir Nugent. "No, dash it, Pett, you *can't* be ill!"

"Sir," said Pett, "I *must*!"

With these tortured words, he disappeared with great precipitancy from the cabin, his exit being accelerated by the deck's rising suddenly at a steep angle as the *Betsy Anne* triumphantly lifted her bows over the trough of the waves.

"Edmund!" cried his anguished parent. "Speak to me!"

"Don't be so ridiculous!" said Phoebe, out of all patience. "Can't you *see* what's the matter with him, poor child?"

Master Rayne, game to the last, raised his head from Phoebe's shoulder, and spoke gallant words. "I'm not dead, Mama. J-just cast up me accounts!"

Tom, who had no sooner set eyes on him than he had started, with great presence of mind, to search for a basin, now handed this homely article to Phoebe, saying, with a grin: "That's the dandy, old chap! You're a prime gun!"

But Master Rayne had shot his bolt. His lip trembled. "I want to go home!" he sad tearfully. "I don't *like* it!"

"Dearest, *try* not to be ill!" begged his mother. "Think of something else!"

"I *can't* think of anything else!" wept Edmund, once more in the throes.

Ianthe, who was growing steadily paler, shuddered, and sank back with the smelling-salts to her nose, and her eyes shut.

"You feeling queasy too, my love?" asked Sir Nugent, concerned. "Now, I'll tell you what: I'll get you a drop of brandy, and you'll be as right as a ram's horn! Nothing like it!"

"No!" faintly moaned his love.

"Extraordinary thing, ain't it?" said Sir Nugent, addressing himself to Tom. "Some people only have to look at a ship for their stomachs to start turning over; other people wouldn't be sick in a hurricane. Runs in families, I daresay. Take my father: excellent sailor! Take me: the same! Famous for it! Made the crossing two years ago with George Retford. Now, that *was* a rough passage! People hanging over the rails all the way: most diverting spectacle! 'Nugent,' George said to me—and as game a man as ever lived, mind you! 'Take your choice!' he said. 'Either that cigar of yours goes overboard, or I do!' Curious, wasn't it? Nothing else turned him queasy, never blenched at his dinner: in fact——"

But at this point his bride brought his reminiscences to a close by requesting him, in a voice of loathing, to go away.

"Well, if there ain't anything I can do, I was thinking Orde and I might crack a bottle," he said. "Very willing to remain, however. Swore I'd cherish you, didn't I? Nugent Fotherby is not the man to go back on his word. Ask anyone!"

"Go away, go *away*!" screamed Ianthe. "Do you wish to *kill* me?"

Seeing that Sir Nugent was about to assure her that he had no such desire, Tom thrust him out of the cabin. "I'd better go too," he said, with an uneasy glance at Ianthe. "Unless you'd like me to stay, Phoebe?"

"No, no, there's nothing for you to do here. There, there, Edmund! Let Phoebe tuck you up warmly, and you'll soon be better!"

"Well, call, if you need me," said Tom. "I won't go out of earshot."

He then withdrew, in the comfortable conviction that both sufferers would probably fall asleep, leaving Phoebe nothing to do but to watch over their slumbers. He was astonished, and considerably concerned, when he heard her calling to him from the foot of the companion-way less than an hour later, and learned that Edmund was very much worse. He saw that Phoebe was looking pale herself, and exclaimed: "I say, Phoebe, you aren't feeling seasick, are you?"

"I? No, indeed! I have no time to be seasick!" she replied acidly. "Don't come down! I want you to ask that wretched man if I may carry Edmund into the other cabin. I believe it is his, but he can't want it, after all. And, Tom, try if you can come by a hot brick! Edmund shivers all the time, and do what I will I can't get him warm."

"Good God, he must be pretty bad! You don't mean to say he's still sick?"

"Not actually sick, no, but those dreadful paroxysms go on, and it hurts him so, poor little man, that he can't help but cry. I've never seen a child so utterly knocked-up, and I've helped to nurse my sisters often and often. It was *wicked* to have brought him on such a journey! She must have known how it would be! She *did* know, and all she will say is that he could be well if he would but make an effort! *She* makes no effort! She is feeling far too ill herself, and her sensibility is so exquisite that she can never bear to be near him when he is ailing! It gives her palpitations. She has them now, so he must be removed from her cabin. Tom, if I could be taken back to Dover on a magic carpet I would not go! No! Or leave that child until I see him safe in Salford's charge! Whatever his

sentiments may be towards Edmund he *cannot* be more unfeeling than that *creature*!"

"Steady, steady!" said Tom. "Throwing your tongue too
much, my girl!"

She gave an unsteady laugh, brushing her hand across her
brow. "I know. But only to you, Tom! I've been running mute
enough, I promise you." She raised her finger suddenly, listening, and called: "I'm coming, darling!"

Not his greatest enemy could have denied that Sir Nugent
was as compliant as he was amiable. Upon hearing what was
required, he instantly went below to beg Phoebe to consider
his cabin her own. He was very much shocked by Edmund's
appearance, and said: "Poor little fellow! Burned to the socket!"
so many times that it irritated Ianthe's nerves. Informed of
this, he withdrew his attention from Edmund, and said solic-
itously: "Still a trifle out of sorts, my love? Now, see if I don't
tell you something that'll do you good! With this wind we shall
be in Calais in only four hours!"

"Four hours!" Ianthe said, in a hollow voice. "Oh, how
could you be so brutal as to tell me? Four more hours of this!
I shall never survive it. My head! oh, my head!"

"What's to be done?" whispered Sir Nugent in Phoebe's
ear. "Seems to be bellows to mend with her. Devilish distressing: wouldn't have had it happen for the world!"

"I expect," said Phoebe, somewhat woodenly, "that she will
feel better when she is alone. Lady Ianthe, will you tell me
where I may find a nightshirt for Edmund? Were they packed
in your trunk? May I look for them there?"

But Ianthe had been unable to bring away any of Edmund's
raiment without arousing suspicion in her parents' household.

Phoebe looked wonderingly at the smart new trunk, at a
pile of bandboxes, and dress-boxes. "But——"

"I had to purchase *everything* new! And in such haste that
I was quite distracted," said Ianthe, in failing accents.

"Told her la'ship to rig herself out in the first style of
elegance, and have everything sent to my house," explained
Sir Nugent. "Good notion, don't you agree?"

Her ladyship, in fact, had forgotten, in an orgy of expensive
shopping, to provide for her son's needs.

Removed to the smaller cabin, tucked up in its berth, with
a champagne bottle full of hot water produced by Tom, Edmund
seemed to grow easier. Phoebe had the satisfaction presently

231

of seeing him drop asleep, and was about to snatch a little rest herself when Sir Nugent came to beg the favour of her attendance on Ianthe. Her la'ship, he whispered, was in devilish queer stirrups, and wished for assistance in an affair of too much delicacy to be mentioned.

Mystified, Phoebe went back to the larger cabin, leaving Sir Nugent to maintain a watch over his stepson. The affair of delicacy proved merely to be a matter of untieing Ianthe's stay-laces, but one glance at her was enough to inform Phoebe that Sir Nugent had not exaggerated her condition. She looked to be in extremely queer stirrups, and when Phoebe felt her pulse she discovered it to be tumultuous.

Phoebe was absent from Edmund's side for a considerable period. Unfortunately he woke up while she was away, and no sooner saw Sir Nugent than he repudiated him. Sir Nugent remonstrated with him, pointing out that for Edmund to order him out of his own cabin was coming it a trifle too strong. However, when he heard himself apostrophized as a Bad Man he realized that Edmund was lightheaded, and strove to reassure him. His efforts failed. During his late agony Edmund had had no leisure to consider anything but his body's ills. It was otherwise now. No longer racked by paroxysms, but only a very small boy pitchforked into nightmare, a pressing need presented itself to him. His face puckered. "I want my Button!" he sobbed.

"Eh?" said Sir Nugent.

Edmund, turning his face into the pillow, repeated his desire in muffled but passionate accents.

"Want a button, do you?" said Sir Nugent. "Now, don't cry, dear boy! Seems a devilish queer thing to want, but—*which* button?"

"*My* Button!" said Edmund, in a perfect storm of sobs.

"Yes, yes, precisely so!" said Sir Nugent hastily. "Be calm, dear boy! I assure you there's no need to put yourself in a taking! If you would but tell me——"

"Button, Button, Button!" wept Edmund.

Tom, looking into the cabin five minutes later to ask Phoebe if all was well, found a distressing scene in progress, bitter sounds of grief issuing from the blankets under which Edmund had wholly retired, and his harassed stepfather feverishly turning out the pockets of a small pair of nankeen pantaloons.

"Good God, what's the matter?" Tom demanded, coming into the cabin, and shutting the door. "Where's Miss Marlow?"

"With her la'ship. Don't care to fetch her away!" said Sir Nugent distractedly. "Left me to mind Edmund! Extraordinary boy! Took me for a bad man: doesn't seem to know me at all! Now he wants a button."

"Well, give him a button!" said Tom, limping to the berth, and trying to draw the blanket back. "Hi, Edmund, what's all this?"

"I—want—my—Button!" wailed Edmund, diving deeper into the blankets.

"Never knew such a corkbrained boy!" fumed Sir Nugent. "Can't get another word out of him. It's my belief he hasn't brought it with him. What's more, I don't see that it would be a bit of use to him if I *could* find it. Well, I put it to you, Orde, would *you* want a button in such a case?"

"Oh, children often have a liking for odd toys!" said Tom. "I did myself. Give him one of your own buttons!"

"Dash it, I haven't got any!" A dreadful possibility reared its head. "You don't mean *cut one off*?"

"Lord, why not?" said Tom impatiently.

Sir Nugent reeled under the shock, but rallied. "*You* cut one off!" he countered.

"Not me!" replied Tom crudely. "This is the only suit of clothes I have, thanks to you! Besides, *I'm* not the boy's papa-in-law!"

"Well, he won't have it I am either, so that doesn't signify. To own the truth, I'd as lief I wasn't. Dashed embarrassing, you must agree, to have a son-in-law telling everyone I'm a bad man."

Tom, not thinking it worth while to reply to this, merely adjured him to find a suitable button. Sighing heavily, Sir Nugent unstrapped one of his numerous portmanteaux. It took him a little time to decide which of his coats he would be least likely to need in the immediate future, and when he made up his mind to the sacrifice of an elegant riding-coat, and started to saw off one of its buttons with his pocket-knife it was easy to see that the operation cost him considerable pain. He was slightly cheered by the reflection that the presentation of so large and handsome a button must raise him in Edmund's esteem. Advancing to the berth, he said winningly: "No need to cry any more, dear boy! Here's your button!"

The sobs ceased abruptly; Edmund emerged from the blankets, tearstained but joyful. "Button, Button!" he cried, stretching out his arms. Sir Nugent put the button into his hand.

There was a moment's silence, while Edmund, staring at this trophy, realized to the full Sir Nugent's perfidy. To blinding disappointment was added just rage. His eyes blazing through his tears he hurled the button from him, and casting himself face downward gave way to his emotions.

"For the lord's sake——!" expostulated Tom. "What *do* you want, you silly little lobcock?"

"My *own* Button!" wailed Edmund.

Fortunately, the noise of his lamentations reached Phoebe's ears. She came quickly into the cabin, and upon being assured by Sir Nugent that so far from bullying his son-in-law he had ruined one of his coats to provide him with the button he so insistently demanded said contemptuously: "I should have thought you must have known better! He means his nurse, of course! For heaven's sake, go away, both of you! There, my dear, come to Phoebe, then! *Poor* little man!"

"He s-said it was my Button!" sobbed Edmund into her shoulder. "He is *bad*! I won't have him, I won't, I won't!"

CHAPTER

22.

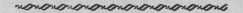

The Lion d'Argent was Calais' most fashionable inn. A parlour and its two best bedchambers had been engaged by Sinderby, the courier hired by Sir Nugent to smooth the furrows from the path of what promised to be a protracted honeymoon. Sinderby had crossed to Calais to be sure of securing accommodation worthy of his wealthy patron, both at the Lion d'Argent and at Abbeville's best hôtel. He had also hired a *bonne* to wait on Master Edmund; and he returned to Dover to superintend the embarkation of the party, feeling that he had provided for every eventuality.

He could not like the chariot of Sir Nugent's design but he accepted it; the arrival of my lady without her maid was harder to accept, for he foresaw that he would be expected to produce a first-rate abigail as soon as he landed again in France, which would be impossible. Her ladyship would have to be content with the services of some quite inferior person until she came to Paris, and she did not bear the appearance of a lady easily contented. With the arrival on board the *Betsy Anne* of Miss Marlow and Mr. Orde his spirits sank. Not only did the addition of two more people to the party overset his careful plans, but he could not approve of these unexpected travellers. He speedily came to the conclusion that there was something smoky about them. They had no baggage; and when, on arrival at Calais, he had requested Mr. Orde to give into his charge his and Miss Marlow's passports Mr. Orde, clapping a hand to his pocket, had uttered an exclamation of dismay. "Don't say you haven't got the passports!" had cried Miss Marlow. "Oh, no!" had been Mr. Orde's grim response. "I've got 'em all right and tight! *All* of 'em!" Upon which Miss Marlow had looked ready to faint. Something very havey-cavey about Miss Marlow and Mr. Orde, decided Sinderby.

He had foreseen that a wearing time awaited him in Calais, but he had not bargained for a search amongst the haberdashers' shops for a nightshirt to fit a six-year-old child. Furthermore, neither Sir Nugent's wealth nor his own address could procure two extra bedchambers at the Lion d'Argent, as full as it could hold. He was obliged to accept for Miss Marlow the apartment hired for my lady's abigail, and to put Mr. Orde in with Sir Nugent, an arrangement which was agreeable to neither of these gentlemen. The Young Person he had found to wait on my lady clearly would not do: she lacked quality. There would be complaints from my lady.

When he returned from scouring the town for a nightshirt it was to discover that another of his arrangements had been overset. Master Rayne had flatly refused to have anything to do with the excellent *bonne* provided for him. "Had to send her off," said Sir Nugent. "Silly wench started gabbling French to him! He wouldn't stand that, of course. Took it in snuff immediately. I knew he would, the moment she said bong-jaw. 'Mark me,' I said to Miss Marlow, 'if *her* tale ain't told!' Which it was. However, it don't signify: Miss Marlow means to look after him. Devilish good thing we brought her with us!"

Lady Ianthe having retired to bed as soon as she had arrived at the Lion d'Argent, only three of the party sat down to dinner in the private parlour. Edmund, who had revived the instant he had set foot on land, had providentially dropped asleep in the little bed set up for him in Phoebe's attic, and Pett was mounting guard over him. He was also washing and ironing his only day-shirt, an office which he promised to perform every evening until the young gentleman's wardrobe could be replenished.

Phoebe was too tired to talk, and Tom too much preoccupied

with the problems besetting them, so the burden of conversation fell on Sir Nugent, who maintained throughout the meal a stream of amiable reminiscences. However, when the covers were removed he excused himself, and went off to enjoy one of his cigars downstairs.

"Thank the lord!" said Tom. "Phoebe, we must discuss what's to be done. I don't want to croak, but the fact is we're in the devil of a fix."

"I suppose we are," she agreed, with remarkable calm. "But at least I know what *I* must do. Should you mind, Tom, if I write two letters before we discuss anything? I have spoken to the courier, and he engages to have them conveyed to England by the next packet, by a private hand. My letter to Grandmama, and the passports, will be taken directly to the Ship, but the courier warns me that if this wind continues the packet may not sail tomorrow." She sighed, and said resignedly: "I hope it may, but if it doesn't there's no other way of reaching poor Grandmama, so it's no use fretting."

"Who is the other letter for? Salford?" asked Tom shrewdly.

"Yes, of course. If he is unable to discover in which direction Ianthe fled——"

"I shouldn't think that likely," interrupted Tom. "Not if he gets wind of that carriage!"

"No, that's what I hope," she agreed. "But he might not, you know. So I shall send him word, and tell him also that I don't mean to leave Edmund, and will contrive somehow to leave word for him wherever we stop on the road."

"Oh!" said Tom. "So that's it, is it? Never mind the letters yet! We'll discuss this business first. How much money have you?" She shook her head. "None, eh? I thought not. Well, all I have is the ready in my pockets, and it don't amount to more than a couple of Yellow Boys, fifteen shillings in coach-wheels, and a few ha'pence. The roll of soft Father gave me is locked in my portmanteau. I daresay I could borrow from Fotherby, but I don't mind telling you it'll go against the shins with me to do it! I've had to borrow one of his shirts already, and a few neckcloths and handkerchiefs, you know. What about you?"

"Oh, isn't it *horrid*?" she exclaimed. "I've had to borrow from Lady Ianthe, and one would so much prefer not to be beholden to either of them! But perhaps we may be able to set it right again, if things go as I hope they may. Grandmama will receive those passports with my letter, and *surely* she must set out at once, whatever the weather?"

"I should think so," he agreed. "And a rare tweak she'll be in! Phew!"

"Yes, and how could one blame her? And if I were obliged to go beyond Paris—No, I think Salford must have overtaken us before that could happen, even if he doesn't start until he has read my letter. I know that Sir Nugent means to take four days on the road to Paris, and I fancy he will find he must take more, with Edmund on his hands. If he leaves Calais at all!"

"Leaving tomorrow, aren't they?"

"Yes, that's what they mean to do, but I shouldn't wonder at it if they find themselves fixed here for several days. Tom, I think Lady Ianthe really is ill!"

"Well, I own that would be nuts for us, but what if she ain't?"

"Then I am going with them," said Phoebe. "I won't leave Edmund. Oh, Tom, for all his quaint ways he's the merest baby! When I kissed him good-night he put his arms round my neck, and made me promise not to go away! I nearly cried myself, for it was so very affecting. He can't understand what is happening to him, and he was afraid I might slip away if he let me out of his sight. But when I said I would stay until he has Button again he was quite satisfied. I don't mean to break faith with him, I assure you."

"I see," Tom said.

She looked gratefully at him. "I knew you would. But I have been thinking whether it might not be best, perhaps, if you borrowed enough money from Sir Nugent to buy your passage back to Dover, to escort Grandmama?"

"You needn't say any more!" he interrupted. "If you think I'll leave you to career across France with this ramshackle pair you were never more mistaken in your life!"

"Well, to own the truth I didn't think you would," she said candidly. "And I must say I am thankful for it! Not but what Sir Nugent is very good-natured."

"Oh, he's good-natured enough!" Tom said. "But don't you get it into your head that he's a man of character, because he ain't! He's a pretty loose fish, if you want the truth! He was talking to me for ever aboard the schooner, and it's as plain as a pack-saddle he hobnobs with a set of dashed Queer Nabs:

all sorts up on the lark! In fact, he's what my father calls half flash and half foolish. Well, good God, if he had any principles he wouldn't have kidnapped Edmund!"

She smiled. "A Bad Man!"

"Ah, there's a deal of sense in young Edmund's cock-loft!" he said, grinning.

On the following morning Phoebe led Edmund down to breakfast to find that Ianthe was still keeping her bed; but her hopes of delay were dashed when Sir Nugent informed her with an air of grave concern that although her la'ship was feeling devilish poorly she was determined to leave Calais that morning. She had not closed her eyes all night. People had tramped past her door; boots had been flung about in the room above hers; doors had been slammed; and the rumble of vehicles over the *pavé* had brought on her nervous tic. Though it killed her she would drive to Abbeville that day.

Edmund, who was seated beside Phoebe at the table, a napkin knotted round his neck, looked up at this. "You wish to kill Mama," he stated.

"Eh?" ejaculated Sir Nugent. "No, dash it——! You can't say things like that!"

"Mama said it," replied Edmund. "On that boat she said it."

"Did she? Well, but—well, what I mean is its a bag of moonshine! Devoted to her! Ask anyone!"

"And you told lies, and——"

"You eat your egg and don't talk so much!" intervened Tom, adding in an undervoice to his perturbed host: "I shouldn't argue with him, if I were you."

"Yes, that's all very well," objected Sir Nugent. "He don't go about telling people *you* are a regular hedge-bird! Where will he draw the line, that's what I should like to know?"

"When Uncle Vester knows what you did to me he will punish you in a terrible way!" said Edmund ghoulishly.

"You see?" exclaimed Sir Nugent. "Now we shall have him setting it about I've been ill-using him!"

"Uncle Vester," pursued his small tormentor, "is the terriblest person in the world!"

"You know, you shouldn't talk like that about your uncle," Sir Nugent said earnestly. "I don't say I like him myself, but I don't go about saying he's terrible! Top-lofty, yes, but——"

"Uncle Vester doesn't *wish* you to like him!" declared Edmund, very much flushed.

"I daresay he don't, but if you mean he'll call me out—well, I don't think he will. Mind, if he chooses to do so——"

"Lord, Fotherby, don't encourage him!" said Tom, exasperated.

"Uncle Vester will grind your bones!" said Edmund.

"Grind my bones?" repeated Sir Nugent, astonished. "You've got windmills in your head, boy! What the deuce should he do that for?"

"To make him bread," responded Edmund promptly.

"But you don't make bread with bones!"

"Uncle Vester does," said Edmund,"

"That's enough!" said Tom, trying not to laugh. "It's you that's telling whiskers now! You know very well your uncle doesn't do any such thing, so just you stop pitching it rum!"

Edmund, apparently recognizing Tom as a force to be reckoned with, subsided, and applied himself to his egg again. But when he had finished it he shot a speculative glance at Tom under his curling lashes, and said: "P'raps Uncle Vester will nap him a rum 'un."

Tom gave a shout of laughter, but Phoebe scooped Edmund up and bore him off. Edmund, pleased by the success of his audacious sally, twinkled engagingly at Tom over her shoulder, but was heard to say before the door closed "We Raynes do not like to be carried!"

The party left for Abbeville an hour later, in impressive style. Sir Nugent having loftily rejected a suggestion that the heavy baggage should be sent to Paris by the *roulier*, no fewer than four vehicles set out from the Lion d'Argent. The velvet-lined chariot bearing Sir Nugent and his bride headed the cavalcade; Phoebe, Tom, and Edmund followed in a hired postchaise; and the rear was brought up by two cabriolets, one occupied by Pett and the Young Person hired to wait on my lady, and the other crammed with baggage. Quite a number of people gathered to watch this departure, a circumstance that seemed to afford Sir Nugent great satisfaction until a jarring note was introduced by Edmund, who strenuously resisted all efforts to make him enter the chaise, and was finally picked up, kicking and screaming, by Tom, and unceremoniously tossed on to the seat. As he saw fit to reiterate at the top of his voice that his father-in-law was a Bad Man, Sir Nugent fell into acute embarrassment, which was only alleviated when Tom reminded him that the interested onlookers were probably unable to understand anything Edmund said.

Once inside the chaise Edmund stopped screaming. He bore up well for the first stages, beguiled by a game of Travelling Piquet. But as the number of flocks of geese, parsons riding gray horses, or old women sitting under hedges was limited on the post-road from Calais to Boulogne, this entertainment soon palled, and he began to be restive. By the time Boulogne was reached Phoebe's repertoire of stories had been exhausted, and Edmund, who had been growing steadily more silent, said in a very tight voice that he felt as sick as a horse. He was granted a respite at Boulogne, where the travellers stopped for half an hour to refresh, but the look of despair on his face when he was lifted again into the chaise moved Tom to say, over his head: "I call it downright cruel to drag the poor little devil along on a journey like this!

At Abbeville, which they reached at a late hour, Sinderby was awaiting them at the best hôtel with tidings which caused Sir Nugent to suffer almost as much incredulity as vexation. Sinderby had to report failure. He had been unable to persuade the best hôtel's proprietor either to eject his other clients from the premises, or to sell the place outright to Sir Nugent. "As I ventured, sir, to warn you would be the case," added Sinderby, in a voice wholly devoid of expression.

"Won't sell it?" said Sir Nugent. "You stupid fellow, did you tell him who I am?"

"The information did not appear to interest him, sir."

"Did you tell him my fortune is the largest in England?" demanded Sir Nugent.

"Certainly, sir. He desired me to offer you his felicitations."

"He must be mad!" ejaculated Sir Nugent, stunned.

"It is curious that you should say so, sir," replied Sinderby. "Precisely what *he* said—expressing himself in French, of course."

"Well, upon my soul!" said Sir Nugent, his face reddening with anger. "That to *me*? I'll have the damned ale-draper to know I ain't in the habit of being denied! Go and tell him that when Nugent Fotherby wants a thing he buys it, cost what it may!"

"I never listened to such nonsense in my life!" said Phoebe, unable any longer to restrain her impatience. "I wish you will stop brangling, Sir Nugent, and inform me whether we are to put up here, or not! It may be nothing to you, but here in this unfortunate child nearly dead with fatigue, while you stand there puffing off your consequence!"

Sir Nugent was too much taken aback by this sudden attack to be able to think of anything to say; Sinderby, regarding Miss Marlow with a faint glimmer of approval in his cold eyes, said: "Bearing in mind, sir, your instructions to me to provide for her ladyship the strictest quiet, I have arranged what I trust will be found to be satisfactory accommodation in a much smaller establishment. It is not a resort of fashion, but its situation, which is removed from the centre of the town, may render it agreeable to her ladyship. I am happy to say that I was able to persuade Madame to place the entire inn at your disposal, sir, for as many days as you may desire it, on condition that the three persons she was already entertaining were willing to remove from the house."

"You aren't going to tell us that they *were* willing, are you?" demanded Tom.

"At first, sir, no. When, however, they understood that the remainder of their stay in Abbeville—I trust not a protracted one—would be spent by them in the apartments I had engaged at this hôtel for Sir Nugent, and at his expense, they expressed themselves as being enchanted to fall in with his wishes. Now, sir, if you will rejoin her ladyship in the travelling chariot, I will escort you to the Poisson Rouge."

Sir Nugent stood scowling for a moment, and pulling at his underlip. It was left to Edmund to apply the goad: "I want to go home!" announced Edmund fretfully. "I want my Button! I'm not *happy*!"

Sir Nugent started, and without further argument climbed back into the chariot.

When he saw the size and style of the Poisson Rouge he was so indignant that had it not been for Ianthe, who said crossly that rather than go another yard she would sleep the night in a cowbyre, another altercation might have taken place. As she was handed tenderly down the steps, Madame Bonnet came out to welcome her eccentric English guests, and fell into such instant raptures over the beauty of miladi and her enchanting little son that Ianthe was at once disposed to be very well pleased with the inn. Edmund, glowering upon Madame, showed a tendency to hide behind Phoebe, but when a puppy came frisking out of the inn his brow cleared magically, and he said: "I like this place!"

Everyone but Sir Nugent liked the place. It was by no means luxurious, but it was clean, and had a homelike air. The coffeeroom might be furnished only with benches and several very hard chairs, but Ianthe's bedchamber looked out on to a small garden and was perfectly quiet, which, as she naïvely said, was all that signified. Moreover, Madame, learning of her indisposition, not only gave up her own featherbed to her, but made her a tisane, and showed herself to be in general so full of sympathy that the ill-used beauty, in spite of aching head and limbs, began to feel very much more cheerful, and even expressed a desire to have her child brought to kiss her before he went to bed. Madame said she had a great envy to witness this spectacle, having been forcibly reminded of the *Sainte Vierge* as soon as she had set eyes on the angelic visages of miladi and her lovely child.

A discordant note was struck by Phoebe, who entered upon this scene of ecstasy only to tell Ianthe bluntly that she had not brought Edmund with her because she had a suspicion that what ailed his doting mother was nothing less than a severe attack of influenza. "And if he were to take it from you, after all he has been made to undergo, it would be beyond everything!" said Phoebe.

Ianthe achieved a wan, angelic smile, and said: "You are very right, dear Miss Marlow. Poor little man! Kiss him for me, and tell him that Mama is thinking of him all the time!"

Phoebe, who had left Edmund playing with the puppy, said: "Oh yes! I will certainly do so, if he should ask for you!" and withdrew, leaving Ianthe to the more agreeable companionship of her new admirer.

Upon the following day a physician was summoned to Ianthe's sick-bed. He confirmed Phoebe's diagnosis, and with very little prompting said that with persons of miladi's delicate constitution the greatest care must be exercised: miladi should beware of overexertion.

"So I fancy we may consider ourselves as fixed here for at least a week," Phoebe said, setting out with Tom and Edmund to buy linen for Edmund. "Tom, did you contrive to leave word at that hôtel where we were to be found? For Salford, you know!"

"Leave word!" echoed Tom scornfully. "Of course I didn't! You don't suppose they will forget Fotherby there in a hurry, do you? Trying to purchase the place! Well, of all the gudgeons!"

"Gudgeon," repeated Edmund, committing this pleasing word to memory.

"Oh, lord!" said Tom. "Now, don't you repeat that, young Edmund! And another thing! You are not to call Sir Nugent a moulder!" He waited until Edmund had run ahead again, and then said severely to Phoebe: "You know, Phoebe, you've no business to encourage him to be rude to Fotherby!"

"I don't *encourage* him," she said, looking a little guilty. "Only I can't help feeling that it would be foolish to stop him, because that might make Sir Nugent wish to keep him. And you can't deny, Tom, that if he were to take him in dislike it would make it much easier for—it would make it much easier to persuade Lady Ianthe to give him up!"

"Well, of all the unprincipled females!" gasped Tom. "Take care Fotherby ain't goaded into murdering him, that's all! He ain't in the humour to stand the roast much longer, and the way that young demon keeps on asking him if he can take a fly off a horse's ear, or some such thing, and then saying that his Uncle Vester can, is enough to drive the silly chuckle-head into a madhouse!"

Phoebe giggled, but said: "I must say, one can't wonder at his being out of humour! With an ailing bride and a son-in-law who detests him I do think he is having a *horrid* honeymoon, don't you?"

But neither of these disagreeable circumstances was, in fact, at the root of Sir Nugent's loss of equanimity, as Phoebe was soon to discover. Finding her alone in the coffee-room that afternoon it was not long before he was confiding to her the true cause of his dissatisfaction. He disliked the Poisson Rouge. Phoebe was rather surprised at first, because Madame Bonnet, besides being a notable cook, treated him with all the deference and anxiety to please that the most exacting guest could have demanded; and everyone else, from the waiter to the boots, scurried to obey his lightest commands. After listening to his discourse for a few minutes she understood the matter better. Sir Nugent had never before so lowered himself as to put up at any but the most fashionable and expensive hostelries. Both his consequence and his love of display had suffered severe wounds. More sensitive souls might shrink from attracting public notice; to Sir Nugent Fotherby, the wealthiest man in England, it was the breath of life. He had hugely enjoyed the sensation caused by Ianthe's opulent chariot; it afforded him intense pleasure to be ushered by landlords, bent nearly double in obsequiousness, into the best apartments, and to know that his sauntering progress was watched by envious eyes. No such eyes were to be found at the Poisson Rouge. To be sure, had he been able to purchase the Hôtel d'Angleterre, and to eject from it all other guests, he would have found himself similarly bereft; but what a gesture it would have been! how swiftly would the news of his eccentricity have spread over the town! with what awe would the citizens have pointed him out whenever he had sallied forth into the street! To have commandeered an unfashionable inn in a quiet road might be eccentric, but conveyed no sense of his fabulous wealth to the inhabitants of Abbeville. It was even doubtful if anyone beyond Madame Bonnet's immediate circle knew anything about it.

Naturally, he did not phrase his grievance so plainly: it rather crept through his other complaints. Acquainted as Phoebe was with another kind of pride, she listened to him with as much amazement as enjoyment. It would have been idle to have denied enjoyment, which was tempered only by regret that the rich mine of absurdity underlying his foppish appearance had been unknown to her when she had caused his image to flit through the pages of *The Lost Heir*. She found herself weaving a new story round him, and greeted with relief (since the outcome of her first literary adventure had been so appalling) the entrance into the room of Master Rayne, his new friend prancing at his heels.

Madame had bestowed the name of Toto upon the puppy, but he was known to her guests as Chien, a slight misunderstanding having arisen between Madame and Master Rayne. Edmund, overcoming his dislike of foreigners in his desire to pursue his acquaintanceship with Toto, had nerved himself to seek him in the kitchen, and even to demand his name of Madame. Chien was what Madame had said, and when he had repeated it she had nodded and clapped her hands. So Chien the puppy had to be.

Sir Nugent eyed his stepson with apprehension, but Edmund addressed himself to Phoebe. He wanted the coloured chalks Tom had bought for him, Chien having expressed a desire of having his likeness drawn. Having been supplied with the chalks and some paper he disposed himself on the floor and abandoned himself to art. The amiable Chien sat beside him, thumping his tail on the floor, and gently panting.

Seeing that Edmund was absorbed in his own affairs Sir Nugent resumed his discourse, walking up and down the room while he enumerated his grievances.

He had arrayed himself that morning in the nattiest of town-wear. His costume, besides such novel features as white pantaloons, and the Fotherby Tie, included a pair of Hessian boots, never before worn, and decorated with extra-large gold tassels. Hoby had made them to his design, and not Lord Petersham himself had ever been seen in more striking footwear. As Sir Nugent strode about the coffee-room the tassels swung with his every step, just as he had hoped they would. No one could fail to notice them: not even a puppy of dubious lineage.

Chien was fascinated by them. He watched them with his head on one side for several minutes before succumbing to temptation, but they beckoned too alluringly to be withstood. He rose to investigate them more nearly, and snapped at the one bobbing closest to his nose.

An exclamation of horror broke from Sir Nugent, followed by a stentorian command to Chien to drop it. Chien responded by growling as he tugged at the bauble, and wagging his tail. Edmund burst into a peal of joyous laughter, and clapped his hands. This outburst of innocent merriment drew from Sir Nugent so fierce an expletive that Phoebe thought it prudent to go to his rescue.

Tom entered on a scene of turmoil. Chien was barking excitedly in Phoebe's arms; Edmund was still laughing; Pett, attracted by his master's anguished cries, was kneeling before him, tenderly smoothing the tassel; and Sir Nugent, red with fury, was describing in intemperate language the various forms of execution of which Chien was deserving.

Tom acted with great presence of mind, commanding Edmund so peremptorily to take Chien away that Edmund obeyed him without venturing on argument. He then frowned down Phoebe's giggles, and mollified Sir Nugent by promising that Chien should not be allowed in the coffee-room again.

Informed of this ban Edmund was indignant, and had to be called to order for begging Tom to give Sir Nugent a pelt in the smeller. He retired in high dudgeon with Chien to the kitchen, where he spent the rest of the afternoon, playing with a lump of dough, and being regaled with raisins, marchpane and candied peel.

On the following day Sir Nugent wisely forbore to wear his beautiful new boots; and Edmund surprised his protectors by behaving in such a saintly fashion that Sir Nugent began to look upon him with reluctant favour.

It came on to rain in the afternoon, and after drawing several unconvincing portraits, which he kindly bestowed on Phoebe, Edmund became a trifle disconsolate, but was diverted by rain-drop races on the window-pane. He was kneeling on a chair, reporting the dilatory progress of her allotted drop to Phoebe, when a post-chaise and four came along the street, and drew up outside the Poisson Rouge.

Edmund was interested, but not more so than Phoebe, who no sooner heard the clatter of the approaching equipage than she came over to the window. It was the sound she had been hoping to hear, and as the chaise drew to a standstill her heart began to beat fast with hope.

The door was opened, and a figure in a caped overcoat of white drab sprang lightly down, turned to give some order to the postilions, and strode into the inn.

A long sigh escaped Phoebe; Master Rayne uttered a piercing scream, scrambled down from his chair, and tore across the room, shrieking: "Uncle Vester, Uncle *Vester*!"

CHAPTER

23

Edmund succeeded in opening the door, still shrieking *Uncle Vester!* at the top of his voice, just as Sylvester reached the coffee-room. He was halted on the threshold by having his legs embraced, and said, as he bent to detach himself from his nephew's frenzied grip: "Well, you noisy brat?"

"Uncle Vester, Uncle Vester!" cried Edmund.

Sylvester laughed, and swung him up. "Edmund, Edmund!" he mocked. "No, don't strangle me! Oh, you rough nephew!"

As yet unperceived, Phoebe remained by the window, watching with some amusement Edmund's ecstatic welcome to his wicked uncle. She was not so very much surprised, though she had not expected him to be cast into quite such transports of delight. If anything surprised her it was Sylvester's amused acceptance of Edmund's violent hug. He did not look at all like a man who disliked children; and he did not look at all like the man who had said such terrible things to her at Lady Castlereagh's ball. That image, which had so painfully obsessed her, faded, and with it the embarrassment which had made her dread his arrival almost as much as she had hoped for it.

"Tell that Bad Man I am *not* his little boy!" begged Edmund.

"Mama says I don't belong to you, Uncle Vester, but I *do*, don't I?"

This was uttered so passionately that Phoebe could not help laughing. Sylvester looked round quickly, and saw her. Something leaped in his eyes; she had the impression that he was going to start towards her. But the look vanished in a flash, and he did not move. The memory of their last meeting surged back, and she knew herself to be unforgiven.

He did not speak immediately, but set Edmund on his feet. Then he said: "A surprise, Miss Marlow—though I daresay I should have guessed, had I put myself to the trouble of considering the matter, that I should be very likely to find you here."

His voice was level, concealing all trace of the emotions seething in his breast. They were varied, but uppermost was anger: with her for having, as he supposed, assisted in the abduction of Edmund; with himself for having, for an unthinking moment, been so overjoyed to see her. That made him so furious that he would not open his lips until he could command himself. He had been trying, ever since the night of the ball, to banish all thought of her from his mind. This had not been possible, but by dint of dwelling on the injury she had done him he had supposed he had at least cured himself of his most foolish tendre for her. It had been an easy task to remember only her shameful conduct, for the wound she had inflicted on him could not be forgotten. She had held him up as a mockery to the world: that in itself was an offence, but if the portrait she had drawn of him had been unrecognizable he could have forgiven her. He had thought it so, but when he had turned to his mother, who had given the book to him to read, prepared to shrug it off, to tell her that it was too absurd to be worth a moment's indignation, he had seen in her face not indignation but trouble. He had been so much shocked that he had exclaimed: "This is not a portrait of me! Oh, I grant the eyebrows, but nothing else!" She had replied: "It is overdrawn, of course." It had been a full minute before he could bring himself to say: "Am I like this contemptible fellow, then? Insufferably proud, so indifferent—so puffed up in my own esteem that—Mama!" She had said quickly, stretching out her hand to him: "Never to me, Sylvester! But I have sometimes wondered—if you had grown to be a little—uncaring—towards others, perhaps."

He had been stricken to silence, and she had said no more.

There had been no need: Ugolino was a caricature, but a recognizable one; and because he was forced to believe this, his resentment, irrationally but inevitably in one of his temperament, blazed into such rage as he had never known before.

As he looked at Phoebe across the coffee-room he knew her for his evil genius. She had embroiled him in her ridiculous flight from her home; she had led him to pay her such attentions as had brought them both under the gaze of the interested ton. He forgot that his original intention had been to win her regard only to make her regret her rejection of his suit: he had forgotten it long ago. He knew that her book must have been written before she had become so well acquainted with him, but she had neither stopped its publication not warned him of it. She had been the cause of his having behaved, at that accursed ball, in a manner as unworthy of a man of breeding as anything could well have been. What had made him do it he would never know. It had been his intention to treat her with unswerving civility. He had meant to make no mention, then or thereafter of her book, but to have conducted himself towards her in such a way as must have shown her how grossly she had misjudged him. He had been sure that he had had himself well in hand; and yet, no sooner was his arm round her waist and his hand clasping hers than his anger and a sense of bitter hurt had mastered him. She had broken from his hold in tears, and he had been furious with her for doing it, because he knew he had brought that scene on himself. And now he found her in Abbeville, laughing at him. He had never doubted that it was she who had put the notion of a flight from England into Ianthe's head, but he had believed she had not meant to do so. It was now borne in upon him that she must have been throughout in Ianthe's confidence.

Knowing nothing of what was in his mind Phoebe watched him in perplexity. After a long pause she said, in a constricted tone: "I collect you have not received my letter, Duke?"

"I have not had that pleasure. How obliging of you to have written to me! To inform me of this affair, no doubt?"

"I could have no other reason for writing to you."

"You should have spared yourself the trouble. Having read your book, Miss Marlow, it was not difficult to guess what had happened. I own it did not occur to me that you were actually aiding my sister-in-law, but of course it should have. When I discovered that she had taken Edmund away withou his nurse I ought certainly to have guessed how it must be. Are you filling that position out of malice, or did you feel, having made London too hot to hold you, that it offered you a chance of escape?"

As she listened to these incredible words Phoebe passed from shock to an anger as great as his, and not as well concealed. He had spoken in a light, contemptuous voice; she could not keep hers from shaking when she retorted: "From malice!"

Before he could speak again Edmund said, in an uneasy tone: "Phoebe is my *friend*, Uncle Vester! Are—are you vexed with her? Please don't be! I love her next to Keighley!"

"Do you, my dear?" said Phoebe. "That is praise indeed! No one is vexed: your uncle was funning, that's all!" She looked at Sylvester, and said as naturally as she could: "You must wish to see Lady Ianthe, I daresay. I regret that she is indisposed—is confined to her bed, in fact, with an attack of influenza."

His colour was rather heightened; for he had forgotten that Edmund was still clinging to his hand, and was annoyed with himself for having been betrayed into impropriety. He said only: "I trust Fotherby is not similarly indisposed?"

"No, I believe he is sitting with Lady Ianthe. I will inform him of your arrival directly." She smiled at Edmund. "Shall we go and see if that cake Madame said she would bake for your supper is done yet?"

"I think I will stay with Uncle Vester," Edmund decided.

"No, go with Miss Marlow. I am going to talk to Sir Nugent," said Sylvester.

"Will you grind his bones?" asked Edmund hopefully.

"No, how should I be able to do that? I'm not a giant, and I don't live at the top of a beanstalk. Go, now."

Edmund looked regretful, but obeyed. Sylvester cast his driving-coat over a chair, and walked over to the fire.

He had not long to wait for Sir Nugent. That exquisite came into the room a very few minutes later, exclaiming: "Well, upon my soul! I declare I was never more surprised in my life! How do you do? I'm devilish glad to see your grace!"

This entirely unexpected greeting threw Sylvester off his balance. *"Glad to see me?"* he repeated.

"Devilish glad to see you!" corrected Sir Nugent. "Ianthe was persuaded you wouldn't follow us. Thought you wouldn't

251

wish to kick up a dust. I wouldn't have betted on it, though I own I didn't expect you to come up with us so quickly. Damme, I congratulate you, Duke! No flourishing, no casting, and how you picked up the scent the lord only knows!"

"What I want, Fotherby, is not your congratulation, but my ward!" said Sylvester. "You will also be so obliging as to explain to me what the devil you meant by bringing him to France!"

"Now, there," said Sir Nugent frankly, "you have me at Point Non-Plus, Duke! I fancy Nugent Fotherby ain't often at a loss. I fancy you'd be told, if you was to ask anyone, that Nugent Fotherby is as shrewd as he can hold together. But that question is a doubler. I don't mind telling you that every time I ask myself why the devil I brought that boy to France I'm floored. It's a great relief to me to hear you say you want him—you *did* say so, didn't you?"

"I did, and I will add that I am going to have him!"

"I take your word for that," Sir Nugent said. "Nugent Fotherby ain't the man to doubt a gentleman's honour. Let us discuss the matter!"

"There is nothing whatsoever to discuss!" said Sylvester, almost grinding his teeth.

"I assure your grace discussion is most necessary," said Sir Nugent earnestly. "The boy has a mother! She is not at the moment in plump currant, you know. She must be cherished!"

"Not by me!" snapped Sylvester.

"Certainly not! If I may say so—without offence, you understand—it's not your business to cherish her: never said you would! I daresay, being a bachelor, you may not know it, but *I* did. I'm not at all sure I didn't swear it: it sounded devilish like an oath to me."

"If all this is designed to make me relinquish my claim on Edmund——"

"Good God, no!" exclaimed Sir Nugent, blenching. "You mistake, Duke! Only too happy to restore him to you! You know what I think?"

"No! Nor do I wish to!"

"He's like some fellow in the Bible," said Sir Nugent, ignoring this savage interpolation. "Or was it a pig? Well, it don't signify. What I mean is, he's possessed of a devil." He added rather hastily: "No need to take a pet: you can rely on my discretion: shouldn't dream of spreading it about! Well, by Jove, now I know why you're so anxious to get him back, and what's more, I don't blame you. He's your heir too, ain't he? Tut, tut, tut, it's a nasty business! Very understandable you should wish to keep him hidden away. Shouldn't be surprised if he got to be dangerous when he grows up."

Sylvester said with ominous calm: "Will you have the goodness, sir, first to stop talking nonsense, and second to ask Lady Ianthe, without more ado, if she will receive me—for five minutes! No longer!"

"Five minutes! Why, she can be cast down in five seconds!" exclaimed Sir Nugent. "In fact, she would be cast down by the very sight of you, Duke. This business must be handled with delicacy. Her la'ship hasn't a suspicion in her noddle that you are here. It was a near-run thing, though. I came out of her room just as Miss Marlow was about to knock on the door. I instantly charged her not to breathe a word to her la'ship. 'Miss Marlow,' I said—Good God!" he ejaculated, with a sudden change of tone. "The abigail! the landlady! Must crave your grace's indulgence—not a moment to be lost! They must be warned! Obliged to leave you!"

He hurried over to the door as he spoke, and collided with Tom on the threshold. "The very person!" he said. "Allow me to present Mr. Orde to your grace! It's Salford, Orde: beg you will entertain him while I'm gone! Feel sure you'll be pleased with one another!"

"No need to put yourself about," Tom said. "I want a few words with his grace myself."

"You do? Well, that's a devilish fortunate circumstance because I think I should take a look in at her la'ship, in case she's got wind of Salford."

Tom shut the door upon him, and turned to confront Sylvester, standing by the table, his eyes as hard as agates, and as glittering. Tom met their challenge unwaveringly, and limped forward.

"If there was one person whom I never expected to have lent himself to this damnable affair it was you," said Sylvester very evenly. "What, if you please, am I to understand by it?"

"From all I've been able to make out," said Tom, continuing to look him in the eye, "you're riding too damned rusty to understand anything, my lord Duke! What the devil do you think I'm doing here? Trying to serve you a backhanded turn?"

Sylvester shrugged, and turned away to lean his arm along

the mantelshelf. "I suppose you to be here in support of Miss Marlow. The distinction between that and serving me a backhanded turn may be plain to you: it is not so to me."

"The only persons who have been trying to serve you a backhanded turn, my lord Duke, are Lady Ianthe and the court-card she's married!" said Tom. "As for Phoebe, the lord knows I didn't wish her to meddle in this business, but when I think of all she's done for you, and the thanks she's had for it, damme, I'd like to call you out! Oh, I know you wouldn't meet me! You needn't tell me I'm not of your rank!"

Sylvester turned his head, and looked at him, a puzzled frown in his eyes. "Don't talk to me like that, Thomas!" he said, in a quieter tone. "You had better sit down: how is that leg of yours?"

"Never mind my leg! It may interest you to know, my lord Duke——"

"For God's sake, will you stop calling me my lord Duke every time you open your mouth?" interrupted Sylvester irascibly. "Sit down, and tell me what Miss Marlow has done for me to earn my gratitude!"

"Well, that's what I meant to do at the start, but you made me lose my temper, which was the one thing I meant *not* to do," said Tom. "And what with you fit to murder the lot of us, and Phoebe swearing she'll starve in a ditch before she travels a yard in your company it'll be as well if I don't do it again!"

"She will not be asked to travel an inch in my company!"

"We'll see that presently. If *you* will sit down I'll tell you just how we both come to be here. But first I'd be glad to know if Lady Ingham's still at Dover. Or didn't you come by way of Dover?"

"I did, but I have no idea where Lady Ingham may be."

"I hoped you might have passed her on the road. Looks as though she couldn't face the jump. I take it you didn't put up at the Ship?"

"I didn't put up anywhere. I came down by the night-mail," said Sylvester.

"Oh! Well, I daresay the old lady is still there. Now, the long and the short of it is, Salford, that Phoebe and I were dashed well kidnapped! I'll tell you how it was."

Sylvester heard him in unresponsive silence, and at the end of the recital said coldly: "I regret having done Miss Marlow

254

an injustice, but I should feel myself obliged to her if she would confine her love of romantic adventure to her novels. If she felt she owed me some form of reparation she might, with more propriety and better effect, have written to me from Dover to tell me that Edmund had been taken to France."

"If Fotherby hadn't told the skipper to set sail I expect that's what she would have done," replied Tom equably.

"She had no business to go aboard the schooner at all. My nephew's movements are not her concern," said Sylvester, so haughtily that Tom had much ado not to lose his temper again.

"So I told her," he said. "But she thought them very much her concern, and you know why! I don't blame you for being angry with her for having written that dashed silly book. I didn't even blame you for having given her a trimming—though I did think that it was ungentlemanly of you to have done so in public. You may be a duke, but——"

"That will do!" Sylvester said, flushing. "That episode also—I regret!—deeply regret! But if you imagine that I think my rank entitles me to behave—*ungentlemanly*—you are doing me as great an injustice as any that I have done Miss Marlow! You appear to believe that I set inordinate store by my dukedom: I do not! If I have pride it is in my lineage! You should understand that: your father has the same pride! *We Ordes* was what he said to me, when we sat at dinner together: not *I am the Squire!*"

"Beg pardon!" Tom said, smiling a little.

"Yes, very well! but don't throw my rank in my face again! Good God, am I some money-grubbing Cit, sprung from obscurity, decorated with a title for political ends, and crowing like a cock on its own dunghill?" He broke off, as Tom shouted with laughter, and regarded him almost with hostility. "It was not my intention to divert you!"

"I know it wasn't," said Tom, wiping his eyes. "Oh, don't fall into a miff! I see precisely how it is! You are *very* like my father, Salford! It's as natural for you to be a duke as it is for him to be the Squire, and the only time when either of you remembers what you are is when some impudent fellow don't treat you with respect! Oh, lord, and I shall be just the same myself!" He began to laugh again, but gasped: "Never mind! The thing is that you take it in snuff that Phoebe meddled in your affairs, as though she were encroaching! Well, she wasn't.

The only idea she had in her head was how to undo the harm she never meant to bring on you!"

Sylvester got up, and went back to the fire, and said, as he stirred a log with one booted foot: "You think I should be grateful to her, do you? No doubt her intentions were admirable, but when I think how easily I might but for her interference have recovered Edmund without creating the smallest noise, I am not at all grateful."

"Yes, I *do* think you should be grateful!" retorted Tom. "If it hadn't been for her looking after him on board the *Betsy Anne* he might have stuck his spoon in the wall! I never saw anyone in worse case, and there was no one else to care what became of him, let me tell you!"

"Then I am grateful to her for that at least. If my gratitude is tempered by the reflection that Edmund would never have been taken to sea if *she* had not put the notion into his mother's head——"

"Salford, can't you forget that trumpery novel?" begged Tom. "If you mean to brood over it all the way home, a merry journey we shall have!"

Sylvester had been looking down at the fire, but he raised his head at that. *"What?"*

"How do you imagine I'm to get Phoebe home?" asked Tom. "Was you meaning to leave us stranded here?"

"Stranded! I can't conceive what need you can possibly have of my services when you appear to be on excellent terms with a man of far greater substance! I suggest you apply to Fotherby for a loan."

"Yes, that's what I shall be forced to do, if you're set on a paltry revenge," said Tom, with deliberation.

"Take care!" said Sylvester. "I've borne a good deal from you, Thomas, but that is a trifle too much! If I had a banking correspondent in France you might draw on me to any tune you pleased, but I have not! As for travelling Tab with Miss Marlow—no, by God, I won't! Ask Fotherby to accommodate you. You may as well be indebted to him as to me!"

"No, I may not," returned Tom. "You may not care for the mess Phoebe's in, but I do! You know Lady Ingham! That business—all the kick-up over Phoebe's book!—tried her pretty high, and she wasn't in the best of humours when I saw her last. By now I should think she's in a rare tweak, but *you* could bring her round your finger. If we go back to England with you, and you tell the old lady it was due to Phoebe you were able to recover young Edmund, all will be tidy. But if I have to take Phoebe back alone, and all you care for is to keep the business secret, we shall be lurched. You won't be able to keep it secret, either. What about Swale? What about——"

"The only one of my servants who knows where I have gone is Keighley. Swale is not with me. I am not as green as you think, Thomas!"

A slow grin spread over Tom's face. "I don't think you *green*, Salford!" he said. "Touched in the upper works is what you are!"

Sylvester looked frowningly at him. "What the devil are you at now? Do you think me dependent on my valet? You should know better!"

"Should I? Who is going to look after Edmund on the journey?"

"I am."

"*Have* you ever looked after him?" enquired Tom, grinning more widely.

"No," said Sylvester, very slightly on the defensive.

"You *will* enjoy the journey! You wait till you've had to wash him half a dozen times a day, my lord Duke! You'll have to dress him, and undress him, and tell him stories when he begins to feel queasy in the chaise, and see he don't eat what he shouldn't—and I'll wager you don't know, so the chances are you'll be up half the night with him!—and you won't even be able to eat your dinner in peace, because he might wake up, and start kicking up a dust. He don't like strange places, you know. And don't think you can hand him over to a chambermaid, because he don't like foreigners either! And if you're gudgeon enough to spank him for being an infernal nuisance he'll start sobbing his heart out, and you'll have every soul in the place behaving as if you were Herod!"

"For God's sake, Thomas——" Sylvester said, half laughing. "Damn you, I wish I'd never met you! Is it as bad as that?"

"Much worse!" Tom assured him.

"My God! I ought to have brought Keighley, of course. But what you don't realize is that when I drew from my bank what I supposed I should need I didn't bargain for two more persons being added to my party. We should come to a standstill before we reached Calais!"

"I hadn't thought of that," admitted Tom. "Well, we shall have to pawn something, that's all."

"*Pawn* something?" repeated Sylvester. "Pawn what?"

"We must think. Have you got that dressing-case of yours with you?"

"Oh, it's I who must pawn something, is it? No, I am happy to say I didn't bring anything but a portmanteau!"

"It will have to be your watch and chain, then. It's a pity you don't sport diamond tie-pins and rings. Now, if only you had a spanking great emerald, like the one Fotherby's dazzling us with today——"

"Oh, be quiet!" said Sylvester. "I'll be damned if I'll pawn my watch! Or anything else!"

"I'll do it for you," offered Tom. "*I* ain't so high in the instep!"

"What *you* are, Thomas, is a——" Sylvester stopped, as the door opened, and Phoebe came into the room.

She was looking so haughty that Tom nearly laughed; and her voice was more frigid than Sylvester's at its coldest. "Excuse me, if you please! Tom——"

"Miss Marlow," interrupted Sylvester, "I understand that I did you an injustice. I beg you will accept my sincere apology."

She threw him a disdainful glance. "It is not of the slightest consequence, sir. Tom, I came to tell you that I meant what I said to you on the stairs, and have settled what I shall do. I mean to beg Lady Ianthe to allow me to accompany her as far as to Paris. Once there I can await Grandmama at the Embassy. I am persuaded Sir Charles and Lady Elizabeth will permit me to remain with them when I tell them who I am. If you will go back to Dover with his grace——"

"Yes, that's a capital scheme!" said Tom. "What's more, I'd give my last coachwheel to see the Ambassador's face when you tripped in, and said you was Lady Ingham's granddaughter, and had come to stay because you'd mislaid her ladyship on the road, *with* all your baggage! For heaven's sake, don't be so shatterbrained! Do you want to set Paris talking as well as London?"

She flinched at this, and Sylvester, seeing it, said: "That's enough! Miss Marlow, you must see that that scheme is quite ineligible. Pray accept my escort to England!"

"I had rather hire myself out as a cook-maid!" she declared. "*Anything* would be preferable to travelling in your company!"

Having expressed himself in much the same terms, Sylvester was instantly nettled, and retorted: "You endured my company for a se'enight not so long since without suffering any ill-effect, and I daresay you will survive a few more days of it!"

"I wish with all my heart I had never gone aboard that ship!" said Phoebe, with deep feeling.

"So do I wish it! For a more ill-judged—I beg your pardon! I believe you meant well!"

"I shall never mean you well again!" she told him fierily. "As for your *condescension*, my lord Duke———"

"Phoebe, take a damper!" commanded Tom sternly. "And listen to me! I've gone along with you till now, but I'm going no farther. You'll do as I tell you, my girl. We shall go home with Salford, and you will *not* be beholden to him, if that's what frets you, because he needs you to look after Edmund. Yes, and let me remind you that you promised that boy you wouldn't leave him until he had his Button again!"

"He won't care for that *now*!" she said.

But as Edmund peeped into the coffee-room at that moment, and, upon being applied to by Tom, instantly said that he would not let Phoebe go away, this argument failed. She did suggest to Edmund that his uncle would suffice him, but he vigorously shook his curly head, saying: "No, acos Uncle Sylvester is *damned* if he will be plagued with me afore breakfast."

This naïve confidence did much to alleviate constraint. Phoebe could not help laughing, and Sylvester, wreaking awful vengeance on his small nephew, lost his stiffness.

But just as Edmund's squeals and chuckles were at their height the company was startled by a roar of rage and anguish from above-stairs. It seemed to emanate from a soul in torment, making Sylvester jerk up his head, and Edmund stop squirming in his hold.

"What the devil———?" exclaimed Sylvester.

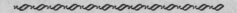

"*Now* what's amiss?" said Tom, limping to the door. "It sounds as if the Pink of the Ton has found a speck of mud on his coat."

"Pett! Pett!" bellowed Sir Nugent, descending the stairs. "Pett, where are you? *Pett*, I say!"

As Tom pulled the door wide Sylvester set Edmund on his feet, demanding: "What in God's name ails the fellow?"

With a final appeal to Pett as he crossed the hall Sir Nugent appeared in the doorway, nursing in his arms a pair of glossy Hessians, and commanding the occupants of the coffee-room to look—only to look!

"Don't make that infernal noise!" said Sylvester sharply. "Look at what?"

"That cur, that mongrel!" Sir Nugent shouted. "I'll hang him! I'll tear him limb from limb, by God I will!"

"Oh, sir, what is it?" cried Pett, running into the room.

"Look!" roared Sir Nugent, holding out the boots.

They were the Hessians of his own design, but gone were their golden tassels. Pett gave a moan, and fell back with starting eyes; Tom shot one quick look at Edmund, tried to keep his countenance, and, failing, leaned against the door in a fit of unseemly laughter; and Phoebe, after one choking moment, managed to say: "Oh, dear, how very unfortunate! But p-pray don't be distressed, Sir Nugent! You may have new ones put on, after all!"

"New ones——! Pett! if it was you who left the door open so that that mongrel could get into my room you leave my service today! Now! *Now,* do you hear me?"

"Never!" cried Pett dramatically. "The chambermaid, sir! the boots! *Anyone* but me!"

Balked, Sir Nugent rounded on Tom. "By God, I believe it was you! Laugh, will you? *You* let that cur into my room!"

"No, of course I didn't," said Tom. "I'm sure I beg your pardon, but of all the kick-ups only for a pair of boots!"

"*Only*——!" Sir Nugent took a hasty step towards him, almost purple with rage.

"Draw his cork, Tom, draw his cork!" begged Edmund, his angelic blue eyes blazing with excitement.

"Fotherby, *will* you control yourself?" Sylvester said angrily.

"Sir, there is no scratch on them! At least we are spared that!" Pett said. "I shall scour Paris day and night, sir. I shall leave no stone unturned. I shall——"

"My own design!" mourned Sir Nugent, unheeding. "Five times did Hoby have them back before I was satisfied!"

"Oh, sir, shall I ever forget?"

"What a couple of Bedlamites!" Sylvester remarked to Phoebe, his eyebrows steeply soaring, his tone one of light contempt.

"Gudgeon," said Edmund experimentally, one eye on his mentor.

But as Tom was telling Sylvester the tale of Chien's previous assault on the Hessians this essay passed unheeded. Sir Nugent, becoming momently more like an actor in a Greek tragedy, was lamenting over one boot, while Pett nursed the other, and recalling every circumstance that had led him to design such a triumph of modishness.

Sylvester, losing all patience, exclaimed: "This is ridiculous!"

"Ridicklus!" said Edmund, savouring a new word.

"You can say that?" cried Sir Nugent, stung. "Do you know how many hours I spent deciding between a plain gold band round the tops, or a twisted cord? Do you——"

"I'm not amused by foppery! I shall be——"

"Ridicklus gudgeon!"

"—obliged to you if—*What* did you say?" Sylvester, arrested by Edmund's gleeful voice, turned sharply.

The question, most wrathfully uttered, hung on the air. One scared look up into Sylvester's face and Edmund hung his head. Even Sir Nugent ceased to repine, and waited for the answer. But Edmund prudently refrained from answering. Sylvester, with equal prudence, did not repeat the question, but said sternly: "Don't let me hear your voice again!" He then turned back to the bereaved dandy, and said: "I shall be obliged to you if you will bring this exhibition to a close, and give me your attention!"

But at this moment the Young Person arrived on the scene, with an urgent summons from Ianthe. Miladi, alarmed by the sounds that had reached her ears, desired her husband to come up to her room immediately.

"I must go to her!" announced Sir Nugent. "She will be in despair when she learns of this outrage! 'Nugent,' she said, when I put them on yesterday—the first time! only once worn! 'You will set a fashion!' she said. I must go to her at once!"

With that, he laid the boot he was still holding in Pett's arms, and hurried from the room. Pett, with a depracating look at Sylvester, said: "Your grace will forgive us. It is a sad loss— a great blow, your grace!"

"Take yourself off!"

"Yes, your grace! At once, your grace!" said Pett, bowing himself out in haste.

"As for you," said Sylvester, addressing his sinful nephew, "if ever I hear such impertinence from you again it will be very much the worse for you! Now go!"

"I won't do it again!" said Edmund, in a small, pleading voice.

"I said, *Go!*"

Scarlet-faced, Edmund fled. This painful interlude afforded Phoebe an opportunity to resume hostilities, and she told Sylvester that his conduct was brutal. "It is extremely improper, moreover, to vent your own ill-temper on the poor child! It would have been enough for you to have given him a quiet reproof. I was never more shocked!"

"When I wish for your advice, Miss Marlow, be sure that I will ask for it," he replied.

She got up quickly, and walked to the door. "Take care what you are about!" she said warningly, as a parting shot. "*I* am not one of your unfortunate servants, obliged to submit to your odious arrogance!"

"One moment!" he said.

She looked back, very ready to continue to do battle.

"Since Fotherby appears to be unable to think of anything but his boots, perhaps you, Miss Marlow, will be good enough to inform Lady Ianthe of my arrival," said Sylvester. "Will you also, if you please, pack Edmund's clothes? I wish to remove from this place as soon as may be possible."

This request startled her into exclaiming: "You can't take him away at this hour! Why, it's past his bedtime already! It may suit you to travel by night, but it won't do for Edmund!"

"I have no intention of travelling by night, but only of removing to some other hôtel. We shall leave for Calais in the morning."

"Then you will remove without me!" said Phoebe. "Have you *no* thought for anyone's convenience but your own? What do you imagine must be *my* feelings—if you can condescend to consider anything so trifling? While I was one of Sir Nugent's party my lack of baggage passed unheeded, but in yours it will not! And if you think I am going to one of the fashionable hôtels in a travel-stained dress, and nothing but a small bandbox for luggage, you are very much mistaken, Duke!"

"Of what conceivable importance are the stares or the curiosity of a parcel of hôtel servants?" he asked, raising his brows.

"Oh, how like you!" she cried. "How *very* like you! To be sure, the mantle of your rank and consequence will be cast over me, won't it? How delightful it will be to become so elevated as to treat with indifference the opinions of inferior persons!"

"As I am not using my title, and my consequence, as you are pleased to call it, is contained in one portmanteau, you will find my mantle somewhat threadbare!" Sylvester flung at her. "However, set your mind at rest! I shall hire a private parlour for your use, so you will at least not be obliged to endure the stares of your fellow-guests!"

At this point Thomas entered a caveat. "I don't think you should do that, Salford," he said. "You're forgetting that the dibs aren't in tune!"

A look of vexation came into Sylvester's face. "Very well! We will put up at some small inn, such as this."

"The inns are most of 'em as full as they can hold," Tom warned him. "If we have to drive all over the town, looking for a small inn that has rooms for the four of us, we shall very likely be up till midnight."

"Do you expect me to remain *here*?" demanded Sylvester.

"Well, there's plenty of room."

"If there is room here there will be———"

"No, there will not be room elsewhere!" interpolated Phoebe. "Sir Nugent is hiring the whole house, having turned out the wretched people who were here before us! And why you should look like that I can't conceive, when it is just what you did yourself, when you made Mrs. Scaling give up her coffee-room for your private use!"

"And who, pray, were the people I turned out of the Blue Boar?" asked Sylvester.

"Well, it so happened that there weren't any, but I don't doubt you *would* have turned them out!"

"Oh, indeed? Then let me tell you———"

"Listen!" begged Tom. "You can be as insulting to one another as you please all the way to Dover, and I swear I won't say a word! But for the lord's sake decide what we are to do first! They'll be coming to set the covers for dinner soon. I don't blame you for not wanting to stay here, Salford, but what with pockets to let and young Edmund on our hands, what else can we do? If you don't choose to let Fotherby stand the nonsense you can arrange with Madame to pay your own shot."

"Well, I am going to put Edmund to bed!" said Phoebe. "And if you try to drag him away from me, Duke, I shall tell him that you are being cruel to me, which will very likely set him against you. Particularly after your cruelty to him!"

On this threat she departed, leaving Sylvester without a word to say. Tom grinned at him. "Yes, you don't want Edmund to tell everyone *you* are a Bad Man. He's got Fotherby regularly blue-devilled, I can assure you! Come to think of it, he's already set it about that you grind men's bones for bread."

Sylvester's lips twitched, but he said: "It seems to me that Edmund has been allowed to become abominably out of hand! As for you, Thomas, if I have much more of your damned impudence———"

"*That's* better!" said Tom encouragingly. "I thought you

264

were never coming down from your high ropes! I say, Salford——"

He was interrupted by the return of Sir Nugent, who came into the room just then, an expression of settled gloom on his countenance.

"Have you told Ianthe that I am here?" at once demanded Sylvester.

"Good God, no! I wouldn't tell her for the world!" replied Sir Nugent, shocked. "Particularly *now*. She is very much distressed. Feels it just as I knew she must. You will have to steal the boy while we are asleep. In the middle of the night, you know."

"I shall do nothing so improper!"

"Don't take me up so!" said Sir Nugent fretfully. "No impropriety at all! You are thinking you would be obliged to creep into Miss Marlow's bedchamber——"

"I am thinking nothing of the sort!" said Sylvester, with considerable asperity.

"There you go again!" complained Sir Nugent. "Dashed well snapping off my nose the instant I open my mouth! No question of creeping into her room: she'll bring the boy out to you. You'll have to take her along with you, of course, and I'm not sure that Orde hadn't better go too, because you never know but what her la'ship might bubble the hoax if he stayed behind. The thing is——"

"You needn't tell me!—Thomas, either you may stop laughing, or I leave you to rot here!—Understand me, Fotherby! I have no need to steal my ward! Neither you nor Ianthe has the power to prevent my removing him. Well, though I am going to do so I have enough respect for her sensibility as to wish not only to inform her of my intention, but to assure her that every care shall be taken of the boy. Now perhaps you will either conduct me to Ianthe, or go to tell her yourself that I am taking Edmund home tomorrow!"

"No, I won't," said Sir Nugent. "You may have the right to do it—well, I know you have! asked my attorney!—but does her la'ship know it? What I mean is will she own she knows it? If you think she will, Duke, all I can say is that you don't know much about females! Which is absurd, because you don't bamboozle me into believing you didn't offer a *carte blanche*, not a year after your come-out, to—what was that little light-skirt's name? You know the one I mean! A regular high flyer, with yaller curls, and——"

"We will leave my affairs out of this discussion!" said Sylvester, rigid with anger.

"Oh, just as you wish! Not but what I've often wanted to ask you—However, I can see you'll fly up into the boughs, so never mind that! The thing is, if I was to tell her la'ship what was in the wind she'd expect me to stop you making off with the brat. And let alone I don't want to stop you, how the devil could I? You know what females are, Duke—no objection to my saying that, is there?—She'll think I ought to pull out a sword, and it wouldn't be a mite of use telling her I haven't got a sword, because the trouble with females is they ain't rational! And a pretty time I should have of it, while you were running off with the boy, as merry as cup and can! Why, I shouldn't wonder at it if she didn't forgive me for a twelve-month!"

"That," said Sylvester, "is your affair!"

"Well, of all the scaly things to say!" gasped Sir Nugent. "Here's me, anxious to help you to the boy, and instead of——Oh, my God, haven't you gone to bed yet?"

This exclamation was caused by the appearance on the threshhold of Master Rayne, bearing all the look of one who, having reached a painful decision, was not to be turned from it. He was followed by Phoebe, who said: "Edmund wishes to speak to you before he does go to bed, Sir Nugent."

"No, no, take him away!" said Sir Nugent. "I've had a very unpleasant shock—not by any means in prime twig!"

"It isn't *wish*, ezzackly," said Edmund, walking resolutely up to his chair, and standing before him with his hands behind his back. "If you please, I beg pardon for having called you a gudgeon, sir. *Ridicklus* gudgeon," he added conscientiously.

Sir Nugent waved him peevishly away. "Oh, very well!"

"And also," said Edmund heroically, "it wasn't Chien. It was me. And I'm sorry, and—and here they are!"

As he spoke he brought his hands from behind his back, and opened them disclosed two dishevelled tassels. Phoebe, unprepared for this gesture, gave a gasp of consternation; Sir Nugent, after staring for a tense moment at the tassels, said chokingly: "You—you——! By God, if I don't——"

"Fotherby!"

Sylvester's voice, ripping across the room, checked the

infuriated dandy as he started up menacingly from his chair. Sylvester came quickly forward, and Edmund, though he had stood his ground, breathed more easily. "You *dare!*" Sylvester said through his teeth.

"I was only going to give him a shake," said Sir Nugent sulkily. "Damn it, I'm his father-in-law, ain't I?"

Sylvester uttered a short, contemptuous laugh, and looked down at Edmund. "Give me those tassels, brat, and be off to bed!"

Edmund relinquished them, but said dolefully: "I thought you wouldn't be angry any more if I said I was sorry!"

"I'm not angry," Sylvester said, tickling his cheek with one careless finger. "Word of a Rayne! Good-night, you imp! Don't keep Miss Marlow waiting!"

"*You're* not angry!" exploded Sir Nugent. "I wonder you don't *reward* the young viper!"

"I may yet," replied Sylvester coolly. "He has done what I could not: given you your own again! When you kidnapped that boy, Fotherby, you knew yourself safe from me, because I would not publish my affairs to the world! I doubt if anything I could have done would have caused you such anguish as Edmund has made you suffer! Bless him, he's full of pluck! *How* his father would have laughed!"

"I have a good mind to call you out! Upon my soul I have!" Sir Nugent threatened.

"I don't think you have!" Sylvester tossed at him. "I am accounted a fair shot, my hero!"

"I fancy," said Sir Nugent, fulminating, "that Nugent Fotherby is as game a man as ever lived! I fancy, if you were to ask anyone, that would be the answer. The thing is her la'ship wouldn't like it. Must cherish her! But if she thinks I'm going to take that changeling of hers along with us——!"

The very thought of Edmund seemed to choke him, for he broke off, his choler mounting again, snatched up the tassels, which Sylvester had dropped disdainfully on the table, and stormed out of the room.

Tom could not but feel that Edmund's confession had still further complicated matters; for the Poisson Rouge now seemed hardly big enough to hold both Sylvester and Sir Nugent. But Edmund's villainy was soon found to have exercised a good effect. Ianthe, when the story was poured into her ears, said that Edmund must be punished. Sir Nugent told her bitterly that Sylvester would not allow it. So the secret of Sylvester's arrival was out. Ianthe fell back on her pillows with a shriek; but Sir Nugent, forgetting his marriage vows, informed her (smiting her dressing-table with his clenched fist so that all the gold-topped bottles on it jumped) that she might there and then choose between him and her hell-born brat. This show of violence quite overawed her. She was also a good deal impressed, for it was clearly a proof of masculine superiority, to which she instinctively responded. Her protests, though maintained tearfully, began to lack conviction; and when Sylvester, taking the law into his own hands, knocked on her door, and entered the room hard upon his knock, his reception was less daunting than might have been expected. He was certainly greeted with reproaches, but these were largely directed against his having encouraged Edmund to behave badly. As she blamed him for not having punished Edmund her subsequent declaration that nothing would induce her to abandon her child to his unkindness sounded lame even in her own ears. She then burst into tears, and said that no one had any consideration for her nerves.

This outbreak of lamentation brought Phoebe into the room, to beg her to restrain herself for Edmund's sake. "I am persuaded you cannot wish to distress him!" she said. "Only think how disturbing for such a little boy to hear his mama crying!"

"You are as heartless as Sylvester!" wept Ianthe. "None of you cares for my sufferings!"

"Not I, certainly," said Sylvester.

"*Oh!*" gasped Ianthe, bouncing up in her bed. Indignation brought her sobs to an abrupt end; an angry flush reddened her cheeks; and her lovely eyes darted fire at Sylvester.

"Not the snap of my fingers!" said Sylvester. "You see, I am quite honest with you, Ianthe. And before you resume this affecting display of sensibility listen to what I have to say to you! It has pleased you to remember for four years a foolish thing I once said to you. You have cast it in my teeth so often that you have come to believe I meant it. No, don't turn away your head! Look me in the face, and answer me! Do you think that I could treat with unkindness all that I have left to me of Harry?"

She said sulkily, picking at her handkerchief: "I am sure *I* never thought you cared so very much for Harry! You didn't shed a tear when he died!" She stopped, frightened by the expression on his face.

It was a moment before he spoke. Watching him, Phoebe saw that he was very pale, his satyr-look pronounced, his lips tightly compressed. When he unclosed them it was to say in a curt voice: "When Harry died—I lost a part of myself. We will not discuss that. I have only this to add: you are Edmund's mother, and you may visit him whenever you choose to do so. I have told you so many times already, but I'll repeat it. Come to Chance when you please—with or without your husband!"

Sir Nugent, who had been listening intently, exclaimed as the door shut behind Sylvester: "Well, upon my soul, that's devilish handsome of him! Now, you must own, my love, it *is* devilish handsome! Damme if I ever thought he'd invite me to Chance! The fact is I had a notion he didn't like me above half. I shall go, I think. I don't say it won't be a dead bore: no fun and gig, and the company pretty stiff-rumped, I daresay. But visiting at Chance, you know! I'll tell you what I'll do: I'll invite him to drink a glass of wine with me! No, by Jove, I'll invite him to dine with me! Do you think I should change my dress, my love? No! might put him out of countenance. I shall put on a fresh neckcloth: that will exactly answer the purpose!"

Full of these amiable plans he hurried from the room. Ianthe dissolved again into tears, but showed signs of recovering her spirits when Phoebe assured her she would take every care of Edmund upon the journey back to London.

"Oh, dear Miss Marlow, were it not for your going I could not consent to his being taken from me!" Ianthe said, clasping Phoebe's hand. "I am sure you will care for him as well as I could myself! And if anyone is so unjust as to say that I deserted my child *you* know it is untrue!"

"If anyone should say such a thing to me I shall reply that he was torn from your arms," promised Phoebe. "Excuse me! I must go back to him, and blow out his candle."

But when she reached the bedchamber she shared with Edmund she checked on the threshold, for Sylvester was sitting on the edge of Edmund's crib. He got up at once, saying with some constraint: "I beg your pardon! I should not be here, but Edmund called to me."

"Of course! It's of no consequence!" she said, in a more friendly tone than she had yet used to him.

"Phoebe, Uncle Vester says my papa would have cut off

one tassel, and he would have cut off the other!" Edmund told her, his eyes sparkling.

She could not help laughing. "I wonder how he would like it if you cut the tassels from *his* boots!"

"Ah, I have explained to him that it is a thing which must on no account be done to uncles!" Sylvester said. He ruffled Edmund's curls. "Good-night, vile brat!"

"You won't go away?" Edmund said, assailed by a sudden fear.

"Not without you."

"And Phoebe? And Tom?"

"Yes, they will both come with us."

"Good!" said Edmund, releasing his clutch on Sylvester's coat. "I daresay we shall be as merry as grigs!"

CHAPTER

25

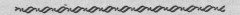

The party reached Calais two days later, having broken the journey at Etaples, where they stayed in what Sylvester unequivocally described as the worst hostelry ever to have enjoyed his patronage. Only Tom might have been said to have fulfilled Edmund's expectations.

Sylvester's temper had been ruffled at the outset, for not even the pledging of Phoebe's little pearl brooch as well as his own watch and chain provided him with enough money to enable him to travel in the style to which he was accustomed. He was extremely vexed with Tom for suddenly producing the brooch in the pawnbroker's shop, which piece of folly, he said, would now make it necessary for him to send one of his people over to France to redeem it. He disliked haggling over the worth of his watch; he disliked still more to be in any way beholden to Phoebe; and he emerged from this degrading experience in anything but a sunny humour. He then discovered that the hire of two post-chaises and four would result in the whole party's being stranded half-way between Abbeville and Calais, and was obliged to make up his mind which of two evils was likely to prove the lesser: to cram four persons, one of whom was a small boy subject to travel-sickness, into one

271

chaise and four; or to hire two chaises, and drive for well over a hundred and twenty kilometres behind a single pair of horses. The reflection that Edmund, before he succumbed to his malaise, would fidget and ask incessant questions decided the matter: he hired two chaises, and in so doing made the discovery that Mr. Rayne, a man of modest means, did not meet with the deference accorded to his grace of Salford. The postmaster was not uncivil: he was uninterested. Sylvester, accustomed his whole life long to dealing with persons who were all anxiety to please him, suffered a slight shock. Until he had landed at Calais he had never made a journey in a hired vehicle. He had thought poorly of the chaise supplied by the Lion d'Argent; the two allotted to him in Abbeville filled his fastidious soul with disgust. They were certainly rather dirty.

"Why hasn't this carriage got four horses?" demanded Edmund.

"Because it only has two," replied Sylvester.

"Couple o' bone-setters!" said Edmund disparagingly.

They were found to be plodders; nor, when the first change was made, was there much improvement in the pace at which the ground was covered. There was a world of difference between a team and a pair, as Phoebe soon discovered. The journey seemed interminable; and although the more sober pace seemed to affect Edmund less than the swaying of a well-sprung chaise drawn by four fast horses, he soon grew bored, a state of mind which made him an even more wearing companion than when he was sick. She could only be thankful when, at Etaples, Sylvester, after one look at her, said they would go no farther that day. She desired nothing so much as her bed; but to her suggestion that some soup might be sent up to her room Sylvester returned a decided: "Certainly not! Neither you nor Edmund ate any luncheon, and if you are not hungry now you should be." He gave her one of his searching looks, and added: "I daresay you will like to rest before you dine, Miss Marlow. Edmund may stay with me."

She was led upstairs by the boots to a room overlooking a courtyard; and having taken off her dress and hung it up, in the hope that the worst of its creases might disappear, she lay down on the bed and closed her eyes. The suspicion of a headache nagged at her, but she soon discovered that there was little chance of being able to rid herself of it. To judge by the noises that came from beneath her window the kitchens had

272

access on to the yard, and were inhabited by a set of persons who seemed all to be quarrelling, and hurling pots and pans about.

Just as she was about to leave her room again Tom came to see how she did. He was carrying a glass of wine, which he handed to her, saying that Salford had sent it. "He says you are doneup. And I must say," added Tom critically, "you do look hagged!"

Having studied her reflection in the spotted looking-glass she was well aware of this, and it did nothing to improve her spirits. She sipped the wine, hoping that it might lessen the depression that had been creeping on her all day.

"What a racket these Frenchies make!" observed Tom, looking out of the window. "Salford cut up stiff when he found this room gave on to the yard, but ours is directly above the *salle des buveurs*, and that wouldn't have done for you at all. There seems to be a fair going on: the town's packed, and no room to be had anywhere."

"Have you to share a room with Salford? He won't like that!"

"Oh, that ain't what's making him ride grub!" said Tom cheerfully. "He don't care for the company, and he ain't accustomed to being told by waiters that he shall be served *bientôt*! I left him coming the duke in the coffee-room, to get us one of the small tables to ourselves. He'll do it too: the waiter was beginning to bow and wash his hands—and all for no more than his grace's high-bred air and winning smile!"

They found, on descending to the coffee-room, that Sylvester had indeed procured a small table near the door, and was awaiting them there, with Edmund, who was seated on an eminence composed of two large books placed on his chair. Edmund was looking particularly angelic and was exciting a good deal of admiration.

"A little more of this sort of thing," said Sylvester in an undervoice, as he pushed Phoebe's chair in for her, "and his character would be ruined!"

"Except that he doesn't care for it," she agreed.

"No, thank God! I have ordered what I hope you will like, Miss Marlow, but there is very little choice. What we should call an ordinary, at home."

He turned to speak to a harried waiter, and Edmund, apparently reconciled to the French language by his uncle's fluency, suddenly announced that he too could talk French.

"Oh, what a bouncer!" said Tom. "What can you say?"

"I can say *words*," replied Edmund. "I can say *bonjour* and *petit chou* and——" But at this point he lost interest, the waiter having dumped in front of him the *plat* of his careful choice.

The dinner was good, and, although the service was slow, the meal might have passed without untoward incident had Edmund not been inspired to favour the assembled company with a further example of his proficiency in the French tongue. An enormously fat woman, seated at the end of the table that ran down the centre of the room, after incurring his displeasure by nodding and smiling at him every time he looked up from his plate, was so much ravished by his beauty that when she passed his chair on her way out of the coffee-room she not only complimented Phoebe on his seraphic countenance but was unable to resist the temptation of swooping down upon him and planting a smacking kiss on his cheek. *"Petit chou!"* she said, beaming at him.

"Salaude!" returned Edmund indignantly.

For this he was instantly condemned to silence, but when Sylvester, after explaining to the shocked lady that Edmund had picked the word up without an idea of its meaning, offering her his apologies, and enduring the hearty amusement of all those within earshot, sat down again and directed a look at his erring nephew that boded no good to him, Phoebe took up the cudgels in Edmund's defence, saying: "It is unjust to scold him! He *doesn't* know what it means! He must have heard someone say it at the Poisson Rouge, when he was in the kitchen!"

"Madame says it to Elise," said Edmund enigmatically.

"Well, it isn't a very civil thing to say, my dear," Phoebe told him, in gentle reproof.

"I didn't think it was," said Edmund, in a satisfied voice.

"It seems to me an extraordinary thing that he should have been allowed to keep kitchen company," said Sylvester. "I should have supposed that amongst the four of you——"

"Yes, and it has often seemed extraordinary to me that amongst how many people he should have been allowed to keep stable company!" flashed Phoebe.

This was so entirely unanswerable that silence reigned until Tom, to relieve the tension, asked Sylvester some question about the next day's journey. As soon as they left the coffee-room Phoebe took Edmund up to bed, bidding Sylvester a chilly goodnight, and Tom a very warm one.

At breakfast on the following morning punctilious civility reigned, Sylvester addressing suave remarks to Phoebe, and Phoebe replying to them with formal courtesy.

But formality deserted Phoebe abruptly when she discovered that instead of Edmund she was to have Tom for her travelling companion. She said at once: "No, no! Please leave Edmund with me! It was to take care of him that I came with you, Duke, and I assure you I am very happy to do so!"

"You are very good, ma'am, but I will take him today," he replied.

"But why?" she demanded.

He hesitated, and then said: "I wish it."

It was spoken in his indifferent voice. She read in it a reflection on her management of Edmund, arising possibly from his overnight solecism, and turned away that Sylvester might not have the satisfaction of seeing how mortified she was. When she next glanced at him she found that he was watching her, she thought with a shade of anxiety in his rather hard eyes. He moved towards her, and said: "What did I say to distress you? I had no such intention!"

She put up her brows. "Distress me? Oh, no!"

"I am taking Edmund with me because I am persuaded you have the head-ache," he said bluntly.

It was true, but she disclaimed, begging him to let Edmund go with her. His thought for her disarmed her utterly; her constraint vanished; and when she raised her eyes to his face they were shyly smiling. He looked down at her for a moment, and then said almost brusquely, as he turned away: "No, don't argue! My mind is made up."

By the time Calais was reached her head-ache had become severe, a circumstance to which she attributed her increasingly low spirits. Edmund, when he heard of it, disclosed that Uncle Vester had the head-ache too.

"I?" exclaimed Sylvester. "I've never had the head-ache in my life, brat!"

"Oh!" said Edmund, adding with a confiding smile: "Just a bit cagged-like!"

Since Tom had had the forethought to consult Sinderby, the inn which housed them that night, though a modest establishment in the unfashionable quarter of the town, was both quiet and comfortable. A tisane, followed by a night's undisturbed sleep, cured Phoebe's head-ache. Her spirits, however, remained low, but as she opened her eyes to see wet window-panes and a sky of a uniform gray this was perhaps not to be wondered at.

"We are in for an intolerably tedious crossing," Sylvester said, when he joined the rest of the party at breakfast. "There is very little wind—which has this advantage, I suppose, that it will be better for one of our number. I have been able to procure a cabin for you, Miss Marlow, but I fear you will be heartily sick of the crossing—particularly if it continues to rain, as it shows every sign of doing."

"Why," demanded Edmund, "am I not let have an egg? I do not want this bread-and-milk. Keighley says it is cat-lap."

"Never mind!" said Phoebe, laughing. "You may have an egg tomorrow."

"I may not be hungry tomorrow," said Edmund gloomily. "I am hungry *now*!"

"Oh, dear! Are you?"

"Fair gutfoundered!" said Edmund.

Sylvester, who was glancing through a newspaper, lowered it, and said sternly: "You never learned *that* from Keighley!"

"No," admitted Edmund. "Jem says it."

"Who the devil is Jem?"

"The one with the spotty face. Don't you *know*, Uncle Vester?" said Edmund, astonished.

"One of the stable-hands?"

Edmund nodded. "He tells me very good words. He is a friend of mine."

"Oh, is he?" said Sylvester grimly. "Well, unless you want to feel my hand, don't repeat them!"

Quelled, Edmund returned to his bread-and-milk. Over his head Sylvester said ruefully: "I make his apologies, Miss Marlow. It is the fault of too old a nurse, and by far too old a tutor. I must find a younger man."

"I don't think that would answer nearly as well as a sensible female," said Phoebe. "Someone like my own dear governess, who doesn't get into a fuss for torn clothes, and likes animals, and collecting butterflies and birds' eggs, and—oh, *you* know, Tom!"

"My dear Miss Marlow, only furnish me with her name and her direction!" begged Sylvester.

"You have met her," she reminded him. "But I am afraid I cannot spare her to you. She and I mean to set up house together, as soon as I come of age."

"Set up house together!" he repeated incredulously.

"Yes. *She* is going to keep house, and *I*— —" She stopped suddenly, gave a little gasp, and continued defiantly: "And I am going to write novels!"

"I see," he said dryly, and retired into the newspaper again.

CHAPTER

26

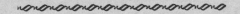

They went aboard the packet in a light drizzle, and with less opposition from Master Rayne than might have been expected. When it was borne in upon him that his all-powerful uncle was unable to waft him miraculously across the sea he did indeed hover on the brink of a painful scene, saying: "No, no, no! I won't go on a ship, I won't, I *won't*!" on a rising note that threatened a storm of tears. But Sylvester said: "I *beg* your pardon?" in such blighting accents that he flushed up to the ears, gave a gulp, and said imploringly: "If you please, I don't want to! It will give me that dreadful pain in me pudding-house!"

"In your *what*?"

Edmund knuckled his eyes.

"I thought there was more steel in you," said Sylvester contemptuosly.

"There is steel in me!" declared Edmund, his eyes flashing. "Keighley says I have good bottom!"

"Keighley," said Sylvester, in a casual tone, "is waiting for us at Dover. Miss Marlow, I must beg you won't mention to him that Edmund found he couldn't throw his heart over. He would be very much shocked."

278

"I will go on that ship!" said Edmund in a gritty voice. "We Raynes can throw our hearts over *anything!*"

His heart shyed a little at the gangway, but Sylvester said "Show us the way, young Rayne!" and he stumped resolutely across it.

"Edmund, you're a great gun!" Tom told him.

"Game as a pebble!" asserted Edmund.

For Phoebe the crossing was one of unalleviated boredom. Sylvester, wrapping his boat-cloak round Edmund, kept him on deck; and since there was clearly nothing for her to do, and it continued to rain, she could only retire to her cabin and meditate on a bleak future. The packet took nine hours to reach Dover, and never had nine hours seemed longer. From time to time she was visited by Tom, bringing her either refreshments, or the latest news of Edmund. He had been a little sick, Tom admitted, but nothing to cause alarm. They had found a sheltered spot on deck, and were taking it in turns to remain there with him. No, there was nothing for her to do: Edmund, having slept for a time, now seemed pretty bobbish.

Towards the end of the crossing the rain ceased, and Phoebe went on deck. She found Edmund in a boastful mood, and Sylvester civil but curt. It was the first time Sylvester had been called upon to look after his nephew, and he was devoutly hoping it would be the last.

When the packet entered the Tidal Harbour it was nearly eight o'clock, and all four travellers were tired, chilled, and not in the best of spirits. The sight of Keighley's face, however, exercised a beneficial effect on two of the party: Edmund fell upon him with a squeal of joy, and Sylvester said, with a perceptible lightening of his frown: "Thank God! You may have him, John!"

"That's all right, your grace," said Keighley, grinning at him. "Now, give over, do, Master Edmund, till I have his grace's portmanteau safe!"

He was surprised to see Phoebe, and still more so when Tom hailed him: but he accepted with apparent stolidity Sylvester's explanation that he was indebted to Miss Marlow and Mr. Orde for the recovery of Edmund's person. All he said was: "Well, to be sure, your grace! And how do *you* do, sir? I see that leg's a bit stiff-like still."

Keighley had engaged rooms for Sylvester at the King's Head. He seemed to think there would be no difficulty in securing two more, but Phoebe said that she must lose no time in rejoining Lady Ingham.

"It would be wiser to ascertain first that she is still there," Sylvester said, his frown returning. "May I suggest that you accompany us first to the King's Head while Keighley makes enquiries at the Ship?"

"No need to send Keighley," Tom interposed. "I'll go there. Take care of Phoebe till I get back, Salford!"

Phoebe was reluctant to let him go without her, for she felt it to be unfair that he should be obliged to bear the brunt of Lady Ingham's displeasure; but he only laughed, told her that he could stand a knock far better than she would ever be able to, and went off.

The King's Head was less fashionable than the Ship. Keighley thought that there was no one putting up there who was at all likely to recognize his grace. He had engaged a parlour, and was soon able to assure Phoebe that there was a good bedchamber to be had, if she should need it. Phoebe, who was sitting beside Edmund while he ate his supper, said: "Thank you, but—oh, surely I shan't need it?"

"How can I tell?" Sylvester replied. "It occurs to me that you have been absent above a se'enight. I must own I shouldn't expect Lady Ingham to kick her heels in Dover for so long, but you should know her better than I."

"I wrote to her," she faltered. "She must have known I should return. Or, if I could not, that Tom would."

"Then no doubt she is awaiting his arrival," he said.

It was his indifferent voice again; she said no more, but as Edmund finished his supper she took him away to put him to bed. A plump chambermaid came to offer her services and, as Edmund took an instant liking to her, Phoebe was able to leave him to her supervision. It seemed probable that he would detain her for a considerable period, entertaining her with his saga, for as Phoebe closed the door behind her she heard him say chattily: "I am a great traveller, you know."

She found, on re-entering the parlour, that Tom had returned from his mission. He was talking to Sylvester, and she saw at once that he was looking grave. She paused, an anxious question in her eyes. He smiled at her, but what he said was: "She ain't there, Phoebe. Seems to have gone back to London."

Her eyes went from his face to Sylvester's. Sylvester said: "Come and sit down, Miss Marlow! It is disappointing for you not to find her here, but of no great consequence, after all. You will be with her by tomorrow evening."

"To have gone back to London! She must be very vexed with me!"

"Nothing of that!" Tom said, in a heartening tone. "She never had your letter. Here it is! You'd have thought the gudgeons would have forwarded it to London, but not they! Well, I never did think the Ship was half the place it sets up to be! Not since I found the boot-catcher's thumb-mark on my new top-boots!"

"Then she cannot know where I went! All these days—— Oh, good God, what must she be thinking?"

"Well, she knows I was with you, so she can't have thought you'd fallen into the sea, at all events. I only hope she ain't thinking I've eloped with you!"

She pressed a hand to her temple. "Oh, she must know better than that! Was she alarmed? Did she try to discover where we had gone, or—What did they tell you at the Ship?"

"Precious little," confessed Tom. "You know what it's like there! All hustle and bustle, with people arriving and leaving at all hours. What I did discover is that your grandmother had a spasm, or some such thing, and went back to London the day after we disappeared, in rather queer stirrups. They had a doctor to her, but she can't have been very bad, you know, or she couldn't have travelled."

But Phoebe, quite appalled, had sunk into a chair, and covered her face with her hands.

"My dear Thomas," said Sylvester, in an amused tone, "Lady Ingham's spasms are her most cherished possession! She adopted them years ago, and must find them invaluable, for while they never interfere with her pleasures they always intervene to prevent her being obliged to engage in anything that might bore her. Depend upon it, she posted back to town to pour out her troubles to Halford."

"I daresay that's exactly so," agreed Tom. "The lord knows I had the deuce of a time bringing her up to the scratch at all. It's plain enough what happened: I let go the rein, and she bolted back to the stable. No need to fall into a fit of the dismals, Phoebe."

"How can I help but do so?" she said. "I have been so troublesome to her——" She broke off, turning away her face.

After a short pause she said more quietly: "She left no message?"

"Well," said Tom reluctantly, "only about our baggage! Muker told them at the Ship that if anyone was to ask for it they were to be told it was at the coach-office."

"Very sensible," said Sylvester, walking over to the sideboard. "Obviously she guessed you would be returning. Miss Marlow, I know your tastes too well to hope you will let me pour you out a glass of sherry, so ratafia it must be."

She accepted the glass he handed her, and sat holding it. "At the coach-office——to be called for! She thought, then— She believed me capable of deserting her?"

"More likely took a pet," said Tom.

"Much more likely," said Sylvester. "Madeira or sherry, Thomas? Until we confront Lady Ingham, Miss Marlow, it must be all conjecture—and singularly profitless. I'll engage to convince her that without your aid Edmund would have been irretrievably lost to me."

"You have said yourself, Duke, that I had nothing to do with his recovery," she said, with a faint smile. "It is quite true, moreover."

"Oh, I shan't tell her that!" he promised.

"But I shall!"

"Thank the lord she didn't take our baggage back to Green Street!" said Tom somewhat hastily. "I'm going with Keighley to collect it the first thing tomorrow morning, and shan't I be glad to be able to leave off the clothes I have on!"

"When I consider," said Sylvester, "that the shirt you are wearing is mine, not to mention the neckcloth, and that I could very ill spare them, I resent that remark, Thomas!"

Phoebe, recognizing an attempt to give her thoughts a more cheerful direction, dutifully laughed, and made no further reference to Lady Ingham. A waiter came to lay the covers for dinner; and a perfectly spontaneous laugh was drawn from Phoebe when Tom, as soon as the first course was laid before them, recommended his host to send it back to the kitchens at once.

"Send it back?" repeated Sylvester, taken off his guard. "Why should I?"

"To puff off your consequence, of course. Ask the waiter if he knows who you are! And if you have any trouble, offer to buy the place. *We* are accustomed to being entertained in the first style of elegance, I can tell you!"

Fascinated, Sylvester demanded the whole history of the journey to Abbeville. He was so much amused by it that he retaliated with a graphic account of Sir Nugent Fotherby's warm welcome to himself, which he had not hitherto thought in the least diverting. Not only present anxieties were forgotten, but past quarrels too. The good understanding that had been reached at the Blue Boar seemed to have returned; and Tom, seeing how easily Phoebe and Sylvester were sliding into their old way of exchanging views on any number of subjects, was just congratulating himself on the success of his tactics when an unthinking remark destroyed all the comfort of the evening. "Like the villain in a melodrama!" Sylvester said, wiping the mischievous smile from Phoebe's lips, bringing the colour rushing into her cheeks, transforming her from the gayest of companions into a stiff figure reminding Tom forcibly of an effigy. Constraint returned. Sylvester, after the tiniest of checks, continued smoothly enough, but the warmth had left his voice; he had withdrawn behind his film of ice, perfectly affably and quite unapproachably.

Tom gave it up in despair. He had a very fair notion how matters stood, but there seemed to be nothing he could do to promote a lasting reconciliation. He was pretty sure Sylvester had forgotten Ugolino when he had uttered that unfortunate remark, but it was useless to say that to Phoebe. She was so morbidly sensitive about her wretched romance that even the mention of a book was liable to overset her. And however little Sylvester had remembered *The Lost Heir* when he spoke of a villain, he was remembering it now.

Phoebe retired immediately she rose from the dinner-table, Sylvester merely bowing when she said that she was tired, and would bid them good-night. And when he had closed the door on her retreating form, Sylvester turned, and said, smiling: "Well, what is to be, Thomas? Piquet? Or shall we try whether there is a chessboard to be had?"

It was really quite hopeless, thought Tom, deciding in favour of chess.

He ate a hasty breakfast next morning, and went off with Keighley to the coach-office. When he returned, he found Sylvester standing by the window and reading a newspaper, and Phoebe engaged in the homely task of wiping the egg-stains from Edmund's mouth. He said: "I've got all our gear downstairs, Phoebe. Keighley's waiting to know which of your valises you wish him to take up to your room. And I found this as well: here you are!"

She took the letter from him quickly, recognizing Lady Ingham's writing. "The smaller one, if you please, Tom. Edmund! where are you off to?"

"Must speak to Keighley!" Edmund said importantly, and dashed off in the direction of the stairs.

"Unfortunate Keighley!" remarked Sylvester, not looking up from the newspaper.

Tom departed in Edmund's wake, and Phoebe, her fingers slightly trembling, broke the wafer that sealed her letter, and spread open the single, crossed sheet. Sylvester lowered the newspaper, and watched her. She did not say anything when she had finished reading the letter, but folded it again, and stood holding it, a blind look in her eyes.

"Well?"

She turned her head towards the window, startled. She had never heard Sylvester speak so roughly, and wondered why he should do so.

"You may as well tell me. Your face has already informed me that it is not a pleasant missive."

"No," she said. "She supposed me—when she wrote this—to have persuaded Tom to take me home. I think Muker must have encouraged her to think it, to be rid of me. She is very jealous of me. She may even have believed me to be running away with Tom. That—that was my fault."

"Unnecessary to tell me that! You have a genius for bringing trouble upon yourself."

She looked at him for a moment, hurt and surprise in her eyes, and then turned away, and walked over to the fire. It seemed so needlessly cruel, and so unlike him, to taunt her when he knew her to be distressed that she felt bewildered. It was certainly a taunt, but there had been no mockery in his voice, only anger. Why he should be angry, what she had done to revive his furious resentment, she could not imagine. She found it a little difficult to speak, but managed to say: "I am afraid I have. I seem always to be tumbling into a scrape. Hoydenish, my mother-in-law was used to call me, and did her best to teach me prudence and propriety. I wish she had succeeded."

"You are not alone in that wish!" he said savagely.

The harsh, angry voice was having its inevitable affect on her: she began to feel sick, inwardly shivering, and was obliged to sit down, digging her nails into the palms of her hands.

"You tumbled into a scrape, as you are pleased to call it, when I first made your acquaintance!" he continued. "It would be more correct to say that you flung yourself into it, just as you flung yourself aboard that ship! If you choose to behave like a hoyden it is your own affair, but that is never enough for you! You don't scruple to embroil others in your *scrapes*! Thomas has been a victim, *I* have been one—my God, have I not!—and now it is your grandmother! Does she cast you off? Do you think yourself hardly used? You have no one but yourself to thank for the ills you've brought on your own head!"

She listened to this tirade, rigid with shock, scarcely able to believe that it was Sylvester and not a stranger who hurled these bitter accusations at her. The thought flitted across her brain that he was deliberately feeding his wrath, but it was overborne by her own anger, which leaped from a tiny spark to a blaze.

He said suddenly, before she could speak: "No—no! It's of no use! Sparrow, Sparrow!"

She hardly heard him. She said in a voice husky with passion: "I have one other person to thank! It is yourself, my lord Duke! It was your arrogance that caused me to make you the model for my villain! But for you I should never have run away from my home! But for you no one need have known I was the author of that book! But for you I should not have *flung* myself aboard that schooner! *You* are the cause of every ill that has befallen me! You say I ill-used you: if I did you are wonderfully revenged, for you have ruined *me!*"

To her astonishment, and, indeed, indignation, he gave the oddest laugh. As she glared at him he said in the strangest voice she had yet heard: "Have I? Well—if that's so, I will make reparation! Will you do me the honour, Miss Marlow, of accepting my hand in marriage?"

Thus Sylvester, an accomplished flirt, making his first proposal.

It never occurred to Phoebe that he had shaken himself off his balance, and was as self-conscious as a callow youth just out of school. Still less did it occur to her that the laugh and the exaggerated formality of his offer sprang from embarrassment. He was famed for his polished address; she had never, until this day, seen him lose his mastery over himself. She believed him to be mocking her, and started up from her chair, exclaiming: "How *dare* you?"

Sylvester, burningly aware of his own clumsiness, lost no time in making bad worse. "I beg your pardon! you mistake! I had no intention—Phoebe, it was out before I well knew what I was saying! I never meant to ask you to marry me—I was determined I would not! But——" He broke off, realizing into what quagmires his attempts to explain himself were leading him.

"That I *do* believe!" she said hotly. "You have been so obliging as to tell me what you think of me, and I believe that too! You came to Austerby to look me over, as though I had been a filly, and decided I was not up to your weight! *Didn't* you?"

"What *next* will you say?" he demanded, an involuntary laugh shaking him.

"Didn't you?"

"Yes. But have you forgotten how you behaved? How could I know what you were when you tried only to disgust me? It wasn't until later——"

"To be sure!" she said scathingly. "*Later,* when I first made you a victim, embroiling you in my improper flight from Austerby, and next wounded your pride as I daresay it was never wounded before, *then* you began to think I was just the wife that would suit you! The fervent offer which you have been so flattering as to make me springs, naturally, from the folly that led me to thrust myself into your affairs, and so make it necessary for you to undertake a journey under circumstances so much beneath your dignity as to be positively degrading! How green of me not to have known immediately how it would be! You must forgive me! Had I dreamt that my lack of conduct would attach you to me I would have assumed the manners of a pattern of propriety whenever you came within sight of me! You would then have been spared the mortification of having your suit rejected, and I should have been spared an intolerable insult!"

"There was no insult," he said, very pale. "If I phrased it— if it sounded to you as though I meant to insult you, believe that it was not so! What I said to you before, I said because the crazy things you do convinced me you were *not* the wife that would suit me! I wanted never to see you again after that night at the Castlereaghs'—I *thought* so, but it wasn't so, because when I did see you again—I was overjoyed."

Not a speech worthy of a man who made love charmingly, but Sylvester had never before tried to make love to a lady seething with rage and contempt.

"Were you indeed?" said Phoebe. "But you soon recovered, didn't you?"

Nettled, he retorted: "No, I only *tried* to! Stop ripping up at me, you little shrew!"

"Phoebe, don't you mean to change your dress?" said Tom, entering the room at this most inauspicious moment. "Keighley took your valise up——" He broke off, dismayed, and stammered: "Oh, I b-beg pardon! I didn't know—I'll go!"

"Go? Why?" Phoebe said brightly. "Yes, indeed I mean to change my dress, and will do so immediately!"

Tom held the door for her, thinking that if only Sylvester, interrupted in the middle of an obvious scene, would drop his guard, grant him an opening, he could tell him just how to handle her. He shut the door, and turned.

"Good God, Thomas! This sartorial magnificence! Are you trying to put me to the blush?" said Sylvester quizzically.

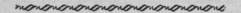

They left Dover just after eleven o'clock, by which time Miss Marlow had quarrelled with both her escorts. Emerging from her bedchamber in the guise of a haughty young lady of fashion she encountered Tom, and instantly asked him whether he had recovered the money he had left in his portmanteau. Upon being reassured on this point she asked him if he would hire a chaise for their conveyance to London. "No," said Tom, never one to mince his words. "I've got a better use for my blunt!"

"I will repay you, I promise you!" she urged.

"Much obliged! When?" said Tom brutally.

"Grandmama——"

"Mighty poor security! No, I thank you!"

"If she will not do it I'll sell my pearls!" she declared.

"That *would* make me cut a fine figure, wouldn't it?"

"Tom, I don't wish to travel at Salford's expense!" she blurted out.

"That's easily settled. Sell your pearls, and pay him!"

She said stiffly: "If you won't do what I particularly wish, will you at least request the Duke to tell you how much money he has expended on my behalf since we left Abbeville?"

"When I make a cake of myself it will be on my own account, and not on yours, Miss Woolly-crown!" said Tom.

Two vehicles had been provided for the journey. One was a hired post-chaise, the other Sylvester's own phaeton, and to each was harnessed a team of four horses. They were job horses, but they had been chosen by Keighley, and therefore, as Master Rayne pointed out to his uncle, prime cattle. When Tom brought his haughty charge out of the inn he found Master Rayne seated already in the phaeton, and Sylvester standing beside it, drawing on his gloves. He went up to him, exclaiming: "Are you driving yourself all the way to London, Salford?"

"I am," replied Sylvester. "I would offer to take you with me, but I'm afraid Keighley must have that seat."

"Yes, of course, but you don't mean to take Edmund too, do you? Had you not better let him come with us in the chaise?"

"My dear Thomas, my only reason for telling Keighley to bring my phaeton to Dover was to save that brat as much travelsickness as I could! He is invariably sick in closed carriages, and never in open ones. Will you accompany Miss Marlow? I hope she will not find the journey too fatiguing: we are a little late in starting, but we should reach town in time for dinner."

Tom, though strongly of the opinion that Sylvester, in his present humour, would be happy to part with his nephew on any terms at the end of the first stage, raised no further demur, but went back to hand Phoebe up into the chaise.

For the first five miles not a word was uttered within this vehicle, but at Lydden, Phoebe (recovering a trifle, in her faithful friend's opinion, from the sullens) asked Tom where he meant to put up in London.

"At Salford's house. He has invited me to spend a few days there. As long as I choose, in fact."

"Good gracious!" said Phoebe. "What an honour for you! No wonder you were so unwilling to oblige me! I must be *quite* beneath your touch!"

"You'll precious soon wish you were beneath my *touch,* if you don't take care, my girl!" said Tom. "If you've any more pretty morsels of wit under your tongue, reserve 'em for Salford! He's far too well-bred to give you your deserts: *I* ain't!"

Silence reigned for the next mile. "Tom," said Phoebe, in a small voice.

"Well?"

"I didn't mean to say that. It was a *horrid* thing to say! I beg your pardon."

He took her hand, and gave it a squeeze. "Pea-goose! What's the matter?" He waited for a moment. "I know I walked smash into a turn-up between you and Salford. What are you trying to do? Break your own silly neck?"

She withdrew her hand. "Excuse me, Tom, if you please! It would be quite improper in me to repeat what passed between us. Pray say no more!"

"Very well," said Tom. "But don't *you* choke yourself with pride, Phoebe!"

At Sittingbourne a halt was called, and the travellers partook of refreshment at the Rose. When they came out of the inn again, and Tom was about to hand Phoebe into the chaise, Sylvester said: "Do you care to tool the phaeton for a stage or two, Thomas?"

"By Jove, yes!—if you think I shan't overturn it!" Tom replied, with a rueful grin. "And if——" he hesitated, glancing at Phoebe.

"Do just as you wish!" she replied at once. "I can very well finish the journey in one of the Accommodation coaches!"

Sylvester turned, and strode towards the phaeton. "Get in!" said Tom curtly. He added, as he took his seat beside Phoebe: "That's the first time I've ever been glad you are *not* my sister!"

She returned no answer. Scarcely half a dozen sentences were exchanged during the remainder of the journey; but although Phoebe pretended to be asleep for the greater part of the way sleep was never farther from her, so torn was she by conflicting emotions. Beside her Tom sat gazing out of the window, wondering what Sylvester could have said to have made her so angry; and wishing that there was something he could do for Sylvester, even if it were no more than relieving him of Edmund's company.

But Keighley was shielding Sylvester from Edmund. "Give over plaguing his grace, Master Edmund!" said Keighley. "Now, that's quite enough, Master Edmund! There's no good to be got out of flying into one of your tantrums!" said Keighley, thinking what a pity it was that he could no longer say the same to Sylvester.

It was after six when the carriages drew up in Berkeley Square, before Salford House. "Why do we stop here?" demanded Phoebe.

"To set down my portmanteau, of course," replied Tom, opening the chaise-door. "Also, I daresay, to allow Salford to take leave of you! Try for a little civility!"

He climbed down from the chaise as he spoke. The doors of the great house were already flung open, and several persons emerged. "Reeth, Reeth, I've been to France!" shouted Edmund, dashing up the steps. "Where's Button? She'll be 'stonished when she hears the things I've done! Oh, Button, I have needed you! Did you miss me, Button? Phoebe doesn't do things the right way. Do you know, I had to tell her, Button?"

"Repellent brat!" remarked Sylvester. "Reeth, Mr. Orde is staying with me for a few days: take care of him for me! Will you go in with him, Thomas? I'll escort Miss Marlow to Green Street."

This scheme seemed so fraught with disaster that Tom could not help saying, in an urgent undervoice: "I wouldn't, Salford! Leave her to come about!"

"Go in with Reeth, Thomas: I shall be with you presently," replied Sylvester, as though he had not heard this advice.

He mounted into the chaise, and almost before the door was shut grasped Phoebe's hands, saying: "Phoebe, you must listen to me! I know I made wretched work of it. I can't explain it to you now—there is too little time—but I won't let you go like this! You can't think I would ask you to marry me in jest, or to insult you!"

"You have told me already that you never meant to ask me," she replied, trying to pull her hands away. "I fancy you will be truly thankful, when you have recovered from the mortification of having your suit rejected, that I didn't snap at so brilliant an offer. Will you please to release me, my lord Duke?"

"But I love you!" he said, gripping her hands rather more tightly.

"You are very obliging, but I cannot return your affection, sir."

"I'll make you!" he promised.

"Oh, no, you will not!" returned Phoebe, thoroughly ruffled. "Will you let me go? If you have no more conduct than to behave in this fashion in the middle of the street, I have! Make me love you, indeed! If I were not so angry, I could laugh to think how exactly I hit you off when I wrote of Ugolino that, try as he might to appear conciliating, he could not open his lips without betraying his arrogance!"

"Do you call it arrogance when I tell you that I love you, and wish to make you my wife?" he demanded.

"Yes, and folly too! You have never suffered a rebuff, have you, Duke? When any female has shown herself not to be disposed to like you it has been a sport with you to *make* her like you very much too well, I daresay, for her comfort. You even lay bets that where others have failed *you* will succeed!"

"What nonsense is this?" he exclaimed. *"I?"*

"Yes, *you*! Was there not an heiress who was called the *Citadel*? Or are your conquests too numerous to be remembered by you?"

"I remember," he said grimly. "You had that from Ianthe, did you? Did she also tell you that it was a piece of funning between my brother and me—discreditable, if you like, but never meant to go beyond the pair of us?"

"In fact, you *didn't* storm the Citadel, Duke?"

"For God's sake, Phoebe, must you throw in my face the follies I committed when I was a boy?"

"I would not if you had outgrown that conceit! But you haven't! Why did you make yourself so agreeable to me? You must have had a great deal of practice, I think, for you did it beautifully! If I had not known what your object was I am sure you must have succeeded in it! But I did know! Tom told you that I ran away from Austerby because the thought of becoming your wife was repugnant to me, and you were so piqued that you determined I should fall in love with you, and afterwards be sorry!"

He had so entirely forgotten that pettish resolve that he was thunderstruck.

"Well?" said Phoebe, watching him. "Can you deny it Duke?"

He released her hands at last, and uttered his crowning blunder. "No. I *was* piqued, I *did*, in a fit of—conceit—arrogance—anything you please to call it!—form some such contemptible scheme. I beg you to believe it was of very short duration!"

"I *don't* believe it!" declared Phoebe.

The chaise turned into Green Street. Miss Marlow, having discharged much of the wrath she had been obliged to keep bottled up for so many painful hours, had begun to feel very low. The Creature beside her, not content with humiliating her in public, and regarding all the disagreeable experiences she had undergone on his behalf with indifference and ingratitude, had stormed at her, and insulted her, and now, when any but a monster of cold-hearted self-consequence must have known how tired and miserable she was, and how desperately in need of reassurance, he sat silent. Perhaps he needed encouragement? She gave it him. "Having become acquainted with your other flames, Duke—all diamonds of the first water!—I should have to be uncommonly green to believe that you preferred me! You asked me to marry you because you are so determined not to be obliged to own yourself worsted that you will go to any lengths to achieve your object!"

Now or never was the time for Sylvester to retrieve his character! He said very levelly: "You need say no more, Miss Marlow. It would be useless, I realize, for me to attempt to answer you."

"If you wish to know what I think of you," said Phoebe, in a shaking voice, "it is that you are a great deal *worse* than Count Ugolino!"

He was silent. Well! now she knew how right she had been. He was not in the least in love with her, and very happy she was to know it. All she wanted was a suitable retreat, such as a lumber-room, or a coal-cellar, in which to enjoy her happiness to the full.

The chaise drew to a standstill, and Sylvester got out, and with his own hands let down the steps. Such condescension! Pulling herself together, Phoebe alighted, and said with great dignity: "I must thank you, Duke, for having been so kind as to have brought me back to England. In case we should not meet again, I should like, before we say goodbye, to assure you that I am not unmindful of what I owe you, and that I wish you extremely happy."

This very beautiful speech might just as well have remained unspoken, for all the heed he paid to it. He said: "I am coming in with you," and sounded the knocker.

"I beg you most earnestly not to do so!" she said, with passionate sincerity.

He took her hand in his. "Miss Marlow, let me do this one thing for you! I know Lady Ingham, and what her temper is. I promise you she shall not be angry with you, if only I may see her first."

"You are very good, Duke, but I assure you I need no intervention!" she said proudly.

The door opened. Horwich ejaculated: *"Miss Phoebe!"* He then encountered a most unnerving stare from Sylvester, and bowed, and stammered: "Your g-grace!"

"Have Miss Marlow's baggage carried into the house!" said Sylvester coldly, and turned again to Phoebe. It was clearly useless to persist in argument; so, knowing that Horwich was listening to every word he said, he held out his hand, and said: "I will leave you now, Miss Marlow. I can never be sufficiently grateful to you for what you have done. Will you present my compliments to Lady Ingham, and inform her that I hope to call upon her shortly, when I shall tell her—for I know well that *you* will not!—how deeply indebted to you I am? Goodbye! God bless you!" He bent, and kissed her hand, while Horwich, consumed with curiosity, goggled at him.

To Phoebe, long past being able to recognize what his intention must be, this speech was the last straw. She managed to say: "Certainly! I mean—you exaggerate, Duke! Goodbye!" and then hurried into the house.

"When the baggage has been taken off, drive back to Salford House!" Sylvester told the chief postilion. "You will be paid there. I am going to walk."

When Reeth presently opened the doors to his master he was a good deal shocked. He had rather suspected that something was wrong, and he perceived now that something was very wrong indeed. He had seen that look on his grace's face once before. It wouldn't do to say anything about it, but at least he could tell him something that would do him good to hear. As he helped Sylvester out of his driving-coat, he said: "I didn't have the time to tell your grace before, but——"

"Reeth, what the devil are you doing here?" demanded Sylvester, as though he had only just become aware of him. "Good God, you don't mean to say my mother is here?"

"In her own sitting-room, your grace, waiting for you to come in," beamed Reeth. "And stood the journey very well, I am happy to be able to assure your grace."

"I'll go to her at once!" Sylvester said, walking quickly to the great stair.

She was alone, seated on one side of the fireplace. She looked up as Sylvester came in, and smiled mischievously.

"Mama!"

"Sylvester! Now, I won't be scolded! You are to tell me that you are delighted to find me here, if you please!"

"I don't have to tell you that," he said, bending over her. "But to have set out without me——! I ought never to have written to tell you what had happened! I did so only because I was afraid you might hear of it from some other source. My dear, have you been so anxious?"

"Not a bit! I knew you would bring him back safely. But it was a little too much to expect me to stay at Chance when such stirring events were taking place in London. Now, sit down and tell me all about it! Edmund's confidences have given rise to the wildest conjectures in my mind, and that delightful boy you have brought home with you thinks that perhaps I shall like to hear the story better from your lips. My dear, who is he?"

He had turned aside to pull forward a chair, and as he seated himself the Duchess saw him for the first time in the full light of the candles burning near her chair. Like Reeth, she suffered a shock; like Reeth, she recognized the look on Sylvester's face. He had worn it for many months after Harry's death; and she had prayed she might never see it again. She was obliged to clasp her hands together in her lap, so urgent was her impulse to stretch them out to him.

"Thomas Orde," he replied, smiling, as it seemed to her, with an effort. "A nice lad, isn't he? I've invited him to stay here for as long as he cares to: his father thinks it time he acquired a little town bronze." He hesitated, and then said: "I daresay he may have told you—or Edmund has—that he is a friend of Miss Marlow's. An adopted brother, as it were."

"Oh, Edmund was very full of *Tom* and *Phoebe*! But how they came to be mixed up in that imbroglio I can't imagine! Phoebe seems to have been very kind to Edmund."

"Most kind. It is rather a long story, Mama."

"And you are tired, and would rather tell it to me presently. I won't tease you, then. But tell me about Phoebe! You know I have a particular interest in her. To own the truth, it was to see her that I came to London."

He looked up quickly. "To see her? I don't understand, Mama! Why should you——?"

"Well, Louisa wrote to tell me that everyone believed her to be the author of that absurd novel, and that she was having a very unhappy time, poor child. I hoped I might be able to put a stop to such nonsense, but I reached London only to discover that Lady Ingham had taken her to Paris. I can't think why she shouldn't have written to me, for she must have known I would help Verena's daughter."

"It's too late!" he said. "*I* could have scotched the scandal! Instead——" He broke off, and looked keenly at her. "I can't recall. Was my busy aunt Louisa at the Castlereaghs' ball?"

"Yes, dearest."

"I see." He got up jerkily, and moved to the fireplace, standing with his head turned a little away from the Duchess. "I am sure she told you what happened there."

"An unfortunate affair," said the Duchess calmly. "You were naturally very angry."

"There was no excuse for what I did. I knew her dread of——I can see her face now!"

"What is she like, Sylvester?" She waited, and then prompted: "Is she pretty?"

He shook his head. "No. Not a beauty, Mama. When she is animated, I believe you would consider her taking."

"I collect, from all I have heard, that she is unusual?"

"Oh, yes, she's unusual!" he said bitterly. "She blurts out whatever may come into her head; she tumbles from one outrageous escapade into another; she's happier grooming horses and hobnobbing with stable-hands than going to parties; she's impertinent; you daren't catch her eye for fear she should start to giggle; she hasn't any accomplishments; I never saw anyone with less dignity; she's abominable, and damnably hot at hand, frank to a fault, and—a *darling*!"

"Should I like her, Sylvester?" said the Duchess her eyes on his profile.

"I don't know," he said, a suggestion of impatience in his voice. "I daresay—I hope so—but you might not. How can I possibly tell? It's of no consequence: she won't have me." He paused, and then said, as though the words were wrung out of him: "O God, Mama, I've made such a mull of it! What am I to *do*?"

CHAPTER

28

After a troubled night, during which she was haunted, waking or dreaming, by all the appalling events of the previous day, which had culminated in a shattering scene with Lady Ingham, Phoebe awoke to find the second housemaid pulling back the blinds, and learned from her that the letter lying on her breakfast-tray had been brought round by hand from Salford House not ten minutes earlier. The housemaid was naturally agog with curiosity, but any expectation she had of being made the recipient of an interesting confidence faded before the seeming apathy with which Miss Phoebe greeted her disclosure. All Miss Phoebe wanted was a cup of tea; and the housemaid, after lingering with diminishing hope for a few minutes, left her sitting up in bed, and sipping this restorative.

Once alone, Phoebe snatched up the letter, and tore it open. She looked first at the signature. *Elizabeth Salford* was what met her eyes, and drew from her a gasp of fright.

But there was nothing in the letter to make her tremble. It was quite short, and it contained no hint of menace. The Duchess wished very much not only to make the acquaintance of a loved friend's daughter, but also to thank her for the care she had taken of her grandson. She hoped that Phoebe would be able, perhaps, to visit her that day, at noon, when she would be quite alone, and they could talk without fear of interruption.

Rather a gratifying letter for a modest damsel to receive, one would have supposed, but the expression on Phoebe's face might have led an observer to conclude that she was reading a tale of horror. Having perused it three times, and failing to detect in it any hidden threat, Phoebe fixed her attention on the words: *I shall be quite alone,* and carefully considered them. If they were meant to convey a message it was hard to see how this could be anything but one of reassurance; but if this were so, Sylvester must have told his mother—*what*?

Thrusting back the bedclothes Phoebe scrambled out of bed and into her dressing-gown, and pattered down the stairs to her grandmother's room. She found the afflicted Dowager alone, and held out the letter to her, asking her in a tense voice to read it.

The Dowager had viewed her unceremonious entrance with disfavour, and she at once said in feeble accents: "Oh, heaven! what now?" But this ejaculation was not wholly devoid of hope, since she too had been told whence had come Miss Phoebe's letter. Poor Lady Ingham had slept quite as badly as her granddaughter, for she had had much to puzzle her. At first determined to send Phoebe packing back to Somerset, she had been considerably mollified by the interesting intelligence conveyed to her (as Sylvester had known it would be) by Horwich. She had thought it promising, but further reflection had sent her spirits down again: whatever might be Sylvester's sentiments, Phoebe bore none of the appearance of a young female who had either received, or expected to receive, a flattering offer for her hand. Hope reared its head again when a letter from Salford House was thrust upon her; like Phoebe, she looked first at the signature, and was at once dashed down. "Elizabeth!" she exclaimed, in a flattened voice. "Extraordinary! She must have come on the child's account, I suppose. I only trust it may not be the death of her!"

Phoebe watched her anxiously while she mastered the contents of the letter, and when it was given back to her said imploringly: "What must I do, ma'am?"

The Dowager did not answer for a moment. There was food for deep thought in the Duchess's letter. She gazed inscrutably before her, and the question had to be repeated before she said, with a slight start: "Do? You will do as you are bid, of course!

A very pretty letter the Duchess has writ you, and why she should have done so—but she hasn't, one must assume, read that abominable book!"

"She has read it, ma'am," Phoebe said. "It was she who gave it to Salford. He told me so himself."

"Then he cannot have told her who wrote it," said the Dowager. "That you may depend on, for she dotes on Sylvester! If only she could be persuaded to take you up—But someone is bound to tell her!"

"Grandmama, I must tell her myself!" Phoebe said.

The Dowager was inclined to agree with her, but the dimming of a future which had seemed to become suddenly so much brighter vexed her so much that she said crossly: "You must do as you please! *I* cannot advise you! And I beg you won't ask me to accompany you to Salford House, for I am quite unequal to any exertion! You may have the landaulet, and, for heaven's sake, Phoebe, try at least to *appear* the thing! You must wear the fawn-coloured silk, and the pink—no, it will make you look hideously sallow! It will have to be the straw with the brown ribands."

Thus arrayed, Miss Marlow, shortly before noon, stepped into the landaulet, as pale as if it had been a tumbrel and her destination the gallows.

Such was the state of her mind that she would not have been surprised, on arrival at Salford House, to have been confronted by a host of Raynes, all pointing fingers of condemnation at her. But the only persons immediately visible were servants, who seemed, with the exception of the butler, whose aspect was benevolent, to be perfectly uninterested. It was well for her peace of mind that she did not suspect that every member of the household who had the slightest business in the hall had contrived to be there to get a glimpse of her. Such an array of footmen seemed rather excessive, not to say pompous, but if that was the way Sylvester chose to run his house it was quite his own affair.

The benevolent butler conducted her up one pair of stairs. Her heart was thumping hard, and she felt unusually breathless, both of which disagreeable symptoms would have been much aggravated had she known how many interested persons were watching from hidden points of vantage every step of her progress. No one could have told whence had sprung the news that his grace had chosen a leg-shackle at last, and was finding his path proverbially rough; but everyone knew it, from the agent-in-chief down to the humblest kitchen-porter; and an amazing number of these persons contrived to be spectators of Miss Marlow's arrival. Most of them were disappointed in her; but Miss Penistone and Button found nothing amiss, one of these ladies being sentimentally disposed to think any damsel of dear Sylvester's choice a paragon, and the other regarding her in the light of a Being sent from on high to preserve her darling from death by shipwreck, surfeit, neglect, or any other of the disasters which might have been expected to strike down an infant of tender years taken to outlandish parts without his nurse.

Phoebe heard her name announced, and stepped across the threshold of the Duchess's drawing-room. The door closed behind her, but instead of walking forward she stood rooted to the ground, staring across the room at her hostess. A look of naïve surprise was in her face, and she so far forgot herself as to utter an involuntary: "Oh——!"

No one had ever told her how pronounced was the resemblance between Sylvester and his mother. At first glance it was startling. At the second one perceived that the Duchess had warmer eyes than Sylvester, and a kinder curve to her lips.

Before Phoebe had assimilated these subtle differences an amused laugh escaped the Duchess, and she said: "Yes, Sylvester has his eyebrows from me, poor boy!"

"Oh, I *beg* your pardon, ma'am!" Phoebe stammered, much confused.

"Come and let me look at you!" invited the Duchess. "I daresay your grandmother may have told you that I have a stupid complaint that won't let me get out of my chair."

Phoebe stayed where she was, clasping both hands tightly on her reticule. "Ma'am—I am very much obliged to your grace for having—honoured me with this invitation—but I must not accept your hospitality without telling you—that it was I who wrote—that dreadful book!"

"Oh, you *do* look like your mother!" exclaimed the Duchess. "Yes, I know you wrote it, which is why I was so desirous of making your acquaintance. Come and give me a kiss! I kissed you in your cradle, but you can't remember *that*!"

Thus adjured, Phoebe approached her chair, and bent to plant a shy kiss on the Duchess's cheek. But the Duchess not only returned this chaste salute warmly but said: "You poor, foolish child! Now tell me all about it!"

To hear herself addressed so caressingly was a novel experience. Miss Battery was gruff, Mrs. Orde matter-of-fact, and Lady Ingham astringent, and these were the three ladies who had Phoebe's interests most to heart. She had never met with tenderness, and its effect was to make her tumble down on her knees beside the Duchess's chair, and burst into tears. Such conduct would have earned her a sharp reproof from Lady Ingham, but the Duchess seemed to think well of it, since she recommended her unconventional guest to enjoy a comfortable cry, removed her hat, and patted her soothingly.

From the moment of discovering that Sylvester had lost his heart to Phoebe the Duchess had been determined to like her, and to put out of her mind all thought of the book she had written; but she had expected to find it hard to do either of these things. It was one thing to nourish private doubts about her son: quite another to find him depicted as a villainous character in a novel that had taken the ton by storm. But no sooner did she see Phoebe and read the contrition in her frank eyes than her heart melted. It rejoiced too, for although Sylvester had said that Phoebe was not beautiful she had not expected to find her a thin slip of a girl, with a brown complexion and nothing to recommend her but a pair of speaking gray eyes. If Sylvester, who knew his own worth, and had coolly made out a list of the qualities he considered indispensable in his bride, had decided that only this girl would satisfy him, he had fallen more deeply in love than his mother had thought possible. She could have laughed aloud, remembering all he had once said to her, for there seemed to her to be no points of resemblance between Phoebe and that mythical wife he had described. She thought there would be some lively fights if he married Phoebe: certainly none of that calm, rather bloodless propriety which he had once considered to be the foundation of a successful alliance.

Well, the marriage might prove a failure, but the Duchess, who had conceived a profound dislike of five unknown but eligible ladies of quality, was much inclined to think that it might as easily turn out to be the making of both parties to it; and by the time the whole history of *The Lost Heir* had been sobbed into her lap, and a passionate apology offered to her, she was able to assure the penitent author, with perfect sincerity, that on the whole she was glad the book had been published, since she thought it had done Sylvester a great deal of good. "And as for Count Ugolino's shocking conduct towards his nephew, that, my dear, is the least objectionable part of it," she said. "For as soon as you embroiled him in his dastardly plots, you know, all resemblance to Sylvester vanished. And Maximilian, I am afraid, is quite unlike my naughty grandson! From all Mr. Orde told me I feel that Edmund would have very speedily put Ugolino in his place!"

Phoebe could not help giving a tiny chuckle, but she said: "I *promise* you it was a coincidence, ma'am, but he—the Duke—did not think so."

"Oh, he knew it was, whatever he may have said! Nor did he care a button for it. Ianthe has been spreading far worse stories about him (because more credible) for years, and he has treated them with perfect indifference. What he cared for was the sketch you drew of him when you first brought Ugolino on to your stage. It is not too much to say that that almost stunned him. Oh, don't hang your head! It was a salutary lesson to him, I believe. You see, my dear, I have lately been a little worried about Sylvester, suspecting that he had become—to use your word for him—arrogant. Perhaps you will feel that I should have noticed it long ago, but he never shows that side of himself to me, and I don't now go into company, so that I've had no opportunity to see what he is to others. I am really grateful to you for telling me what no one else has liked to mention!"

"Oh, no, no!" Phoebe said quickly. "It was a caricature, ma'am! His manners are always those of a well-bred man, and there is no appearance in him of self-consequence. It was very wrong of me: he had given me no real cause! It was only——"

"Go on!" the Duchess said encouragingly. "Don't be afraid to tell me! I might imagine worse than the truth, you know, if you are not open with me."

"It—it seemed to me, ma'am, that he was polite not to honour others but himself!" Phoebe blurted out. "And that the flattery he receives he—he doesn't notice because he takes it for granted—his consequence being so large. I don't know why it should have vexed me so. If he had seemed to hold others cheap I should only have been diverted, and that would have

302

been a much worse fault in him. I think—it is his indifference that makes me so often want to hit him!"

The Duchess laughed. "Ah, yes, I understand that! Tell me: he's not above being pleased?"

"No, ma'am, never!" Phoebe assured her. "He is always affable in company: not a bit stiff! Only—I don't know how to express it—*aloof*, I think. Oh, I didn't mean to distress you! Pray, pray, forgive me!"

The Duchess's smile went a little awry. "You haven't distressed me. It distressed me only to know that Sylvester was still living in some desolate Polar region—but it was only for a moment! I don't think he *is* living there any longer."

"His brother, ma'am?" Phoebe ventured to ask, looking shyly up into her face.

The Duchess nodded. "His twin-brother. They were not alike, but the bond between them was so strong that nothing ever loosened it, not even Harry's marriage. When Harry died—Sylvester went away. I don't mean bodily—ah, you understand, don't you? I might have been sure you would, for I know you to have a very discerning eye. Sylvester has a deep reserve. He will not have his wounds touched, and *that* wound——" She broke off, and then said, after a little pause: "Well, he kept everyone at a distance for so long that I believe it became, as it were, an engrained habit, and is why he gave you the feeling that he was aloof—which exactly describes him, I must tell you!" She smiled at Phoebe, and took her hand. "As for his indifferent air, my dear, I know it well—I have been acquainted with it for many years, and not only in Sylvester! It springs, as you so correctly suppose, from pride. *That* is an inherited vice! All the Raynes have it, and Sylvester to a marked degree. It is inborn, and it wasn't diminished by his succeeding, when he was much too young, to his father's dignities. I always did think that the worst thing that could have befallen him, but comforted myself with the thought that Lord William Rayne—he is Sylvester's uncle, and was guardian to both my sons for the two years that were left of their minority—that William would quickly depress any top-loftiness in Sylvester. But unfortunately William, though the kindest man alive, not only holds himself very much up, but is also convinced that the Head of the House of Rayne is a far more august personage than the Head of the House of Hanover! I have the greatest affection for him, but he is what I expect you would call gothic! He tells me, for instance, that society has become a mingle-mangle, and that too many men of birth nowadays don't keep *a proper distance*. He would have given Sylvester a thundering scold for showing incivility to the humblest of his dependants, but I am very sure that he taught him that meticulous politeness was what he owed to his own consequence: *noblesse oblige,* in fact. So, what with William telling him never to forget how exalted he was, and far too many people looking up to him as their liege-lord, I am afraid Sylvester became imbued with some very improper notions, my dear! And, to be candid with you, I don't think he will ever lose them. His wife, if he loved her, could do much to *improve* him, but she won't alter his whole character."

"No, of course not, ma'am. I mean——"

"Which, in some ways, is admirable," continued the Duchess, smiling a little at this embarrassed interjection, but paying no other heed to it. "And the odd thing is that some of his best qualities spring directly from his pride! It would never occur to Sylvester that anyone could dispute his hereditary right of lordship, but I can assure you that it would never occur to him either to neglect the least one of the duties, however irksome, that attach to his position." She paused, and then said: "The flaw is that his care for his people doesn't come from his heart. It was bred into him, he accepts it as his inescapable duty, but he hasn't the love of humanity that inspires philanthropists, you know. Towards all but the very few people he loves I fear he will always be largely indifferent. However, for those few there's nothing he won't do, from the high heroical to such tedious things as giving up far too much of his time to the entertainment of an invalid mother!"

Phoebe said, with a glowing look: "He could never think that tedious, I am persuaded, ma'am!"

"Good gracious, of all the boring things to be obliged to do it must surely be the worst! I made up my mind not to permit him to trouble about me, too, but—you may have noticed it!—Sylvester is determined to have his own way, and never more so than when he is convinced he is acting for one's good."

"I have frequently thought him—a trifle high-handed, ma'am," said Phoebe, her eye kindling at certain memories.

"Yes, I'm sure you have. Harry used to call him The Dook, mocking his overbearing ways! The worst of it is that it's so hard to get the better of him! He doesn't *order* one to do things: he merely makes it impossible for one to do anything else. Some idiotish doctor once convinced him it would cure me to take the hot bath, and he got me to Bath entirely against my will, and without ever mentioning the name of the horrid place. The shifts he was put to! I forgave him only because he had taken so much trouble over the iniquitous affair! His wife will have much to bear, I daresay, but she will never find him thoughtless where *her* well-being is concerned."

Phoebe said, flushing: "Ma'am—you mistake! I—he——"

"Has he put himself beyond forgiveness?" enquired the Duchess quizzically. "He certainly told me he had, but I hoped he was exaggerating."

"He doesn't wish to marry me, ma'am. Not in his heart!" Phoebe said. "He only wished to make me sorry I had run away from him, and fall in love with him when it was too late. He couldn't bear to be beaten, and proposed to me quite against his will—he told me so himself!—and then, I think, he was too proud to draw back."

"Really, I am quite ashamed of him!" exclaimed the Duchess. "He told me he had made a *mull* of it, and that, I see, is much less than the truth! I don't wonder you gave him a set-down, but I am delighted to learn that all his famous address deserted him when he proposed to you! In my experience a man rarely makes graceful speeches when he is very much in earnest, be he never so accomplished a flirt!"

"But he *doesn't* want to marry me, ma'am!" averred Phoebe, sniffing into a damp handkerchief. "He told me he did, but when I said I didn't believe him—he said he saw it was useless to argue with me!"

"Good heavens, what a simpleton!"

"And then I said he was w-worse than Ugolino, and he didn't s-say anything at all!" disclosed Phoebe tragically.

"That settles it!" the Duchess declared, only the faintest of tremors in her voice. "I wash my hands of such a ninny! After having been given all this encouragement, what does he do but come home in flat despair, saying you won't listen to him? He even asked me what he should do! I am sure it was for the first time in his life!"

"F-flat despair?" echoed Phoebe, between hope and disbelief. "Oh, *no*!"

"I assure you! And very disagreeable it made him, too. He brought Mr. Orde up to take tea with me after dinner, and even the tale of Sir Nugent and the button failed to drag more than a faint smile from him!"

"He—he is *mortified,* perhaps—oh, I know he is! But he doesn't even *like* me, ma'am! If you had heard the things he said to me! And then—the very next instant—proposed to me!"

"He is clearly unhinged. I daresay you had no intention of reducing him to this sad state, but I feel you ought, in common charity, to allow him at least to explain himself. Very likely it would settle his mind, and it won't do for Salford to become addle-brained, you know! Do but consider the consternation of the Family, my dear!"

"Oh, *ma'am*——!" protested Phoebe, half laughing.

"As for his not liking you," continued the Duchess, "I don't know how that may be, but I can't recall that he ever before described any girl to me as *a darling*!"

Phoebe stared at her incredulously. She tried to speak, but only succeeded in uttering a choking sound.

"By this time," said the Duchess, stretching out her hand to the embroidered bell-pull, "he has probably gnawed his nails down to the quick, or murdered poor Mr. Orde. I think you had better see him, my dear, and say something soothing to him!"

Phoebe, tieing the strings of her hat in a lamentably lopsided bow, said in great agitation: "Oh, no! Oh, pray——!"

The Duchess smiled at her. "Well, he is waiting in anxiety, my love. If I ring this bell once he will come up in answer to it. If I ring it twice Reeth will come, and Sylvester will know that you would not even speak to him. Which is it to be?"

"Oh!" cried Phoebe, scarlet-cheeked, and quite distracted. "I can't—but I don't wish him to—oh, dear, what shall I do?"

"Exactly what you wish to do, my dear—but you must tell him what that is yourself," said the Duchess, pulling the bell once.

"I don't know!" said Phoebe, wringing her hands. "I mean, he *can't* want to marry me! When he might have Lady Mary Torrington, who is so beautiful, and good, and well-behaved, and——" She stopped in confusion as the door opened.

"Come in, Sylvester!" said the Duchess calmly. "I want you to escort Miss Marlow to her carriage, if you please."

"With pleasure, Mama," said Sylvester.

The Duchess held out her hand to Phoebe, and drew her down to have her cheek kissed. "Goodbye, dear child: I hope I shall see you again soon!"

In awful confusion, Phoebe uttered a farewell speech so hopelessly disjointed as to bring a smile of unholy appreciation into the eyes of Sylvester, patiently holding the door.

She ventured to peep at him for one anxious moment, as she went towards him. It was a very fleeting glance, but enough to reassure her on one point: he did not look at all distracted. He was perhaps a little pale, but so far from bearing the appearance of one cast into despair he was looking remarkably cheerful, even confident. Miss Marlow, assimilating this with mixed feelings, walked primly past him, her gaze lowered.

He shut the door, and said with perfect calm: "It was most kind in you to have given my mother the pleasure of making your acquaintance, Miss Marlow."

"I was very much honoured to receive her invitation, sir," she replied, with even greater calm.

"Will you do *me* the honour of granting me the opportunity to speak with you for a few minutes before you go away?"

Her calm instantly deserted her. "No—I mean, I must not stay! Grandmama's coachman dislikes to be kept waiting for long, you see!"

"I know he does," he agreed. "So I told Reeth to send the poor fellow home."

She halted in the middle of the stairway. "Sent him home?" she repeated. "And, pray, who gave you——"

"I was afraid he might take a chill."

She exclaimed indignantly: "You never so much as thought of such a thing! And you wouldn't have cared if you had!"

"I haven't reached that stage yet," he admitted. "But you must surely own that I am making progress!" He smiled at her. "Oh, no, don't eat me! I promise you shall be sent back to Green Street in one of *my* carriages—presently!"

Phoebe, realizing that he was affording her an example of the methods of getting his own way lately described to her by his mother, eyed him with hostility. "So I must remain in your house, I collect, until it shall please your grace to order the carriage to come round?"

"No. If you cannot bring yourself even to speak to me, I will send for it immediately."

She now perceived that he was not only arrogant but unscrupulous. Wholly devoid of chivalry, too, or he would not have done anything so shabby as to smile at her in just that way. What was more, it was clearly unsafe to be left alone with him: his eyes might smile, but they held besides the smile a very disturbing expression.

"It—it is—I assure you—quite unnecessary, Duke, for you to make me any—any explanation of—of anything!" she said.

"You can't think how relieved I am to hear you say so!" he replied, guiding her across the hall to where a door stood open, revealing a glimpse of a room lined with bookshelves. "I am not going to attempt anything of that nature, I assure you! I should rather call it *disastrous* than unnecessary! Will you come into the library?"

"What—what a pleasant room!" she achieved, looking about her.

"Yes, and what a number of books I have, haven't I?" said Sylvester affably, closing the door. "No, I have not, I believe, read them *all*!"

"I wasn't going to say *either* of those things!" she declared, trying hard not to giggle. "Pray, sir, what is it you wish to say to me?"

"Just *my darling*!" said Sylvester, taking her into his arms.

It was quite useless to struggle, and probably undignified. Besides, it was a well-known maxim that maniacs must be humoured. So Miss Marlow humoured this dangerous lunatic, putting her arm round his neck, and even going so far as to return his embrace. She then leaned her cheek against his shoulder, and said: "Oh, Sylvester! Oh, Sylvester!" which appeared to give great satisfaction. "Sparrow, Sparrow!" said Sylvester, holding her still more tightly.

Convinced by the great good sense of this reply that the Head of the House of Rayne had recovered his wits, Phoebe heaved a sigh of relief, and offered a further palliative. "I didn't mean that *wicked* thing I said to you!"

"Which one, my precious?" enquired Sylvester, relapsing into idiocy.

"That—that you are worse than Ugolino. I wonder you didn't *hit* me!"

"You know very well I wouldn't hurt a hair of your head, Sparrow. I am sure this is a very smart hat, but do allow me to remove it!" he said, pulling the bow loose as he spoke, and casting the hat aside. "That's better!"

"I *can't* marry you after writing that book!" she said, softening the blow, however, by clinging rather closer.

"You not only can, but must, if I have to drag you to the altar! How else, pray, is my character to be re-established?"

She considered this, and was suddenly struck by an inspiration. She raised her head, and said: "Sylvester! I know the very thing to do! I will write a book about you, making you the hero!"

"No, thank you, darling!" he replied with great firmness.

"Well, how would it be if I wrote a *sequel* to *The Lost Heir*, and made Ugolino become quite *steeped* in infamy, and end up by perishing on the scaffold?"

"Good God! Sparrow, you are, without exception, the most incorrigible little wretch that ever drew breath! *No!*"

"But then everyone would know he *couldn't* be you!" she pointed out. "Particularly if I dedicated it to you—which I could do with perfect propriety, you know, if I were just to subscribe myself *The Author.*"

"Now, that *is* a splendid thought!" he said. "One of those pompous epistles, with my name and style set out in large print at the head, followed by *My Lord Duke*—which you are so fond of calling me—and then by several pages interlarded with a great many *Your Graces,* and such encomiums as may occur to you, and——"

"*None* would occur to me! I should have to rack my brain for *weeks* to think of anything to say of you except that you are odiously arrogant, and——"

"Don't you dare to call me arrogant! If ever I had any arrogance at all—which I deny!—how much could I possibly have left after having been ridden over rough-shod by you and Thomas, do you imagine?" He stopped, and turned his head towards the door, listening. "And that, if I mistake not, *is* Thomas! I think, don't you, Sparrow, that he deserves to be the first to offer us his felicitations? He *did* try so hard to bring us about!" He went to the door, and opened it, to find Tom, who had just been admitted into the house, about to mount the stairs. "Thomas, come into the library! I have something of an interesting nature to disclose to you!" He added, as his eyes alighted on the tight posy of flowers in Tom's hand: "Now, what's all this, pray?"

"Oh, nothing!" Tom replied, blushing, but very off-hand. "I chanced to see them, and thought her grace might like to have them. She was saying last night that she missed the spring flowers at Chance, you know."

"Oh, indeed! Dangling after my mother, are you? Well, don't think I'll have you for a father-in-law, for I won't!"

"I don't think that is at all a proper way to speak of her grace," said Tom, with dignity.

"You are very right!" approved Phoebe, as he came into the room. "And the flowers are a very pretty attention: exactly what Mrs. Orde would say you ought to do!"

"Well, that's what I——Oh, by Jove!" Thomas exclaimed, looking from Phoebe to Sylvester in eager enquiry.

"Yes, that's it," said Sylvester.

"Oh, that's famous!" Tom declared, shaking him warmly by the hand. "I never was more glad of anything! After you were such a goose, too, Phoebe! I wish you excessively happy, both of you!" He then hugged Phoebe, recommended her to learn how to conduct herself with propriety, and said, with rare tact, that he would take himself off at once.

"You will find her in her drawing-room," said Sylvester kindly. "But you would be better employed, let me remind you, in making your peace with Lady Ingham!"

"Yes, I shall do so, of course, but later, because she don't like morning-callers above half," replied Tom.

"What you mean," retorted Sylvester, "is that your nerves are losing their steel! Tell her that you left me on the point of writing to Lord Marlow, to request his permission to marry his daughter, and fear nothing! She'll fall on your neck!"

"I say, that's a dashed good notion!" exclaimed Tom, his brow clearing. "I think, if you've no objection, I *will* tell her that!"

"Do!" said Sylvester cordially, and went back into the library, to find himself being balefully regarded by his love.

"Of all the arrogant things I've heard you say——"

"My lord Duke!" interpolated Sylvester.

"——that remark was the most insufferable!" declared Phoebe. "What makes you so sure Grandmama will be pleased, pray?"

"Well, what else am I to think, when it was she who proposed the match to me?" he countered, his eyes full of laughter.

"Grandmama?"

"You absurd infant, who do you suppose sent me down to Austerby?"

"You mean to tell me you came at *Grandmama's* bidding?"

"Yes, but with the *utmost* reluctance!" he pleaded outrageously.

"*Oh*——! Then—then when you sent me to her—Sylvester, you are *atrocious*!"

"No, no!" he said hastily, taking her in his arms again. He then, with great presence of mind, put a stop to any further recriminations by kissing her; and his indignant betrothed, apparently feeling that he was too deeply sunk in depravity to be reclaimable, abandoned (for the time being, at all events) any further attempt to bring him to a sense of his iniquity.

THE EXTRAORDINARY BESTSELLER!

THE WOMEN'S ROOM

BY MARILYN FRENCH

FOR EVERY MAN WHO EVER
THOUGHT HE KNEW A WOMAN.

FOR EVERY WOMAN WHO EVER
THOUGHT SHE KNEW HERSELF.

FOR EVERYONE WHO EVER
GREW UP, GOT MARRIED
AND WONDERED WHAT HAPPENED.

$2.95/05739-8

ON SALE WHEREVER
PAPERBACKS ARE SOLD

SK 16